Acknowledgements

Thanks – again – to Charlotte Hobson, this time for teaching me how to swear like a Russian trooper (and she seems like such a *nice* girl when you meet her . . .). Thanks, also, to Peter F. Hamilton for coming up with a name for the lightwarp generators and for the loan of 'terminal terminus'; to Irene Hind for airline information; and, last but far from least, to Antony Harwood, non-berserker agent.

BERSERKER

BERSERKER
The Guardians BOOK 2

J. M. H. Lovegrove

Copyright © J M H Lovegrove 1999

All rights reserved

The right of J M H Lovegrove to be identified as the author of this work
has been asserted by him in accordance with the Copyright, Designs and
Patents Act 1988.

First published in Great Britain in 1999 by
Millennium

An imprint of Victor Gollancz Books Ltd
Orion House, 5 Upper St Martin's Lane,
London WC2H 9EA

To receive information on the Millennium list, e-mail us at:
smy@orionbooks.co.uk

A CIP catalogue record for this book is available
from the British Library

ISBN 1 85798 555 9

Typeset at The Spartan Press Ltd, Lymington, Hants
Printed in Great Britain by Clays Ltd, St Ives plc

I never saw no miracle of science
That didn't go from a blessing to a curse
I never saw no military solution
That didn't always end up as something worse

– Sting, 'If I Ever Lose My Faith in You'

Prologue

Five figures in a freezing desert landscape.

Fanned out at twenty-yard intervals, crunching through the grey pre-dawn light, following the course of a deep, narrow wadi. An SAS patrol. Five men in brown-and-khaki disrupted-pattern-material combat fatigues. Faces tiger-striped with smears of camo cream. Two-oh-three Armalites and Minimi light machine-guns in their hands. Webbing scarves around their necks. Grenades and NBC masks dangling from their belts. The breath wisping from their mouths in twists and tangles of chilly vapour.

Nearing their target: the point where the wadi broadens out and shallows. There, an Iraqi infantry detachment is bivouacked.

A hundred yards from the encampment, the patrol's leader – the tallest among them by half a head – raises his hand to signal a halt. Immediately, wordlessly, the other four obey. The leader gestures to the right, and the four men move off in that direction. The leader, meanwhile, takes himself up to the top of a shallow rise, which affords him a good naked-eye view of the wadi encampment. Flattening himself out on his stomach, he surveys the scene.

He sees a score of two-man tents erected in rows, half a dozen khaki Toyota Land Cruisers and a pair of armoured personnel carriers fitted with turret-mounted 7.62 machine-guns. Tethered to the rear bumper of one of the Land Cruisers is a skanky, slat-ribbed mongrel. The dog is silent and somnolent now, lying with its head on its paws and its eyes closed, but a couple of hours earlier it was barking with a moon-maddened frenzy. This sound was what first drew the patrol to the encampment.

There are, as far as the patrol leader can determine, six enemy soldiers on sentry duty. Two are stationed near the only visible point of vehicular access into the wadi, where a section of the dried-up riverbed's bank has crumbled and collapsed to create a kind of natural ramp. Another two are positioned on the far side of the encampment. The remaining two rove independently among the rows of tents, meeting up at intervals to exchange a few words and, at one point, share a cigarette. All six sentries are armed with AK-47s. None is exhibiting a high degree of vigilance. Indeed, one of the pair by the 'ramp' is sitting cross-legged on the ground, slumped forward, with his rifle across his knees – fast asleep. This and the fact that the Iraqis have no qualms about letting the dog bark would suggest that either they have no idea that Allied forces have already penetrated behind their lines or, perhaps more likely, that they do not consider a solitary infantry detachment to be a strategic target of the order of a Scud launcher or an AAA emplacement.

The first pewter streaks of dawn have appeared on the eastern horizon and the last stars are winking out. A spectral mist is rising from the ground. The Iraqis are stirring, waking up, coming out of their tents. A few go to relieve themselves against the bank of the wadi, standing or squatting as appropriate. The patrol leader did not notice this earlier when first reconnoitring the encampment, but the soldiers look young. Bony, angular physiques. Scarcely older than boys.

And for a moment – but only for a moment – he questions the morality of what his squad is about to do. Is it fair that these gawky young conscripts should suffer as a consequence of Saddam's megalomania?

He dismisses the doubt. It is war. In war, everyone is a victim. Besides, Saddam has been gassing Kurds and

Marsh Arabs since 1988. This mission, if nothing else, will go some way towards evening out that injustice.

The patrol leader's task now is to observe, in order to deliver an eye-witness report for the Intelligence Corps spooks back at Forward Operations Base. He watches carefully as his four comrades make their way to a point directly upwind of the encampment. Private Kevin Hensher – a brawny Devonian, dedicated lifter of weights and pint-glasses. Sergeant Ian Gleason – the patrol's 2i/c, small, trim, ginger-haired, freckled. Private Derek Jones – the patrol's radio operator, known variously as 'Toby', 'Dumbo', 'Radar' and 'Charles' on account of his prominent jug-ears. Private Jerry Palmer – the most athletic among them, an avid hiker and rock-climber in his spare time.

It is Palmer's job to put together and position the weapon that the patrol have come here to deploy. As he creeps forward, the other three keep their guns trained on the encampment, ready to open fire if Palmer should happen to be spotted. In his arms Palmer is gently cradling an oblong canister and its pair of tripod bases. Roughly the size of a telephone directory, with rounded-off corners, the canister is made of matt-black metal. On one side, the following words are stencilled in white:

FRONT TOWARDS ENEMY

At the lip of the wadi Palmer fits the tripod bases into slots on the canister's underside, then places the assembled weapon on the ground, turning it to face in the recommended direction. He preps the device, setting the timer. Then, having hit the activating switch, he retreats on all-fours from the canister. Though he makes every effort to move slowly and stealthily, it is obvious that he wants to get away from the device as quickly as possible. Even from two hundred yards, his apprehension is clearly visible to the patrol leader. The body language of the other three men tells a similar story.

The timer has been set for fifteen minutes. The patrol leader prays that the wind will not change in that time, but keeps his NBC mask close to hand just in case.

He hears a soft, chuffing sound, and something tightens in his guts like a coiling snake. Suddenly dense black smoke is billowing from the canister, spilling into the air like ink into water. He sees his four comrades freeze stock-still, staring at the device first in disbelief, then in abject horror. He himself refuses initially to accept what his eyes are reporting. He wants the dark cloud to be an optical illusion, a trick of vision caused, perhaps, by a temporary thickening of the ground-mist.

But the cloud continues to swell and blossom like time-lapse footage of some hideous black fungus growing . . . and the sickening knot in the patrol leader's stomach tightens yet further as he realises that the gas is travelling against the prevailing wind; is being expelled by the canister away from the enemy encampment . . .

. . . towards the four patrol-members.

Palmer, Jones, Hensher and Gleason lay down their guns and reach for their NBC masks to begin fitting them on clumsily. All manage to secure the masks in place just as the first tendrils of black gas reach them. A few seconds later they are engulfed, lost from view.

Time passes with hideous slowness. Distantly the patrol leader is aware of the dog down in the wadi, awake again, and howling and baying like a demented thing. There are shouts coming from the encampment. Two of the sentries have rushed up the 'ramp' to see what is happening. But the patrol leader's attention is focused primarily on the burgeoning gas cloud. More and yet more gas is pouring from the canister, massing around the spot where his four comrades are. From his remote, godlike vantage point, he is unable to do anything but look on – and fear.

Abruptly the canister ceases to spew out its contents. The gas cloud hangs in the air, a dense clot of blackness that seems to hover with a will of its own, with a malevolent sentience, throbbing like some sinister ebony jellyfish.

At that moment the dog ceases its howling and, tucking its tail under its belly, crawls beneath the Land Cruiser to which it is tied.

4

The next instant, the first of the monsters comes lurching out of the cloud, uttering a hoarse, inarticulate roar.

It is nearly seven feet tall, a mass of sinewy, vein-crazed flesh, its physique a caricature of the human body, every muscle pumped up to absurd proportions, and asymmetrically, so that its posture is distorted. Its head has been pushed forwards and to the side by an overdeveloped trapezius. One arm is twisted out at an ungainly angle by a deltoid the size of a watermelon. Its back is humped by an immense set of laterals and a reptilian ridge of spine. One leg drags under the weight of its own distended calf. Shreds of clothing cling to this creature – the remnants of a combat blouse flap around its neck and chest; torn trousers hang from its waist, every seam in them split; swollen feet protrude from a ruined pair of boots.

Its pallid scalp is furred with sparse patches of ginger hair.

Gleason.

No sooner has the patrol leader identified this misshapen monster as his second-in-command than the other three patrol-members also emerge from the black cloud. Jones first – a hulking, elongated, bat-eared mockery of the man he once was. Then Hensher, whose beer-drinker's belly is inflated to Sumo-wrestler size and whose weight-lifter's pectorals have assumed silicone-breast-implant proportions. And finally Palmer, still wearing his NBC mask although it is askew on his head, hyper-trophied scalp-flesh bulging between its rubber straps. As with Gleason, their uniforms hang on them in tattered shreds. Palmer, indeed, is all but naked. And, like Gleason, they are all screaming. Madness is on their faces. Bloodlust is in their eyes.

They start lumbering towards their leader.

They are coming for him, and he knows what they will do when they get their hands on him. Tear him apart. Rip him to pieces like a rag doll.

He pushes himself to his feet.

Turns to run.

Finds he cannot.

From the ankles down, his feet are mired in the ground. The hard desert floor has somehow liquefied beneath him. Has turned to mud. Densely, intensely sticky mud. He cannot prise his feet out. His struggles to free himself only make him sink deeper. Now he is embedded up to his shins, his boots and puttees no longer visible. Now the mud has risen to his knees. Where is his gun? Somehow he has mislaid his Armalite. It is nowhere to be seen. He is weaponless. Defenceless.

And the four man-monsters are still coming for him, pounding towards him, roaring, raging, raving. He knows what they can do to a human being, these things that were his comrades, his friends. He knows how terrible their strength is, how hard they are to kill. They will dismember him. Disembowel him. Dismantle him. He knows this.

Ten yards away. He can see the blood-webbed whites of their eyes. Their screams have merged into one huge rumbling growl, like the engine of a juggernaut . . .

. . . thundering by outside the window.

MacGowan snapped awake in his armchair like a man falling to earth. An involuntary spasm ran through his body, causing the glass ashtray that was perched on his knee to spin up into the air and tumble to the floor, disgorging an afternoon's worth of butts and ash-tappings. He gulped for breath, hiccuping the air into his lungs. His heartbeat was an erratic jackhammering throb that threatened to explode every vein in his body.

'Christ,' he hissed, and began repeating the word over and over, using it as a mantra to calm himself, control himself.

Gradually his breathing steadied, and with it his pulse-rate. Soon his cardiopulmonary system was operating normally once more. He groped for the packet of Marlboro and the disposable lighter on the sofa arm like an infant in need of the nipple. Lighting one of the cigarettes, he inhaled gratefully.

'Christ,' he said once more. This time, the word came

6

out as a long, trembling sigh, accompanied by a bluish billow of smoke.

He reached down for the fallen ashtray and set it in his lap, then glanced around him at the fixtures and fittings of his bedsit home. The dreary, messy normality of his surroundings helped reassure him that he was no longer in the world of the nightmare. There was the narrow kitchen counter, piled high with unwashed crockery, empty beer-cans, old pizza boxes and burger cartons. There was the torn wallpaper – like the upholstery of the chair he was sitting on, blotched with all manner of indefinable stains. There were the browned, threadbare net curtains, offering a hazy view of the night-lit street outside. There, in the corner, was his sagging single bed, the sheets and blankets spilling in rumpled swags onto the floor, where they merged with strata of strewn clothing. When was the last time he had made the bed? Or been to the laundrette? He had no idea. Could not remember.

A portable television with a twisted coat-hanger for an aerial sat in front of him on an upturned cardboard box. He had fallen asleep watching *Countdown*. Now it was the Channel Four news. John Major was bleating on about the Conservative Party's policy on Europe, or lack of same. MacGowan regarded the country's prime minister with a bleary, sardonic eye while he slowly, gratefully sucked on the Marlboro.

The nightmare. The fucking nightmare.

It came to him at least once a fortnight, sometimes more often than that. Each time it was the same, and each time it left him panic-stricken and feeling like he was about to have a heart attack. Always he awoke before the charging, monstrously mutated soldiers reached him, but while he was dreaming the dream there was never any certainty of that. While he was dreaming the dream, there was only ever the build-up – the step-by-step re-enactment of the mission – and then the detonation of the canister, the appearance of the black gas . . . and then the terror.

He had done his best to forget all about the mission. To

forget what he had seen out there in the Gulf. To forget he had ever heard the words 'Codename: Bearskin'.

But, hard though he had tried, it seemed that the memories would not forget him.

When he had smoked the cigarette down to the filter, he stubbed it out, placed the ashtray on the floor again and got shakily to his feet. Grabbing his overcoat, he switched off the TV and headed out.

It was a rainy, blustery evening in December of 1992. Two days ago, MacGowan had received a phone call from his solicitor notifying him that as of ten o'clock that morning – at which time, in his absence, a decree absolute had been granted in court – he was no longer a married man. MacGowan still did not know whether to feel sorry for himself or relieved, but he was, at any rate, glad for Sarah. The way he was now, she was well shot of him.

He made his way along the gusty, blackly shimmering streets in the direction of the Pen and Sword, a pub just off Hornsey Lane at which he had, in recent months, become a valued customer. He was still feeling the after-effects of the nightmare. Ghostly echoes of it seemed to manifest all around him. People he passed – strange shambling silhouettes, huddled and barely human in their thick winter clothing – reminded him of his comrades' freakishly disfigured forms. The darkness, the inky wetness of the pavements, made him think of the black gas. The cold brought back tingling memories of the subzero desert nights.

Head down against the rain, he thought of Sarah, and of the last time he and she had talked in person, rather than over the phone or through the medium of solicitors. That had been six months ago, the day she had finally had enough and had turfed him out of their flat in Camden. There had been tears in her eyes as she had dumped his bags on the front doorstep, but at the same time her face had been set into an expression of determined resolve. She was doing what she hoped was best for both of them. That was what she had said, at any rate, and she was probably right. She had arranged the Crouch End bedsit for him, and she told him he should stay there until he had sorted himself out. Until he had rebalanced his inner karmic scales.

The chances of that happening, though, were a big fat zero. Nothing in MacGowan's life would ever be sorted out as long as he kept having the nightmare.

Thanks to the nightmare, MacGowan seemed to be living constantly in fear – fear that stemmed not just from the nightmare itself but from knowledge of its existence, from never knowing when it was going to visit him again, never knowing how long a respite he would have before its next appearance. Alcohol was the best way he had found to blur and nebulise that fear. Which was why the local pub, along with his nearest off-licence, had become a haunt of his.

His drinking was also the principal reason why Sarah had kicked him out of their home – but he did not like to think about that. He did not like to think about the way he had behaved towards her while drunk. He had never hit her. That was something in his favour, at any rate. Even deep in his cups, he had never so much as raised a hand against her (which was just as well, because there was nothing he despised more than a wife-beater, except perhaps a child-molester). All the same, some of the things he had said to her had been as bad as blows. He bitterly regretted each and every occasion when he had raged at her, wounding her with words. But he knew that no amount of regret – or apologies, which he had offered her in profusion each time he sobered up – could fully atone for the hurt he had inflicted with his drunken tongue.

It was getting on for eight o'clock when he reached the Pen and Sword. Letting the door swing shut behind him, he stamped his boots and nodded his head to shake the rain off, then peered around. There were three other patrons on the premises. Two of them were old men, regulars. They were playing dominoes in one of the booths. The third was a white-haired man in a velvet-lapelled overcoat, who was sitting on a stool at the bar,

9

nursing a cup of tea. MacGowan offered this man a curt, formal nod as he strode up to the bar. The white-haired stranger returned the nod. MacGowan ordered a pint of Guinness with a Jack Daniel's chaser from the publican, and while the publican was pouring the drinks, the white-haired man spoke.

'They tricked you, you know,' he said.

MacGowan turned to the stranger and asked if he was talking to *him*.

The white-haired man calmly nodded and repeated his remark.

MacGowan, frowning, enquired politely what the fuck he was going on about.

'The canister was boobytrapped,' the white-haired man said. 'There was never any fifteen-minute delay on the timer.'

MacGowan, startled, told the man he had better explain himself sharpish, or was he looking for a smack in the mouth?

At this the white-haired man merely smiled, not in the least perturbed to have been threatened with violence by a rough-looking, six-foot-seven, sixteen-stone ex-squaddie. Addressing the publican, he said he would like to pay for Mr MacGowan's drinks, at which MacGowan demanded, 'And how do you know my sodding name?'

'I take it I have your attention, then?' said the white-haired man.

'Yes, you have my fucking attention.' MacGowan was thoroughly annoyed and unnerved now. 'Just who the hell *are* you?'

'Rest assured, Mr MacGowan, that I mean you no harm whatsoever. I wish simply to have a drink with you and discuss a couple of matters.'

The publican set MacGowan's pint and chaser down on the bartop. His blithe expression suggested that he had found nothing peculiar about the foregoing exchange of dialogue, and indeed that he had been a silent third party to far stranger conversations in his time. 'Which of you gentlemen's going to pay, then?' he asked, looking from MacGowan to the white-haired man.

MacGowan continued to stare at the white-haired man, unable to fathom him. It had occurred to him, fleetingly, that the man might be an IRA revenge-squad hitman who had somehow managed to track him down. But his accent was pure, authentic London, not Londonderry, and, more to the point, if he was here to carry out an execution, he would have done so already. The thing was, there was something definitely *off* about the way the bloke looked, something that made MacGowan, at a gut-instinct level, leery of him. His skin was so waxily smooth it was almost unnatural, as though he had been sprayed with some sort of preservative coating, and his forehead was unusually large and protuberant, so much so that it cast his eyes into deep shadow. And the eyes somehow did not belong to the face. They were clear and bright and intelligent, but none the less seemed considerably older than the rest of the man. What with that and his snow-white hair, appearance-wise the man just did not add up. Then there was the fact that he seemed to know about Codename: Bearskin and, moreover, had echoed MacGowan's own deepest, darkest suspicions. *They tricked you, you know.*

In the end, MacGowan's curiosity got the better of his caution. He took a deep breath and unwittingly, just by uttering three innocuous little words, made what would turn out to be one of the most momentous decisions of his life.

'He can pay,' he said to the publican.

They sat down at a table well away from the bar and out of earshot of the publican and the dominoes-players. There, the white-haired man, having removed his overcoat and draped it over the back of an empty chair, introduced himself as John Rattray. As MacGowan set to sipping his Guinness, Rattray proceeded to tell him what he knew about him – which, it turned out, was almost everything.

William Patrick MacGowan. Born 29 December 1957, only offspring of Liam and Jeannie MacGowan. Brought up on a council estate in Hounslow. Aged eleven, watched his father – a bricklayer by trade – walk out on the family. During his teens, appeared in court a number of times on juvenile misdemeanour charges. Joined the army as a cadet in 1973. Applied to join the Special Air Service in 1978. Failed the first Selection but got through on the second attempt. Served several tours of duty in Ireland between 1979 and 1983. Took part in the Iranian Embassy siege in 1980, as a rooftop sniper. And, of course, played a role in the reclamation of the Falkland Islands. In 1984, started going out with Sarah Kingsley, then an aerobics instructor, now an aromatherapist. Continued to serve on a number of covert missions to protect British interests around the world. Wed the aforementioned Miss Kingsley in June 1986. No progeny from the union. Marriage dissolved earlier this year, the decree absolute just come through. Resigned from the SAS at the beginning of this year. Currently subsisting on a meagre army pension with no other form of employment.

'Well done,' said MacGowan, with a slow, sardonic hand-clap. 'All you forgot to include was which side I dress to.'

'The right.'

MacGowan glanced down at his own crotch, then up again. 'Now I'm impressed.'

'A lucky guess,' said Rattray, with a shrug. 'A fifty-fifty chance of being correct.'

MacGowan drained his pint and then knocked back the whisky chaser. 'OK,' he gasped, slamming the shot-glass down on the tabletop, 'so you've been through my personnel files and you've had access to my legal records. I don't know how the fuck you managed it, but I'm willing to let that go for the moment. Tell me what you meant when you said the canister was boobytrapped.'

'Ah yes,' said Rattray. He beckoned to the publican. 'Same again for Mr MacGowan,' he said. 'And I'll have what he's having, too.'

*

12

'In January 1991,' Rattray said after the drinks had arrived, 'you formed part of a five-man SAS patrol tasked with a special mission behind enemy lines in Iraq. You were, in fact, the patrol's designated leader. The mission was carried out under conditions of the utmost secrecy. All you were told by your Intelligence Corps supervisors was that you were to deploy a new, highly advanced non-persistent biological agent against a "soft" target. The nature of the agent was not revealed to you, so that your observations of its effects would be impartial and un-prejudiced, unmuddied by any preconceptions. You were told that the agent worked by inhalation rather than through skin-contact, and that therefore your NBC masks' filters would protect you from it, should some mishap occur. All of this is true so far?'

MacGowan nodded and gestured at Rattray to go on.

'Four days into the mission, you located a suitable target some hundred kilometres north of the Saudi Arabian border. An Iraqi infantry detachment. Poorly guarded. Poorly defended. You proceeded to deploy the agent as instructed. You yourself took the position of observer, while your four colleagues unleashed the agent on the Iraqis. But something went wrong.'

'It was human error,' MacGowan intoned. This was what the Intelligence spooks had decided, at the end of a debriefing that lasted nearly two weeks – that human error was to blame for the exposure of the patrol-members, rather than the Iraqi soldiers, to the agent. Private Palmer, the spooks had said, must have prepped and primed the device incorrectly. Clearly, in the heat of the moment Palmer had made two crucial mistakes: he had failed to set the timer properly and he had positioned the canister the wrong way round. Such things, regrett-ably, did occur in the theatre of combat, and no amount of careful pre-planning could prevent that.

MacGowan had begged to differ. He had seen the gas jetting out from the canister *against* the prevailing wind. He had seen the four patrol-members put their NBC masks on. The spooks, however, would not accept his version of events, and in the end he had given up trying to make them.

'It was not human error,' Rattray replied. 'That's what the Intelligence Corps wanted you to believe, but that's not what happened. And I think you know that that's not what happened.'

'Sometimes I think . . .' Scratching his cheek distractedly, MacGowan gathered his thoughts and started again. 'I have a pretty clear recollection of what those four . . . *things* did after the gas got them. They went down and they waded in among the Iraqis and they . . . they took them apart with their bare hands. Killed them. Slaughtered them. In their dozens. It was carnage. They were so strong. Gleason and that lot – what they had become. So strong. They were just about unkillable. The jundies pumped round after round into them, and they just kept on coming. Fucking AKs blowing bloody great chunks out of them, and they just kept on coming. But . . .'

'But the Intelligence people told you that you must have imagined it, or at any rate that your perception of events must have become exaggerated in your memory. They were prepared to accept that your comrades attacked the Iraqis, but they did not believe you when you talked about them taking bullets point-blank and laughing and when you described the extreme physiological mutations wrought on them by the gas.'

'I'd been wandering in the desert for two days – without my bergen, without rations, with just a canteen of water to survive on – before I was spotted and picked up. According to the RAF blokes in the Chinook that retrieved me, I was half-dead from exposure and babbling like a madman. After what I'd seen, hardly surprising really. It's possible . . . I mean, I was in shock, and, you know, after forty-eight hours lost in the desert . . . I *could* have got things muddled up, I suppose.'

MacGowan had tried to convince himself of this hundreds, perhaps thousands of times over the past couple of years. He longed to believe that his comrades, driven crazy by the lethally toxic agent, had hurled themselves at the Iraqis and had, in their death-frenzy, managed to kill maybe one or two of them before being brought down by gunfire. He wanted nothing more on earth than to know that this was true . . .

But then there were his memories of screaming Iraqis being torn apart. One poor sod being snapped in two like a Christmas cracker (or whatever the Moslem equivalent). Another having his lungs pulled out. Another being tugged apart by the legs like a human wishbone. Yet another being introduced – sadistically – to his own bowels. Blood gushing in crimson freshets from stumps of limbs, from decapitated necks, from ripped-open ribcages, staining the *wadi* floor dark brown. Terrified, suicidal cries of '*Allah'u akbar!*' as the Iraqis vainly launched themselves against their vicious, monstrous attackers, only to die horribly. Mutilated corpses strewing the ground. And then one raghead hurling himself at Hensher with a grenade in his hand, the pin pulled – sacrificing himself and destroying Hensher at the same time, both of them disintegrating in a cloud of vaporised flesh. And Jones, strafed by salvoes from the armoured personnel carrier's 7.62 guns, being whittled down to shattered bone and muscle, and still fighting as he went down, still snarling and lashing out around him. And Gleason, blown to pieces by a shell from a shoulder-mounted rocket launcher. And Palmer, run over by an APC, knocked flat, surrounded by Iraqis and eventually succumbing to long, concentrated bursts of gunfire.

All of this he remembered vividly.

And then there was the nightmare, during which he relived the moments leading up to the slaughter in realistic detail, with the typically ghastly dream-variation that it was he, not the Iraqis, whom the patrol-members turned on.

'No,' said Rattray firmly, 'there's nothing wrong with your recollection of the incident, Mr MacGowan, and let me tell you why. Let me tell you a little bit about Codename: Bearskin.'

*

Codename: Bearskin, Rattray said, was developed in the late eighties by a company called PetriTech PLC. Biologists carrying out research in the field of human-friendly bacteria succeeded in engineering a strain of bacillus that had the effect of stimulating intense muscle-fibre growth and tissue regeneration in mammals. The medical benefits seemed potentially enormous. The bacillus might be used to speed up the healing process for accident victims and patients after operations, taking away much of the pain and trauma of recuperation.

However, it seemed that PetriTech's biologists had done their job too well, or not well enough, depending on your viewpoint. When tested on laboratory animals, not only did the bacillus cause extreme and ultimately fatal levels of physical overdevelopment, it triggered the release of large quantities of adrenocorticotrophic hormones, resulting in greatly increased aggression. In short, it lent the test-subjects immense strength while at the same time driving them into a blinding, pathological rage. One lab assistant, while trying to put down a rhesus monkey that had been injected with the bacillus, had most of his face torn off by the little animal and nearly died as a result of his injuries.

Realising that what its biologists had created had no viable commercial use, PetriTech was on the point of discontinuing the project. However, it so happened that someone high up in British Army Intelligence got wind of the existence of the bacillus and decided it might have a military application.

The army purchased a single batch of the bacillus. Shortly after that, PetriTech's laboratories burned to the ground in a mysterious, unexplained fire. At the same time, several of the biologists involved in developing the bacillus died in a series of random and apparently unrelated accidents.

'An extraordinary set of coincidences,' Rattray added, with just a ghost of a smile. He seemed to be enjoying some dark private joke.

'Yeah, well, whatever,' said MacGowan. 'So this

bacillus they made became the Codename: Bearskin agent?'

'Correct.'

'And let me get this straight – the army only had the one lot of the agent, but they decided to field-test it anyway.'

'Shame to let their investment go to waste.'

'And me and my team were the guinea pigs.'

Rattray nodded.

'And the canister was rigged to emit the gas backwards.'

Rattray nodded again.

'I knew it.' There was ferocious triumph in Mac-Gowan's voice. 'I fucking knew it. *Bastards!*' He clenched his fists and looked around the pub as though searching for someone to hit. In the past few minutes a handful of other patrons – wet, wind-blown – had drifted into the Pen and Sword. Innocents. Just as *he* had been an innocent. Slowly his anger subsided; his fists relaxed into hands again.

'After all,' said Rattray, 'it wouldn't be the first time the British army has experimented on its own troops. It's a matter of public record now that, back in the fifties and sixties, British soldiers were used as human lab-rats at Porton Down. Many suffered agonising deaths as a result, or had to endure debilitating ailments for the rest of their lives, as a result of exposure to toxic gases, nerve agents, radiation and chemicals. Your comrades, Mr MacGowan, were merely the latest to "benefit" from this tradition.'

'But what were the intelligence boys hoping to prove?'

'I assume you've heard of the Viking berserker warrior?'

'Yeah. Supposed to be the hardest of the hard, weren't they?'

'Indeed. You might even call them the Early Norse SAS.'

MacGowan lifted one corner of his mouth to show that, however subtly it was phrased, he knew bullshit flattery when he heard it. 'What about them?'

'Before battle, berserker warriors would work themselves up into a trance-like frenzy which allegedly left them immune to the pain of wounds. Some historians have suggested that, in order to facilitate this frame of mind, they ingested fly agaric – magic mushrooms – and were thus able to fight like men possessed, feeling neither pain nor pity. Traditionally, berserkers went into combat unarmed and clad in the pelt of a bear.'

'The pelt of a . . . Ah.' MacGowan nodded slowly. 'I thought the name must have something to do with the Guards. Obviously not.'

'Obviously not.'

'And that's what the four guys in my patrol were supposed to be? Berserker warriors?'

'Imagine it,' said Rattray. 'In a contemporary theatre of war a battalion of berserker ground troops, unleashed on the enemy, would be virtually unstoppable. Your patrol proved that beyond a doubt, each man being worth at least ten ordinary opponents. What was also proved was that the bacillus produced just as extreme effects in humans as it did in rhesus monkeys. Even if the four human test-subjects hadn't been killed by the enemy, it's doubtful they would have survived for long following exposure to Codename: Bearskin, given the extraordinary stresses and strains that their bodies were being subjected to. Not only that, but troops infected by the bacillus would be very difficult to control, which would call into doubt its use as a weapon for one's own side.'

'So the test was a failure, in other words.'

'Yes.'

'That's something, I suppose.' MacGowan's eyes narrowed in suspicion. 'So tell me: how come you know all this?'

'If I explain that, I'll have to explain a lot of things,' Rattray replied. 'Therefore, before we go any further, Mr MacGowan, I need to know whether I can trust you.'

'You can trust me,' said MacGowan, after a moment's thought, 'for as long as I keep trusting *you*.'

'Fair enough,' said Rattray. 'Another round?'

'Why not? Let me get this.'
'No, let me.'

The pub filled and emptied and filled and emptied, a tide of patrons coming and going, ebbing and flowing. At times everyone seemed to be shouting, while the CD jukebox blared. At other times, the jukebox was mute and the pub was all but silent, here and there a low-murmured conversation, and the thud of dart into dartboard the loudest sound in the room.

MacGowan and Rattray each drank their way through another five pints of beer with accompanying chasers, and while they drank Rattray told a tale which initially seemed to MacGowan the most preposterous thing he had ever heard but which, the more he listened and drank, began to take on a strange ring of authenticity.

There existed, Rattray said, a race of beings much like ourselves who lived at one remove from what we would consider to be reality. Their world and ours were adjacent, just a hair's breadth apart, a fraction of a second out of synch, yet at the same time separated by an immense gulf. Linked in several places, yet divided. Like Siamese twins, two bodies sharing certain organs and functions in common. Like the two tines of a tuning fork, both emanating from a common stem, both shimmering in harmonic sympathy, but neither quite touching its counterpart. The concept was hard to get across by any other means than metaphor, Rattray added apologetically, and MacGowan told him that, if it was any consolation, he had not the faintest idea what Rattray was on about, to which Rattray replied, with a mild, ironic laugh, 'I wouldn't be surprised if that made two of us.'

This race, he continued, were known as the paraterrestrials, and though their existence was now a well-guarded secret, once – many millennia ago – they and we had a close relationship and would converse freely via the points at which their world and ours were connected. Far superior to us in terms of technological, civic and spiritual development, the paraterrestrials adopted a kind of benevolent older-sibling role and began cultivating us while we were still cave-dwelling hunter-gatherers, teaching us what they knew, nurturing us, sharing with us their science and their wisdom, shaping us. With their help we emerged from our caves and began building towns, cities, nations, empires. We learned speech and writing and agriculture. We became political animals. We made tools and with those tools constructed simple machines. Civilisations grew and flourished across the globe – but the greatest of them all, the star pupil, the favourite child on which the paraterrestrial lavished the finest gifts, the most care and attention, was Atlantis.

'*The* Atlantis?' said MacGowan.

'None other,' said Rattray.

It was a place of breathtaking magnificence, Rattray continued. Its City of the Golden Gates was a wonder of the world, concentrically arranged, with broad, tree-shaded streets, gardens and balconies overflowing with shrubs and orchids and climbing plants, and gleaming towers that brushed the stars. A myriad of cunning mechanisms made life easier and more comfortable for the continent's inhabitants: levitation discs; gongs that could raise huge weights by means of pure sound; crystals that transmitted energy from the sun; machines that channelled the earth's magnetic currents to generate power. Cars thrummed along electromagnetic roads, jewelled aircraft flashed through the skies, and automated devices took care of the menial chores. Atlantis's democratic system was the model that all others sought to emulate. Atlantis's citizens led lives of peace and ease and contemplation. Art and culture were highly prized. Leisure activities were keenly pursued. Religion was tolerant, humanistic and aligned with nature.

In short, the Atlanteans had everything human beings could possibly wish for. But, of course, it was not enough. They knew that the paraterrestrials had more to offer them, were still keeping some secrets to themselves, and they came to the conclusion that if the paraterrestrials

20

would not surrender this extra knowledge voluntarily, then it must be taken from them by force.

The Atlanteans set to adapting the technology they already possessed. With typical human ingenuity, they transformed harmless inventions into weapons of war. They worked out a means of bridging the gap between the human and paraterrestrial realms, and then breached their way into that counterpart reality.

The paraterrestrials, though taken by surprise, were none the less able to repulse the Atlanteans' incursion without too much trouble. Not content to leave it at that, however, they decided that these upstart and ungrateful humans should be taught a lesson. Atlantis was destroyed. The entire continent was subjected to a tectonic shift and was moved from its position in the middle of the Atlantic Ocean ninety degrees of latitude southwards to where it now lay, buried beneath a miles-thick sheath of ice and snow – Antarctica.

Then the paraterrestrials, as a further demonstration of their affront, closed off the channels of communication between their world and ours. Other nations would not now benefit from their attentions the way the Atlanteans had.

A handful of Atlanteans survived the cataclysm, but too few to keep the flame of knowledge alight. The planet entered a Dark Age. Civilisations crumbled and fell apart. Mankind reverted to primitive ways.

This state of affairs continued for some eight thousand years, after which the paraterrestrials, who still retained a fondness for us, felt that we had been consigned to purdah long enough. It was time to resume relations with us.

This decision provoked discord. Some of the paraterrestrials felt that it would be foolhardy and dangerous to deal with the human race again. We had proved that we were not to be trusted. The experiment had been a failure. We should be left well alone.

The majority of the paraterrestrials felt otherwise, however, and so the process of educating and refining mankind commenced anew. It was agreed, though, that this time we would not be granted so much knowledge at once.

'Because we'd behaved like a kid with a big bag of sweets,' said MacGowan. 'We couldn't eat just one or two. We had to scoff the lot, and then we felt sick.'

'If you like,' said Rattray.

'Hey, you're not the only one who can talk in metaphors, you know.' Smiling, MacGowan lit up another Marlboro. 'D'you mind?' he asked, fanning away a wreath of smoke.

Rattray shook his head.

'Not worried about passive smoking, then?'

'Not greatly.'

Rattray resumed his narrative.

The paraterrestrials devised a timetable for us, he said, a gradual progression of technological and social evolution by which no new scientific discovery and no new mode of thought would gain currency until it was considered that mankind, as a race, had collectively acquired the moral sophistication necessary to cope with the ramifications and consequences. Anything that did not fulfil this criterion would be deemed 'contratemporal' and would be suppressed or eradicated.

As a concession to the paraterrestrial minority who were opposed to further contact with the human race, it was decreed that there would be no more direct interaction between us and them. The paraterrestrials' involvement in our affairs would be conducted at arm's length, covertly.

In order to ensure that the plan for Progress was adhered to, the paraterrestrials realised they would need human agents to act on their behalf. To this end, they established the Guardians.

A hand-picked cadre of women and men, the Guardians were entrusted with the task of regulating mankind's development and preserving knowledge from the world and the world from knowledge.

This task the Guardians had been carrying out, in secret, throughout recorded history. For instance:

In Ancient Greece, the inventor Daedalus constructed a means of man-powered flight for himself and his son Icarus. The Guardians showed him the error of his ways.

Aztec murals depict rocket-ships, men hunkering at the controls. The Guardians saw to it that these ships never flew.

In the library at Alexandria could be found several books and scrolls dating back to the Atlantean era, some of which contained blueprints for contratemporal devices. The Guardians lit the fire and fanned the flames that burned the library to cinders.

Leonardo da Vinci's tanks and flying machines could have changed the face of war for ever. The Guardians made sure that they never left the drawing board.

Nikolai Tesla's aether energy transmission device could easily have been adapted to serve as a devastating death ray. The Guardians put the dampers on it.

The Philadelphia Experiment, ostensibly an attempt to degauss the hull of a destroyer, the USS *Eldridge*, so that it would not be susceptible to magnetic mines, was, in fact, a crude, tentative attempt at a radar cloaking device. The Guardians arranged for the experiment to fail drastically, so that it would not be repeated.

These were just a few examples of Guardian operations. Rattray claimed he could have cited several hundred more.

'What about flying saucers?' said MacGowan, stubbing out the dog-end of his cigarette in a Kronenbourg 1664 ashtray. 'Is that these parawhatsits visiting us?'

'To the best of my knowledge, the paraterrestrials' – Rattray enunciated the word carefully – 'have never physically visited this reality. In fact, most UFO encounters can be explained as hoaxes, mass hallucination, the misidentification of natural or manmade phenomena, or delusions brought on by attacks of temporal lobe epilepsy. There have, however, been a few instances when a UFO sighting has arisen as a consequence of Guardian activity, usually when we've had to bring down a human-built aircraft that was employing a form of contratemporal propulsion.'

'"We",' said MacGowan.

'I am, of course,' said Rattray, 'a Guardian.'

'Of course.' MacGowan peered at him over the rim of a near-empty, froth-streaked pint-glass. 'But what about the paraterrestrial minority?' he said. 'The ones who wanted to have nothing to do with us any more? I have a feeling they've got a part to play in this somehow.'

'How very astute of you.'

The minority, Rattray said, were not appeased by the policy advocating no direct intervention in human affairs. They formed a splinter faction whose stated aim was to prove mankind's unreliability, to show to the rest of their race that our belligerence and avarice were innate, immutable qualities, and that like the proverbial leopard we could not change our spots. The splinter faction set about attempting to disrupt the course of our development, using oblique methods. They supplied inspiration through dreams, visions, trances and various other apparently 'ordinary' processes. They secreted items of contratemporal hardware where they might be accidentally discovered. They used human agents – sometimes with their knowledge, usually not – to disrupt the carefully ordered sequence of social and technological evolution which was intended to bring us, eventually, to a state of parity with the paraterrestrials.

The splinter faction came to be known as the Anarchs.

'As in "anarchists"?'

'The words are derived from the same Greek root, but the meanings are subtly different.'

In order to distinguish them from the Anarchs, the paraterrestrials for whom the Guardians worked were also given a name: the Librans.

'My wife's into that astrology stuff,' MacGowan remarked, adding ruefully, 'my *ex*-wife.'

'Again, the same root, but with a distinct meaning of its own.'

Behind most of the incidents mentioned earlier, the

hand of the Anarchs could be discerned. However, over the past two centuries their efforts had become more concerted and determined. It seemed they were losing patience with us and were keen for the whole 'human problem' to be resolved as soon as possible, and so were interfering more than ever before, their goal nothing less than our utter destruction, which they intended that we ourselves would bring about, either by committing collective suicide through nuclear war or self-inflicted ecological catastrophe, or by once again attempting to break through into the paraterrestrials' reality and having to be violently – and this time permanently – put in our place.

'And how do you know all this?' MacGowan asked.

'We know all this,' Rattray replied, 'because the Librans tell us so.'

'And you believe everything they tell you.'

'It's an article of faith.'

'So why are you telling *me* all this?'

'I should have thought that was obvious.'

'Yeah, it is, kind of, but I want to hear you say it.'

'We want you to join us, Mr MacGowan. We want you to become a Guardian.'

For the duration of one whole pint of Guinness, MacGowan pondered sombrely and deeply on Rattray's request. Finally, at the whisky-chaser stage of the round, he said, 'Why me?'

The Guardians, he was told, had need of military operatives. Most of their missions called for men and women who could handle weapons, who had undergone professional combat training, and who were prepared, if necessary, to take lives.

'And your next question,' said Rattray, 'is what if you refuse? What if you think everything I've just told you is absolute arrant nonsense and you want to have nothing further to do with me because I am quite clearly a stark raving lunatic?'

'As a matter of fact,' said MacGowan, 'my next question was going to be, "How come you don't seem to be drunk?" Because you've matched me pint for pint, chaser for chaser, and we've had three so far – or is it four?'

'Five, actually.'

'Exactly. There you go. Five. And you're not swaying or slurring your words or anything. I mean, I thought *I* had a hard head . . .'

Rattray's lips twisted into a grim kind of smile. 'I would try and explain, but I've given you enough weirdness to mull over for one evening. Another time, perhaps.'

'Then,' said MacGowan, 'let's go back to *your* question. What if I refuse?'

'To be brutally frank, Mr MacGowan—'

'God, I hate it when people are brutally frank.'

'—what choice do you have? I'm offering you a chance to use the only real skills you possess, in return for a handsome stipend.'

'Ah, money. You didn't mention money before.'

'The Guardians are well funded,' said Rattray. 'We have substantial interests in certain corporations that deal in cutting-edge technology.'

'Paraterrestrial technology.'

'Exactly. Inventions that have been approved by the Librans as safe for human consumption. Not only that, but we are bankrolled by a number of privately wealthy individuals whose family fortunes have been accumulated over the centuries through the auspices of the Librans.' Rattray reeled off a list of surnames, each internationally famous and synonymous with Croesian riches.

'In each family,' he said, 'only one member actually knows where the funds allotted to the Guardians are going. It's his or her task to keep that a secret from the others, and to select a candidate from the next generation to carry on the tradition.'

'Well, it all sounds very tempting . . .' said Mac-Gowan, as the publican, unbidden, brought them another round.

'But you're still uncertain,' said Rattray.

'Of course I am. Half of me believes you, and half of me thinks you belong in one of those places where they give you crayons instead of pencils to write with and where knives and forks aren't allowed.'

'Then consider this,' said Rattray. 'Paraterrestrial science was involved in the manufacture of Codename: Bearskin. Anarch-influenced biologists created the agent that cost your four comrades their lives and left you the way you are now – divorced, jobless and clinically depressed.'

MacGowan winced. 'You're doing that "brutally frank" thing again, aren't you?'

'What I'm doing,' said Rattray, 'is offering you the opportunity to redress the wrongs that have been done. Not directly. The Guardians have already taken care of Codename: Bearskin's inventors. But you can do your bit to make sure that there are no more Codename: Bearskins.'

Neither man said anything for a while. MacGowan sat with his chin on one fist, sipping and brooding. Then Rattray reached into an inner pocket of his jacket for his wallet, from which he produced a business card. 'You have twenty-four hours to decide,' he said, handing the card to MacGowan and getting up to leave. The tide of pubgoers was in full spate just then.

The card simply had the words JOHN RATTRAY printed on it, along with a cell-phone number. Mac-Gowan squinted at it, nodding.

'One last thing,' he said, looking up at Rattray, who was putting on his overcoat. 'If I was to try to tell the rest of the world what you've just told me . . .'

'I wouldn't advise it, Mr MacGowan. I wouldn't advise it at all.'

'Right. Yes. I get it. OK.'

'Twenty-four hours, Mr MacGowan.'

And with that, Rattray strode through the milling throng of patrons and exited the Pen and Sword.

All the rest of that night MacGowan sat up in his bedsit and mused on everything that Rattray had said, turning the information over and over in his mind. He held and toyed with Rattray's business card so much that it became dog-eared and finger-smeared. He did not sleep. He did not feel like sleeping. Come dawn, he went out walking. He walked all over North London, through Highgate to Hampstead to Belsize Park and beyond, looking around him at the city he knew well, seeing it as if for the first time, with fresh eyes.

A twin race. Another world just a fraction of a second out of synch with this one.

Everything – buildings, lamp-posts, parked cars, trees – seemed new and suffused with a deeper significance. From the milkman trundling along in his whirring, tinkling float to the fruit-and-veg stall owner setting out his wares – who was in on the secret? Who was not? Everything seemed less simple, yet at the same time somehow clearer.

The weirdest part of it was, MacGowan felt that he had been aware all along of the things Rattray had told him. It was as though he had, in the past, caught occasional, brief, corner-of-the-eye glimpses of the secret machinations that were going on beneath the surface of the everyday world, but had not recognised them at the time for what they were. It made sense. That was what was so crazy. Rattray's bizarre story made absolute, perfect sense.

At a greasy-spoon café in Chalk Farm, MacGowan munched his way slowly through a full English breakfast. As he ate, he contemplated the second chance that had been presented to him.

Redressing the wrongs that had been done. Rebalancing the karmic scales.

Having finished and paid for the meal, he went in search of a telephone box.

He made two calls.

The first was to Sarah. As soon as she picked up and said hello, he said, 'Sarah, I love you. I'm sorry. It's going to be all right.' He hung up before she could reply.

Then he took out Rattray's business card and dialled the number on it.

'Rattray.'

'Rattray, Bill MacGowan here.'

'Mr MacGowan.'

'I'm in.'

'I'll contact you again soon,' said Rattray, and broke the connection.

It might not stop the nightmares, MacGowan thought as he replaced the receiver. I'll probably be stuck with those for the rest of my life.

But he had the feeling that as long as he did what he could in memory of Hensher, Gleason, Jones and Palmer, then their dream-spectres would never reach him. They would charge at him, hell-bent on tearing him to pieces . . .

But they would never reach him.

PART 1

PART 4

1

There were four of them, boys, none of them older than
eighteen, all of them dressed in brand-name sportswear:
baggy anoraks, sweatshirts and tracksuits, chunkily ba-
roque basketball boots. The clothing made it hard to tell
them apart, masking differences in colouring, physique
and physiognomy – a casual uniform. They walked along
the pavement in a four-square phalanx, arms dangling
by their sides, feet louchely dragging. Their pace was
unhurried. They were young, invulnerable. They owned
the streets.

It was nine o'clock on a cloudy but warm September
night, and the four teenagers, unable to think of a better
way to occupy themselves, had decided to do over a
tramp. They had nothing against tramps particularly, but
tramps were easy and safe targets, either too fucked-up on
meths or too enfeebled by lack of food to offer much
resistance.

So the four teenagers made their way through the
sodium-lit thoroughfares of South London to a small
park they knew of, one which was often used as an open-
air dormitory by vagrants, and one whose gates were
easily scaled.

Inside the park, three of them waited while the fourth
urinated long and hard against a tree. Then, in a pack,
they set off in search of prey.

They soon found what they were looking for.

The tramp was lying curled up in the foetal position on

33

a bench. From a distance, he resembled a large heap of rags. Up close, the four teenaged boys could see that he was a tall, rangy man with a bushy, unkempt beard. He was bundled up inside a huge, heavy army-surplus great-coat whose cuffs and hems were frayed. His laceless brogues were worn through at the soles. He was fast asleep, and in his arms was a quarter-full 500-ml bottle of cheap whisky, which he was clutching to his breast as tightly as a slumbering child clutches a teddy bear.

The four teenaged boys grinned at one another.

Cecil Evans was woken by several pairs of hands grabbing him roughly and rolling him off his makeshift bed, on to the ground.

The bench was set into a concrete base. Cecil landed hard, pain spiking into his left shoulder and ribs. The whisky bottle slipped from his grasp but, miraculously, did not break. He tried to struggle to his feet, but the hands that had dislodged him from the bench now held him down. He peered up, blinking blearily, trying to focus. He had an impression of man-shaped silhouettes looming over him, black against the starless magenta field of the urban night sky.

'Please,' he mumbled. 'Please, you don't know what you're doing.'

All he received in reply was a round of mocking, malicious laughter. He saw bone-white grins hovering in the dark. Then, out of the corner of one eye, he glimpsed a foot swooping through the air, a pale blur, and suddenly his thigh ignited with pain.

Cecil groaned and clutched his leg. Through gritted teeth he continued to speak. He had to warn them. 'I mean it,' he said. 'You don't know what you're getting yourselves into.'

'Twat,' he heard one of his assailants sneer. 'Thinks he's Steven fucking Seagal, innit?'

'What's the old pisshead gonna do?' said another of them. 'Gonna knock us out with his BO, is he?'

'You don't understand,' Cecil said urgently. He could

sense Mr L. Brain stirring inside him, awakening from dormancy, uncurling, emerging. 'I can't control him. If I'm in danger, he takes over. He protects me. Please! Listen to me! Run while you still can! It may not be too late.'

But there was just more laughter, and then Cecil was punched in the cheek, the impact jarring his brain inside his skull, sending his head slamming against the concrete . . .

And then, for an immeasurable period of time, Cecil was unaware of anything.

And then he found himself standing about five metres away from the bench. His knuckles were throbbing achingly, there was sweat on his face, and he was panting hard. He felt as though he had just run the 400 metres, punching steel girders along the way.

Around him, the four teenagers lay sprawled on the ground. One was partly propped up against the bench, his head tilted at an awkward angle, as if he had fetched up in this position after being bodily *hurled*. Another was face-down on the grass, both forearms twisted around, broken at the elbows. These two were still alive, but neither was conscious. As for the other two, one was on his back, moaning softly and wheezing air in through a mashed mouth and a swollen nose that resembled a ripe, split plum, while the other was writhing on his side, gagging and mewling in agony, his arms clasped around his belly.

Cecil, his head whirling like a cyclotron, made for the bench. Plumping himself down, he retrieved the whisky bottle from the ground and unscrewed the cap. The whisky was bitter, raw stuff, but a few swigs of it helped restore clarity and equilibrium.

Grimly he surveyed Mr L. Brain's handiwork. The four youngsters had brought this punishment on themselves, of course. He had warned them, and it was hardly his fault that they had chosen to ignore the warning. All the same, Cecil could not help but feel *some* compassion for them. How could they have known that he was not the defenceless target that he appeared to be? How could they have known that he had his very own, as it were, 'Guardian' angel?

He decided to head for the nearest phone-box and (anonymously) summon an ambulance. Though the juvenile would-be muggers had richly deserved the beating they had received at his – or rather Mr L. Brain's – hands, it wasn't right that any of them should die as a result. The one clutching his belly, in particular, appeared in urgent need of medical attention. Cecil was no doctor, but he suspected that some of the kid's internal organs had been ruptured.

He took one more swig of whisky, then stowed the bottle away in an inner pocket of his greatcoat and got to his feet.

And teetered.

And collapsed to his knees.

And saw:

a pair of large, sinister-looking, cubic concrete buildings – empty and long-abandoned – nearby, a clay-grey sea, heaving against a shingle beach

a flash – and now, as though in an X-ray photograph, the ghostly embers of a dead fire visible at the heart of each of the buildings – a memory of glowing, deep inside – and within the glow, a face – an inordinately famous face – that of an elderly man with a shock of white, wild hair, wrinkled skin and warm, wise eyes – Albert Einstein

then, of all things, a Siamese cat – sitting sphinx-like – its slanting blue eyes slightly crossed – its face a chocolate-brown smudge – its ears, paws and tail the same colour, shading to pale ochre along its torso

and then figures in white coats – faceless, featureless people moving industriously to and fro amid a forest of test-tubes and retort stands and glass tubes – ministering to a creation

and the object of their attentions: something dark and wormlike – a grotesque pupa, curled up, fat with evil promise – ready to be born

With that, the vision dissolved, and the night-time park and the quartet of injured teenagers glimmered into view again. For a moment, superimposed over the scene, Cecil saw Mr L. Brain's signature-symbol. It hovered gibbously like the afterimage of a bright light temporarily retained by his retinas: a mouth in front of another mouth, the two slightly misaligned, so that the lower mouth looked like the shadow of the upper. But the mouths were dissimilar. One was tight, grim, forbidding, perhaps even hateful; the other was more tender, almost a smile, though it still had a touch of sternness about it.

As the signature-symbol faded, Cecil braced himself for the inevitable consequence of one of Mr L. Brain's visions. Sure enough, it came. A clench of reverse peristalsis, and then Cecil was doubled over and puking his guts out on to the ground. The evening's supper had been predominantly liquid. The whisky burned his throat on the way up as it had on the way down, but altogether less pleasantly this time.

He vomited until his stomach was empty, cursing soundly in the lulls between bouts of retching and heaving. Finally the nausea abated. Settling back on his haunches, Cecil cleaned off his lips and beard with his sleeve. Spatters of regurgitated whisky speckled his trousers. His digestive system felt as though it had been scoured from the inside out with wire wool.

And he had a feeling that there was something odd, something out of place. A nagging, snagging feeling that things were not entirely as they ought to be. Like entering a favourite room and realising, at a glance, that a single item of furniture has been shifted a few inches from its customary position, but being unable to establish *which* item of furniture.

What was it? What was wrong?

Cecil racked his brains.

The vision itself was no different from any other, at least in tone. It was as violently vivid as his visions always were. Nor was its content particularly unusual. Indeed, the motif of white-coated people surrounded by laboratory apparatus was a recurrent one in Mr L. Brain's cryptic instructions, a stock image.

No, what was amiss was not in the vision itself, but in what had followed. The signature-symbol.

Cecil conjured up Mr L. Brain's double-mouths in his memory. Yes, that was it.

The mouths had been back-to-front. Usually the tender smile was overlaid on the grim grimace. This time, it had been the other way round.

Had this inversion of the mouths happened before? It might have, and Cecil had simply not noticed. Was it significant? Maybe. Maybe not. It was not his place to determine such things. That job belonged to the man with whom he now had to arrange a rendezvous.

John Rattray.

2

The door-buzzer sounded. Rattray, dressed in pyjamas, leather slippers and a Paisley-patterned silk dressing gown, went to the video-entryphone unit mounted on the wall in the hallway of his flat, next to the main entrance.

The entryphone's small black-and-white screen showed Cecil Evans, in profile, standing on the building's porch. He was checking the number on the front door, making sure he had the right house.

Rattray pressed the intercom button. 'Cecil?'

Cecil turned to look into the camera lens. 'Yeah, John. It's me.'

'Come on in.' Rattray hit the button that unlatched the front door. 'Third floor. Keep going up till you can't go any further.'

'I remember.'

A minute later, Rattray was ushering Cecil into his living room.

'Nice to see you again, John,' said Cecil, as they shook hands.

A strong odour of stale alcohol and unwashed body and clothes reached Rattray's nostrils. 'You, too, Cecil,' he said, tuning down the sensitivity of his olfactory nerve-receptors so that the smell ceased to trouble him. 'Take a seat.' He gestured at a damask-covered sofa.

Cecil removed his greatcoat and draped it over one arm of the sofa. He made an elaborate show of brushing the back of his trousers before sitting down. As he sank into the comfort of the sofa's upholstery, he sighed.

'Ahh, that's nice,' he said. Then, noticing Rattray's clothing, he frowned. 'I didn't get you out of bed, did I? When I rang?'

'It wouldn't matter if you had,' replied Rattray. 'But, as it happens, I'd just had a bath and was up watching *The X-Files* when you called.'

'Ah. And how was it? *The X-Files*, that is. I don't need to know about the bath.'

'A reasonably entertaining episode. A few factual inaccuracies, but then that's only to be expected, given that the majority of the scriptwriters work for us. Keeping the waters muddied.' Rattray gestured in the direction of the kitchen. 'Can I fix you something to eat?'

'Sandwich'd be great.'

'What would you like in it?'

'Don't mind. Whatever you've got in the fridge.'

'How does ham and cheese sound?'

'Lovely. And some tea'd be nice, if it's not too much trouble.'

'You know me. A cup of tea's never too much trouble.'

Rattray disappeared into the kitchen and began busying himself there. Cecil, to pass the time, glanced appraisingly and approvingly around the flat. The decor was timelessly tasteful, the furnishings expensively classic. Shelves of books lined one wall – old books, the kind without jackets. There were paintings from every decade of the century, and a large gilt-framed mirror over the fireplace. Cecil decided that if he ever had a flat – if, by some miracle, his dream of a normal life ever became a reality – he would decorate it in exactly this style. And he would keep it as spotlessly clean as Rattray kept this place.

A few minutes later Rattray returned carrying a tray, on which were the promised ham-and-cheese sandwich, a pot of Earl Grey tea, two cups, a small milk jug, a bowl of sugar and a plate of shortbread biscuits. He set the tray down on the marble-topped coffee-table in front of Cecil and seated himself in an armchair on the opposite side of the table.

Cecil rubbed his hands together and tucked in to the food. He polished off the sandwich in half a dozen bites, then wolfed down all of the biscuits almost as swiftly.

Rattray, his expression inscrutable, watched as Cecil wetted an index finger and began running it around the biscuit plate, gathering up crumbs and sucking them off the finger. When the plate was gleamingly clean, Cecil sank back in the sofa, sated.

'Much appreciated,' he said to Rattray. 'Cheers.'

'Not at all,' replied Rattray. 'You know, you really ought to have let me come and pick you up in the car. There was no need to walk all the way over here from – where was it you rang from? Streatham?'

'Balham. And I didn't mind the walk. It wasn't that far. Helped clear my head a bit.'

'You said a gang of teenagers attacked you.'

Cecil nodded.

'But you're all right?'

'Couple of bruises, but basically fine.' Cecil tapped his temple. 'Chap up here took over and sorted them out.'

'Of course he did,' said Rattray. 'You're a valuable asset, Cecil. It would be foolish of the Librans to leave you undefended. Speaking of which . . . In your opinion, was the attack Anarch-initiated?'

Cecil frowned briefly. 'Doubt it. Nah, it was just kids out for kicks. Otherwise Mr L. Brain would've killed them, wouldn't he?' He gave a hollow, humourless chuckle. 'Instead of just crippling and maiming them.'

'So no need for the Domestic, then.'

'Nope. No food for the big kitty. I called an ambulance, though. Least I could do, though I didn't hang around to see it arrive. I figured there was a chance police would turn up as well, and the last thing I need is yet another run-in with *them*.'

'Yeah, bastard pigs,' said the former Detective Inspector John Rattray of Her Majesty's Metropolitan Police wryly.

They both laughed.

The contrast between these two men could not have been much more pronounced. One was clean-shaven and neatly groomed; the other, abundantly, was not. One had once been a figure of authority; the other had never held any public position of rank. One was urbane and – to judge by the fact that he could afford a maisonette flat on one of Kensington's smarter thoroughfares – affluent; the other was a dweller of the streets, someone who moved all-but-ignored through the interstices of society, with few other possessions than the clothes on his back.

Looking at the two of them together, you might have thought that Cecil was the senior by a margin of perhaps ten years, but in fact Cecil's face, seamed and coarsened by the vicissitudes of his harsh existence, made him appear to be about fifty when he was actually in his late thirties. Rattray, on the other hand, though he, too, appeared to be in his fifties, was considerably older than that. Ten decades older, to be precise. Cecil was prematurely aged; Rattray was, by artificial means, kept ageless. Time etched its marks deeply in Cecil; Rattray, time could not touch, at least not physically.

Yet in spite of the many differences between them, they were equals. Each was aware of the burdens that the other man had to carry, and this gave them something in common: suffering. Different qualities of suffering, to be sure, but similar quantities, inasmuch as such things can be objectively measured. That was the bond they shared, and that was what made them close comrades, perhaps even friends.

Now Rattray, judging that the tea had brewed to the perfect strength, leaned forwards and filled each of the cups. Cecil helped himself to milk and sugar, lavish amounts of both. Rattray, in turn, poured a modicum of milk and a sprinkling of sugar into his own cup. Then, settling back, he reached for the pencil and the spiral-bound notepad which he had laid out on the occasional table next to the armchair, in readiness, prior to Cecil's arrival.

Observing this action, Cecil nodded soberly. 'All right,' he said, taking a sip of his tea. 'I understand. Down to business. Here goes.'

When he had finished recounting the vision in as much detail as possible, Cecil paused. 'There *was* something else,' he said. 'Only I'm not sure if it's worth mentioning or not.'

'Every little bit helps,' said Rattray.

'I don't know if I've told you this before, but when Mr L. Brain finishes "talking" to me, he always signs off with this one particular image.'

'You have referred to it on a couple of occasions. The two mouths?'

'Well, yes. I think they're meant to reassure me, or as an apology for inconveniencing me. Maybe both.'

'And what about them?' said Rattray, regarding Cecil carefully. For all the unwrinkled smoothness of Rattray's features, there was one aspect of his face that belied his true age. His eyes. In them, the accumulated weariness of a century and a half of living was deeply ingrained. Overshadowed by a heavy forehead, Rattray's eyes peered out at the world with painful understanding, like hermits from caves. Fixed now by their dark, glittering scrutiny, Cecil felt suddenly ill at ease.

'You can see one through the other, like in a double-exposure photograph,' he said, 'but they're not the same as each other. One's a smile, the kind of smile your mum'd give you when you were a kid and you did something stupid but endearing. The other mouth's more serious. Cold. Exasperated. Like when you were in school and your teacher asked you a question and you got the answer completely wrong – the sort of mouth you'd see her make then. Like she *knew* you were going to get it wrong, it was no more than she expected.'

At the foot of the last page of his shorthand notes on Cecil's vision, Rattray made a quick sketch of how he imagined the two mouths to look.

'It's probably not important,' Cecil went on, 'but

normally the mother-mouth sits on top of the teacher-mouth. Tonight, though, I'm almost certain it was the other way round.'

He waited for Rattray to speak, but for a long time the erstwhile policeman said nothing and simply stared at the two mouths he had drawn, side by side.

'Well?' Cecil prompted. He was worried that he might have annoyed Rattray. Perhaps he should not have raised the subject of Mr L. Brain's signature-symbol. It was just too trivial a detail. He should not have wasted Rattray's time with it.

'Interesting,' said Rattray, quietly.

'Does it mean anything?'

'Hard to say. It may well. Recently certain aspects of Guardianship have begun to seem . . . problematic to me.'

'Problematic?' Rattray had hesitated over choosing the word, and it seemed to Cecil that he had been intending to use another, more emotive adjective but had changed his mind at the last moment.

'I've become aware of implications, of a certain, deeper level of complexity to what we do.' Rattray shook his head. 'But it's not *your* concern, Cecil. The difficulty, if it lies anywhere, lies within me.'

'I'm sure, whatever it is, you'll be able to sort it out, John,' said Cecil in an encouraging tone of voice. 'You're the smartest bloke I know. You apply your grey matter to it, and you'll be able to think it through. I have confidence in you.'

'Thank you,' said Rattray.

'Maybe you think too much. Maybe that's what the trouble is. Think too much and take too little for granted.'

'Maybe. Maybe.' Rattray inclined his head forwards in a slow, contemplative nod. Then, abruptly, he clapped the notepad shut and slid the pencil into the pad's spiral binding. 'Cecil,' he said, all brisk and businesslike again, 'as ever, you've performed a sterling service.'

'Just doing my job,' said Cecil. 'If job's the right description for something you have no choice about doing,' he added, ruefully.

'I think for most of us it is.' Rattray rose to his feet. 'I've got some money for you, of course. Fifty pounds, the going rate for visions these days. But I was wondering . . . I don't have a guest room as such, but I could make up a bed for you on the floor here, if you'd like.'

'Oh, no.' Cecil stood up, too, and gathered up his greatcoat. 'No, I couldn't possibly. Wouldn't dream of it.'

'It'd be no trouble.'

'No, John. Thank you, but it wouldn't be right.'

Cecil seemed genuinely embarrassed by the offer, so Rattray refrained from pressing him further. While he did not think for a moment that Cecil enjoyed the life he led, he understood that Cecil had grown to accept the limitations imposed on him by his role as a conduit for communiqués from the paraterrestrial world. Clearly he would not feel comfortable sleeping under Rattray's roof, and might not even sleep at all. It would be a reminder of the ordinary, everyday existence that he could not have, that was forever denied him. A painful reminder.

Rattray showed Cecil to the door, and as they shook hands slipped a folded wad of pound notes – two twenties and a ten – into Cecil's coat pocket. Cecil acknowledged receipt of the payment with the merest of nods.

'Look after yourself, mate,' he said to Rattray.

'You, too,' Rattray replied.

Cecil turned, went downstairs and let himself out by the front door.

3

Back in the living room, Rattray examined the notes he had taken.

As usual, the instructions conveyed in Cecil's vision were vague and imprecise, but Rattray, through familiarity, was immediately able to discern that some form of contratemporal biological experimentation was taking place. When interpreting Cecil's visions it was often necessary to think laterally and make oblique verbal associations. In this instance the sinister chrysalised pupa – an image which had been used by the Librans in the past – represented a symbolic play on the word 'bug'. The mission, therefore, was going to entail the suppression of the development of a bacteriological or viral agent, doubtless one with a potential military application.

So far, so good. Less easy to deduce, however, was the location of the laboratory where the biowarfare agent was being developed. Some kind of abandoned sea-fort or coastal defence bunker? Probably not, if the Einstein reference was anything to go by. And in which country? The Siamese cat suggested Thailand, but if so, why had the Guardians' Pacific Rim chapter not been entrusted with the mission? Besides, shingle beaches were not, as far as Rattray was aware, a common coastal feature of the former kingdom of Siam.

Kawai Kim would be able to work it out. She was far better than he was at making sense of the Librans' enigmatic messages. With the immense global encyclopaedia of the World Wide Web at her fingertips, she was able to sieve probabilities from possibilities and certainties from probabilities, and thus translate the crude images supplied by the Librans into hard facts. *She* would be able to furnish the Guardians with precise mission parameters.

Rattray turned his attention to the matter of the mismatched mouths. Here was something new, something that merited pondering.

He inspected the sketches he had made of the mouths. They did not look all that dissimilar (but, then, he had never been much of an artist). Cecil, however, had made it clear that they were quite distinct from each other. Cecil's visions operated on an instinctual level as well as on a visual. What he saw while immersed in one of his trance-like states was intimately linked with a set of emotional responses, for which reason Rattray was always at pains to ask him not just for superficial descriptions but for visceral impressions as well. It built up a more fully rounded picture.

For Cecil, then, one of the mouths was that of a fond, forgiving mother, the other that of a stern teacher. He felt, seeing them, the same way he had felt when either kind of facial expression had been directed at him while as a boy.

For Rattray, however, Mr L. Brain's signature-symbol seemed to represent something else. Something more.

Duplicity.

He did not *want* to construe it that way. He would have much preferred to have come up with a more innocent interpretation. But, try as he might, he could not.

Duplicity.

Five months ago, Rattray and his fellow members of the North Europe chapter had been sent by the Librans to the American South-West to suppress the production of an antigravity-propulsion drive. The mission – assuming you discount one serious hitch that had nearly cost three of them their lives – had been a success. However, in the course of events Rattray had discovered that the woman who in 1901 had recruited him to the Guardians, the only woman, moreover, whom he had ever truly loved, Valentina Aleksandrovna Popkova, had, it appeared, been killed in 1908 while engaged on an action-to-suppress in a remote and inhospitable region of her native Russia. Rattray had no means of being certain that this was what had happened, but the evidence was compelling.

It was not the fact of her untimely death that had disturbed him, however, since he and Valentina had parted for good in 1905, both acknowledging that they would not see each other again. Rather, it was the fact that he had not been *informed* of her death. Deliberately or otherwise, he had been kept in the dark.

This revelation had sown a seed of doubt which, in the stony ground of a less questioning brain, might not have germinated, but which found fecund soil in the mind of the innately introspective John Rattray, and took root and flourished.

The Librans demanded much of their agents on Earth. A Guardian was expected to obey orders without hesitation and kill without compunction, like a good foot-soldier. A Guardian had to accept that the Librans were wisely and benevolently shepherding the human race through the minefield of its own ingenuity, and had to take it on trust that the Librans knew best which theories and inventions should and should not be permitted to exist and when the time was right for a social change or a piece of new technology to be handled wisely by its creators. A Guardian had to believe, too, that the Anarchs had tried numerous times in the past to disrupt the Librans' plans, and were continuing to do so today, more strenuously than ever. A Guardian had to make it his or her goal to oppose the Anarchs' efforts to hothouse the human race to self-destruction, and had to be prepared to sacrifice his or her life, and take the lives of others, in the furtherance of that goal.

This was the creed to which Rattray had adhered for nearly a century, in large part because Valentina, by her example and by the force of her personality, had convinced him that he should, that it was the correct thing to do. Indeed, his initial decision to accept Valentina's invitation to become a Guardian was heavily influenced by his admiration for her (though he had not realised this at the time and was reluctant to admit it even now). This is not to say he thought that she had been sent to seduce him, to beguile him into joining. After all, he had not recognised – or even confessed to himself – his feelings for her until *after* he had undergone the series of hideous operations that had transformed him into a near-invulnerable and effectively immortal being, the price of his Guardianship. Nor was he in any doubt that her love for him had been as passionate and sincere as his for her. There had been no deception involved, nor any *self*-deception. Nevertheless, had anyone other than Valentina been sent to recruit him, it was debatable whether he would have enlisted as a Guardian so readily, or even at all.

And having queried the Librans' motives in one instance, it was hard not to begin to look askance on everything else they did. Having spotted one serious-looking crack in the plasterwork, it was hard not to start noticing – or imagining – others, and not to wonder whether the entire edifice might not have been built on shaky foundations and be ready to fall.

The Librans moved in mysterious ways – that was the accepted policy among Guardians when the Librans asked them to do something that was, by normal human standards, morally or ethically equivocal. The Librans, in their otherworldly wisdom, knew best.

But what if they did not?

This was why Rattray was now dwelling on the matter of the two mouths. Hitherto what Cecil referred to as 'Mr L. Brain's signature-symbol' had seemed to Rattray to stand for the Librans' attitude towards humanity, one of care tempered by concern. Now, in its duality, he could not help but see an element of deceitfulness; in its inversion, a shift in viewpoint, albeit one whose significance he could not yet determine.

Perhaps Cecil was right. Perhaps he *did* think too much. His colleague Lucretia Fisk had implied something similar at the outset of the previous mission five months ago. 'What we do as Guardians isn't easy to justify all the time,' she had said, 'and if you think about it too hard, you may find yourself starting to have doubts, starting to ask yourself the kind of questions to which there are no good answers.' Perhaps this was so, and he was divining deeper meanings where there were none.

Perhaps.

Rattray shook his head, as though you could rid yourself of a troublesome thought the same way you could rid yourself of a bothersome fly. But the thought would not be dismissed so easily. It had been lodged in his mind for five months, and had been preying on him like a parasite all that time, fastening and fattening itself on his doubt.

In an effort to ignore it, he had immersed himself in miscellaneous items of day-to-day Guardian business. He had:

– checked with the Guardians' various sources of funding and made sure that they had, as he had advised them, sold off their riskier assets and moved their money into safer, blue-chip stocks (Kim's financial-trend projection programs had predicted the current slump in the global economy);

– contacted all of the North Europe chapter's disinformation experts and been brought up to date on their latest efforts (these included some gloriously faked-up camcorder footage of cold fusion failing to take place under laboratory conditions, and a book that offered a radical reinterpretation of the Koran, suggesting among other things that the angels Mohammed famously met were actually beings from an alternate realm, to which assertion Islamic historians and Muslim religious leaders were responding with the expected outrage and vilification, although the sales-boosting *fatwa* the book's publishers were hoping for had yet to be declared);

– spoken at length with Arnold X, by default the

current head of the North American Guardians, who was still in the process of putting his chapter back together following the Oregon Massacre two and a half years earlier (Arnold's tone had been frostily polite – he had not yet entirely forgiven Rattray and the North Europe chapter for embroiling him in the near-disaster that had been the antigravity-propulsion action-to-suppress);

– telephoned the Guardians' government contacts in Westminster, Brussels, the Hague and Bonn and ensured that they were continuing to do their best to cover up, repudiate and deny all reports and rumours of anomalous phenomena, whether those phenomena did or did not relate to Guardian activity (on a couple of occasions he had felt it necessary to remind the individuals concerned that it was still within his power to make their unusually unpleasant private vices public knowledge).

Through these and other routine tasks Rattray had hoped to keep himself distracted and not allow his doubts to develop into full-blown fears . . . but the parasitic thought had continued to cling and suck and suckle and swell.

Now, at last, there was some proper work to be done, work he could focus and concentrate on to the exclusion of all else. Now, at last, there was a chance he might be free from nagging, insistent uncertainty, even if only for a while.

He went through to his study, booted up his computer and composed an e-mail to Kim.

4

The reply was waiting for him with his service provider the following morning. Logging on after breakfast, he retrieved and opened the e-mail. Immediately he was asked for his password and given fifteen seconds in which to enter it. With ten swift, confident finger-strikes he stabbed out 'METHUSELAH'. The password was accepted. Private-key decryption software went to work. Kim had beefed up her code and security protocols recently, so Rattray's PC took longer than usual to unscramble the content of the e-mail.

'My dear Mr Rattray,' the e-mail began, in characteristically mock-formal tones. 'Another conundrum from the Librans, but one which it was not beyond the powers of the Otaku Queen to unravel . . .'

Kim proceeded to supply an interpretation of Cecil's vision that, as Rattray read through it, seemed to him to fit together and make sense. He nodded approvingly as he scrolled down through the e-mail. Good work, Kim.

The final few paragraphs of the e-mail, however, had nothing to do with the vision, and their tone was more intimate and direct.

On to the matter of Emperor Dragon, who has been stepping up his efforts to embarrass and discredit me. I enclose, as an attached file, a copy of his latest flame against me: pictures of my avatar in pornographic situations. Emperor Dragon calls them a 'Late Valentine' to me, although, as you will see, he can't even spell 'Valentine' properly. (That should give you some idea of the intelligence of this person!)

I feel it's only fair to warn you, John, the pictures are quite explicit. Which, of course, means they've been *extremely* popular among 'Net-users, most of whom are mentally, if not actually, adolescents. (And before you suggest it, there's no point in me trying to erase the pictures. It's too late. Copies have been duplicated across mirror-sites all across the world. I'd never be able to locate and dispose of them all.) I thought you should see them, anyway, as they are typical of Emperor Dragon's infantile 'sense of humour'.

Really, John, he is a tiresome and infuriatingly elusive opponent. So far, all my attempts to retaliate in kind to his slurs and slanders have met with little success. His 'Net persona is nowhere near as high-profile as mine, so I cannot properly deal with him on that level. It's a bit like trying to fight back against guerrilla warfare – no matter how great your firepower, it's hard to hit what you cannot see.

There is some good news, though. <g> As you are aware, I have been attempting to unearth Emperor Dragon's Real Life whereabouts. Until now, his digital trail has led me to countless ghost sites, false addresses and dead ends. He has been covering his tracks well – amazingly well, if even the Otaku Queen cannot unearth him! However, I have managed to narrow his location down to the Japanese archipelago. It makes sense to me that Emperor Dragon is Japanese. His onscreen avatar is that of an oriental dragon with three talons on each foot. A Chinese dragon traditionally has four or five talons per foot. A Japanese dragon has three.

I'm now busy pursuing various further avenues of investigation, and I'm optimistic that I will shortly be able to establish which city he lives in, and perhaps even obtain a street address.

In the light of this, I would like to beg a favour of

you, John, as an operative of unique capabilities and as, I hope, my friend. Would you come to Tokyo and help me find and confront Emperor Dragon in person? Between us we might be able to persuade him to desist in his attacks on me. I would not go so far as to suggest invalidation, but perhaps some other form of permanent discouragement.

I await your reply.

She signed off, 'Yours hopefully, Kim,' adding the unhappy emoticon ':-('.

Rattray knew about Emperor Dragon. He had first made his presence known during the action-to-suppress five months ago in America. Shortly after that, he had begun to post 'slash fiction' about Kim on various sites across the 'Net – sweaty, fetid fantasies in which Kim was portrayed as the victim of the grossest kind of lusts and perversions. Kim had been the subject of slash fiction before (after the Andersons, Pamela and Gillian, she was the third most fantasised-about female on the 'Net). Mostly the tone of the pieces about her had been respectful and rather sweet, but once Emperor Dragon's violent and depraved stories started to appear, the floodgates were opened, and copycats were soon coming up with their own equally sordid works of prose about her, trying to outdo one another in their imaginative vileness.

Emperor Dragon had then switched to criticising Kim openly, posting diatribes against her everywhere, saying among other things that her reputation as one of the world's foremost hackers was undeserved and that her sexy online image was a fraud – in Real Life, she was as stupid as a sheep and as ugly as a pig. To provide himself with a soapbox for these opinions, Emperor Dragon had set up a homepage, the Kill Kawai Kim Korner. Dozens of new subscribers were signing up to it daily.

He had also resorted to sabotage. At one point he had hacked into the chatroom Kim moderated, Kawai Kim's Koven, and altered the site's hyperlinks, rerouting them so that they led users to various unsavoury homepages, including one that belonged to an international paedo-phile ring and another that belonged to a sect of extremely humourless millenarian fundamentalists who were holed up in South America, the Children of Elijah. It had taken Kim several hours of hard work to repair the damage.

In short, a concerted effort was under way to besmirch Kim's name and bring her down, and its instigator was the pretender to her crown, Emperor Dragon. And it appeared that his campaign of defamation and vilification was beginning to have some effect. Loyalty to and admiration for the Otaku Queen were on the wane. The Koven, once one of the most frequently hit chat-room sites on the 'Net, was losing popularity fast. Kim's opinions were no longer considered as valid as once they had been. A handful of diehard Kovenites remained faithful to her and were doing their best to defend her reputation, but the pack mentality was at work among the virtual community. 'Net-users were rallying in their droves behind the challenger to Kim's supremacy, the new, usurping, would-be alpha-dog.

Throughout it all, Kim had striven to maintain a brave face and rise above Emperor Dragon's assaults on her dignity, but Rattray could tell that deep down she was upset and worried. In telephone conversations he had had with her in recent weeks, her voice, normally calm and confident, would fracture and falter whenever the name of her tormentor was mentioned. Kim lived so much of her life through her vicarious cyber-self that, although it was not really *her* being travestied and pilloried online, she felt the distress almost as acutely as if it was.

She was right. Emperor Dragon should not be allowed to compromise the effectiveness of a Guardian asset. Some kind of 'permanent discouragement', as Kim so delicately put it, was in order. And if she *could* find out where he lived, then a personal visit might do the trick. Rattray doubted, however, that he was the right man for the job. Far better that one of the local Guardians should deal with the matter. Fond though he was of Kim, Rattray did not think it was appropriate for him to travel all the way to Japan to tackle a problem that was not really the North Europe chapter's business.

No, he would have to tell Kim, regretfully, that he could not help her. To lend weight to his decision, he would point out that the Librans had yet not decreed that Emperor Dragon was a threat. Until they did, the Guardians did not technically have the authority to act.

Something he saw while viewing Emperor Dragon's pictures caused him to change his mind.

In her Koven, Kim presented herself to the world by means of a realistically rendered onscreen avatar: a busty, pneumatic, Lycra-clad caricature of young Asian womanhood which bore only a passing resemblance to the actual Kim. In his pictures, Emperor Dragon had appropriated the avatar and modified her, stripping her of her already skimpy and suggestive clothing and portraying her, in a variety of poses, being obscenely abused by aliens.

The aliens were of the classic 'Grey' variety, slender and insect-eyed, but whereas in ufological tradition Greys were genderless creatures, these ones were equipped with huge male genitalia. In one picture Kim was strapped face-down to an operating table on board a spaceship and was being sodomised by one of the prodigiously endowed extraterrestrials. In another, she was orally servicing one Grey while at the same time masturbating another two. In a third, a group of the aliens were standing around her in a circle, ejaculating copious amounts of green semen onto her naked body.

There were half a dozen other such images. All of them were executed to a high degree of digital draughtsmanship and with an incongruous elegance, an ill-befitting delicacy of composition. Nothing *in* the pictures themselves, however, particularly offended Rattray. As a police officer he had laid eyes on much more explicit material, even in the Victorian era.

It was after he had examined all the pictures that he remembered Kim deriding Emperor Dragon in her e-mail for misspelling the title of his 'Late Valentine' to her.

Curious to see which of the two words Emperor Dragon had typed incorrectly and how, Rattray glanced at the filename at the top of the screen.

It was at that moment that he decided he would, after all, be making a trip to Japan.

Emperor Dragon had got just one letter of 'Valentine' wrong – an error which, to anyone other than Rattray, would have been inconsequential, but which, to Rattray, could hardly have seemed of greater significance.

The filename was 'Late Valentina'.

Rattray sat back in the leather-upholstered chair before his computer desk and stared at the latter of the two words, frowning, fingers tapping lower lip.

It could have been a coincidence, nothing more. An unfortunate mistyping. If Emperor Dragon was Japanese, as Kim suspected, then it was not surprising that he might accidentally exchange one vowel of an English word for another.

Even so . . .

It was logical to assume that Emperor Dragon knew about the Guardians. He appeared to have access to paraterrestrial-grade software, which did not in itself mean that he was anything more than an unwitting Anarch stooge. However, the timing of the first assault on Kim's mainframe, which he had instigated, was such that it could only have been intended to cause the maximum possible damage to the Guardian action-to-suppress in America. In which case, it was not unreasonable to believe that Emperor Dragon had been regularly monitoring Kim's electronic communications for some time before the attack and was aware that she and Rattray were in frequent touch with each other. Even if this was not so, he still must have known that there was a strong likelihood of Rattray noticing his pictures of Kim, or having his attention drawn to them by another Guardian, and spotting the little verbal clue he had planted.

Might Emperor Dragon know something about Valentina and her death? And if so, what?

Rattray brooded on the matter for some considerable time. Then, finally, addressing himself to the computer again, he called up mail-composition mode and typed Kim a letter. He squirted it off to her, then made a series of phone calls.

An hour later, he armed his maisonette's security system, locked the main door and headed downstairs with a packed suitcase. His Mercedes 600 SEC was parked out on the street in a resident's permit space. He placed the suitcase in the boot, then drove off.

A little over an hour later he was passing through the gates of Bretherton Grange in Surrey.

5

In 1968 Lucretia Fisk's younger brother Ron was driving home along the A24 to his home, Bretherton Grange, when his Aston Martin DB6 veered off the road and into a tree. The accident – in which both occupants of the car, Ron and his young female passenger, were killed – made headlines. Ron was the drummer in a band called the Royals, who were currently in vogue thanks to their chart-topping single, 'Strawberry Sunshine'.

Had their drummer not died in this manner, the Royals would probably have never amounted to more than a footnote in the history of popular music. Ron's death, however, gave them a new lease of life, conferring on them a whiff of credibility that sustained them through lean times and clung to them even to this day. Although the band did eventually break up in the early eighties, citing the usual 'irreconcilable musical differences', it carried on in two incarnations, the Real Royals and the True Royals, both of which could still be found performing in small venues all across Europe. This was Ron's legacy to his fellow band-members: lifetime careers.

Ron's legacy to his sister Lucretia was far stranger. For, in addition to plying his trade as a sticksman, Ron Fisk was a Guardian. Whoever owned Bretherton Grange was invested with the responsibility for looking after the vast array of contratemporal hardware that was stowed in the labyrinthine network of cellars beneath the main

building, and Ron had inherited the house and estate –
with attendant duties – from his first cousin once removed, Raymond Farquhar-Colquhoun, in the early
sixties. Farquhar-Colquhoun had, in turn, inherited the
Grange from his maiden aunt, the minor poetess Bridget
St Swithin, who had inherited it from her father, the emin-
ent Victorian astronomer Professor Archibald St Swithin,
and so on, in a succession of generational handing-downs
dating back to the middle of the eighteenth century, when
the house had been founded.

Ron discharged the obligations of the role of custodian
of the Guardians' hoard as efficiently as he could, but his
heart was never in it. The yoke of responsibility chafed on
his shoulders. Whenever talking about Guardianship with
his sister, he would often cry with frustration, complain-
ing that he was being torn two ways, like the rope in a
tug-of-war. All he wanted to do was play in a band and
enjoy all the fringe benefits that the life of a rock musician
brought (by which Lucretia knew him to mean drugs,
booze, money and easy sex). He wasn't cut out for this
Guardian stuff at all. Too serious for him by far. It was
freaking his head out.

Ron and Lucretia kept few secrets from each other.
He had revealed to her all about the Guardians, what
they were, what they did, safe in the knowledge that
she would never breathe a word of what he told her
to anyone else. Hence Lucretia knew exactly what she
was letting herself in for when she offered to assume
Ron's role for him. Farquhar-Colquhoun, if he had
had any sense, would have chosen Lucretia as his
successor anyway. She – practical, methodical, focused
– was far better suited to the task than Ron –
wild, intemperate, ill disciplined – ever was. Farquhar-
Colquhoun, however, had been a male chauvinist of
the old school, and had not believed a woman up to
the job.

Ron accepted his sister's offer readily and, relieved of
the burdens of Guardianship, went mad with freedom.
His death was all but inevitable, but at least he was able

to indulge in a few heady, halcyon months of sheer rock 'n' roll Babylon before his car met the tree and he met his Maker.

The funeral service, held at a church a few miles from the village of Bretherton, was a muted affair.

At the end of the afternoon, as the last few funeral-goers departed, Lucretia's mother came up to her. Mrs Fisk had had little to say during the ceremony and the wake, spending most of her time sobbing into a handkerchief or silently receiving the condolences of friends, relatives and complete strangers, but now she had composed herself and was ready to give her daughter a piece of her mind. She approached Lucretia in the hallway of the Grange while Lucretia's father was out bringing the car round.

'This never would have happened if it hadn't been for you, Lucretia,' Mrs Fisk said in chillingly cold tones. 'You wanting to be an artist. Setting Ron a bad example. Filling his head with all sorts of ideas. He would have done something sensible, had a normal career, a normal life, if it hadn't been for you.'

Over the course of her adolescence Lucretia had managed to develop an immunity to her mother's vicious tongue, and could normally shrug off or ignore even her most waspish remarks. That day, though, her defences were down, and her mother's words stung.

'I have never seen you happier,' she replied, with imperious calmness, 'than on the day the Royals got a single into the Top Five. You looked like you were ready to burst with pride. "My boy," you said as they played "Strawberry Sunshine" on the radio. "That's my son," you said. "My little Ronnie." You boasted about it to all your friends. You told the neighbours, the milkman, the newspaper-delivery boy, anyone who would listen. His choice of career didn't bother you *then*, did it? It only bothers you now, when it gives you a chance to get at *me*. Because that's the problem, isn't it? *I'm* the one who's not following a "sensible" career. *I'm* the one who's not prepared to settle for the drudgery of being a housewife, who's going to make her own way in life using the skills she was born with.'

'Are you?' retorted her mother, narrow-eyed, vituperative. 'It's been three years since art college and you haven't sold a single sculpture.'

'I don't yet have the facilities to do the kind of work I'd like to do.'

'If it wasn't for your father supporting you . . .'

'And Ron. Don't forget, Ron helped me out, too. With some of the money he earned from not choosing a "sensible" career.'

'Still,' said Mrs Fisk, 'you encouraged him in his irresponsibility. Getting him to hand this place over to you. This house was what kept his feet on the ground.'

'Wrong! This house and all that went with it were never anything more than a millstone around Ron's neck.' As she said this Lucretia waved her arm irritably in the direction of the bookcases that covered the hallway's west wall, an entirely reflexive gesture whose significance was lost on her mother. The bookcases hid the secret entrance to the cellars, whose seemingly limitless extent Lucretia had only just begun to explore.

At that point Lucretia's father entered by the front door to find the two women standing in the middle of the hallway, bent angrily towards each other like a pair of black-garbed pugilists. A seasoned arbiter of disputes between his wife and his daughter, Mr Fisk discerned immediately what was going on and stepped forward to intervene.

'Theresa, Lucretia,' he said in a placatory tone. 'This is neither the time nor the place . . .'

They both swung round and glared at him witheringly. Mr Fisk was visibly shaken to see such antagonism in their eyes. He beat a hasty retreat to the car, where he remained until his wife came striding out of the Grange a minute later and demanded he drive her home.

It was a defining moment for all three family-members. Thereafter none of them was able to look at or speak to either of the other two without the feeling that something, somewhere, had been irrevocably cracked and ruined, like a chipped china cup that, no matter how skilfully it is repaired, can never be restored to its original integrity. There had been family arguments before, of course, but Ron's death cast everything in a new light. Their anger at him for dying in such a stupid, unnecessary manner was transferred to each other. Because Ron was not there to take the blame, they blamed each other.

Lucretia's parents never visited her after she took up residence at Bretherton Grange. Her father said it was because he and her mother associated the place too much with Ron, but all of them were aware of the real reason.

Lucretia had lived at the Grange for thirty years now, twenty-six of those in the company of her common-law husband, Dennis Holman. Following on in the tradition of previous owners, each of whom had added to the building or grounds in some way, immediately upon moving in Lucretia had tacked a large conservatory on to the back of the house, which she put to use as a studio. There she constructed the huge, mechanistic, ineffable sculptures that had made her internationally renowned and in demand over the past three decades. She had also, in those thirty years, given birth to two daughters, Daisy and Alice, and had attended countless Guardian mission-briefings and taken part in a number of actions-to-suppress.

Lucretia was tall and tended to wear her auburn hair tied back in a thick plait. Her hands, from years of working with frequently intractable materials, were rough and ruddy and strong. Her figure was subsiding into late-middle-age shapelessness, but her eyes remained quick and alert, even behind the half-moon spectacles she sometimes had to wear. By no stretch of the imagination could she be considered a beautiful woman, but now that she had achieved her mid-fifties, her toothsome and somewhat horselike features were settling into a sort of composure that in certain lights could be quite handsome. Her face had grown comfortable with its sags and wrinkles.

63

This was the woman who appeared at the front door of the Grange to greet Rattray as he arrived. She embraced him and gave him a peck on the cheek. Rattray reciprocated the affectionate gesture stiffly. There was a certain warmth in his voice as he enquired after Lucretia's health, but a more extrovert display of his undoubted fondness for her would have been entirely out of character.

'I'm well,' Lucretia replied. 'And you?' She laughed at herself. 'Silly question, really, to ask of a man who can't even catch a cold. Come on in.'

Dennis Holman was also on hand to welcome Rattray into the house. He apologised for his appearance. He was in the midst of some interior redecoration, knocking down partition walls in an annexe of the Grange which had so far not been used for anything and which he intended to convert into a games room for playing billiards, table tennis and darts. There was concrete dust all over his denim workshirt and his head, powdering his beard and his thinning thatch of hair.

The two Holman-Fisk girls were currently away, Daisy at Cambridge, Alice at boarding school. The hallway echoed Lucretia's, Rattray's and Holman's footsteps resoundingly as they walked across it, as though the house were trying to compensate for the absence of its two noisiest residents.

Rattray noted the absence. 'The girls aren't here. Bill will be relieved about that.'

'Yes, poor Bill,' said Holman. 'They were pretty cruel to him on the croquet lawn last time.'

'I don't think it's *croquet* Bill's worried about,' said Lucretia, with the slightest and slyest of smiles.

'You mean Daisy?' said Rattray.

'It's quite sweet, really,' said Holman. 'Daisy acts so grown-up most of the time, but then you see the way she pricks up her ears whenever one of us mentions Bill's name and the way she always smartens herself up whenever she knows he's coming down, and you remember it was only a few months ago that she was a teenager.'

'She's sent him letters, too,' said Lucretia, 'and phoned

him.' The three of them were passing through into the dining room at this point. 'Poor old Bill. The worst of it is, he's done nothing to encourage her. It's strictly a one-way affair, and he's been behaving like the perfect gentleman.'

'For now, maybe,' said Holman. 'But I know men. If someone as determined as Daisy has her sights set on Bill, I doubt he'll be able to hold out long.'

'If you ask me,' said Rattray, 'Bill won't dare to so much as touch her. He's too scared of what you, Lucretia, would do to him if he did.'

'And what *would* you do to him, Lu?' Holman asked.

'Nothing,' said Lucretia, seating herself at the head of the dining table. 'Daisy's an adult. She can make her own choices. And to be frank, the age gap between them notwithstanding, she could do a lot worse than Bill. She probably thinks he's wonderfully unsuitable, but Bill's honest and thoughtful and a lot cleverer than he acts, which is more than can be said for *some* of the boyfriends Daisy's brought home. And, as John says, he's scared of me, which is another point in his favour.'

'You're a wicked woman, Miss Fisk,' said Holman with a fond grin. 'So. John. How many more of you are coming?'

'Just Bill,' said Rattray, sitting down in the space next to Lucretia.

At that moment, as if on cue, a chime reverberated through the house, announcing that another Guardian had arrived at the gates of the Grange.

6

As soon as Rattray had phoned him that morning,
MacGowan had sprung from his bed, dressed, breakfasted, packed and leapt into his slate-grey Saab 9000i.
He would have reached Bretherton Grange sooner, but he
was held up by the morning rush-hour traffic and road-
works on the North Circular.

The wrought-iron gates of the Grange parted automatically for MacGowan as he neared them. Each Guardian
carried on his or her person at all times the symbol of
Guardianship, an egg-shaped talisman composed of
tightly interlocking segments, which usually took the
form of an item of jewellery or some small practical
accessory such as, in MacGowan's case, a keyring. These
puzzle-eggs, as they were known, unlocked doors all over
the world for Guardians, providing them with access to
places ordinary people could not go. At the Grange, the
approach of a Guardian bearing a puzzle-egg was
detected by instruments hidden within the intercom pillar
that stood beside the apron of Tarmac that led up to the
main gates. When the Guardian came within a certain
proximity, the gate-opening mechanism was triggered.

As the gates parted, MacGowan gunned the Saab's
engine and swerved the car deftly into the gap while it was
still widening. Judging the timing just right, he grinned as
the wing-mirrors missed the inner vertical edges of the
gates by a whisker. Putting himself through this little test
of nerve and driving skills was a habit he had developed

over the six years he had been regularly coming to the Grange as a Guardian. For as long as he continued to pass the test and did not prang the gates or the car, this was proof to him that his hand–eye co-ordination was as sharp as ever, that even though he was nearly forty years old he was not losing it, that he still had what it took.

He cruised along the winding driveway to the house. He passed by several clusters of the stone pyramids that Bridget St Swithin had had erected all across the grounds in patterns reflecting those of the constellations, the size of each pyramid corresponding to the magnitude of brightness of the star it represented. He passed by the wooden windmill that was the architectural contribution of the Grange's second owner, Anders van der Pool. He passed by the row of cedars that obscured the long, low, single-storey concrete block which the unimaginative Raymond Farquhar-Colquhoun had attached to the house during the 1950s. This was the portion of the Grange which, for want of any other use, Dennis Holman had begun to convert into a games-room annexe.

The driveway terminated in a turning circle, the centre-piece of which was one of Lucretia's sculptures, a lopsided hurricane of mangled metal and aeroplane parts she called *Da Vinci's Dreams Downcast*. To MacGowan, the thing was pretty ugly. And yet there was *something* about it that stirred his fascination each time he laid eyes on it. Maybe it was just the way the sculpture teetered top-heavily, looking as if it was in danger of tipping over at any moment, even though it was clearly not going to. MacGowan might not have the first clue about modern art, but he could admire a cunning feat of engineering.

He drew to a halt outside the Grange, pulling in beside Rattray's Mercedes. He killed the engine and climbed out of the car, bracing himself for another awkward bout of bluff and parry with Daisy Holman-Fisk. Daisy had phoned him twice and written him two lengthy letters in the five months since he last visited here. One of the phone calls had been to invite him to be her escort at one of the Cambridge May Balls. During the other phone call, she had told him she was going to one of the summer's outdoor rock festivals and asked if he would like to accompany her. ('Tents and mud,' she had said. 'An ex-soldier should feel right at home.') On both occasions he had tactfully declined, and had been pained to hear the false, brittle breeziness in Daisy's voice as she had said, 'Oh, well,' and, 'If you're sure.' His conscience had been pricked, and he had been *this* close to caving in and agreeing to come – anything so that Daisy would not be upset. Somehow, though, he had managed to hold his tongue both times. Guilt, he knew from experience, was a poor reason for going on a date with someone.

Daisy was persistent, he had to give her that. But it just wasn't going to work. Couldn't she see that? Couldn't she just take the hint, without him having to come right out with it and tell her? She was good-looking and sexy and lively and smart, a pretty irresistible package in his book. Under any other circumstances he would have been in there like Flynn. But she was also half his age and, more pertinently, she was the daughter of a friend and colleague. For those reasons, it simply could not happen.

Daisy, if she knew MacGowan was coming to the Grange, was usually waiting by the front door, ready to pounce. When, on this occasion, the door was opened not by her but by her father, MacGowan was both relieved and, to his surprise, a little disappointed. The thought flitted across his mind that Daisy had lost interest in him, and he found the idea vaguely upsetting. It was as if – absurdly – she had cheated on him.

Then he remembered. It was term-time. Daisy was away at university. He chided himself for forgetting that. Could have saved himself a bit of anxiety there.

He trotted up the steps to shake Holman's hand. He did a double-take at the dusty state of Holman's clothing and head.

'I'm busy with a spot of DIY,' Holman explained, and he ushered MacGowan indoors and through to the dining room.

Smoky autumn sunshine filtering in through french

windows steeped the dining room with a soft yellow glow. Through the windows could be seen a tidy expanse of lawn dotted with more of those stone pyramids. Beyond lay well-tended shrub beds, and beyond them oaks and beeches whose leaves were beginning to wither and brown.

MacGowan greeted Rattray and Lucretia, and took his seat on Rattray's right. 'Mr International Playboy on his way?' he remarked, referring to the youngest member of the North Europe Guardians, Piers Pearson.

Rattray shook his head. 'I didn't think Piers would be needed this time out.'

'That's a shame,' said MacGowan. 'I was looking forward to topping up my pop-culture references.'

'Tea, Bill? Coffee?' Holman enquired.

'I'm all right, thanks,' said MacGowan.

'I'll leave you to it, then.' Holman exited, closing the dining-room's double doors behind him.

'So how're you doing?' MacGowan asked Lucretia. 'Working on something new?'

'A piece for an inner-city children's recreation area in Manchester. One of those non-paying jobs I occasionally do.'

'One of your cool climbing-frame-type things?'

'An Obstaclimb, yes.'

MacGowan's eyes gleamed with a genuine, boyish excitement. 'Those are brilliant. They make me wish I were thirty years younger.'

'As I recall, Bill,' said Lucretia, 'your age didn't seem to matter the last time I built one.'

'Well, it would have been rude not to try it out. Besides, *someone's* got to road-test those things for you, haven't they?'

'And I remember Daisy and Alice thinking it was the funniest thing they'd ever seen – a grown man, scampering about on a child's plaything.'

Lucretia, feeling as wicked as could be, watched for MacGowan's reaction to the mention of Daisy's name. Sure enough, MacGowan abruptly became forthright and businesslike. 'Yes, well. Let's get down to work, shall we?'

Rattray, nodding, picked up the hard-copy he had brought with him of Kim's e-mail.

'Right,' he said. 'As you might expect, we have another scientific advance on our hands.' He laid a light, sarcastic emphasis on the word *advance*. 'The Librans have presented us with a grand total of two pieces of information to go on. Firstly, a location. The decommissioned nuclear power station at Seal Point, down on the South Coast.'

'Seal Point?' said MacGowan. 'Not sure I've heard of it.'

'Perhaps you'd know it by its previous name,' said Lucretia. 'Brightsea.'

'Oh, yes. That's where there were all those radiation-leak scares back in the seventies.'

'And leukaemia clusters in the surrounding community,' Lucretia added.

'The very same,' said Rattray. 'At first, British Nuclear Fuels Limited kept strenuously denying that the two pressurised-water reactors at the power station were faulty in any way, and dismissed the high incidence of leukaemia among local children as a "statistical blip". BNFL claimed that the power station's safety record was second to none, and the higher the evidence mounted that *somehow* radioactive materials were escaping into the surrounding environment, the more emphatic the denials became. Eventually the company was forced to admit that there had been "a few undesirable events" at the plant, but said that these were "minor", that they had all been "safely contained" and that the emission levels remained within "acceptable safety-limits".'

'The usual drill,' remarked Lucretia.

'Quite,' said Rattray. 'Whatever the truth about the power station's safety, or lack of it, Brightsea gained such notoriety that after a while it was hard to find trained technicians willing to work there for anything less than top pay – danger money. Brightsea became, like Windscale, synonymous with all the drawbacks of atomic energy, and the power station itself became economically unviable. The whole thing was a PR fiasco, and in the end BNFL had no choice but to take the reactors offstream, shut the station down and close the site.'

'And then the local tourist board gave the area a nice bright shiny new name,' said MacGowan.

'Seal Point,' said Lucretia, and chuckled wryly. 'I remember a TV reporter commenting at the time that no seals have actually ever been sighted on that particular stretch of the British coastline.'

Rattray shuffled through the pages of the hard-copy. 'This – the location – Kim was able to infer from two mental images Cecil was granted. One was of the power station itself and its geographical situation, accompanied by a picture of Einstein to convey the message that atomic energy was involved. The other image was of a Siamese cat.'

'A cat?' said MacGowan.

'Seal-point. It's the most common variety of the breed.'

'Oh, you've got to be kidding.'

Rattray shrugged. The nature of Cecil's visions – the fact that, unlike those of his predecessor Frazier Hamilton, they were visual and not aural – necessitated this type of serendipitous linkage when interpreting them, particularly when it came to place-names and proper nouns.

'So what's going on at this power station, John?' Lucretia asked. 'Guardians tried to suppress the development of nuclear fission sixty years ago and failed, and for better or worse we're stuck with it. That particular genie is out of the bottle. So it must be something else. Correct?'

'Correct. Since Brightsea was decommissioned in the mid-eighties, the place has remained a vacant shell. BNFL have tried to sell off the site, to no avail. No one, not even the most rapacious property developer, will touch it. So the buildings have just been left to moulder and rot. Now, however, it appears that someone *has* shown an interest in the place. Kim chased down various leads and discovered evidence that a fortnight ago a company called Gene Genius paid BNFL for the use of the buildings as a temporary laboratory in order to undertake some – and I quote verbatim from the rental agreement – "delicate experiments".'

'What sort of experiments?' MacGowan asked.

'Gene Genius is an agritech research outfit specialising in the genetic modification of plants. The company engineers disease-resistant strains of wheat, genetic herbicides, that sort of thing. Or, at least, so it claims.'

'Meaning?' said Lucretia.

'Perhaps it would help if I pointed out here that, like Seal Point, Gene Genius used to go by another name. In a previous incarnation, before it was bought out and taken over by a larger conglomerate, Gene Genius was known as PetriTech PLC.'

MacGowan stiffened.

'And we have reason to believe,' Rattray went on, 'that they haven't learned their lesson from last time. That they've started to diversify into other branches of research again.'

'Oh, God,' said Lucretia. 'They've developed a bio-weapon.'

'Precisely. Now, we have no data concerning this weapon's capabilities, but if past experience is anything to go by, then we're looking at a bacteriological agent of considerable potency and virulence. Needless to say, once the agent, whatever its capabilities, becomes available on the open market, there are certain military dictators who will be only too keen to get their hands on it, and not only will they purchase it in great quantities, but they'll be willing to use it. And then there are the doomsday cultists and the terrorist organisations, and even our very own military—'

'Yeah, yeah, we get the picture, John,' MacGowan interrupted brusquely. His hands were fisted on the table, their knuckles white, and he was speaking through clenched teeth. 'It's nasty and we've got to suppress it.'

'Do we really have no data about this bacteriological

agent, John?' said Lucretia. 'Kim couldn't dredge up even a hint about what it can do?'

Rattray shook his head slowly. 'We're in the dark.'

'But we don't *need* to know what it can do,' MacGowan insisted. 'We know where they're making it. That's enough. Just tell me how many men you want me to get together, John, and how many bullets you want me to put into the heads of the stupid bloody arseholes who're making the stuff.'

'In answer to both questions, Bill: however many you wish – as long as the agent itself and all traces of its method of production are eradicated.'

'Oh, they will be, don't you worry.'

Rattray laid the hard-copy aside on the tabletop. 'It would appear, therefore, to be a relatively straight-forward assignment,' he said. 'Bill, you'll be in charge of assembling a combat team to infiltrate the power station and suppress production of the agent, and you, Lucretia, will furnish Bill with all the hardware he needs.'

'While you, John . . . ?' said Lucretia, eyebrows raised.

'With everyone's permission,' said Rattray, and he gave a little sideways twitch of the head that some might interpret as a sign of awkwardness, 'I would like to be excused from involvement in this particular mission.'

'Excused?' said MacGowan, with a frown. 'What on earth for?'

'I'm needed elsewhere. In Japan, to be precise.'

'Japan?' said Lucretia. 'Have the Pacific Rim chapter asked for your assistance on something?'

'Not exactly, no. You remember how, earlier this year, Kim's mainframe was invaded by half a dozen hackers?'

'Like I could forget,' said MacGowan grimly.

'Since that unfortunate incident, Kim has been trying to establish what happened – how it was that a half-dozen hackers were able to penetrate her system. Kim's firewall security software is paraterrestrial-grade. You'd need software of comparable sophistication to crack through it.'

'In other words, someone may have access to para-terrestrial-grade software,' said Lucretia. 'Quite a few people, in fact.'

'Quite a few people were involved in the attack, but Kim believes just *one* person made the attack possible – a Japanese hacker known as Emperor Dragon.'

'I don't understand the first thing about all this cyber-space guff,' said MacGowan, 'but why would this Emperor Dragon bloke help Kim out, then turn on her? It doesn't make sense.'

'Emperor Dragon instigated the assault on Kim's mainframe,' said Rattray, 'in order to manoeuvre Kim into a position where he could offer her help and she would have no choice but to accept. That, in hacker terms, made him one up on her.'

'And if he has access to paraterrestrial-grade software,' MacGowan said, 'then he needs to be stopped.'

'He also needs to be stopped,' said Rattray, 'because for the past few months he's been hard at work destroying Kim's reputation among the online community.' He gave a brief synopsis of the various acts of sabotage and traduction that Emperor Dragon had visited on Kim.

'John, I'm sure you're keen to see the problem resolved so that Kim is free to continue her work,' said Lucretia. 'I'm sure we all agree that's important. But what can *you* do in Japan that the Pacific Rim chapter can't? Why do *you* have to go all the way over there?'

'I'm under obligation,' Rattray replied. 'Kim asked me personally.'

'The way I see it, if John wants to go, let him,' remarked MacGowan. 'He's right – this Seal Point job looks like a pretty straightforward infil-exfil affair. We can manage without him just *once*, can't we?'

'Well, I don't approve,' said Lucretia. 'I think it sets a bad precedent. And Hiro Masamunow isn't going to like you muscling in on his chapter's territory, John.'

'If no one tells him, Hiro will never have to know,' said Rattray.

'You'd carry out a Guardian action on another chapter's turf without informing them?' Lucretia sounded shocked at the notion.

'It would be simpler that way. Besides, this isn't officially a Guardian action.'

'What is it, then?'

Rattray selected his words with a lawyer's precision. 'It's an action the Librans have not ordained but couldn't possibly object to.'

'A fine distinction. John, we have to observe certain rules as Guardians, certain orthodoxies. You can't go around ignoring them just because you feel like it.'

'What I'm proposing may be something of a – for want of a better word – freelance measure, Lucretia, but it doesn't signify that I'm any less committed to the Guardian cause.'

'I never said it did. But think about it. What if, even as we speak, the Guardian oracle in Osaka is receiving orders to invalidate Emperor Dragon? What if you and Hiro's team run into each other while you're out there? It could get messy. I can't believe you haven't considered that possibility.'

'I've considered it, and if it happens then explanations will have to be made and ruffled feathers smoothed. It's nothing that couldn't be solved by gentle diplomacy and a certain amount of grovelling. We *are* all on the same side, after all.'

Lucretia remained unconvinced. You could see it in the set of her jaw, the straightness of her spine, the knotty latticing of her work-roughened fingers. 'Because I've known you for a long time and I respect you, John,' she said, 'I'm not going to prevent you doing this if you feel you must. I'd like to go on record, however' – and here she looked at MacGowan, her expression making it clear to him that his eye-witness testimony might be required at a later date – 'as saying that I have deep reservations about one of us thinking he can act as a free agent. It runs counter to the whole spirit of Guardianship.'

'Your reservations are noted, Lucretia,' Rattray said, feeling considerably relieved. He had not been comfortable arguing with her, partly because she was a friend and ally, but principally because he knew she was in the right. 'I wouldn't even have considered going to Japan if the circumstances weren't what they are. Without wishing to sound patronising, I have every confidence that the two of you, and Bill in particular, will pull off this action-to-suppress successfully without me.'

'Damn right we will,' said MacGowan. There was a hard edge to his voice. He was looking forward to getting his hands on the Gene Genius scientists and showing them what he felt about what they did for a living. He was looking forward to it very much indeed.

7

In the dining hall of his dilapidated château overlooking the Loire, Gérard de Sade, with his computer configured into teleconference mode, began conversing with a jade-scaled Oriental dragon.

'She has done it?' were his first words to the dragon, whose glittering jewelled head almost entirely filled the onscreen teleconference window.

'Calm yourself, de Sade,' came the reply. 'This eagerness is unbecoming. Whatever happened to formalities? To politeness?'

'Yes, I apologise.' De Sade aimed what he hoped was a look of contrition at the blue-black lens of the QuickCam that perched, like a dark grey eyeball, on top of his monitor. 'Good morning, Emperor Dragon. Or, I should say, good evening.'

The dragon drew back its mouth in a ferociously fangsome grin. De Sade could not help but marvel at the speed and complexity of the graphics software Emperor Dragon was using to generate this real-time avatar. When the dragon grinned, its ruby eyes even seemed to twinkle with amusement.

'That's better,' Emperor Dragon said. His English was Japanese-accented, spoken a little too quickly, with a faint American twang. De Sade assumed that, like him, Emperor Dragon had learned English – the Esperanto of the online world – with some fluency because it was essential to his work.

'And how is the weather with you in France?' Emperor Dragon enquired. 'Oh, but, then, you wouldn't know, would you? Not being the outdoors type.'

'If you have called up merely to mock me . . .'

'Of course not.' The dragon, still grinning, shook its head. 'I was being unfair. After all, you are not a *total* agoraphobe, are you, de Sade? I understand that sometimes you venture as far as a hundred metres from your château.'

De Sade's lugubrious features clouded over. 'I will terminate this conversation.' He reached for the keyboard to demonstrate the seriousness of his intent.

'You won't, de Sade,' Emperor Dragon replied, his avatar's eyes narrowing to ruby slits, 'because you know that if you do, you will never hear from me again.'

De Sade's fingers came to rest meekly, weakly, on the keyboard keys. Control, he told himself. Curb your temper, Gérard. Endure what you have to endure in the name of the *Société Pour la Vérité*, in the memory of Jean-Claude. 'Then,' he said to the dragon, 'I beg you to stop these games and answer my first question. Has she done it? Has Kawai Kim summoned help?'

'She has. There's little she does electronically that I don't know about. And, as I predicted, the person she has asked to help her isn't one of her fellow-countrymen, it's the Englishman.'

'The Englishman – the one whom you describe as very dangerous.'

'Very dangerous,' Emperor Dragon confirmed, 'but also very important to the Guardians. He is their lynchpin, you might even say a legendary figure among them.'

De Sade thought he detected a whiff of hyperbole. 'But dangerous,' he reiterated. 'To attempt to catch him is not without risks.'

'Winning any worthwhile prize involves risks. You would prefer I brought you one of the lesser Guardians? You would prefer a minnow to a salmon?'

It would be cheaper for me, de Sade thought. Cheaper, but not nearly so useful.

'As I thought,' said Emperor Dragon, and he gave a self-righteous snort that was translated onscreen as two little puffs of smoke issuing from the dragon's gold-rimmed nostrils. 'Of all the Guardians in the world, this man has the most experience of their working methods. If you wish to expose their organisation, bring them into the light of public scrutiny, he is the way to do it. Get him to confess to the Guardians' misdeeds, and their whole operation will come crumbling down. Put him on trial in the European Court of Human Rights, and you put *all* the Guardians on trial.'

'Your price for capturing him, though, is . . . high.'

'The choice is yours, de Sade. Small fry or big fish.'

Perhaps attracted by all this piscine talk, one of the many cats with whom de Sade shared his château leapt up on to the dining table and insinuated herself between him and his computer keyboard, draping her tail along his face like a showgirl teasing a member of the audience with a feather boa. The cat – an overweight, pink-nosed silver tabby – confidently expected to be petted, and hence was shocked when de Sade testily swiped her off the table with his elbow. She landed plumply on the floor and trotted off to a corner of the room, where she sat down and began washing herself, licking smooth her ruffled dignity.

'Well?' said Emperor Dragon. 'The bait is on the hook, but I can pull the line out of the water any time I wish. I need an answer, de Sade. If you want me to proceed, I will proceed. If not, then we have no more to say to each other and our brief alliance is at an end.'

'You know that I can only say yes, proceed.'

'Then, the money.'

'I can transfer thirty per cent to you straight away,' de Sade said. 'The remaining seventy per cent will take a little longer.'

Fire erupted from the dragon's mouth, rippling along the bottom of the teleconference window and licking up the sides. As the flames dispersed, they revealed that the dragon's expression had soured to an angry frown.

'Don't fuck with me, de Sade,' Emperor Dragon intoned. 'We agreed fifty per cent. A non-returnable deposit, whether I succeed or fail.'

The hacker had beefed up the bass and reverb on his voice in order to make himself sound more threatening, but all de Sade could think of was the climax of *The Wizard of Oz* ('Pay no attention to the man behind the curtain!'). He knew then that he had the upper hand in the negotiation. Emperor Dragon was in this for the money, nothing else, and no one but de Sade was prepared to pay to have the Englishman captured; no one but de Sade had the desire and the wherewithal to see the Guardians brought to justice for their crimes against humanity. Emperor Dragon could not 'sell' the Englishman to anyone else. This was strictly a one-customer market, which meant the customer set the rules.

'Thirty per cent,' he repeated. 'You get the rest, in cash, only when the Englishman is brought to me.'

'I have expenses,' Emperor Dragon said. 'Overheads.'

'Thirty. Take it or leave it.'

Onscreen, the dragon-avatar breathed fire again – but this time there was, de Sade thought, a sigh of resignation buried amid the crackling of flames.

'Thirty-five,' Emperor Dragon said.

'I am a reasonable man,' said de Sade, with a reasonable man's shrug. 'Thirty-two point five. My final offer.'

'Very well.' The dragon scowled. 'Non-refundable.'

'Of course.'

'Then I will let the Otaku Queen know where I can be found. Or rather, I will let her think she has discovered my location by herself.'

'And I will look forward to hearing from you again when the Englishman is in your custody.'

The dragon emitted another huge belch of fire that swelled to fill the whole screen from edge to edge, corner to corner. When the flames burned themselves out, the teleconference window was blank. Conversation over.

De Sade slumped back in his gilded rococo chair and surveyed the expanse of mahogany dining table in front of him. The table, which, like the chairs surrounding it, dated back to the *Époque Regence*, was laden with every kind of up-to-the-minute telecommunications device imaginable.

After a few moments of sober contemplation, his fingers steepled to his lips, de Sade leaned forward again and reached for perhaps the simplest piece of equipment in front of him, a humble telephone. He dialled the number of his bank in Paris and asked to speak to the manager, whom he authorised to transfer a sum of money – in the region of half a million francs – from his checking account to an account at a Tokyo clearing bank.

Next he rang a Monsieur Chaigne, a dealer specialising in rare and vintage wines. He told Monsieur Chaigne that he needed to realise some more of his 'liquid assets', to the tune of approximately one million francs. A meeting was arranged for the following day. Monsieur Chaigne would come to the château and go through de Sade's cellars, selecting bottles from the superb range of vineyards and vintages that had been accumulated by de Sade's fore-bears, principally by his grandfather and great-grand-father.

For Monsieur Chaigne, who was not just a wine dealer but a wine connoisseur as well, exploring de Sade's cellars was always a thrill. As he inspected the racks of cobweb-wreathed bottles, he would let out little murmurs of pleasure and admiration, and sometimes the occasional gasp of joyous surprise. Brushing the dust off a mildewed label, he would hold a particular find up to the light and admire the glow of its contents, sighing like a young man with a new lover.

For de Sade, however, the prospect of yet again plundering the only significantly valuable capital asset he owned – the only thing of any real worth he had inherited, other than the château – filled him with little delight. In ten years he had nearly half emptied his cellars in order to fund his quest to expose *les Gardiens*. Once the wine was gone, the quest would be over, and if, by that time, he had not succeeded in his intentions, then there would be no other course open to him but to take his own life. He would be penniless. Ruined. He would have sacrificed all he possessed, for nothing. Worse, he would have failed to keep his vow to avenge Jean-Claude's death. What use, then, would living be?

De Sade rose and went to a window to look out over the Loire, some two hundred metres below. Beyond the river lay a rolling expanse of virgin forest that stretched in waves to the horizon. There were patches of amber and orange among the green. The rumour of autumn was taking root and beginning to spread.

A beautiful, spectacular view on this bright, clear afternoon, but all de Sade could think about was going out on to the terrace that ran along the riverfront side of the château, climbing up on to the parapet, stepping off and plummeting to his death.

He tried to imagine how it would feel, to be outdoors, beneath the achingly, oppressively wide sky, for the last time ever; to be standing on the parapet at the top of that two-hundred-metre-high cliff, with the Loire, placid, broad and brown, waiting for him below; to take that final, irrevocable step and be embraced by the uprushing wind of his descent; to plunge acquiescently to his doom, and the neck-cracking, spine-shattering suddenness of *impact*.

De Sade was wont to entertain fantasies of this and other methods of suicide. To contemplate ending it all made him, perversely, happy. He had resolved from a very young age that for him there would be neither a long, lingering terminal illness such as that which had carried his grandfather away nor a slow slide into the degrading incompetence of senility, a condition he had watched his grandmother, and later his father, ineluctably succumb to. A quick death, a romantic death – that was what he yearned for, and the idea of such a death was often a source of consolation and comfort when his mind was troubled.

Jean-Claude, he knew, would have chided him for such morbid musings. Would have told him he was being melodramatic and self-pitying. But Jean-Claude, for whom life had been as light and inconsequential as a child's balloon, was dead, while he, de Sade, for whom life was heavy and hard to bear, remained alive. It was as though life held you to itself harder the less you liked it. As though life was an enemy who wanted to be your friend.

Jean-Claude, were he still around, would have said to de Sade now, *Find something to hope for, and feel hopeful*. De Sade decided to try. He thought of the Englishman, John Rattray. All he knew about the man was what Emperor Dragon had told him: that he was intelligent, dangerous and hard to kill. He thought of how he would feel if Emperor Dragon *was* able to bring this particular Guardian to the château. He thought of the sense of triumph that would come when he finally had a member of that clandestine paramilitary organisation – an important member, moreover – in his clutches.

And, for a while at least, it seemed to work. De Sade's gloom partially lifted, and as he continued to gaze out over the river and forest, something not unlike a smile found itself a home on his saturnine face.

8

MacGowan's first port of call after leaving Bretherton Grange was a Georgian terraced house in Mayfair which, like most such houses in that area of central London, had been converted from residential to office use. Next to the front door, the names of the companies conducting business within the building were etched in capitals in a column of slim, discreet brass plaques. MacGowan was here this afternoon to visit the OVERSEAS OUTCOMES AGENCY on the second floor. He pressed the appropriate bell button and spoke his name into the microphone grille when prompted. A moment later he was buzzed inside.

On the second-floor landing MacGowan was greeted by a willowy young blonde woman whose name he knew but, having a bad head for names – especially, for some reason, women's first names – could not remember. The receptionist ushered MacGowan into a modest-sized room furnished with a desk, a potted rubber plant and seats of black leather and chromed tubular steel. Framed posters of foreign lands adorned the walls: smiling African natives outside mud huts; a gaggle of East European children crocodiling happily towards school; some Middle Eastern women weaving carpets; a group of gap-toothed, grinning goatherds in Kurdistan; workers toiling without complaint on a Nicaraguan coffee plantation.

The receptionist told MacGowan that Mr Templeton would see him straight away, and invited him to follow her. This MacGowan happily did, for the receptionist was wearing a brief PVC miniskirt which adhered to her pert buttocks like shrinkwrap over two juicy cuts of meat and revealed nearly all of a pair of long, shapely, stocking-clad legs. It seemed to MacGowan that the receptionist could sense his admiring gaze on her lower half as she led him through the panelled oak door into Templeton's office. He thought she might even be putting an extra sway into her stride, a bit more of a swing into her hips, purely for his benefit.

'Bill,' said Roger Templeton, getting to his feet as the receptionist and MacGowan entered. Templeton extended his left hand across the Moroccan leather work-surface of his huge, burled-walnut desk. 'Good to see you again.'

'Roger.' MacGowan gripped Templeton's hand with his own left hand. 'How's it hanging?'

Templeton glanced at his limp right arm, which the action of shaking hands was causing to swing like a pendulum. 'Uselessly by my side, as usual,' he replied.

MacGowan cringed. 'Sorry.'

'Think nothing of it,' said Templeton, with an unoffended laugh.

Roger Templeton was a greying-haired man in his forties, with the looks and the gentlemanly affability of a matinée idol just past his prime. He dressed expensively – his navy-blue suit was from Ede and Ravenscroft, his white silk shirt from Gieves and Hawkes, his solid-gold cufflinks from Asprey's – and he kept himself in shape. He had been educated at one of the finest public schools in the country, had undergone officer training at Sandhurst, and had accepted a commission as a captain in the Royal Green Jackets, whose green-red-and-black-striped regimental tie he habitually wore. However, he was not your typical overprivileged, undertalented 'rupert' – not one of those chinless wonders who regarded a stint in the army as a means of whiling away a few years before taking that sinecure in the City or assuming management of daddy's farm in the shires. For one thing, MacGowan had it on good authority that Templeton would have risen even further in the army, perhaps all the way to the top, had his career not been abruptly cut short by the skiing accident that had left his right arm paralysed. And for another thing, MacGowan could only admire the way Templeton had learned to cope with his disability. Naturally right-handed, Templeton had taught himself to write legibly with his left. Not only that, but he still jogged and played tennis, with his right arm tied up in a sling so that it would not get in the way, and he still pursued the opposite sex with undiminished vigour. Rather than upbringing, it was Templeton's determination not to let a little thing like a non-functioning limb hinder him in any way that, in MacGowan's opinion, gave the man class.

'Shelley?' Templeton said to his receptionist. 'Coffee for Mr MacGowan and myself, if you'd be so kind. Or perhaps you'd prefer something stronger, Bill?'

'I'm driving. Coffee'll be fine.'

The receptionist left the office, closing the door.

Templeton sat back down in his desk chair and invited MacGowan to make himself comfortable in a wing-backed chair positioned opposite.

'Thanks for agreeing to an appointment at such short notice,' MacGowan said, seating himself.

Templeton waved his hand. 'Not a problem. I'm used to it in this line of work. So, another of your little jobs, eh?'

MacGowan nodded.

'I'm assuming a five-man team?'

'Including me,' said MacGowan.

'Your old regiment seem to think that four's a better number these days.'

MacGowan understood the psychology behind the SAS's decision to switch from five-man patrols to four-man. People had a natural tendency to pair off, and thus, in a group of five, for the inevitable mathematical reasons one person was going to wind up feeling excluded. Four was better, therefore, for morale.

'I know,' he said. 'But in my day' – he adopted the voice

of a miserable old codger – 'we didn't worry about namby-pamby things like "group morale". In my day we had five-man patrols because if one gets wounded, it's easier for four men to carry him than three. Besides' – he reverted to his normal speaking voice – 'I don't think the team we're going to assemble today is going to be together long enough for group morale to become a concern.'

The receptionist, Shelley, re-entered with two steaming cups of coffee on a tray. She set the tray on Templeton's desk and said she would see to it that the two men were not disturbed.

Templeton thanked her, and after she had left the room said to MacGowan, 'I can give you her home phone number, if you like.'

MacGowan realised he had disguised his enchantment with the receptionist's figure poorly.

'Aren't you and she . . . you know?'

'Alas not,' said Templeton, shaking his head. 'Work-place relationships – bad idea.'

'Well, maybe I'll take you up on your offer,' said MacGowan, taking a sip of his coffee, 'but not until this operation's out of the way.'

'Sound attitude. Now, where were we? A five-man team, including yourself. Any particular specialities required?'

'One munitions expert.'

'Indeed.'

'And I want D.B., if he's free.'

'Of course. Anything else?'

'They've all got to have NBC training and night-combat skills.'

'Fine. Let's take a peek in the database, shall we?'

There was a PC sitting on the desk to Templeton's left, its monitor angled towards him. Templeton turned to the computer, powered it up and gestured to MacGowan to come round and view the screen over his shoulder.

MacGowan looked on as Templeton gained access to his files by typing in a set of complex passwords. Then, moving his hand from the keyboard in order to manipulate the mouse, he clicked open a document folder. The head of a long list of names of ex-servicemen appeared onscreen, many of them followed by the letters 'NCA' – 'Not Currently Available'.

Templeton scrolled through the list, which comprised approximately five hundred names in all. Every so often he paused and used the mouse to highlight one. Then, when he had been through the list, he clicked the 'Open File' icon on the toolbar. The hard drive hummed and chattered as the computer pulled up data on the selected names.

One after another, three dozen CVs with accompanying photographs came up onscreen. The CVs detailed, among other things, each individual's age, marital status, training, rank attained, decorations, weapons skills, battlefield experience and post-discharge civilian employment. Under the last heading the most common job descriptions were 'Security Consultant', 'Prison Officer' and 'Personal Bodyguard'.

MacGowan recognised at least half of the names and faces displayed. Either they were men he had served with or they were men he had hired, through the Overseas Outcomes Agency, for previous Guardian operations.

Together with Templeton he went through the files one by one, evaluating the merits and capabilities of each man. Templeton was personally acquainted with everyone on his database and so was able to supply character assessments as well. He knew which of them had problems working with people of a certain race or sexual orientation. He knew which needed to kept away from alcohol or women for the duration of an operation. He knew which were likely to fold under torture, if captured.

Eventually the three dozen potential candidates were narrowed down to a shortlist of six. After further debate, two were put in reserve, and MacGowan was left with a team of four: a former member of the Russian Spetsnaz, a former member of the Australian SAS, a former Royal Engineer and a former Gurkha.

'I'll get in touch with them on your behalf,' Templeton said, making a note of the four men's contact numbers. 'You, of course, will be supplying the ordnance?'

MacGowan nodded.

'You know, it's not my place to be nosy, Bill, but everyone who ever works with you comes back raving about the hardware you manage to get your hands on. State-of-the-art, they tell me. "Stuff so advanced it makes the smart bomb look stupid," one chap said. Out of professional curiosity, where *do* you come by it?'

'Roger, you should know better than to ask that.' MacGowan said this in a friendly enough manner, but there was an unmistakable note of censure in his voice.

'Yes. Absolutely. Forgive me.' Templeton turned back to the computer, where the four successful candidates' files were now displayed simultaneously on the monitor, each reduced to occupy a quarter of the screen. 'Good little squad you've got there,' he said. 'Commendably international.'

MacGowan cast his eye over the four men's pictures. He had worked with two of them before; the other two had excellent reputations.

'They'll do,' he said.

9

In the roof garden of a two-storey mews house in Chelsea, a slender young man sat in the lotus position. He was naked except for a dhoti, a pair of circular mirror-shades and a crystal puzzle-egg suspended around his neck on a silver chain. His brown hair was cut in a modish bob and a long moustache drooped around his mouth.

The roof garden's potted shrubs and dwarf cypresses shivered and rustled in the cool city breeze. The noise of traffic from the nearby King's Road was a constant background grumble, interspersed with horn-blares and the occasional crunch of a bad gear-shift and shout of a disgruntled driver. A bamboo windchime, suspended from a wisteria-wreathed pergola in the roof garden, dangled and tinkled in euphonious counterpoint.

The young man seemed undisturbed by any of these sounds and sensations. He sat on the garden's brick paving like a statue of tranquillity, the backs of his hands resting lightly on his knees, his thumbs and index fingers forming Os.

About three yards away from him, a beautifully groomed Afghan hound looked on. The dog was elegantly sprawled along a low stone bench, and her cornsilk coat rippled and shimmered with the this-way, that-way tugging of the wind. She held her head erect, and her eyes peered out intelligently through her fringe. Her name was Lady Grinning Soul, and her meditating master was Piers Pearson, Freelance Facilitator.

That morning, Rattray had rung Piers to inform him that the Guardians were about to embark on another mission, but that on this particular occasion Piers's services would not be required. Piers had responded to the news with equanimity. His personal talents weren't suited to every Guardian action-to-suppress, and though like any international playboy adventurer he craved excitement and danger, he was just as happy to be left to pursue leisure. He had thanked Rattray for paying him the courtesy of calling, and had been about to put the phone down when Rattray had said, 'Piers, before you hang up, there is one thing I'd like your opinion on.'

'Go ahead, old boy,' Piers had replied.

Rattray had paused for a good ten seconds to collect his thoughts and had then explained about Kawai Kim's situation and her request that he travel to Japan to help her.

'I'm not too hot on computers,' Piers had said, when Rattray had finished. 'All I know about them is, you mustn't build one too big or it'll take over the world and threaten to start a nuclear war, and you mustn't have one on board your spaceship or it'll go mad and start singing old music-hall numbers. However, if Kim feels that you, rather than any member of the Pacific Rim chapter, are the man to come to her aid, then so be it. A chap can't turn down a cry for help from a damsel in distress, after all. Simply not done.'

'But ought I to do something the Librans haven't expressly sanctioned?'

'That, John, is between you and your conscience.'

'My conscience.' Rattray had made it sound as though the concept had been new one to him, something he had heard about but had never had to deal with directly before.

'That's right,' Piers had said. 'That thing in one's head it would be so much more convenient not to have.'

It had been evident to Piers that Rattray was disconcerted by his own readiness to go behind the Librans' backs. The Librans, surely, could not take exception to what he intended to do, but all the same, it was accepted Guardian tradition to act only when the Librans told you to and never to carry out any action that the Librans did not stipulate – a tradition which Rattray, perhaps more than any other Guardian, embodied and espoused. Rattray had served the Librans faithfully and self-denyingly for nigh on a century, constantly putting their needs before his own, like some loyal retainer who could not dare to dream of anything else but attending to the wishes of his lord. Now, it seemed, a spark of independence had been kindled in him. He was doing something slightly off-kilter, slightly wilful, and Piers had to wonder why. He could only conclude that it was to see how the Librans would respond. Rattray was testing the limits of his indenture; giving his bonds a tug to find out how much slack they had in them.

It was understandable. No one could do the same demanding job that Rattray did, for the length of time he had been doing it, and *not* begin to wonder if there was more to life. What concerned Piers were the possible consequences. Rattray had clearly made up his mind already to go to Japan, which was one of the two reasons why Piers had not attempted to dissuade him – the other reason being that he suspected Lucretia would also try, and Lucretia, he knew, would have a better chance of succeeding. But whether, having satisfied himself that he was not the Librans' mindless puppet after all, that he was a man not a number, Rattray would be content to leave it at that, or whether he would take this as carte blanche to keep pushing things a bit further, Piers could not predict.

So he had decided that a consultation was called for. It was an extreme measure, one never lightly taken, but he had felt the situation warranted it. At midday he had driven up to Stoke Newington in his canary-yellow Caterham 7 to procure some premium-grade psychedelics from his usual dealer, and now he was journeying deep within himself, borne along on lysergic wings. Seeking the consensual realm. Seeking Colloquy.

Inside Piers's head, the world was mandala-whorls. A

sparkling, behind-the-eyelids interplay of light and dark. Kaleidoscopic patterns throbbing in time to his heartbeat. He was aware of his body but at the same time of no longer being a part of his body. He was sinking within himself, fleshly concerns falling away. Then, as though penetrating a veil, suddenly he was yogic-flying through a dimensionscape straight out of a Steve Ditko issue of *Dr Strange*, all floating islands and garish colours and twisting, hollowing, impossible geometries. He was descending at a shallow incline towards a glowing horizon, beyond which lay his ultimate destination.

As the horizon neared, Piers's breathing slowed until the rise and fall of his chest was all but imperceptible. Lady Grinning Soul, knowing with canine instinct that her task now was to watch over her master and make sure he was protected, maintained her vigilance as the last tethers that held Piers's mind to physical reality fell away and he crossed the rim of the horizon and entered a bright, immense, measureless void.

He was not alone in the void. All around him, above, beneath, on every side, floated others. An infinity of entities, thronging like starlings. And all around him there was a low babble, much like the sound of London's incessant background rumble, but here composed of voices. A multitude of voices, murmuring.

Colloquy.

The others who were here with Piers, within him and yet not *contained* in him, were an unimaginably diverse assortment of lifeforms. Few resembled each other. Few even resembled human beings. There were living spatial configurations, and organisms that were symmetrical along more than one axis, and things that existed in fewer than three dimensions and things that existed in more than four. There were sentient mathematical equations, and argumentative and highly opinionated microbes, and creatures made up entirely of vapour. There were intelligences the size of nebulae, and group-mind colonies of inorganic objects, and a whole bestiary of animal-like species, vertebrate and invertebrate, legged and finned, slimy and furred. There were representatives of Life in all its manifold variety, and while many of them looked alike, no two belonged to exactly the same race.

All hovered in the void, conversing. Some used speech, some used music, some used other forms and frequencies of sound. Some communicated by scent, some by thought, some by light or colour or configuration of limbs. Whatever the medium of transmission, the overall effect was a massed glossolalia, a constant Babel thrum of information.

As soon as Piers arrived, he was enfolded by a message of greeting. A great throb of welcome was extended to him by all the entities in his immediate vicinity. A spherical cluster of eyeballs like a chrysanthemum's petals blinked an intricate code-sequence of salutation. A twinned, entwined pair of glowing sine waves flickered their recognition. A sweet-smelling botanical being blared a scent of hello from its orchidaceous trumpet-orifices. A quiffed, caped and collared Vegas-era Elvis, whose sweat-streaked face was a chubbier version of Piers's own, twirled a finger at him and sneered, flicking his hips affectionately.

Piers reciprocated with a simple, politely spoken 'Good afternoon'. The utterance radiated out around him, passing in a flash from lifeform to lifeform like a near-instantaneous game of Chinese whispers. His arrival was noted, his presence in the void registered.

He did not need to state why he had come or voice any particular question. His reason for being there was already intimately known. Immersing himself in the rolling river of polylingual speech that flowed all around him, he simply listened.

He understood nothing of what each individual entity was saying, but their words, in combination, *were* intelligible to him. He had no need of specific meaning when he could pick up the general gist. Tone, cadence, expression, inflection – these told him all he needed to know about the mood of the multiplicity of beings around him. There was a distinct trend of feeling among the entities, a definite, discernible consensus, a strong current of opinion in the river of speech that was, in many ways, like a premonition, a portent of things to come.

The opening moves of an endgame had been played, and difficulty lay ahead for Piers. In the immediate future, danger from within would place him in personal jeopardy. In the longer term, loyalties would be strained to breaking, and Piers would have to tread carefully. There were wheels within wheels. Foes within foes. Piers would have to maintain his aloofness, let no one know he was more than he appeared. His impartiality would be crucial.

This was the advice Colloquy had for Piers, and he acknowledged it with mute sombreness.

Then it was time to leave, and a chorus of farewells swelled around him as he buoyed back upwards into himself, refilling the shell of his body, psyche infiltrating flesh like ether into tubes, and external sensations gradually returning – the smells of car exhaust and creosote, the remote urban hubbub and the closer-to tinkling of the windchimes, the coarse texture of the brick paving beneath his backside and thighs, the taste of his own saliva and the chemical aftertang of the acid, and finally – as he opened his eyelids – sunglasses-shaded sight.

He gasped in a lungful of air, like a swimmer surfacing. It was late afternoon, and the sun was reddening over the Chelsea rooftops. Unfurling his knotted legs, he clambered to his feet. As he stood flexing the stiffness out of his limbs, Lady Grinning Soul arose from her semi-recumbent posture and stepped down from the stone bench. She trotted over to her master and raised her head to him. Piers squatted down and started stroking her, fondling her ears and nuzzling her muzzle.

'Looks like there's trouble coming, old girl,' he said. 'But don't you worry. I'll do as I've been told, and everything'll be all right.'

At this, the crystal puzzle-egg around his neck gave a spasm, briefly extending its component parts and then retracting them again.

It did this whenever it detected a lie.

PART 2

10

Since joining the Guardians nigh on a hundred years ago, Rattray had travelled extensively, not least during the first half of the twentieth century when Britain – and the British chapter of the Guardians – had a larger role to play in world affairs than nowadays. As the century progressed, however, and one by one the Empire's colonies and protectorates gained their independence, Rattray and his fellow British Guardians were called upon less and less to make expeditions to far-flung corners of the globe and deal with outbreaks of Anarch activity there. Regions which had previously been served by one or at most two Guardians, acting as sort of local liaison officers to the British chapter, were entrusted by the Librans with full-blown, self-governing chapters of their own.

It was the end of an era, one which Rattray and his compatriots were not altogether sorry to see pass. Battling the armies of tribal warlords who had managed to get their hands on items of contratemporal weaponry; smashing oriental drug rings that peddled strange, powerful opiates of paraterrestrial origin; venturing into remote, 'lost' valleys where thuggish sects had arisen under the sway of priests who, through the Anarchs' auspices, had been endowed with godlike powers – these might seem thrilling stuff, the sort of escapades that would not be out of place in the pages of pulp adventure novels. To the British Guardians, however, they were nothing more than missions, arduous and risky exercises in logistics and tactics. There was one episode from this period that Rattray could not recollect without a certain amount of guilty amusement, namely when his imperviousness to the lethal effects of a poison-tipped blowdart caused an entire New Guinean rainforest tribe to drop to their knees and worship him as a deity – one of those rare, memorable instances when life imitates hoary fictional cliché – but on the whole, as Britain's influence throughout the world waned, Rattray and his colleagues found they were not having to journey beyond the borders of the British Isles and mainland Europe so often, and this came as something of a relief. Travel, in the days before long-haul jumbo jets, was a difficult, uncomfortable and time-consuming business, and the adverse climates and unpleasant diseases in foreign parts all added to the inconvenience.

For less selfish reasons, too, Rattray welcomed the decrease in the British chapter's worldwide responsibilities. It was better, in his opinion, that the task of curbing contratemporal technology should be carried out by members of the indigenous population of a country or continent, since they were familiar with the territory and could do what was required of them less conspicuously and with greater efficiency. Likewise, when in the mid-1970s the Librans decreed that Europe's disparate national chapters should be amalgamated into the broader sovereignty of two larger chapters, Rattray took a positive view of this. It seemed a logical and practical step, in keeping with the times and the shifts in the tides of geopolitics.

His optimism was, at least, proved half-justified. The Guardians living in European nations south of a latitudinal line roughly extrapolated from the border between France and Spain coalesced into a unit that operated with an admirable degree of organisation. Their actions-to-suppress were planned and executed with bravura and brio, and earned them plenty of kudos among their peers. The North Europe chapter, on the other hand, found it hard to emulate the standard set by their southern counterparts. Among the members who made up the new chapter there had long been disagreements over strategy and techniques, mild differences of opinion which, it was hoped, would dissolve in the spirit of unification, but which, in the event, merely consolidated into firmly held and intractably opposed dogmas. In addition, what, in the days when European Guardians seldom met or took part in missions together, had been minor personality clashes blossomed into outright antipathies now that there was regular contact between the parties concerned. Nevertheless, it was generally felt that these difficulties were merely teething troubles, not beyond the ability of rational, adult human beings to iron out.

Things went really awry for the North Europe chapter when, in 1981, the Guardian oracles in Malmö and Nice died within a few weeks of each other, both of natural causes. This left just one oracle to provide the chapter with instructions from the Librans, Scotsman Frazier Hamilton, Cecil Evans's predecessor. In theory, given that the chapter was supposed to be working as a harmonious whole, this should not have posed any great problem. In practice, since Britain now had the only extant oracle in North Europe, Britain's Guardians inevitably came to dominate the chapter.

Rattray was acutely aware that this state of affairs might aggravate existing tensions and exacerbate discord, and did his utmost to appease his colleagues on the mainland, consulting them at every turn and making sure they were involved in every action-to-suppress to the fullest extent. His efforts, alas, were in vain. With no oracle of their own, and the Librans apparently not predisposed to furnish them with one, the non-British members of the chapter had no choice but to rely on the British members to initiate and co-ordinate missions, and naturally this soon came to be a source of resentment.

The non-British members were not slow to voice their discontent. The British, they claimed, had always

101

considered themselves a cut above the rest, a breed apart. And now that the British Guardians had the chance to lord it over the rest of the chapter, they were enjoying their new-found supremacy a little too much. Indeed, it was even hinted that Rattray and his compatriots were actively *suppressing* the whereabouts of new oracles on the continent, and invalidating them when they emerged, in order to maintain their unmerited position of authority.

Such accusations were, it must be said, not made wholly seriously, and bespoke more of frustration and pre-existing national prejudices than anything. They were, though, overt symptoms of the hostility which arose towards the British Guardians during the early eighties and which led to instances of behaviour ill befitting members of a clandestine international cabal dedicated to shaping and securing the destiny of the human race – behaviour more appropriate, in fact, to the school playground: squabbles, prima donna tantrums, point-scoring, name-calling, cronyism, bickering, intransigence bordering on rebelliousness and more. The decade, for Rattray, was one long administrative headache, involving as much pacifying of egos as quelling of contratemporal technology.

It was perhaps inevitable that sooner or later, somewhere along the line, all the back-biting and in-fighting would result in the mishandling of an action-to-suppress. Nobody, however, could have foreseen what a comprehensive botching it would be when it came. What happened in a remote Balkan village in June of 1988 was such an unforgivable lapse of discipline and of reason that Rattray, even though the disaster had been none of his doing and entirely beyond his control, could never think about it without wincing in shame.

One good thing came of the events of that terrible day, which was that they had the effect of sobering everyone up and restoring everyone's sense of perspective. They also, it seemed, forced the Librans to sit up and take notice. Until then, the Librans had either been ignorant of the North Europe chapter's internal difficulties or else had been turning a blind eye. Now, by whatever means they learned about such matters, they were made aware that all was not well with their human representatives in that particular region of the globe, and set about rectifying the situation. A new oracle came to light in Geneva, Johann Schreiber, teenage scion of a wealthy Swiss family.

Throughout his childhood, Johann had been plagued by epilepsy, but all of a sudden his *grand mal* seizures began to be attended by hallucinations of shocking intensity and befuddling content. Posing as a psychiatrist, the Guardian Carlo Dalbagno, an Italian ex-patriot resident in Zürich, offered the Schreiber family his professional services, claiming very persuasively that he could help the boy where some of the best analysts money could buy had failed. Very soon Dalbagno had initiated young Johann into the mysteries of Guardianship, and although, in the end, he was not able to effect a complete 'cure' in his 'patient', Herr and Frau Schreiber were grateful to him none the less, since he did at least manage to get Johann to come to terms with his hallucinations and cease to fear them.

Now, after each of his fits, Johann would phone or e-mail Dalbagno with a detailed description of what he had envisioned in his mind's eye during the seizure. Johann's parents could not quite see *how* this practice helped their son, but it was clear to them that it was doing him some good because he was altogether a more sanguine and purposeful individual these days.

So now the North Europe chapter had two oracles, and its non-British members had the independence from British governance that they craved. However, the rift that had opened up between them and their British colleagues did not close. Instead, the British Guardians decided that it would be better for all concerned if they seceded from the chapter for the time being, a move that met with little opposition. In effect the British chapter was re-established, and now continued to function in all but name, a sub-chapter within the chapter, operating much as it had done before the attempted unification, while Guardians situated across the rest of North Europe assembled for actions-to-suppress in their territory as and when required, under the marshalship of two men: the aforementioned Carlo Dalbagno, and Dieter Braun, a native of Köln.

The Pacific Rim chapter, Rattray knew, was disposed along similar lines. While ostensibly the chapter consisted of members of equal standing from all the industrialised nations of South-East Asia, in practice Japan's Guardians, like Britain's, had found themselves estranged from their cohorts, and, as in North Europe, the Librans had granted the Pacific Rim chapter a second oracle in Kuala Lumpur in addition to the one already active in Osaka.

There was, in fact, an especially good reason why the Librans should have human representatives to deal almost exclusively with Anarch activity within the Japanese archipelago. Japan, the hotbed of global technological innovation in the latter half of the twentieth century, had proved fertile soil for Anarch meddling. Most of the credit for the country's post-war economic prosperity lay, of course, with General MacArthur and, more pertinently, with the will, ingenuity and tremendous social organisation of the Japanese people, but the Anarchs had also contributed through their subtle machinations, covertly inciting and enticing the Japanese to push the technological envelope to its limits. Hiro Masamunow and his team, in short, had a lot on their plate, with the result that Guardians in the other Pacific Rim countries had had no qualms about banding together in a sort of free-floating coalition which, by and large, operated independently of the Japanese Guardians.

Rattray was musing on these thorny matters of Guardian politics as his plane began its descent through a juddering, turbulent layer of raincloud to Tokyo's Narita airport. It struck him as a sad commentary on human nature that, even among a group of men and women who shared such a clear-cut and distinct goal as the Guardians did, there could not be perfect, absolute accord. It seemed there was no cause so noble, so all-surpassing, that its adherents could set aside their differences of opinion and refrain from internal wrangling.

Then again, who was he to judge? For here he was, pursuing his own agenda, encroaching on the territory of others just as if it was the old days and he and the British chapter were flying in to sort out another 'little local difficulty'.

And as the plane's tyres touched down on the runway Tarmac and her speed was reduced with a titanic roar of reverse thrust, Rattray found himself hoping that the Librans were really as tolerant of human foibles and perversities as they seemed to be. Doubtless he would find out soon enough if they were not.

11

The immigration officials at Narita were thorough and, consequently, slow. When at last it came to be Rattray's turn to have his passport inspected, the uniformed man in the high-sided booth scrutinised it closely, flicking through it page by page and frowning over each entry and exit stamp. Opening the passport at the inside back cover, he held it up to compare the photograph of unmarried, middle-aged professor of modern history John Oldman with the face of the passport-holder himself. He then asked Rattray a few formal questions in halting English. Eventually he seemed satisfied, and handed the flawless forgery back to Rattray. With a tiny wave he indicated that Rattray was free to proceed to the baggage carousels.

Rattray retrieved his sole item of luggage, a medium-sized Samsonite holdall, and followed signs – which were in English as well as *kanji* – to the arrivals lounge. The arrivals lounge was bright and bare, bustling with moving bodies. Flight announcements in a trilling, birdlike female voice sang out echoingly over the Tannoy.

As he entered, Rattray scanned the faces of those waiting behind a barrier to greet people off the planes. Some looked expectant, others anxious, a few indifferent. When he had phoned Kim yesterday morning to tell her he was leaving for Heathrow and that he would be with her by noon – her time – the following day, she had insisted she would meet him at the airport. Now Rattray realised, with a twinge of embarrassment, that he was not going to be able to pick her out from the crowd in front of him.

He knew Kim's online image well enough. (A little *too* well, if the truth be told, having viewed Emperor Dragon's pictures. He felt, disconcertingly, as though he had been made a voyeur to the violation not of a computer-generated construct but of an actual person.) The problem was, of course, that Kim's avatar bore only a passing resemblance to Kim herself. Kim's real face Rattray had seen a couple of times in Guardian file photographs, but its features were nowhere near as clearly fixed in his mind as those of her avatar. Any of a dozen dark-haired young women at the barrier in front of him could have been her.

Slowing his pace, he spotted one young woman who was squinting with a particular intensity at the people entering the arrivals lounge. She had short-cut hair that framed her face squarely and severely, and she was wearing patent-leather pumps and a navy-blue suit with a pencil skirt that reached to her knees, revealing calves and ankles that were slightly stubby but, all the same, appealingly well turned. She had a mackintosh folded over one arm, and an umbrella hung from the crook of her other arm. Her skin tone was marginally paler than that of the average Japanese, and her eyebrows were bushier and her eyes' epicanthic folds less pronounced.

As Rattray watched, the young woman heaved a resigned sigh and reached into her inside jacket pocket to produce a spectacles case, from which she took out a pair of heavy-rimmed spectacles which she lodged on the bridge of her nose. Now better equipped to see, she resumed her survey. The moment her gaze alighted on Rattray, she broke into a smile of recognition.

'John!'

Rattray diverted towards her. 'Kawai Kim, I presume.'

'Just plain Kim,' Kim replied humbly, removing her spectacles. 'Not so "kawai" in the flesh.'

If she was fishing for a compliment, she was casting her

line into empty waters. Rattray merely pointed to the end of the barrier and said, 'I'll meet you there.'

A few seconds later they were facing each other again. Kim hesitated, then, with a brave grin, offered up her hand for a handshake. Rattray enclosed her petite fingers briefly in his dry, smooth fist.

'We'll take a taxi,' Kim said, gesturing in the direction of the exit. 'It costs the earth, but . . .' She shrugged. Such luxuries were perks of the job.

Outside, rain was falling in a silky drizzle from a sky that was half grey, half white, like the flank of a shark. Rattray and Kim, huddled under Kim's umbrella, joined the queue at the taxi rank. They did not have to wait long. Soon they were at the head of the queue and a vacant taxi was pulling up beside them. Kim bent down and spoke to the white-gloved driver through his side window. With a few brief bobs of her head, she told him her address, and he nodded curtly. Using buttons on the dashboard, he opened the boot so that Rattray could stow his holdall there, then unlocked the rear doors to allow his passengers to climb in. When his fares were safely on board, the driver pulled away from the kerb, switching his windscreen wipers to intermittent.

It was forty miles from Narita to the centre of Tokyo, and the expressway into the city passed through suburbs of unvaryingly low level, acres of blockish little houses bristling with television aerials and linked to one another with a seemingly inordinate quantity of telephone and electricity cable. During the journey, conversation between the two Guardians was restricted to mundane topics – Rattray's flight, the weather (which, Kim joked, surely must remind him of home), that sort of thing. There was no reason to believe that the taxi driver understood a word of English, but Guardian affairs were never discussed within immediate earshot of a non-Guardian. From his passengers' behaviour and appearance, the taxi driver would reasonably assume that Kim was an 'office lady' who had been sent by her boss to meet a *gaijin* businessman off a plane and escort him into town.

An hour later, Rattray and Kim were dropped off near Kim's condominium in Tokyo's mainly residential Hibiya district. Kim's apartment was on the seventh floor.

'It's hardly the most spacious place in the world,' Kim warned Rattray, as she unlocked the apartment door. 'But, of course, we Tokyoites like to live small. Anyway, if I had somewhere larger, it'd be difficult to explain to the authorities how I could afford it. As long as I've room for all my computer stuff, I'm happy.'

As she opened the door, an alarm buzzer began to sound. She strolled into the narrow entrance lobby and entered a code-number into a keypad mounted on the wall. The buzzer fell silent. If Kim had failed to disable the alarm in time, a series of shaped plastique charges would have detonated inside her computer hardware, destroying every byte of information stored there.

She indicated to Rattray that it was safe to follow her in.

The entrance lobby led to the apartment's main room, which most people would have put to use as a living room but which Kim had filled with computer equipment and made her base of operations. With a proud flourish she invited Rattray to admire the humming array of monitors and TV screens and the plethora of big-meg hardware and top-of-the-line peripherals, all linked together with wreaths of cable and wire. He looked around, nodding and making the appropriate polite noises.

Kim then started going on about the various contra-temporal components that had been obtained for her from a local Node. Her most recently acquired upgrade was a chip that, as far as she could tell, used quantum parallelism, running algorithms simultaneously in parallel universes, thereby speeding up her processing power and increasing her bandwidth by an awesome degree. Evidently, because she knew that Rattray used a PC and was well wired-up, she thought that the concept would excite him as much as it did her, and so as not to disappoint her Rattray did his best to look as though he shared her enthusiasm. To him, though, computers were merely

109

tools, machines that fulfilled a function. He did not view them with anything approaching the hacker's fanatical awe.

Finally Kim led him through to her bedroom and showed him out on to the balcony. The view was of more condominium buildings and, down at ground-level, a children's playground and a small, well-tended area of park where brick pathways meandered between autumn-drooping trees. Hardly picture-postcard stuff, yet Rattray leaned his elbows on the balcony handrail and stared out as though the scene demanded a tourist's contemplation.

'Some tea, perhaps?' Kim asked.

'Why not?'

She went indoors. Rattray let his gaze rove over the windows of the buildings opposite, pausing whenever some vignette of everyday domestic life caught his eye: a middle-aged man doing the washing-up; two children bickering over a toy; an elderly, fragile-looking woman held rapt in her armchair by a soap opera on television. Then his attention turned to the playground, where a pair of spiky-haired, pre-school-age boys were scampering over a climbing frame while their mothers sat on a bench nearby, chatting animatedly. Seeing the boys, Rattray was reminded of Lucretia's current work-in-progress. Two days ago, after the meeting at Bretherton Grange had come to a close, Lucretia had walked out of the dining room, leaving Rattray and MacGowan to go over the fine details of the Seal Point action-to-suppress. Later, after MacGowan had hopped into his Saab and headed back up to London, Rattray had gone in search of Lucretia to make his farewells. He had found her in the large, daylight-drenched conservatory that was her studio. She had been vigorously applying bright green paint to the metalwork of one portion of her 'Obstaclimb'.

The Obstaclimb took up most of the studio's available space, its various sections laid out in approximately the positions they would take when the entire construction was assembled *in situ*. Several of the sections were attached – by means of industrial-size versions of a mountaineer's karabiners – to chains that hung from a system of tracks and pulleys suspended from the ceiling. The chains were operated by a control panel mounted on one wall and were used to raise pieces of sculpture so that Lucretia could work beneath them and could load the finished articles on to the back of a lorry.

To traverse the entire length of the Obstaclimb without touching the ground, which was the object, would tax the abilities of even the most athletic of youngsters. From one end to the other there were about forty metres of ladders, ledges, hoops, slide poles, ropes, rungs, mazes and cat-walks to be crossed, climbed over and negotiated. There was also a certain amount of problem-solving to be done along the way – how to get from one level to another using the limited handholds available, how to negotiate a series of trapdoors that could only be opened in a specific sequence, and so on – so that brain as well as brawn was required.

Rattray's youth was such a long time ago that he could barely remember what it felt like to be a child. None the less, as he looked up at the Obstaclimb, a vestigial boyish urge was stirred in him, and had the apparatus been completed and there been no one around to witness, he might at least have *considered* climbing up on to it and attempting to cross it.

Lucretia had heard Rattray enter the studio but she did not pause from her task. She continued to layer on the paint with strokes so forthright and fierce that she looked as though she was trying to force the bristles of her brush into the metal. The black smock she was wearing over her day clothes was stippled and streaked with fresh splashes of green.

'On your way, then?' she said to Rattray, without looking round.

'Yes. I thought I'd—'

'Ticket already booked? Flying out tonight?'

'Tomorrow.'

'Send Kim my regards.'

'Lucretia . . .'

111

'It's all right, John. I'm not angry.' Everything about the tension in Lucretia's stance and the determination with which she was attacking her work belied the statement.

'If you are, I'm sorry,' said Rattray.

'But I'm not.'

'Then I'm sorry anyway. Look, Lucretia, it's not as if we haven't left Bill to run an action-to-suppress on his own before. He's entirely dependable.'

'Of course he's dependable. He's a soldier. A soldier knows the value of taking orders, of obeying without question.'

'A soldier also knows the value of initiative.'

'What you're doing isn't initiative, John. It's dissension in the ranks.'

'If it is dissension in the ranks, and I'm not saying it is, but if it *is*, why does it annoy you so much? I'd have thought you of all people, an artist, would approve of someone rattling the cage of orthodoxy. You'd have said it was necessary and healthy.'

Now Lucretia stopped painting and turned. Her eyes were wide and bright, and a small curlicue of green paint adorned her left cheek, comma-shaped like a teardrop.

'I'm *not* annoyed, John,' she said. 'Christ, you're supposed to be one of the smartest people alive. Don't you get it? I'm not angry. I'm *scared*.'

Rattray was taken aback. 'Scared? What of?'

'Not "what of". "Who for".'

'For me? You're scared for me?' He attempted a comforting smile. 'Lucretia, I'll be fine. You know as well as I do, I'm exceedingly hard to harm.'

'It's not just you I'm scared for, John.' Lucretia looked as if she was going to say more, but then she simply shook her head. 'Oh, for God's sake, go on, get out of here. Go to bloody Tokyo and do "what a man's gotta do". Just promise me one thing.'

'What?'

'This is the one and only time you pull a stunt like this. Promise me that?'

'I can't predict the future, Lucretia.'

'Just promise me anyway. For my peace of mind.'

'How is it worth anything if you know I don't mean it?'

'Men have always been promising women things they don't mean, and women have always fooled themselves in believing what they hear even though they know they shouldn't. It's a time-honoured tradition. Indulge me.'

'Very well. I promise.'

'Thanks, you liar. Now sod off.' Lucretia dismissed him from her presence with a floor-spattering flap of her brush, and Rattray exited the conservatory, glad that a rapprochement, however fragile, had been achieved.

He valued Lucretia's opinion and her approval. How highly he valued them, he perhaps had not realised until that afternoon, when the former had not been to his liking and the latter had been withheld. Now, standing on Kim's balcony, he made a pact with himself.

He did not think this was going to be the one and only time he tested the limits of Guardianship. He felt, in fact, that he had taken the first step down what was going to turn out to be a steep and treacherous slope. It was not an irrevocable step, not yet, but if he took another, and then another, and another, before long a remorseless momentum would set in and he would be racing helplessly towards the bottom.

All the same, he would *try*, to the very best of his ability, to keep the casual, ironical promise he had made to Lucretia. He would *try* to take just this one step and then pull back.

The decision calmed his troubled conscience.

Women weren't the only ones, he thought, who could derive peace of mind through self-deception.

12

In her apartment's kitchen nook, basically a corridor that led to the bathroom, Kim filled an electric kettle and switched it on. While she stood, arms folded, waiting for the water to heat up, she wondered if there was something the matter with Rattray. The man at present out on her balcony was not the man she was familiar with from several years of telephonic and electronic communication. Online and over the phone, he came across as altogether more personable and friendly, with a line in wry humour that Kim enjoyed and reciprocated as best she could. In the flesh, F2F, he seemed cold, inaccessibly reserved, even – yes – inscrutable.

Perhaps he was tired from his journey, she thought. West-to-east long-haul flights were the worst for jetlag. But then she remembered that Rattray did not tire easily. He could resist such physical weaknesses.

She could only conclude, then, that Rattray was the sort who was more comfortable dealing with people at one remove, from behind a computer keyboard or at the other end of a phone line, when he could not give any of himself away through facial expressions or inadvertent gestures. In Real Life, he felt he had to exert absolute self-control all the time in order to maintain a similar impenetrability, a similar aloofness. A paradox: he could only allow himself to be approachable when he was at a distance.

This she could understand, and even empathise with.

For, in a similar way, were there not two Kims? The shy creature who seldom ventured out of her apartment, and the bold, ballsy, confident and all-conquering Otaku Queen who, Emperor Dragon notwithstanding, ruled cyberspace. But that was just a role she played: Kawai Kim, Otaku Queen, hacker's wet dream. It was not really her. It was, in fact, her polar opposite, the yin to her yang. Was this also true of Rattray, to a lesser extent? All this time, had his respectful, gracious attitude towards her been merely a mask for a cooler and more circumspect nature? In which case, why *was* he here?

At that point Kim – who, when it came to other people, invariably feared the worst – began to worry. Could it be that Rattray resented being here? Had she put him in an awkward position by asking him to help, forcing him out of sheer politeness to agree to come? Had she grievously miscalculated the strength of their relationship?

She did not know. It was possible. Fretfully she began to drum the fingers of one hand against her chin. She tried to console herself by recalling how, that time when her system had been invaded and she had been overcome by a kind of panic-stricken paralysis, Rattray had coaxed her out of it. He had spoken her name and had expressed absolute confidence in her, in her abilities, and he had not been angry, even though he had every reason to be, seeing as she had let him and MacGowan and Arnold X down badly. His voice, from thousands of miles away, had been firm and focused, so calmly authoritative, so suffused with absolute trust, that she had had no choice but to pay attention and comply. It had seemed, in that moment, that there had been no distance between them at all. With the power of speech alone he had reached deep within her, and through his sheer faith in her he had resurrected her own faith in herself. Even now, five months on, the memory made her tingle, and on this occasion it brought the desired reassurance.

Get a grip, she told herself sternly. He would not have come all this way if he had not wanted to.

The kettle bubbled to a boil and clicked itself off.

Two minutes later Kim appeared on the balcony and invited Rattray to come back inside. On the bedroom carpet she had set down a woven-bamboo tray on which she had laid out two cups and a teapot from an *Arita-yaki* tea set, a valuable family heirloom bequeathed to her by her grandmother. The china was of a pellucid delicacy, gorgeously ornamented with detailed blue designs that showed scenes of domestic life from the feudal era. Even when there was nothing in them, the cups seemed filled to the brim with light.

Kim hunkered down cross-legged on the floor on one side of the tray and invited Rattray to do the same on the other.

'Ah, the famous tea ceremony,' said Rattray, hitching up his trousers as he sat so as not to kink the creases.

'My own version. No bamboo whisk, no ladle, no iron kettle, and no green tea – just good honest Earl Grey.' Kim tapped the lid of the pot with a finger. 'I got it from a specialist tea importer in Ginza,' she added. 'Hideously expensive.'

'You went to some trouble,' Rattray said, appreciatively inhaling the tea's sweet tang of bergamot.

'Some,' Kim said. In fact, as she did with all her groceries, she had purchased the tea via modem and had it delivered to her home, but she did not feel the need to share this with Rattray. 'So how long does it need to brew properly? The instructions on the box were a little vague.'

'I usually take a relaxed attitude about that, myself. When you feel it's ready, then it's ready.'

'How Zen.'

'Any milk?' Rattray asked, surveying the tray.

'Oh. I forgot. Sorry.'

Kim got up and went to the kitchen nook, feeling marginally happier about the situation now. Rattray appeared to have relaxed. Either that, or she was adjusting to his Real Life mannerisms. He seemed touched, at any rate, that she had gone to the effort of obtaining his preferred beverage. She had intended the Earl Grey as a small welcoming gesture, to show him that she was grateful for what he was doing for her. Apparently it had worked. She had won his favour.

She returned to the bedroom with a carton of milk from the fridge and knelt down opposite Rattray again. She poured a half-centimetre of milk into each of the cups, and then, guessing that the tea must have attained the proper strength, and hoping that Rattray was right that you could judge such a thing by instinct, she picked up the pot. She filled the cups to just below the brim – aromatic Indian tea, an Englishman's favourite, gurgling into fine Japanese chinaware. She watched as Rattray lifted one of the cups to his lips and took a sip.

'Good,' was his verdict. 'You obviously have the knack. *Domō arigatō.*'

'You're welcome.' Kim reached for the second cup, but Rattray placed his other hand over it.

'I'd wait for that to cool down a bit, if I were you,' he said. '*I* can afford to scald my fingertips. You can't.'

With a laugh, Kim withdrew her hand.

Rattray set his cup back down on the tray. 'Well, I have to ask – what's the word on Emperor Dragon's whereabouts?'

'Kyoto.'

'Definitely Kyoto? When we spoke yesterday, you weren't a hundred per cent sure.'

'I am now. He's been getting very sloppy. Last night he posted another flame at the Koven and left his bang path wide open, past his server, virtually all the way back to his terminal. Not only am I sure he's in Kyoto, but I've narrowed him down to a local area code. One more transmission from him, and I'll have his home phone number.'

'Is it really carelessness on his part, I wonder.'

'If not, then it's overconfidence. And remember, I'm very good at what I do.'

'No argument about that. I'm merely being cautious. We don't want to go charging off into an Anarch trap.'

'Emperor Dragon is a lone hacker, John. Probably just some teenage *otaku* living at home with his parents.'

'But he has paraterrestrial-grade software.'

'Yes, but does he realise it? I don't think so. I think the Anarchs may have boosted his computer's capabilities without his knowledge.'

'And he just accepts that unquestioningly?'

'He's arrogant. He assumes it's because he's more gifted than everyone else.'

'Even so, surely he must wonder sometimes why he's able to do the things he does, why he seems to be so much better than everyone else.'

'OK, maybe, just maybe, he is aware that some of the software packages and applications he has on his hard drive are perhaps a bit – what's a good word? Radical? Maybe there's stuff on his system that he doesn't fully understand and can't remember downloading. But if so, it's not in his nature to question this too closely.'

'I can see that, I suppose,' said Rattray. 'If something works, and it works well, why trouble yourself with *how* it works? The Anarchs count on that time and time again. In fact, if the Anarchs have a coat of arms, it probably has the proverb about a gift horse inscribed on it.'

'Of course, there is another possibility,' said Kim. 'The Anarchs could have pulled a Windows trick on him.'

She was referring to a plot hatched by the Anarchs in the early nineties to insert a latent virus into Windows '95 during its development stage. At a prearranged date and hour, the virus would activate and sabotage every computer in the world currently employing Windows '95 as its multitasking operating environment, crashing it and wiping its memory. To this end, the Anarchs began subjecting one of the programmers working on Windows '95 to a series of subliminal instructions, flashed at him via his workstation monitor at home. Into the hapless programmer's brain were downloaded the code for the virus, knowledge of how to install it and the will to do so. The upshot of this scheme, had it been successful, might merely have been a lot of very annoyed PC-users. Equally, it might have led to the collapse of the world's entire financial system and global chaos of the kind that could quite easily have tipped over into anarchy and international armed conflict. Thanks to a warning from the Librans, however, the North American Guardians were able to invalidate the programmer before he could complete the installation of the virus, and Windows '95 did not go down in history as the Software of the Apocalypse.

Rattray nodded. 'Either way,' he said, 'your assumption is that Emperor Dragon is simply another unwitting Anarch dupe, working on his own, unguarded, unprotected.'

'Yes.'

'At this point our colleague Bill MacGowan would probably say something like, "Assumption is the mother of all foul-ups."'

'Then I'm not assuming,' Kim said, with all the confidence she could muster. 'I'm certain.'

Rattray picked up his cup of Earl Grey again and sipped it for a while, frowning into the middle distance.

Kim sat there, unsure whether to say anything. The silence was eventually broken by her stomach, which chose that moment to emit a voluminous borborygmic rumble. She had risen and breakfasted early that morning in order to give herself time to clean and tidy her apartment in readiness for Rattray's visit. It was now well past lunchtime, and her body had felt the need to give an audible reminder of a fact which her brain, in all the flurry and anxiety of meeting her friend and fellow Guardian, had neglected: she was hungry.

She glanced at Rattray, hoping against hope that he had not heard. It seemed, incredibly, that he had not, for his expression remained unchanged and he continued to drink his tea, his sombre grey gaze fixed on no physical object within the room but focused on some invisible prospect, some horizon of thought. Then, abruptly, he set down his cup and said, 'I'm a bit peckish. Perhaps we should go for a bite to eat.'

It was only as they were setting out for Hibiya subway station that Kim recalled Rattray telling her once, during one of their many phone conversations, that he did not experience the symptoms of hunger. He ate regularly and conscientiously because he needed to, but actual hunger pangs were among the bodily discomforts he no longer suffered from.

Embarrassment and gratitude jostled within Kim all the way to the station.

13

Rattray was intrigued to discover that, on the Tokyo subway, not only was everything sparklingly clean compared with the London Tube, but everything was on a scale about a tenth smaller than he was used to. He could not pass along the station tunnels without ducking his head to avoid brushing the low ceilings with his hair, and the train-carriage doors and seats also did not quite conform to Western proportions. He noted, too, that all the signs had English subtitles, just as they did at the airport, although at the airport you might expect this, whereas on the subway it seemed a generous courtesy.

He remarked on this to Kim, who replied that it was also intended to be slightly patronising to *gaijin* Westerners who could not be bothered to learn Japanese script. He asked if the same applied to the vending machines he had seen, most of which were adorned with words and phrases and even entire poems in English. Kim said no. There, the English was intended to make the vending machines and the products they contained seem sexy and Western and cool.

'I see,' said Rattray.

'Sorry,' said Kim, with a smile. 'We don't do these things deliberately to confuse you.'

Three stops southbound along the Hibiya Line, the two Guardians alighted at Roppongi station, and emerged from the subway exit into the clamour of one of Tokyo's busiest districts. Essentially a haven for tourists and resident foreign nationals, Roppongi was clogged with foot and road traffic even on this cold, rainy afternoon.

Most famous for its nightlife and restaurants, Roppongi catered for the international palate with local franchises of McDonald's, the Hard Rock Café, Häagen Dazs and the like. Tucked away down its narrow side-streets, however, could be found some of the better examples of Japan's native cuisine. Kim took Rattray to an *izakaya* which had been recommended on a Website guide to eating out in Tokyo. Its humble entrance and somewhat dilapidated interior decor were, according to the guide, no reflection on the quality of the food served.

The head waiter, having greeted his two new customers with a warm '*Irrasshaimase!*', directed them to a long, low hardwood table. Since the lunchtime rush was over, Kim and Rattray were the restaurant's only patrons other than a trio of extremely inebriated businessmen who had either forgotten that they had been due back at their desks an hour ago or were too drunk to care. The two Guardians made themselves comfortable on cushions on the tatami-mat floor, sitting catercorner from each other at one end of the table. Rattray invited Kim to order on behalf of both of them.

'I have faith in your judgement,' he said, adding, 'in this as in other matters.'

Heartened by the vote of confidence, Kim got carried away with the ordering. Before long, waiters were bringing a seemingly endless series of dishes – skewered yakitori, neatly wrapped packages of sushi and sashimi, heaped tangles of soba noodles and fried seaweed, and more besides – each course arriving before the two Guardians had had a chance to finish the previous one. At one point Rattray found himself eating batter-fried abalone tempura along with a side order of *poteto furai*, and felt obliged to comment to Kim that ten thousand miles was a long way to come for a plate of fish and chips.

Kim was soon full, and set down her chopsticks with a

gorged sigh, but Rattray kept on eating, not only because he was aware that it was considered polite in Japan to eat everything you were given, but also in order to store up a reserve of extra energy, just in case. This way, in the event that he was injured somehow during the next couple of days, healing the injury would not leave him dangerously debilitated.

Cold, clear sake came with the meal. Kim confined herself to just the one cupful, but made sure that Rattray's cup was kept replenished.

'Do you want me to end up like them, Kim?' Rattray remarked, when the small earthenware sake bottle was nearly empty. He inclined his head discreetly in the direction of the three businessmen, who had begun singing songs tunelessly but with great gusto.

'Just being a good hostess,' Kim replied. 'I know it's not possible to get *you* drunk.'

'It is possible, but only if I allow it to happen.'

Kim shook her head in wonderment. 'It must be incredible – having total control over your meat.'

'My "meat",' said Rattray, reiterating the hacker slang with just a hint of distaste.

'I mean,' Kim went on, 'are there any limitations to what you can do?'

'Plenty.'

'Such as? For example, how extreme would a wound have to be for it to kill you?'

'What a ghoulish question.'

'I'm sorry. Have I offended you?'

'No. It's simply that . . . Well, I've never met anyone who's just come right out and asked.'

'Well, I'm curious.'

'All right, then.' Rattray aimed a sideways glance at the three businessmen, who were still singing lustily away. They appeared oblivious to anyone else in the room but themselves. 'I wasn't handed an instruction manual after the Librans finished operating on me,' he said, his voice slightly lowered, 'but from logic and from experience I've worked out pretty much what level of damage I can and cannot survive. Loss of a limb I can cope with. It takes time, and it's a particularly unpleasant process, but the limb does regrow.'

'How many times has it happened?'

'How many times have I lost a limb? Once. And that's once too often.'

'What about decapitation?'

'That would do for me straight away. Likewise if my heart or my brain were to suffer a massive trauma.'

'Burning?'

'That depends. If you wanted to get rid of me that way, you'd have to incinerate me completely. If, say, all you did was douse me in kerosene and set me alight, I'd be able to regenerate the burned tissue easily enough.'

'Might the shock not kill you?'

'Unlikely. My body has suitable coping systems. It can accelerate blood clotting, the flow of neural messengers, the release of hormones, natural analgesics, endorphins, all that sort of thing.'

'What about poisons? I suppose those can't harm you either.'

'A modern neurotoxin might prove fatal, I don't know. I've never been exposed to one and I've no great desire to be. Anything short of that I know I can withstand. I could probably even eat a badly prepared fugu fish' – he dabbed his lips with a napkin – 'assuming I haven't done so already.'

'Direct hit with a nuclear warhead?'

Rattray gave her a wry look. 'Now you're being facetious.'

Kim laughed. 'All right, then, so you're effectively immortal—'

'As long as I don't meet with some catastrophic mishap, yes.'

'What about modifying your body?'

'What do you mean?'

'I just thought that, since you're capable of mending yourself in this fantastic way, you might also be capable of *changing* yourself.'

'You mean disguise my appearance by shifting the skin on my face around?'

'Yes. And maybe you could also alter your skin tone, the colour of your hair, the colour of your eyes, the timbre of your voice, even. With a bit of practice, you could pass yourself off as somebody completely different. Couldn't you?'

'An intriguing idea,' said Rattray, nodding to himself. 'I'll give it some thought. Although I'm not sure it would work. As far as I can tell, when my body has to heal itself, what it does is restore me to my genetically predetermined shape. The healing process is simply an exaggerated version of the anti-ageing process, which is what my physiology does of its own accord, maintaining me, repairing the cellular degradation that comes with growing old, constantly restoring me to my original, as it were, template – that of me at the age I was when I was recruited and "improved". I imagine that process *could* be overridden, however. Perhaps. I don't know. Intriguing.'

'Do you have any idea what it was that the Librans actually did to you, John?' Kim asked. 'When they "improved" you?'

'I have an inkling. Nanotechnology.'

Kim nodded. 'Yes, that's my theory, too. Hundreds of millions of semi-intelligent, self-replicating submicroscopic machines swarming around your body, constantly fixing you, mending damage wherever they find it, enhancing all your physiological functions.'

'When you put it like that, I get an irresistible urge to scratch myself.'

'You can feel them? Inside you?'

'No, of course not. It's an unappealing mental image, that's all. Tiny things inside you that aren't naturally supposed to be there. It makes me think of a termite infestation.'

'Except that these termites are on your side, they're helping you, not undermining your woodwork.'

'Yes, well, *some* would say that was a good thing.'

125

'Everlasting, illness-free life, John – it's what everyone in the world dreams of having. How could it possibly not be a good thing?'

'You'd know if you'd tried it.'

'Do you honestly mean that? Or is that just something you tell other people to make them feel better about not having what you have?'

'It does sound hypocritical, I admit,' said Rattray, 'and even, in a way, ungrateful. But I can assure you, Kim, what the Librans have given me is a gift I'd willingly return, if I could.'

Kim slapped his wrist mock-angrily. 'How can you *say* that? For me, it would be the biggest kick in the world, knowing that almost nothing can hurt me or kill me. If I were the way you are, I'd wake up every morning and, I don't know, stick my hand in the toaster and electrocute myself, something like that, just to remind myself how fortunate I am.'

Rattray was peering, bemused, at the spot where Kim had playfully hit him. 'The novelty,' he said, looking up at her, 'if there ever *was* any novelty, has long since worn off. I don't particularly enjoy the way I am now. I take no pleasure in the abilities I have. If I've come to some kind of acceptance of my condition, it's because rationally I know that it enables me to do my job better, but that's all. Sometimes I wonder if life might not regain its zest, its savour, if there was just a bit more hazard to it, if death was a strong possibility rather than an outside chance. You appreciate something more if you know it might be taken away from you at any moment.'

'I'm not convinced,' said Kim. 'My grandmother was in her eighties when she passed away. She was sane and fit and active right up until her final illness. She didn't want to die. I'm sure, if she'd been given the opportunity, she'd have gone on living for ever.'

'But I'm nearly twice the age she was. Believe me, there comes a point when you feel you've had enough.'

'If you really felt that way, surely you'd have killed yourself by now.'

Rattray's lips twisted into a grim smile, as if the notion wasn't as outlandish as Kim thought. 'Well, there are the practicalities to consider, aren't there? How does someone like me go about committing suicide?'

'You could find a way,' Kim replied, 'if you really wanted to do it.'

'Yes, I suppose I could.' Rattray surveyed the empty bowls and plates in front of them. 'Are we all done here?'

'I think so.'

'Then shall we make a move?'

Kim caught the head waiter's attention and raised her hands, one index finger crossed over the other. Shortly, the bill was brought.

The first thing Kim did after they arrived back at her apartment was change out of her office-lady attire into a more comfortable outfit – a plain white blouse, a tartan kilt, knee-high socks and sandals. The next thing she did was sit down at her computer console, don her spectacles and pull her split-keyboard towards her on its slide-out shelf. She hit a sequence of keys, and the constantly reconfiguring puzzle-egg screen-saver that was playing on the largest of the screens arrayed before her vanished and was replaced by an animated sprite standing against a plain blue background. The sprite was a slender, large-headed, grey-skinned alien, just like those which Emperor Dragon had depicted committing degrading acts on Kim's avatar, although this one was neatly neuter and not equipped with a monstrously oversized male appendage.

'That's Haiiro No,' Kim explained to Rattray over her shoulder. 'My interactive interface. Cute, isn't he?'

'Very,' said Rattray.

The little elfin creature was hopping up and down on the spot like a child with a full bladder, his large, slanting, expressive eyes flashing like two almond-shaped slivers of jet. To judge by his agitated manner, Haiiro No had some important information to divulge.

'I hope it's good news.' Kim tapped in a command, and Haiiro No started speaking rapid Japanese to her in a high-pitched, strangulated voice that Rattray identified as Kim's own, sped up and electronically treated.

When he had finished talking, Haiiro No executed a bow like an actor taking curtain-call and marched off-screen. The options menu screen of Kawai Kim's Koven appeared.

'Emperor Dragon has posted another flame, I take it,' Rattray said.

'He has,' said Kim ruefully. 'But this will be his last,' she added. 'This will be the one that leads us to him. I know it. I can feel it.'

She quickly pulled up the relevant posting. It was headed, as before, 'Late Valentina' (and seeing those words, Rattray, as before, felt a frisson – it just seemed too artfully contrived, too *pat*, to be a coincidental spelling error).

This time, the posting was verbal rather than visual. It consisted of a series of haikus.

'We don't have to read them,' Rattray said, eyeing the first few.

'We might as well,' Kim said, and, heaving a sigh of resignation, she began scrolling through the posting.

There were two dozen of the haikus all told. They began:

> Kawai Kim bathing
> Big turd floats to the surface
> 'I'm a dirty girl!'

> Kim at her console
> Blank screen – nothing is working
> Where is the On switch?

> Sad and all alone
> Otaku Queen frigging herself
> No boyfriend ever

The rest were in a similar derogatory vein.

'All right,' Kim said, when she and Rattray had read them all. Her lips were compressed tight together. 'He's

128

had his fun. Now I trace him. Did you hear that, Emperor Dragon?' She hunched forwards, addressing the main screen, as though her online tormentor were actually there, lurking inside the cathode-ray tube. 'Now I'm going to hunt you down and find you.'

And with that, she started typing furiously, her fingers moving almost too fast for Rattray to follow. Images appeared on the screens; appeared and went. Long lists of numbers scrolled up and up and up. Windows opened, expanded, closed. Rattray recognised the introductory sequence of Kawai Kim's Koven as it flashed into view, only to vanish again almost immediately. The content of the main screen changed repeatedly, here and there sections of text unfurling that Rattray was unable to read quickly enough to take in (and he doubted he would have understood what the text signified even if he *had* had time to read it). The rack-mounted stack of hard drives in one corner of the room buzzed and droned industriously.

Feeling entirely superfluous to requirements, Rattray none the less stayed in the room. It was fascinating to watch a skilled practitioner of an arcane artform at work. Kim was utterly consumed in what she was doing, her body curved towards the array of screens as though they were exerting a sort of magnetic attraction on her, drawing her in. Occasionally her right hand would stray from the keyboard to use the mouse for a swift point-and-click. Other than that, she just typed and typed and typed, filling the room with a monotone *Flight of the Bumble-Bee* clickety-clack rhythmic rattle.

Finally, with a hissed 'Yes!', Kim stopped typing and threw herself back in her chair. She twisted around to look up at Rattray. Her cheeks were flushed; her eyes, behind the thick lenses of her spectacles, were narrow with fierce satisfaction.

'Success?' said Rattray.

Kim spread out her hands. 'But of course. I told you I would find him.'

'An address?'

'Absolutely. We can leave for Kyoto first thing in the morning.'

'Why wait till tomorrow morning? How long does it take to get to Kyoto?'

'By shinkansen, a couple of hours.'

Rattray glanced at the numeral clock that was blinking away in one corner of the main screen. 'If we leave now, we could be there by six.'

Kim turned back to her keyboard. 'I'll book us tickets.'

Half an hour later, they were travelling by taxi to Tokyo's central Japan Railways station. A quarter of an hour after that, they were aboard the Bullet Train, gliding out of the city on a sibilance of steel, heading from the country's modern capital to its old.

14

Without seeking the permission of the three other men in the hotel room, because he knew it would be granted only grudgingly and with the accompaniment of tiresome wisecracks, Vasily Robirchenko lit up another Byelomorkanal.

The stink from his previous cigarette, smoked half an hour earlier, had only recently dispersed, and as Robirchenko exhaled a fresh cloud of vilely pungent fumes into the air, the rangy, looningly ugly man who was sitting on the opposite side of the table from him, and who was halfway through his umpteenth game of patience, fanned out the cards in his hand and started wafting them in front of his nose, at the same time making melodramatic coughing and gagging noises.

'God strewth!' exclaimed Karl Craddock, when it became clear that his rendition of a man dying of asphyxia was having little effect on Robirchenko. 'What do they make those things out of anyway? Dogshit and old cabbage?'

'*Yob tvoyu mat*,' replied Robirchenko, and sent a smoke-ring drifting across the table in Craddock's direction.

'That didn't sound like a compliment, I must say,' observed Bob Griffith, in whose room the four men were congregated. Griffith was a softly spoken Yorkshireman, compactly built, cubic and bullet-headed. He played prop forward for a minor-league rugby team in his hometown of Bradford, and off the pitch habitually wore his team's shirt. Currently he was stretched out, fully clothed and supine, on the room's saggy-mattressed double divan. His arms were folded behind his head and there was a Sony Discman lying beside him on the salmon-pink candlewick counterpane. He had unplugged one of the Discman's earphones from his ear so that he could hear what was being said and listen to his music at the same time. A track from Bryan Adams's greatest hits album whispered and rustled from the exposed earphone's miniature speaker.

'It was not a compliment,' Robirchenko confirmed. 'I was telling our Australian friend to go fuck his mother.'

'Love to, mate,' Craddock replied breezily, 'but the old girl's been six feet under for a decade and she's probably a bit too dry now. How about I fuck *your* mother instead?'

'*Voniuchaya pizda.*'

'Yeah, you too, Vaseline.'

'Vasily.'

'Whatever.' With a loose, lopsided grin, Craddock set his cards down, pushed his chair back, got to his feet and strode over to the window, saying, 'Reckon we could do with a spot of fresh air in here.' He thrust aside the nylon net curtain and heaved up the window's lower sash, which stiffly and creakily permitted itself to be raised. As the window opened, in came a cool, salty breeze, along with the sound of waves crashing and the straining, elegiac cries of seagulls.

Leaning on the windowsill, Craddock looked out.

The view from the second-floor room was of the beachfront high street of the town of Carvingdean, a small seaside resort on the south coast of England, the kind of place that even at the height of the tourist season still looked shabby and unfrequented and unpopular. Now, in hazy autumn, Carvingdean was all but deserted, and the retail premises that relied on the glut of summer custom to turn over an annual profit – the amusement arcades, fish-and-chip restaurants, ice-cream kiosks and postcard-and-novelty emporia – seemed to be simply going through the motions of plying their trades, remaining open in the same way that the eyes of sleepwalkers remain open.

Immediately in front of the hotel, whose name was the Ship Hotel and whose off-white Victorian façade was in serious need of renovation, there was a promenade lined with unoccupied deckchairs. The deckchairs, their striped canvas tongues flapping gossipily in the onshore wind, sat facing turquoise-painted railings. On the other side of the railings lay a strip of shingle beach that shelved in three steep undulations to the sea. Grey-green waves were hurling themselves at the beach's edge, leaping like hounds, slinking back like curs. A mile out in the Channel, two yachts were being tugged along by their wind-bellied sails. Beyond them, a supertanker gracefully traversed the line of the horizon.

Turning his head to the left and squinting, Craddock was able to discern the outline of a pair of large, grey, cubic buildings that hunkered on the tip of a promontory about three miles east along the coast. Seal Point. From this distance, the disused nuclear power station looked like a pair of gigantic dice that had been rolled and forgotten about.

He glanced impatiently at his watch. It was getting on for midday. 'Where the hell is MacGowan anyway?' he said over his shoulder to the others in the room. 'It's been – what, four hours?'

'He had to go somewhere in Surrey, didn't he say?' replied the fourth man present, a slim, lean-muscled Tibetan. Dor Bahadur Uphadhyay – D.B. to his friends – was kneeling on the floor, busily taking the shine off a pair of combat boots, rubbing dubbin over their uppers but leaving the dubbin unpolished, so that the boots would not reflect light in the dark. As he worked, he smiled. Uphadhyay was forever smiling, whatever he happened to be doing. The skin of his face was scored with deep, fanning creases around the eyes and mouth, the visible emblems of a perennially sunny disposition.

'Well, how far is that from here?' Craddock demanded.

'Fuck it, you can drive from one end of this bloody country to the other in about ten minutes, can't you?'

'No, that is not possible,' Robirchenko stated matter-of-factly.

Craddock rolled his eyes. 'I was exaggerating,' he said, as though explaining himself to a five-year-old. 'For comic effect.'

'I know.' The Russian drew nonchalantly on his cigarette. 'And I was pretending not to realise. For comic effect.'

The two men gazed levelly at each other. Then Craddock broke the contact, turning and resuming his contemplation of the view from the window, while Robirchenko leaned forwards and idly contemplated the sheaf of architectural blueprints that were spread out in front of him on the table. Uphadhyay continued to unshine his boots, and Griffith inserted the second earphone back in his ear and started humming along with the music and swinging his toes together in time to the beat.

Gesturing at the blueprints, Robirchenko said, 'I hope they have decontaminated this place properly.'

'Yeah, like you haven't got cancer already,' Craddock said, pointing to the cheap porcelain ashtray that was holding down one corner of the blueprints. The ashtray brimmed with Byelomorkanal butts.

Robirchenko fixed Craddock with a frosty stare and stolidly stubbed his latest cigarette out.

'Surely there would not be a laboratory there if the power station was still radioactive,' Uphadhyay opined.

'It makes me unhappy all the same,' said Robirchenko. 'I have relatives in Kiev. A cousin and her family. She tells me people are still dying there as a result of Chernobyl.'

Griffith had unplugged one of his earphones again. 'Bill's getting us NBC gear, Vasily, remember?'

'NBC equipment is not a hundred per cent reliable,' said Robirchenko.

'You've not worked for Bill before, have you?'

Robirchenko shook his head.

'Take it from me – whatever we'll be using tonight, it'll

be reliable. Better than the best you've ever used. Isn't that right, D.B.?'

Uphadhyay nodded serenely. 'Mr Bill has connections.'

'But connections to what? This is what I wish to know,' said Robirchenko. 'Ever since I left Spetsnaz and went freelance, I have been hearing about Bill MacGowan from other professionals. He pays well above the going rate, that I know for myself now. But who is paying *him*? No one has yet been able to explain this properly to me.'

'I hate to say this, but Vaseline's got a point,' said Craddock. 'Normally I don't give a shit about why I'm doing a job or who I'm doing it for, but Bill's got an intriguing rep. Any ideas, Bob?'

'I've worked for Bill twice before,' replied Griffith, 'and I'm as much in the dark as you are. D.B.'s the real MacGowan expert here. Aren't you, D.B.? Done about half a dozen jobs with him, isn't that right?'

The Tibetan lowered his head. 'Mr Bill has indeed called on my services several times,' he said, 'and I flatter myself that he and I are friends. But I also know that in our business one does not ask what one should not ask.'

'But possibly he has let something slip by accident,' said Robirchenko. 'Some clue as to who employs him.'

'If so, I have not noticed.'

'Gurkhas,' said Craddock. 'Noted for their loyalty.'

If Uphadhyay detected the faint note of scorn in Craddock's voice, he chose not to show it. 'Their loyalty and their honesty,' he said, beaming as broadly as ever. He lifted up his boots for one last all-over inspection, then, satisfied that he had made them as dull as they could be, set them down on a sheet of newspaper on the floor and picked up his kukri. He drew the boomerang-shaped knife from its leather sheath and set to sharpening it, running a small whetstone back and forth along the blade with a diligent, precise action. The kukri had been a present from the Sultan of Brunei, given to Uphadhyay to replace the combat-worn weapon that had seldom strayed from his side since he joined the Gurkhas in the early seventies. Uphadhyay had spent four years in Brunei as a member of the sultan's private contingent of Gurkha troops.

'So tell us about these two jobs you did for big Bill, Bob,' said Craddock. 'Since Smiley here's being so bloody tight-lipped.'

'One was up in Scotland, the other on the Isle of Wight,' said Griffith, pressing the 'Stop' button on his Discman. 'The Scotland job, it was a bunch of us up against some kind of private army. A terrorist cell, I think, camped up in the Cairngorms. There was a hell of a firefight, though thankfully I was out of the worst of it.'

'A firefight?' said Craddock. 'What did the locals make of *that*?'

'Nothing, as far as I'm aware. There was one report in a local paper about military exercises up in the hills, but that was about it.'

'Which would imply that Bill has friends in high places,' said Robirchenko. 'To be able to keep such a thing quiet.'

'Aye.' Griffith nodded. 'There was some other stuff going on that I didn't really understand – something to do with a kind of new weapons technology. Bill was a bit unclear about it at the pre-op briefing, deliberately I think. He told us that some of us might see some weird stuff when we went in, and it would be better for us if we just sort of *overlooked* it.'

'And did you?' Craddock asked. 'See any weird stuff?'

'I'm not sure. Like I said, I wasn't in the thick of things. I heard some odd sounds and saw these lights hovering in the sky – they could have been parachute flares, I suppose, although they moved against the prevailing wind, some of them . . . I don't know. I had other things to concentrate on, to be honest – like wiring up a roadbridge in case the terrorists tried to escape across it. D.B. would be able to tell you a bit more about it. He was up at the sharp end that night.'

'Well?' Craddock said to Uphadhyay.

'I do not recall encountering anything worth mentioning.'

'Oh, how very bloody diplomatic. You know, it's people like you that give our profession a good name.'

'Thank you, Mr Karl.'

'And on the Isle of Wight, Bob?' said Robirchenko. 'What happened there?'

'That,' said Griffith, 'was a small-scale job. Just three of us: me, Bill, and this other fellow – Rattray, he was called. John Rattray. Bit of a cold fish. Non-service, as far as I could tell. We did an infil into this bloody great big mansion belonging to some aristocrat or other, I forget his name now. Viscount Somebody-or-Other. Lovely old house, it were. Filled with paintings and statues and huge pieces of furniture. And it had a security system like you wouldn't believe. Electric fences, pressure sensors, motion sensors, infrared alarm triggers, the works. We bypassed it all. Piece of cake. Bill and that Rattray fellow had a gadget for everything. Like Batman and Robin with their utility belts, they were.'

'So what were you there to do?' said Craddock. 'Was this viscount a criminal or something?'

'I'm not sure. He was building something nasty in his basement, that's about as much as I know. I never got to see what it was. Rattray and Bill went down to have a look, but I was told to stay up on the ground floor and stand sentry. I overheard Bill say something to Rattray at one point about a "time device", which sounded odd, but maybe I just misheard. He could have said "*timer* device".'

'So it was a bomb he was making, perhaps?' suggested Robirchenko.

'Possibly. Though it beats me why an aristocrat would be putting together a bomb in his basement.'

'Mad as a dingo in a dunny, your Pom aristocrats – that's why,' Craddock averred. 'Comes of generations of screwing their sisters.'

'So what happened to this man?' asked Robirchenko. 'This viscount?'

'We went in at night, of course,' said Griffith. 'He and his wife were asleep in bed. Rattray went into their room and squirted some stuff in their faces. Knockout spray, or maybe something more permanent. Then Bill and I set incendiaries, we got out of there and the place went up in flames. The fire was out of control before the fire brigade were even called, and the house burned down to the ground, and Viscount and Lady Whoever were cremated along with it. No one suspected arson – we did our job too well. "Faulty electrical wiring" was the accident investigator's conclusion.'

'Did you not feel guilty about destroying that house and all those paintings and antiques?' Robirchenko asked.

'Oh, yes. But I suppose Bill didn't want to leave any evidence.'

'And speak of the devil . . .' said Craddock. Out of the window he had spied MacGowan's Saab pulling up outside the hotel.

15

The Bullet Train sighed to a halt at Kyoto station, and Rattray and Kim disembarked. The journey had been smooth, swift and scenic. On the way they had passed snow-capped Mount Fuji, and the approach into the Kyoto basin had taken them through paddy-fields and pastureland which, apart from the presence of the odd item of modern farm machinery, seemed to have changed little since feudal times.

In each coach of the train a digital readout displayed the shinkansen's current speed and the number of minutes remaining till the next stop. As they had neared Kyoto, Kim had watched with mounting nervousness as the latter figure had counted down, and now, as she and Rattray walked along the platform, she was on edge, all knotted up inside. Emperor Dragon was near – physically near. Somewhere in this city he was lurking. The person she had come to fear and despise over these past few months, the person who, until today, had repeatedly evaded her detection, was somewhere out there in the dusk-shrouded jumble of low roofs and ugly urban blocks that hunkered between two low ranges of hill. So close. Unaware that nemesis was coming for him.

In all honesty Kim would have preferred for her conflict with Emperor Dragon to have remained within the digital realm, but since this was apparently not possible, she had been left with no choice but to resort to this tactic, confronting her online opponent in Real Life. She was slightly ashamed of this – for a hacker, it seemed like weakness – but, then, she reminded herself, there were more important things at stake here than simply her pride. Emperor Dragon had meddled in Guardian affairs, and now he was going to reap the consequences.

The two Guardians took a taxi to the address which Kim had obtained by hacking into the national telecommunications database. Kim had not visited Kyoto before and, with only a house number and a street name to go on, had no reason to believe that their destination would not be a residential dwelling.

Imagine her chagrin, then, when the taxi deposited her and Rattray outside a videogame arcade in the city's entertainment district, just east of the Kamo-gawa river.

Inside the arcade, children, teenagers and a few adults were locked in play with the whirring, whizzing, whining machines – shooting at armed terrorists on the screens with plastic pistols, spinning the steering-wheels of motor-racing games, manipulating buttons and joysticks in complex configurations in order to get fighters to perform special combat moves, and repeatedly, repeatedly thrusting coins into the slots. A great blare of sound effects and churning rock music issued from the arcade's entrance, mingling with the racket emanating from all the other videogame arcades and the pachinko parlours along the street. Neon hoardings flickered; lightbulb arrays flashed. Energy was palpable in the air, a hot crackling atmosphere that pulsated against the purple twilight sky.

'Perhaps he has an apartment above,' Kim suggested gamely, peering at the windows of the building's upper storey, which were occluded by venetian blinds.

'Perhaps,' Rattray agreed, with little conviction. 'Or perhaps we've pursued a false trail.'

Kim had been thinking this, but had not wanted to admit it to herself, and even less had wanted Rattray to say so out loud. Inside her, anxiety had given way to a sensation of brittleness, of embarrassment and crumbling hopes. Had they come all this way for nothing? Had

Emperor Dragon misdirected her to a bogus terminal site? Had he got the better of her yet again?

Her thoughts were interrupted by a great blatting roar of exhaust. Turning, she saw three motorcycles come tearing along the street towards her and Rattray. As they drew level with the two Guardians, the motorcycles' riders slammed on the brakes and the bikes screeched to an abrupt, sideways halt in the road. Plumes of tyre-smoke drifted onwards, like souls released by death.

The motorcycles, all Kawasakis, sported skilfully rendered customised paintjobs. One had an airbrushed picture of a naked woman on its petrol tank. The body-work of another had been resprayed metallic blue and was adorned all over with decals showing cartoon characters, brand logos and slogans. The chrome-plated parts of all three bikes shone with a lovingly polished gleam. As for their riders, they were clad in brightly coloured leathers and Caterpillar boots, and their helmets were as customised as the machines they straddled.

The nearest of the motorcyclists, whose helmet bore a Rising Sun design, flipped up his mirrored visor, revealing a nose that had clearly been broken at least once, flanked by eyes whose pupils were so dilated that his irises were reduced to thin brown coronas. The motorcyclist unbuttoned the flap of his jacket and reached inside with a gloved hand to produce a slim, plain white envelope. He offered the envelope to Kim. When she hesitated to take it, Rattray stepped forwards and plucked it from his grasp. The biker, having casually appraised Rattray from head to toe, snapped his visor down and gunned his throttle. His two companions did the same, and with a sudden growl of engaged gears and a squeal of wheels the three of them roared off, leaving behind the reek of petrol fumes and burned tyre-rubber. They hurtled down the street, deliberately swerving and veering in order to alarm pedestrians. Rattray and Kim watched them until the blurred, curving streaks of their taillights were lost in the distance.

'*Bosozoku*,' Kim murmured.

'I'm sorry?' said Rattray, thinking he must have misheard. 'Did you say "berserker"?'

'*Bosozoku.*' Kim spaced out the separate syllables of the word. 'It means "thunderbolt tribe". They're trouble. They're into drugs and drag-racing and fighting over territory, and they have no respect for authority or their elders.' It was evident from her tone that this last was the worst of their crimes. 'Everyone in Japan hates them, but no one really knows what to do about them.'

'I'd have thought a good clip round the earhole would suffice,' Rattray opined. He glanced around. No one in the immediate vicinity appeared to have thought much of the preceding incident. A trio of teenage tearaways menacing a *gaijin* tourist was obviously not an uncommon sight in this city.

He turned his attention to the envelope. He looked for a name on it, but the envelope was blank on both sides. 'Well, let's see what this is all about,' he said, and inserted one index finger beneath the flap.

Inside the envelope there was a single sheet of paper which, when unfolded, revealed a photocopied map on each side. One of the maps was of Kyoto itself, the other of what appeared to be a park of some sort. An X had been drawn in yellow highlighter pen on each map, and running down the right-hand side of the map of the park there were a few lines of hand-written Japanese script.

Kim provided the translation. 'It's from him – Emperor Dragon,' she said. 'He wants us to meet him tomorrow morning, six a.m., here.' She gestured at the park map. 'This is a temple on the outskirts of the city. A shrine. And he emphasises that just the two of us should go. If anyone else comes with us, the meeting does not happen.'

'That's all?'

'That's all. Except this.' She pointed to one of the *kanji* characters, set apart from the rest. It was shaped distinctly like a man holding a spear.

Rattray, recognising the character, nodded. The same character appeared on the options menu of Kawai Kim's Koven, where it served as a gateway for Guardian users, enabling them to access Kim's hidden Guardian information network. It represented the first syllable of the Japanese word for guardian, *hogosha*.

'Then he does know about us,' Kim said, 'about what we are.'

'It would seem that way.'

'You don't sound surprised.' Half joking, she added, 'Is there something you haven't told me, John?'

Rattray made an ushering gesture. 'Shall we walk? Get away from all this racket?'

They set off along the pavement. For a while Rattray seemed lost in thought. Eventually he spoke.

'I regret to say, Kim,' he said, 'that I have something of a confession to make.'

'A confession?'

'Emperor Dragon has been using you.'

'Using me?' Kim shook her head. 'I don't understand.'

'His smear campaign against you has been a calculated attempt to get you to respond in the way you have – by summoning me here to help.'

'But it's me he wants, me he hates. Isn't it?'

'No,' said Rattray. 'I can't really explain to you my reasons for believing what I've just said. It's too complicated, too . . . personal. You'll just have to take it on trust that I've solid grounds for thinking that I'm the target here, not you. Which leads me to a second confession. I, too, have been using you.'

'Now I'm really confused. I invited *you* to come here.'

'And I accepted, but principally because you'd provided me with a useful pretext. I'm as keen to meet Emperor Dragon as you are, perhaps keener. I want to know if he knows something, as I suspect he does – something about my past, something that goes back to the roots of my Guardianship. I've no idea why a Japanese computer hacker, of all people, should possess this knowledge, and it may be that I've come here on a wild-goose chase, deluding myself into seeing a connection where none exists. I'll find out the truth tomorrow morning. The main thing is, because I have too high a regard for you to be anything less than honest with you, Kim, I wanted you to be aware that I had an ulterior motive for making this trip.'

Kim was silent for several minutes while she took in what she had just heard. The revelation that Emperor Dragon had been manipulating her came as a shock, but in retrospect she could see how it might be possible. If he knew about the Guardians and he had been monitoring her unobtrusively for a while – since before he had made himself known during the Nowhere mission, even – then he might reasonably be aware that, of all her fellow Guardians, Rattray was the one she conversed with the most enthusiastically. Her electronic relationships with other Guardians were steadfastly formal and businesslike, but between her and Rattray there had been, almost from the start, a rapport, a reciprocal warmth. Over the years he and she had built up a repertoire of knowing little phrases and penpal-type in-jokes. Sometimes he called her an 'IT-girl'. Sometimes, for fun, she adopted a lofty, cod-Victorian prose style in the cover notes to her interpretations, mimicking the Dickens novels she had studied at school. Sometimes he would make mock-patronising references to her youthfulness. Sometimes she would tease him about his immense old age (it was at her suggestion that he had adopted 'Methuselah' as his online alias).

And Emperor Dragon, by decrypting her e-mails and rifling through her files, had uncovered this affinity between them and had exploited it in order to lure Rattray to Japan.

It was possible, yes. And if Rattray thought that this was what had happened, then it was almost undoubtedly true.

Their footsteps had been taking them west, and now they reached the river. The Kamo-gawa was a leaden, low, slow-moving waterway, and in this section of the city there were restaurants and cafés on its eastern bank, tables under awnings and parasols, illuminated by necklaces of lights. Kyoto's residents were gathering for their evening meals, and genial conversation rippled along the esplanade, along with the sound of piped *gagaku* music, spiky and ethereal. The sky above the city had turned a deep indigo and was flecked with stars.

The two Guardians continued in silence across one of the flat bridges that traversed the river. Halfway, Rattray halted, and Kim halted, too. Leaning on the parapet, Rattray gazed down into the dark, moiling waters.

Finally he spoke again. 'If it's all right with you, Kim, I'd rather you weren't present at the meeting tomorrow morning. It's obvious that Emperor Dragon has set up a trap of some sort for us. There may, therefore, be some risk to yourself if you come, and I'd rather not have that on my conscience.'

A geisha, wearing full make-up and dressed in a heavy black kimono bound with a broad gold sash, came along the pavement towards them, her eyes decorously downcast. Kyoto was one of the few places in Japan where geishas were a common sight, but even so, in these modern surroundings she was a living manifestation of a bygone era, an exquisite ghost from history, and it seemed to Kim somehow inappropriate to continue talking until she had passed by.

'No, John,' she said, with a firm shake of her head, as the geisha's dainty, tripping footsteps faded. 'No way am I staying behind. I *have* to be there.' Why did she have to be there? Was there a valid reason? There was! 'He's expecting both of us, remember? The meeting will be called off if I don't show. But, more to the point, if you're right about him, then I want to be present when he gets his comeuppance.'

'His comeuppance?'

'If he knows about the Guardians, if he's compromised our security that badly, then he's a threat and needs to be invalidated. Simple as that. He can't be allowed to remain alive.'

Rattray's features – his heavy-ridged brow, his deep-set eyes – made him in certain lights gauntly handsome, in others cadaverous. Just then, in the distant glimmering electric glow from the riverside restaurants, he looked the latter; with his pale skin and white hair, he looked skeletal, deathlike.

'Invalidated?' he said grimly. 'Yes, I suppose so.' He nodded to himself. 'Once I've found out what I want to know. Yes . . .'

16

Half an hour before the foregoing conversation took place – or nine and a half hours later, if you factor in the difference between time-zones – MacGowan was at the wheel of his Saab, heading from Bretherton to Carving-dean.

The most direct route between the Guardians' head-quarters and the seaside town contained no stretches of motorway, but MacGowan was making the best of the dual carriageways and A-roads, which were relatively clear. He kept within the speed limit all the way and overtook only when the opposite lane was absolutely empty ahead, taking no risks. With a mix of ten albums on the CD changer in the Saab's boot – old favourites like Pink Floyd and the Beatles, and new pleasures such as Radiohead and Oasis, whom he liked partly because they reminded him of, respectively, Pink Floyd and the Beatles – he had plenty of top-notch music to play at top volume in order to keep him from getting bored.

Also in the Saab's boot were a pair of black backpacks laden with paraterrestrial-grade *matériel* which Lucretia, drawing from an itemised requisitions list MacGowan had faxed her that morning from the Ship Hotel, had retrieved for him from the cellars beneath Bretherton Grange. The Grange was built over a Node, one of those points where Earth and the world of the paraterrestrials interpenetrated. The Librans kept the Nodes stocked with weaponry and equipment, enabling the Guardians to use them as quartermaster's stores.

As he drove, MacGowan deliberated on the mission ahead.

An abandoned nuclear power station seemed, on the face of it, an unusual place to establish a secret bio-weapons lab, but it did make a kind of sense, when you thought about it. After all, you were unlikely to be troubled by interlopers there. Never mind that the site had been scrupulously scrubbed of all residual contamination. Radiation was one of the great modern bogey-men, and even the rumour of its presence was enough to convince most people to keep their distance.

So what could he and his team expect to find within Seal Point? MacGowan knew that the manufacture of bioweaponry did not require much space. A single average-sized room would be big enough, as long as it could be sealed airtight, and a bioreactor itself – the chamber in which the germ agent or viral agent was cultivated – did not have to be much larger than a kitchen swingbin. MacGowan had seen one once, on a previous action-to-suppress: a cylinder of glass and stainless steel, with plastic tubes protruding from it and a transparent hourglass-shaped core, the whole thing filled with a gelatinous, reddish-brown liquid. An innocuous-looking object, like some kind of ornament from the sixties, the sort of kitsch item Piers Pearson doubtless had cluttering his home. But it incubated death. Sinister, silent, agonising, ineluctable death. And on that previous action-to-suppress MacGowan had ruthlessly and unhesitatingly killed the protective-suited scientists who had been ministering to the bioreactor like priests around an altar. And having dealt with them, having rid the world of one kind of pestilence, he had then introduced a paraterrest-rial neutralising solution into the bioreactor in order to eradicate its contents clean down to the last microbe, thereby ridding the world of another kind of pestilence.

So, he and his team could expect to be entering a bacteriological Hot Zone. Lucretia had supplied paraterrestrial-grade NBC suits and hypodermic pressure-gun syringes containing a paraterrestrial vaccine that could counteract the effects of exposure to most known toxins, bacilli and pathogens, which was some comfort. All the same, an Anarch bio-agent was an unknown quantity, and so all possible care could and should be taken within its vicinity.

Next question: was the team likely to encounter any armed resistance within the power station?

In his judgement, the answer was no.

Reconnaissance the previous day had revealed which of the twin reactor buildings was the one being used by the scientists. MacGowan had not been in any doubt that the Librans' instructions – and Kim's interpretation of them – were on the money, but tactical intelligence was worthless if it wasn't backed up by observation with the trusty Mark 1 Human Eyeball. Assumption, after all, was the mother of all fuck-ups.

Through binoculars, from a vantage point on a hilltop about a mile away, MacGowan had watched the power station all morning and all afternoon for activity. Had anyone happened to pass by and ask him what he was up to, he would have told them that he was hoping to spot some of the seals that were reputed to congregate at Seal Point. But no one came by, and for most of the day he did not see another human except the occupants of cars driving along on the coast road. The power station appeared to be deserted, but eventually, around six o'clock, his patience was rewarded. With a faint rumble, the door to the loading bay of one of the buildings rose up several feet, and a man emerged. MacGowan trained the binoculars on him, homing in with the focus dial.

The man was undistinguished-looking: in his forties, bald on top, slim, wearing old worn jeans and a sweat-shirt. He gazed out of the doorway for a few moments, blinking as though unused to the daylight. Then he went back inside.

MacGowan was able to make out three vehicles inside the loading bay: a Ford Transit van with blacked-out windows and a pair of Peugeot 205s, one white, one red. Just the kind of transport he would expect to see. The two cars for personnel, the Transit for equipment. The man got into the white 205, started it up and drove out of the loading bay, stopping just the other side of the entrance. He climbed out, reached up for the base of the door and hauled it down. Then, stepping back into the car, he drove along the sliproad that led to the power station's main gates.

At the gates he got out again, and, taking a key from his pocket, undid the padlock that held together the heavy chain that secured the gates. Then he got back into the car, steered it through, got out once again, re-locked the gates, then headed off along the coastal road towards Carvingdean.

An hour later the white Peugeot returned, and the man repeated the whole laborious gate-opening and -closing procedure in reverse. Through the Peugeot's windows MacGowan spied bulging Sainsbury's carrier bags on the back seat. The man steered the car back down the sliproad to the loading bay, halted outside, got out, raised the door, drove inside and moments later hauled the door down once more.

That had been the only visible indication that the power station was occupied. MacGowan had spotted no guards posted outside either of the reactor buildings, or anywhere within the cordon of the perimeter fence. In fact, as far as he could tell, the Gene Genius eggheads at work within the disused power station were employing no form of security at all. Clearly, as he had thought, they were relying on Seal Point's 'glowing' reputation to keep snoopers and intruders at bay.

In short, it looked like a relatively straightforward in-out job, with only a handful of non-combat personnel for opposition. Not that that meant he was going to be any less careful or ruthless during the mission. Civilians could cause just as much trouble as trained military operatives, as he remembered only too well from the action-to-suppress in Nevada.

Roadsigns to Carvingdean began appearing, and soon MacGowan was driving through lowland countryside along narrow, hedge-banked roads. The light gradually altered, gaining the flatter, cleaner quality that characterised coastal light. Trees and bushes had grown up uniformly bent and bowed in the direction of the prevailing onshore wind, and the land became grassy and rough as its sloped towards the sea. He had a sense of the country unravelling, unmaking itself, as he approached England's edge.

Carvingdean itself was not much of a town. Other than its beachfront high street, it had precious little to offer except small pebbledashed semis and, rising behind the main part of town, row upon row of retirement bungalows boasting sea views and not much else. Carvingdean's guest houses, bed-and-breakfasts and hotels all without exception had names with a marine or a nautical theme, and the place clearly thrived in summer but out of season was as dead as a doornail.

MacGowan parked outside the Ship Hotel, switching off the Saab's engine and cutting off Thom Yorke's tremulous tenor in the middle of 'No Surprises', Radiohead's sweetly sarcastic plea for a life of strife-free, conformist bliss. He climbed out of the car and, glancing up, espied Karl Craddock hanging out of an upstairs window, grinning down at him like a gargoyle. The Australian was truly one of the least handsome individuals MacGowan had ever set eyes on. He had a face even his own mother would have been hard pressed to love, what with its pockmarked skin, its bulging eyes and its mouth that seemed to be permanently drawn into a baggy leer. On the plus side, the bloke had a sense of humour and was, by all accounts, a good soldier.

'G'day, mate!' Craddock called down cheerily, waving at MacGowan.

MacGowan returned the wave. 'I'll be up in a moment.' Unlocking and opening the car's boot, he retrieved the two backpacks. With one of the backpacks slung over each shoulder he made his way, heavily weighed down, up the front steps of the hotel and into the foyer.

The foyer was decked out in crimson flock wallpaper and floral chintz curtains, like a cross between an Indian restaurant and an old lady's sitting room. A young male clerk was on duty at the reception desk, looking bored. MacGowan nodded to him as he passed, heading for the stairs. The clerk twitched a lip in response.

MacGowan had chosen the Ship Hotel as his team's quarters for the simple reason that it was the only halfway decent hotel in all of Carvingdean. By anyone's standards it was not luxuriously appointed, and few of the rooms had en suite bathrooms, but it was large enough to afford him and his team some privacy in their activities. He climbed two flights of stairs and knocked on the door to Griffith's room.

Uphadhyay let him in.

'Afternoon, ladies,' MacGowan said, setting the backpacks down on the floor. 'Miss me?'

'Like a dose of the clap,' said Craddock.

'That much? I'm honoured.' MacGowan sniffed the air. 'Buggeration! Did something die in here?'

With a caustic, defiant chuckle, Robirchenko tapped out a fresh cigarette from the blue-and-white Byelomorkanal pack and lit it.

'Best leave that window open, Karl,' MacGowan advised Craddock. He clapped his hands and rubbed them together. 'All right. Thumbs out of bums, everyone. We've got work to do. D.B., would you help me unpack these?' He gestured at the backpacks. 'Remember – pinch the clasps for a count of five before releasing them, otherwise everything inside the bag gets trashed and I have to go all the way back to bloody Surrey again . . .'

For the next few hours, MacGowan instructed the other four on how to use the equipment he had brought in the backpacks. Then he and the four mercenaries went over the infiltration plan. By the time they were done, the afternoon had faded, dusk was falling and the streetlights were flickering into life all along the promenade. All five men being very hungry by now, they decided to head out for an early supper.

Only one restaurant along Carvingdean's seafront looked as though it had any aspirations to quality. Its sign boasted that it served the best seafood in the area. Inside, there were small tables, laid with cutlery, glasses, napkins folded into bishop's mitres and, as a centrepiece, a carnation in a stem vase. Most of the tables were unoccupied, and the patrons, if they were talking at all, talked at the lowest possible volume. Music tinkled innocuously in the background. Husks of dead blue-bottles littered the windowsills.

The five men were shown to a table by a plump, jolly waitress with apple cheeks and stubby arms. The waitress's frilly-collared nylon blouse and prodigious bosom were engaged in a close-fought battle between fabric and flesh.

She distributed menus and, while the five men were making up their minds what to have, asked them in a light, just-making-conversation tone what had brought them to Carvingdean.

MacGowan trotted out the agreed-upon cover story: they were marine biologists working for an international conservation agency, and they were there to test the waters around Seal Point to see what, if any, harm had been down to the local sea life by emissions from the reactor.

'Oh, you've probably heard the joke about the sea around here,' said the waitress, with a jaunty flap of her arms and a giggle. 'Seal Point – where the fish really do have fingers.'

MacGowan pointed to the menu. 'Speaking of which, what do you recommend?'

'The lemon sole. Definitely. It's delicious.'

'Does it come with fingers and glow in the dark?' Craddock asked. ''Cause if it does, no thanks.'

'Oh, no, "no worries",' the waitress reassured him in a passable imitation of an Australian accent. 'It's not caught locally.'

153

'Your sign says "best seafood in the area",' said Robirchenko.

'*In* the area, not *from* the area. We're not crazy, you know.'

All of them decided to try the lemon sole, with the exception of Uphadhyay, who, although no longer a practising Buddhist, remained a vegetarian. He chose a plain omelette with salad.

'Chips, of course,' the waitress said.

'Chips all round,' MacGowan confirmed.

The waitress began collecting up the menus. 'So, you anything to do with those people up at the reactor, then?'

'There are people up at the reactor?' MacGowan said, feigning mild surprise. 'I thought it'd been closed down.'

'Oh, yes. Been there about a fortnight now, they have. No one's exactly sure what they're doing, but we reckon they must be checking the radiation levels, making sure the place has been cleaned up properly.'

'That's probably what they're doing, then,' MacGowan said, nodding.

On everyone's behalf he ordered mineral water to go with the meal. He was pleased that none of the team raised so much as a murmur of objection to this, not even Craddock, who, Roger Templeton had informed him, was occasionally a little too partial to a drop of the hard stuff. Craddock had enough sense to know that alcohol immediately before a mission was inadvisable.

While they were waiting for the food to arrive, and after it came, the five men chatted about people they knew in common.

For MacGowan, the conversation was not only a chance to catch up on what a number of his contemporaries from the Regiment were up to nowadays, it was a chance to assess how well his team were meshing together and how accurate Templeton's judgement of each man's personality had been. Templeton had predicted that Robirchenko and Craddock would clash. The one was too phlegmatic, the other too abrasive, for there not to be friction between them, he had said. And sure enough,

154

Craddock was taking every opportunity he could to get a rise out of Robirchenko. At one point he even went so far as to cast aspersions on the Spetsnaz's reputation, claiming – not without some truth – that the Spetsnaz were feared more for their brutal, ruthless treatment of civilians and captives than for their military prowess. He was expecting Robirchenko to respond in kind, but instead Robirchenko merely treated his carping with a humorous disdain, knowing that this would annoy the Australian. Each man was scoring points off the other in his own way, and in the process the foundation was being laid for a mutual respect. Templeton had predicted that when the time came, the two men would knuckle down and work well together. MacGowan was inclined to agree.

Uphadhyay's services MacGowan was gladder than usual to have enlisted. Not only did he trust the man with his life, but the Tibetan's natural, unforced cheerfulness was a welcome antidote to the bickering of Craddock and Robirchenko.

As for Griffith, he was a thoroughly reliable sort. Slightly dull, too, to be honest, but every team had to have its bedrock member, its earth wire. MacGowan had no illusions about the fact that he in all probability fulfilled the same role with the Guardians. After all, with the Guardians you had Rattray, who was smart but too lofty and cerebral for his own good; you had Lucretia, who was level-headed enough but, of course, was an artist, and therefore by definition a bit up her own arse; and then you had Piers, who could not be nuttier if he were encased in a brown wrapper and called a Snickers bar. That lot needed someone who was more in touch with reality than they were, in order to bring them back down whenever they started to float off. Rattray might run the show, but MacGowan was the one who underpinned things.

Looking at the four-man team assembled now in the restaurant, MacGowan knew that Templeton had selected well. The dynamics were right.

And he was reminded – how could he not have been? –

of the four men he had led into the Iraqi wilderness eight years earlier. He knew that what had happened to *them* had been none of his fault. He and they had just been stooges, unwitting pawns in one of the army's more sinister games, and had he not drawn the short straw in the lottery to decide who would head up the squad, *he* could have been one of the four who were transformed into slavering, slaughtering monsters, and Gleason or Hensher or Palmer or Jones could have been sitting here in his place. It was just luck that he had survived and they had not. In no way could he be held responsible for their deaths. Yet the unwarranted guilt was hard to shake, and his recurring nightmare – which still afflicted him, though less frequently these days – was always there to remind him of it, in case he should forget.

And so, as he habitually did before an action-to-suppress, MacGowan offered up a prayer. As a lapsed Catholic he did not believe in the God of the Bible, but he did believe in a power or animating principle that ran the universe, and he prayed to it now – briefly, in no more time than it took to think the words – that he and the men under his command today would return from the impending mission alive and unscathed.

When the meal was done, MacGowan picked up the tab, paying with cash and adding a tip for the waitress that was generous but not so generous as to attract attention. Then it was back to the hotel and up to their rooms, to sit and wait and, if possible, grab a couple of hours' sleep.

The twilight darkened to night. Carvingdean quietly shut up shop and settled down to sleep. Midnight came, and the streets were empty as MacGowan and the four mercenaries left the hotel, lugging the two backpacks. Crammed into the Saab, they headed along the coast to Seal Point.

17

In the dead grey light of a dead grey dawn, Rattray and Kim waited.

The two Guardians were in the contemplative garden of a Shinto shrine on the outskirts of Kyoto, part-way up a hillside overlooking the ancient city. In front of them lay an area of grey gravel, raked into comb-patterns that swirled around artfully positioned rocks. Some of the rocks were stolid boulders, others were tall upstanding stones, and all of them were coal-black and gleamed with the dampness of the newborn day. Beyond the gravel area there was an expanse of lawn, clipped to precision, and a short way down the hillside there was a pond spanned by a semicircular wooden footbridge, whose reflection in the water's glass-smooth surface completed its O. Birds occasionally stirred the silence with a sleepy twitter or chirp, but otherwise everything was motionless and subdued. There was stillness here but – at least as far as Kim was concerned – precious little tranquillity.

With her arms folded across her chest and the fur-trimmed hood of her anorak pulled up over her head, Kim sat, hunched, at the foot of a flight of steps that mean-dered up the hillside and disappeared into misty groves of trees – umbrella pines, larches with Hokusai-wave fronds, Japanese maples whose sawtooth leaves were a gorgeous autumn red. Rattray was standing nearby on a pathway next to the gravel area, as static as one of the stones. Every so often Kim would shiver or give some small indication of agitation – a glance at her watch, a twitch of her head in the direction of a sound. Rattray, whatever his inner state, was outwardly placid, and the cold did not trouble him.

Kim knew she ought to be feeling relieved and expectant. She was about to meet Emperor Dragon F2F at last, and, if the meeting went according to plan, its outcome would mean an end to the strain of the past few months. She ought to have been looking forward to this rendezvous, but in the event her sense of anticipation was muted. Mostly she felt nervous, and woozily tired.

She had slept badly. Her mattress at the *ryokan* where she and Rattray had spent the night had been uncomfortable, but what had really made slumber difficult had been the knowledge that in a few short hours she would have to be up again and off to confront her online foe in person. She had wanted to be clear-headed and alert when she met Emperor Dragon, at the peak of her mental faculties so that he could see for himself that she was, and had always been, his superior. However, as she had tossed and turned on the lumpy, unfamiliar mattress, she had begun fretting that she was not going to be sufficiently rested by morning, and the fretting had kept her awake, and the longer she had remained awake the more fretful she had become – a negative feedback loop. In the end, she had managed no more than a couple of hours of fitful dozing before Rattray had roused her at five o'clock with a discreet tap on the door to tell her that their taxi was waiting outside.

And now (another glance at her watch) Emperor Dragon was late, and it occurred to Kim that perhaps he was not going to come after all. Perhaps this was just yet another humiliation, so that now he would be able to boast to everyone how Kawai Kim had sought him out in Real Life, with some sort of *gaijin* minder in tow, and he had arranged an assignation with her and then failed to keep it. He had stood her up, as though she were a jilted girlfriend.

No, she told herself, he would be coming.

Finally, in the hope of relieving her agitation, Kim got up and went to the edge of the area of grey gravel. Those seeking enlightenment and spiritual refreshment were supposed to find the contours of the raked parallel lines and the placement of the stones soothing and inspiring. Kim, not in a meditative mood just then, used the toe of her boot to etch a few small patterns of her own in the gravel – some bird-shapes and a stick-figure. As symbolic gestures went (disrupting centuries of well-tended tradition) it was not an especially brave or indelible act, but it gave her a quick, cheap thrill.

'Kim.' Rattray's voice, a hissed whisper.

Kim looked up.

There were figures coming downhill towards them, through the misty shadows beneath the trees. She counted four people, and a little further behind a fifth, descending the steps. All of a sudden she was no longer tired. She moved closer to Rattray.

The first four emerged into the contemplative garden. *Bosozoku*. These ones were not wearing motorcycling gear. Instead, they were decked out in the *bosozoku*'s other favourite mode of attire: leather jackets, plain white T-shirts, Levis with the cuffs turned up, Timberlands, James Dean haircuts – a kind of fantasy-parody of American cool. One was wearing peardrop mirror-shades. Another was twirling a toothpick in the corner of his mouth. Among them, Kim did not see the broken-nosed one who had presented her and Rattray with the envelope yesterday.

The *bosozoku* strode towards the two Guardians, their fists bulking out the pockets of their leather jackets. Positioning themselves to either side of Kim and Rattray with their legs apart and their hands still in their pockets, like some sort of macho honour guard, they waited while the fifth member of their party reached the foot of the steps and crossed over towards them.

He was older than the others – in his late twenties, like Kim – and he was dressed smartly and fashionably, with a shirt done up to the collar but no tie, a pair of black slacks, a pair of wingtip shoes and a brocade waistcoat on whose front panels two jade-green silk dragons writhed. He walked with a very slight limp, favouring his left leg, which made him seem both frail and affected. His hair was slicked down and gathered at the back in a ponytail, and his irises were an impossibly lustrous and sparkling blue. (Tinted contacts, thought Kim. Had to be.) He looked like a rock star, an impression reinforced by the refined, pretty-boy grace of his face, with its high cheekbones and full, somewhat sneering lips, and by the manner in which he held himself, as though accustomed to nothing but subservience and adulation. In fact, Kim could only assume that he *was* someone famous, or rather had been, because his features were faintly familiar. Teenybop idols came and went at a meteoric rate, and their faces and records were barely distinguishable from one another, so it was perfectly possible that she had glimpsed this person on MTV once, a few years ago perhaps, at some point during his brief, mayfly period of stardom. Somehow, though, she sensed that she knew him from elsewhere. And for some reason – and not just because he was Emperor Dragon – she associated his features with cruelty.

'Ah, the great Kawai Kim,' Emperor Dragon said, bowing so low that the gesture could only be construed as sarcastic. 'And her friend Mr Rattray. An honour to make your acquaintance, sir.' Another deeply sarcastic and sarcastically deep bow. 'Thank you both for coming. I apologise for the earliness of the hour, but at this time of day we should be guaranteed privacy.'

'We would be guaranteed greater privacy,' Rattray said, 'if your associates were to leave.'

'Not possible.' Emperor Dragon pressed his palms together as though begging indulgence. 'You see, I am no fool, Mr Rattray, and I am no fighter. I know that you could overpower me and kill me easily if I were alone. These associates of mine, as you call them, afford me some protection from that. Besides, we may converse freely in front of them. Their grasp of English extends not much further than "Fuck you, asshole" and "Yippee-ki-yay, motherfucker", and being people of culture, we should be able to avoid those phrases.'

Rattray nodded to indicate that he found the presence of the *bosozoku*, if not acceptable, at least tolerable. 'I must then ask if I can call you by some other name than Emperor Dragon.'

Emperor Dragon smiled. 'I would have thought Miss Harada would have been able to tell you my real name.'

Miss Harada? thought Kim, with a jolt of surprise. It was not possible. Hardly anyone knew her family name.

'You don't recognise me, Kimiko-san?'

Kim shook her head warily. 'I feel I ought to, but . . .'

'It's no matter. It may come to you, it may not. It's not important, anyway. Mr Rattray, I take it that you have deduced by now, using that Sherlock Holmesian brain of yours, that it is you all along that I have been interested in. Squashing the great Kawai Kim like a fly has of course been amusing, but it has only been incidental to my aims, a means to an end. And,' he added, fixing his piercing blue gaze on Kim, 'if I may say so, you weren't half the opponent I was expecting you to be, Kimiko-sam. I thought you might present me with something of a challenge, but, oh, no. Not a bit of it. A terrible thing, don't you agree? To lose one's touch so completely.'

Kim smarted and bristled, and a dozen sharp retorts formed in her mind, but in vain. Emperor Dragon had turned his attention away from her, back to Rattray again. 'You have come all this way in a quest for answers, Mr Rattray, forsaking your duties on the slim chance that I might know something about a certain person from your past. The clue was tenuous, wasn't it? Yet you came anyway.'

'It seemed an avenue of investigation worth pursuing.'

Kim noticed that Rattray's lips were compressed tightly together. It was the first time she had seen an expression on his face that had its origins in the realm of the less superficial emotions, ones that ran deeper than mere amusement or resolve.

'Still the police inspector after all these years,' Emperor Dragon jeered. 'No stone unturned, no lead unchased.'

'As it happens, I'm rapidly forming the opinion that you know nothing of any interest at all,' Rattray said evenly. 'Your employers gave you a single item of information, enough to pique my curiosity, nothing more. Anarch stooges are never shown anything other than a tiny corner of the picture, just one piece of the jigsaw puzzle.'

'But I am not merely an Anarch stooge,' Emperor Dragon replied. 'I'm more. So much more.'

'John, this is bullshit,' said Kim. 'We're wasting our time here.'

'Please, Kim,' said Rattray, raising a finger to her. He moved a couple of paces towards Emperor Dragon, and the moment he did so, the four *bosozoku* slid their hands from their jacket pockets, producing weapons: a switch-blade, a motorcycle chain, a set of brass knuckledusters, a small-calibre automatic.

Rattray halted.

'Purely a precaution, Mr Rattray,' Emperor Dragon said, still loftily unperturbed.

'I see nothing that can harm me,' Rattray replied, eyeing the varied array of armaments.

'Maybe not you,' said Emperor Dragon. 'But what about Kim?'

Rattray did not reply, but the flinty glitter in his eyes spoke volumes.

'The question now is, are you going to try to kill me, and in the process risk the life of this young lady here? I doubt it. Pig-ugly Ainu bitch she may be, but you evidently have a soft spot for her.'

Kim bristled again. Bad enough that she had become Rattray's Achilles' heel in this situation, but now Emperor Dragon was *insulting* her? Her hands balled into fists and she made to move forwards, but the *bosozoku* with the switchblade caught sight of her and waved the knife at her in an admonishing manner. Fuming, Kim stayed put.

'I'm unwilling to endanger a colleague,' Rattray said,

laying a gentle but unmistakable stress on the last word. 'However, I'm presuming there's an alternative.'

'How astute of you.' Emperor Dragon reached inside his waistcoat and took out a slim, matt-black box like a spectacles case. He popped the lid. Inside, embedded in pre-formed foam padding, was a small black pistol with a slender, skeletal grip and no trigger guard. The pistol looked as though it was designed to fire something other than bullets.

'You are aware of its provenance, of course,' Emperor Dragon said as he showed the pistol to Rattray. Kim discerned bright blue detailing along its long, narrow barrel.

'I'm supposed to be impressed?' Rattray said.

'No, but knowing where this comes from should at least convince you to take me seriously.'

'Why? Because that device you're holding is capable of killing me? I doubt it is, otherwise you'd have produced it much sooner.'

'Quite correct, Mr Rattray! Really, you do live up to your reputation.' Emperor Dragon aimed a quick glance at Kim. 'Unlike some I could mention.'

'I'm getting tired of this,' Rattray said. 'It's my belief that this entire meeting was called purely as a demonstration of egomania on your part, Emperor Dragon, and as far as I'm concerned there's little to be gained by prolonging it any further. Kim and I are going to leave now. Any attempt to hinder us will be met with extreme resistance.'

'That,' said Emperor Dragon, shaking his head regretfully, 'is a shame. I was hoping we would be able to handle this in a civilised manner. However, since it seems we can't . . .'

He gave a signal to the *bosozoku*.

But Rattray was already moving. Fast.

Kim had seen nothing quite like it before. One moment, Rattray was standing still. The next, he was hurtling towards the *bosozoku* with the automatic. The transition from immobility to inhuman speed was near-instantaneous. It was as though a sudden, intensely localised hurricane had swept Rattray off his feet and was carrying him straight towards the young tough. The *bosozoku* scarcely had time to register an astonished grimace before Rattray was upon him. There was a crunch that sounded to Kim, incongruously, like the noise of someone biting down loudly on a boiled sweet, and then the automatic fell to the ground with a dull clatter. The *bosozoku* did not realise at first what had happened. The penny only dropped when he looked down at his arm and saw that his wrist had been shattered and that his hand was hanging inertly from the broken joint like a bunch of bananas. He raised the hand and stared it for a couple of seconds. Then pain and nausea hit him simultaneously, and he sank to his knees with a groan and vomited copiously on the ground.

Rattray snatched up the pistol and hurled it away. Propelled by his smooth overarm lob, it sailed through the air in a twirling parabola and descended gracefully and accurately towards the pond, landing slap-bang in the middle, shattering the reflecting calm of the water's surface into bullseye ripples.

Rattray, however, had not paused to see where the gun went. No sooner had he thrown it than he was heading for the *bosozoku* with the motorcycle chain. Emperor Dragon, meanwhile, was barking out an order in Japanese which Kim, too absorbed in watching Rattray, did not hear.

The motorcycle chain came up and was whirled in the air, once, twice . . . but before its wielder had a chance to use it properly, Rattray crashed into him, propelling him on to the gravel area. The *bosozoku* lost his footing in the soft gravel and tumbled on to his back. One end of the chain was wrapped several times around his fist, however, so he did not lose his grip on it, and as Rattray straddled him, the *bosozoku* whipped the chain at Rattray's face. The chain struck Rattray's cheek and temple, snapping his head sideways. A bloody weal appeared.

With some difficulty, since he was lying supine, the *bosozoku* drew back his arm in order to lash Rattray again, but as the chain swung towards him, Rattray deflected it with his left hand. At the same time, with his right hand, he dealt the young man a tremendous chopping blow to the throat.

The *bosozoku* lurched and spasmed, heaving for air, but his windpipe had been crushed and each attempted inhalation was a ghastly glottal non-event, a hopeless, abortive hiccup. His face rapidly purpled and his heels scrabbled desperate gouges in the gravel.

As Rattray clambered off the asphyxiating thug, another of the *bosozoku*, the one with the knuckledusters, came darting across the gravel towards him. Kim tried to yell out a warning, but the *bosozoku* reached Rattray before she could find her voice. Rattray was in a half-crouch, off balance. The young man caught him with a mighty roundhouse kick, sending him flailing over. Rattray was on his feet again almost immediately, but the *bosozoku* laid into him before he could recover his balance fully.

His arms working like pistons, the *bosozoku* pounded brass-knuckled blow after brass-knuckled blow into Rattray's torso. He was quite clearly a trained martial artist. His fists found their mark with power, precision and economy, and each punch shoved Rattray backwards and elicited an involuntary huff of air from his lungs.

The young man drove Rattray against one of the standing rocks and kept him there, still punching, not allowing him a moment's respite. The repeated smack of knuckleduster against flesh was appalling to Kim's ears, all-too-bathetically reminiscent of the sound of a slab of beef being tenderised. And Rattray appeared to be succumbing to the onslaught. He was doubled over, taking the blows, but not fighting back. The *bosozoku* was winning!

The instant she perceived that Rattray was in trouble, Kim ran to his aid. Heart thumping, she sprinted out on to the gravel area, intending to leap on to the *bosozoku*'s back and tear at his hair and claw his eyes until he left Rattray alone. A small voice at the back of her mind was telling her that doing this would almost certainly mean *she* would get beaten up, too, but she did not listen to it. There was no way she could just stand by and watch her friend be pummelled mercilessly into oblivion.

She managed to cover no more than a few yards, however, before she was tackled and brought down face-first on to the gravel by the fourth *bosozoku*, the one with the switchblade. She grunted in pain as the gravel tore at her palms and chin, and then shrieked with frustration and rage as the young man dragged her back to her feet. She struggled against him, but he was far stronger than her, and once he had an arm clamped about her neck and the point of the switchblade pressed into her neck, she knew that it was futile to continue to resist.

'That's it, bitch, keep cool,' he muttered into her ear in their native tongue. 'Nothing you can do but let your English boyfriend get what he deserves.'

Moments later, the *bosozoku* with the knuckledusters broke off from hitting Rattray and stepped back. His face shone with sweat and he was breathing hard, although he was not out of breath. He peered contemptuously at Rattray, who was still leaning against the rock, bent over.

'Had enough, asshole?' he growled in gutturally mangled English. 'You no' so tough. I kick seven shade shit outta you, huh?'

By way of a reply, Rattray lifted his head and smiled mirthlessly at the young man. The weal on the side of his face was gone, immaculately healed. Slowly he raised himself to his full height. He did not appear to be in any discomfort at all. It was as if not one of the *bosozoku*'s punches had connected.

He charged at his opponent. The *bosozoku* recovered from his astonishment in time to adopt a defensive stance, one fist by his side, the other level with his stomach, dropping his weight on to his back foot . . . but that was all. Rattray's first punch – a jab to the nose – shattered the bridge of his mirror-shades and also his nasal cartilage. As the two halves of the mirror-shades fell to the gravel with a tinkle of broken glass, blood spurted from the young man's nostrils. Rattray hit him again, a piledriver blow to the sternum that lifted the *bosozoku* off his feet, cracking several of his ribs. The thug staggered backwards, teetered and dropped to the ground on his backside, legs splaying, with an expression of absurd incomprehension on his face. Rattray wasted no time in kicking him in the mouth, where the blood from his nose was streaming down to form a crimson goatee. Teeth splintered, and the young man reeled over and fell to the gravel, clutching his mouth and groaning.

Rattray spun around, searching for the fourth *bosozoku*. When he saw that Kim was being held at knifepoint, a brief flash of annoyance passed across his face, quickly replaced by a resigned, sagging acceptance that the fight was over. Had Kim not been scared to speak with the switchblade at her throat, she would have told him that she would not have allowed herself to be captured in this way if she had not been so intent on rushing to help him. She tried to convey this to him with a plaintive, apologetic look.

Emperor Dragon appeared beside her, as smug as a well-fed cat.

'Problems, problems, Mr Rattray,' he said. 'What to do now? Your hairy-faced little girlfriend has gone and got herself caught, and however fast you move, Kenji will be faster with his blade. A chink in your armour, it seems. Or perhaps that should be a *Jap* in your armour.' He chortled, mightily pleased at his own joke.

'Kill her, and I'll still kill you,' said Rattray.

'Yes, very likely. But you're not going to risk her life, are you?'

Kim almost grunted in her frustration. This was so old fashioned, so gallingly macho-movie – the female sidekick letting the hero down. She squirmed in the *bosozoku*'s grasp, but stopped when she felt a sharp sting at her neck, followed by a sensation of wet warmth as blood oozed from a shallow cut and dribbled down to her collarbone.

'Keep still, Kim,' Rattray said. 'It's all right. They're not going to hurt you. They wouldn't dare.'

'So,' said Emperor Dragon, reopening the matt-black case and taking out the paraterrestrial pistol. 'It appears that I truly have the advantage now.'

'Indeed,' said Rattray, hoarse-voiced with self-restraint. 'The question is, what do you intend to do with it?'

'That's for me to know and you to find out.'

'Promise me one thing, Emperor Dragon. Whatever happens to me, Kim remains unharmed.'

'You have my word on it.' Spoken with such haughty imperiousness by Emperor Dragon that it was hard not to believe him sincere. He was too arrogant not to keep a vow.

'Very well,' said Rattray. 'What do you want me to do?'

'Just hold still.'

Emperor Dragon raised the paraterrestrial pistol and levelled it at Rattray. He took time making certain of his aim, inclining his head to one side and squinching one eye shut, but it was obvious to everyone concerned that this was a sham, and that what he was really doing was savouring the moment, relishing the taste of victory.

Rattray refused to give him the satisfaction of looking worried. Instead, he simply stared at him, his eyes glittering darkly, filled with the implication of acts of violence.

Finally Emperor Dragon deigned to squeeze the trigger.

There was a sharp hiss, and something zipped through the air and hit Rattray's cheek. Rattray reached up, plucked the object from his skin, and looked at it. What he was holding between his thumb and forefinger was the remains of a transparent gel capsule the size of a cod's roe, which had burst open on impact with his cheek to disgorge its contents, a droplet of clear fluid. He peered at the capsule, as though unable to fathom what harm something so tiny could do to him. It was already beginning to dissolve in his fingers, as it was designed to. Then, abruptly, he staggered forwards, swayed, collapsed to his knees and keeled over flat on his face on the ground.

Emperor Dragon sniggered at the ignominy of Rattray's fall. Kim gasped at the impossibility of it.

'Oh, he's not dead,' Emperor Dragon reassured her, amused by the horror in her expression. 'That toxin would kill an elephant, but him it will merely incapacitate for a few hours. This way, he'll be easier to transport.'

'Transport?' said Kim. 'Where are you taking him?'

'You'll find out. You're coming, too.'

Before Kim could say anything else, Emperor Dragon put the index and little fingers of his right hand between his lips and blew a shrill, piercing whistle. Instantly, half a dozen more *bosozoku* emerged from hiding places behind shrubberies and tree trunks. The two *bosozoku* whom Rattray had injured were helped to their feet and borne away limping and moaning. The third, the one with the crushed windpipe, who by now had ceased breathing, was hoisted up by his arms and legs and carried unceremoniously off. Rattray's insensible body was removed from the scene in much the same manner, and, at a signal from Emperor Dragon, Kim, still at knifepoint, was marched downhill after her fellow Guardian to a waiting van.

An hour later, just as the sun was rising, a groundskeeper entered the contemplative garden and was shocked by the state in which he found it: the gravel all churned up, here and there a sprinkling of what looked to be blood, and a spattered puddle of vomit on the grass nearby. He could scarcely conceive what had gone on here, but he suspected that the culprits were either drugged-up teenage tearaways or – an interpretation of the evidence too sinister for comfort – yakuza hitmen. Either way, the disrespect for the sanctity of the garden appalled the groundskeeper, and within minutes he was washing away the vomit with a hose and smoothing out the gravel with a rake, diligently undoing the damage.

Another hour later, just as the first visitors began arriving at the shrine, he was finished. Order had been restored to the contemplative garden, and it was as though whatever had happened there had never occurred.

18

Clad head to toe in black, with only their faces exposed, the five men stole down the shallowly sloping hillside that led from the coastal road to the beach, half a mile to the west of Seal Point. Reaching the beach, they turned left and moved, spaced out at even intervals, along the grassy, hummocky ground that ran above the line where the shingle petered out. Uphadhyay was on point. The lithe Tibetan darted surefootedly along over the uneven terrain, followed by MacGowan, then Griffith, then Robirchenko. Craddock took up the rear.

Each of the team was carrying his personal choice of sidearm, holstered at his waist. Craddock and Robirchenko were also armed with Heckler and Koch MP5K compact submachine guns, which hung at their sides from webbing straps. Uphadhyay was carrying his kukri tucked into his belt.

The one-piece, paraterrestrial-grade NBC suits all five were wearing were made of a lightweight, non-reflective fabric that flowed like silk. The sleeves tapered to thin, flexible gloves, and the legs ended in socks that were thin enough to sit comfortably inside boots. For extra protection, each man had cinched the legs of the suits tightly at their ankles with puttees.

Ahead, the power station loomed, its twin buildings rising dark and blank against the moonlit sky. Soon the team arrived at the perimeter fence, a twelve-foot barrier of chainlink topped with out-curving spikes and loops of barbed wire. They crouched down. The night wind scoured onshore across the promontory, making the scrubby littoral weeds, gorse and heather rustle and shiver and hiss. A rind of grey surf seethed at the edge of the tar-black sea.

Uphadhyay turned, offering his back to MacGowan. The one-time member of the Gurkha Regiment was toting a knapsack, a semi-rigid blister fashioned from some kind of rubbery black material, fastened to his torso by a tight-fitting harness. (Griffith was wearing one identical, his containing non-paraterrestrial explosives and detonators in separate compartments.) Peeling open the knapsack's flap, MacGowan took out an object shaped not unlike a quarter-pint hip-flask. It was black with blue markings along its sides – sinuous, curlicued hieroglyphs that could have been purely ornamental but could, equally, have been brand names or insignia written in some indecipherable ancient language.

MacGowan touched the conical nozzle of the 'hip-flask' to the base of the fence, an inch above the ground, then depressed a thumb-lever on top of the device. A silent blue spark ignited at the tip of the nozzle. With a single swift rotation of his arm he described a circle on the fence with the device. Along the circumference of the circle, which was roughly a metre in diameter, the chainlink wires parted with a staccato ripple of tiny metallic plinks and twangs as the device passed over them.

MacGowan returned the paraterrestrial wire-cutter to Uphadhyay's knapsack, then grabbed the cut-out section of chainlink and bent it forwards until it was flat on the ground. He crawled through the hole, and the other four followed.

Having penetrated the perimeter fence, MacGowan gestured to his team to follow him, and together they set off across the three hundred yards or so of open ground to the nearer reactor building, the one which he had seen the man in the Peugeot emerge from and return to yesterday. They trod as stealthily as they could, the wind carrying away most of the sound of their footfalls and the soft creak and clatter of their equipment.

At the corner of the building, the five men halted again and hunkered down. From Uphadhyay's knapsack Mac-Gowan withdrew five faceplates. Each was a contoured, matt-black, mask-like shell, with a pair of convex oval lenses for the eyes and a smooth-cornered trapezoid protuberance to accommodate the mouth and nose. (When MacGowan had first shown one to his team back at the hotel, Craddock had, predictably, likened it to Darth Vader's mask, and had held it up in front of Robirchenko's face and asked him to wheeze.) Elegant bright-blue designs, similar to the hieroglyphs on the wire-cutter, were engraved on the faceplates' cheeks and around the lenses. From a few yards away, these markings resembled Maori facial tattoos.

MacGowan distributed the faceplates and each team-member put his on. The rim of each faceplate was just large enough to overlap the edge of the hood aperture of the paraterrestrial-grade NBC suit and was lined with a smooth, pliant cushioning material akin to neoprene, which, when the faceplate was held in place, bonded automatically with the fabric of the hood to form an airtight seal. This seal could be broken only by simultaneously depressing a pair of recessed buttons on either side of the faceplate. Although there was apparently no respiratory opening, breathing was not hindered by the faceplate, and MacGowan had assured his team that the faceplates worked far more effectively than army-issue HEPA filters. The air they inhaled would be perfectly pure. Nothing toxic, not a radioactive particle, not a bacillus, could penetrate either the faceplate or the suit.

The five men were already wearing communications sets beneath their hoods, throat-mics and ear-plug receivers linked to belt-mounted shortwave units. As soon as each man's faceplate was securely in place, MacGowan ordered an audio check. His team sounded off in turn with their callsigns, subvocalising so that their utterances were inaudible except through the comms system.

'Baby,' said Uphadhyay.

'Posh,' said Robirchenko.

'Sporty,' said Griffith.

'Scary,' said Craddock.

'Night-vision OK?'

He received four affirmatives.

'Clear as day, Manager,' said Craddock.

'*Bozhe moi*,' said Robirchenko softly, impressed.

Standard paraterrestrial-grade night-goggles gave you a green-hued view of the world, and were, as far as any Guardian could tell, based on the principle of thermal imaging, although with a superior quality of definition to that offered by any terrestrial system, cooled or uncooled, up to and including the Thermal Observation Gunnery Sight fitted to Challenger tanks, which is generally considered to be the acme of modern image-intensification technology. The NBC-suit faceplates, on the other hand, employed an advanced form of available-light enhancement, again with a superior quality of definition to that offered by any technology presently known to mankind. However, for reasons no Guardian had yet been able to determine, the faceplates transformed the nocturnal landscape into a monochrome study in shadows and shades of *blue*, rather than the green of the thermal-imaging goggles.

MacGowan peered around, letting his eyes gradually adjust to their new, blue, brighter reality. The concrete side of the reactor building appeared to him as a field of rough-textured lapis lazuli. Each member of his team was a black silhouette limned with cobalt highlights. The distant sea-surf glimmered cerulean. The moon, as in the song, was blue.

'Right,' he said, when he reckoned that the other four had also had sufficient time for their eyes to adjust. 'Let's hit it.'

The team set off around the corner of the building and moved in single file, at a half-crouch, towards the entrance to the loading bay. With their faceplates in place, the five of them looked eerily insectile and, though of varying height and build, strangely, sinisterly identical.

As they reached the entrance, MacGowan instructed Craddock and Robirchenko to keep watch. The Australian and the Russian immediately moved into position, one to the right of the entrance, the other to the left, each holding his MP5K at shoulder-height, covering a ninety-degree arc of approach.

MacGowan went up to the loading-bay door. There was a person-sized door inset into the larger door. Gently he tried the handle. Locked.

He summoned Uphadhyay over, delved in the Tibetan's knapsack, and took out a black metal rod about eight inches in length and two inches in diameter, with a hollowed, slightly flared tip. He placed the flared tip over the plate of the door's lock and squeezed a blue trigger that was fitted flush into the rod's underside. There was an abrupt, muffled *whump* from the rod, followed by the tinkling clatter of something metallic falling to the floor on the other side of the door.

MacGowan removed the rod, revealing a round hole where the lock's central cylindrical plug had been. The plug had been neatly punched out. MacGowan returned the rod to Uphadhyay's knapsack and tried the door handle again. The door swung unresistingly inwards.

MacGowan eased his Browning 9mm from its holster and stepped through.

The loading bay was thirty yards long on each side and fifteen high. Other than the two Peugeots and the Transit van it was empty. Not a scrap of the original winching and loading equipment had been left behind. Walls, floor and ceiling were bare concrete, and there was a raised concrete platform at the far end, accessible by a short flight of steps. The platform led to a pair of large, hydraulically sprung double doors. Next to the doors sat a petrol-driven generator, which was not in operation.

MacGowan padded past the vehicles towards the platform, skirting a puddle of greasy water and scanning all around him as he went, on the alert for the slightest movement. Uphadhyay, Griffith and Robirchenko followed in triangular formation. Craddock remained beside the open entrance door, covering the rear, until all four of the others had reached the platform. Then he eased the door shut and crossed the loading bay to join them.

Uphadhyay leapt nimbly up on to the platform and approached the generator. He indicated to MacGowan the thick, rubber-insulated flex that led from the generator and ran beneath the double doors.

MacGowan nodded. 'Handy. All we have to do is follow that, and it'll take us where we want to go.' He turned to the three men behind him. 'Posh,' he said. 'You're in front now.'

Robirchenko used the stubby barrel of his MP5K to nudge one of the double doors open a crack. He peered through.

'Corridor,' he said. 'Twenty, twenty-five metres long. Empty.'

'OK.'

The team set off along the corridor, moving with a fluent, synchronised ease. The corridor terminated at the junction between two flights of stairs, one ascending, the other descending. The generator flex led down the descending staircase. The five men followed it down, Robirchenko still in the vanguard.

At the foot of the staircase they emerged into the vast chamber that had once contained the power station's turbogenerator set, but was now a vault of drip-echoing emptiness. The floor was covered with an inch-deep layer of water, and more water was trickling down the walls and spattering down from the roof in chains of droplets that glittered like sapphire necklaces in the faceplates' blue-tinged world. In the decade and a half since Seal Point's decommissioning, rain and sea had been hard at work penetrating the power station's structure. There was a certain irony to this, not to mention a certain natural justice. Once, when it had been Brightsea, the power station had utilised sea water as a coolant, pumping in and expelling thousands of gallons of the stuff daily. Now that the power station was Seal Point, a hulking husk of its former self, the sea was still coming in, but unbidden, incrementally, tide by tide. The briny marine air had eaten away at the power station's concrete shell, allowing in the rain. A slow, seeping process of salty decay was under way. A revenge, some might say.

The generator cable had been strung across a series of tripod-based poles in order to keep it out of the water on the floor. It reached all the way to the other side of the chamber, where, just visible to the faceplates' light-enhancing lenses, lay the entrance to a broad, low, rectangular tunnel.

'Scary, left. Posh, right,' MacGowan ordered.

Craddock and Robirchenko obediently took up position at either wing of the squad, their splashing footfalls merging with the general background cacophony of aqueous sounds.

'Baby, Sporty, stick with me.'

They were halfway to the tunnel entrance when Craddock whispered urgently, 'Hold it!'

Everyone halted.

'What is it?' said MacGowan.

'I dunno, Manager. Thought I saw movement over in the corner, ten o'clock.'

'Go and check.'

'Could have been a rat, maybe. It was kind of at the edge of my vision. Like a blur.'

'Go and check anyway.'

The other four men remained perfectly still while Craddock made his way cautiously over to the corner of the chamber. They watched his black silhouette in the dark-blue twilight as he inspected the spot where he believed he had glimpsed something. Eventually, he turned and lifted his arms in a shrug. 'Nothing. Like I said, could have been a rat. Probably long gone.'

'OK. Proceed.'

Into the tunnel they went, into a pitch-darkness that taxed even the faceplates' night-vision capability. The five men were still able to see where they were going, but the grain of resolution had become coarser and shapes were less well defined, as in a blurred old photograph. The interference patterns in the water around their feet registered like television static.

'Can't be much further now,' MacGowan said, keeping track of the flex, which was pinned along the side of the tunnel.

The tunnel gave on to a chamber even vaster than the previous one, its ceiling and far wall invisibly distant in the dark. Here the reactor itself had once been housed, although there was no trace of it now. It, and the pipes that had fed it, and the gantries from which it had been monitored, were all gone. The chamber was a concrete womb, empty after a monstrous stillbirth.

MacGowan traced the path of the generator flex. It ran along the wall for a dozen yards, then led into a doorway, which was deep-recessed and two steps up from floor-level.

'Bingo,' said MacGowan. 'All right, everybody, listen up. Scary, you stay put by the tunnel. Posh and Sporty, you'll wait by the door after me and Baby have gone in. When Baby and I are done in there, Sporty, I'll give you the all-clear to come in and lay charges.'

'Grand,' said Griffith.

The door, which had been left fractionally ajar in order to admit the flex, was thick and heavy, constructed of lead-lined steel. MacGowan, with Uphadhyay at his side, grasped its handle-lever.

'They're civilians,' he reminded Uphadhyay, 'so I'm not anticipating much resistance.' He added grimly, 'Zero leniency, all the same.'

Uphadhyay hesitated. He had few qualms about killing an armed opponent, but noncombatants were a different matter. Still, he was a professional, and professionals did whatever their paymaster ordered. He unsheathed his kukri. 'Understood.'

Gently MacGowan nudged the door inwards. Up-hadhyay entered the room beyond, kukri poised. MacGowan was right behind him. Browning levelled, he scanned the interior of the room in a series of quick sweeps.

It was a bunker of some kind, perhaps formerly a storage area or a changing room for personnel. Whatever MacGowan had been expecting to find in here – a bioreactor and other laboratory equipment, or maybe a dormitory of scientists bundled up in sleeping bags – he had not been expecting to find the room empty.

Uphadhyay halted in the middle of the floor and crouched down. He picked up the generator flex and held it up for MacGowan to see.

The flex terminated in a splay of its component wires, connected to nothing.

'But that's their only power source,' MacGowan said. 'And they can't have pulled out, because their transportation's still here. So why would they . . . ?'

Realisation dawned. MacGowan felt something cold and heavy sink inside him.

'Oh, Christ,' he breathed.

He was about to tell his team to go on the defensive, get ready for a quick-smart withdrawal, they had been suckered into a trap . . . but before he could get the words out there was a loud, echoing gunshot from the reactor chamber, and he heard Craddock shout, 'What the fuck—!?' The exclamation was not subvocalised, and was mask-muffled but still startlingly loud.

MacGowan wheeled about. 'Bob. Sit-rep! Who fired?'

Griffith: 'It was Craddock, I think.'

Craddock: 'Wasn't me, you dil! Somebody's—'

Another two gunshots, swiftly followed by a stuttering burp of return fire from a submachine gun and Craddock yelling, 'Fucker! Fucker!'

MacGowan made for the door. 'Vasily! Back up Karl!' Like the rest of the team, MacGowan was not consciously aware of having abandoned the use of their callsigns. Under the circumstances, pseudonyms simply did not seem important or appropriate any more.

Robirchenko: 'I am there. At the tunnel entrance. I can see nothing.'

178

Craddock: 'What do you mean, see nothing? *Someone's* in there shooting at us!'

Robirchenko: 'There is no one in the tunnel.'

Craddock: 'Like fuck there isn't! I'll show you.'

Another volley of submachine-gun fire. Another couple of return shots from within the tunnel.

MacGowan lunged through the doorway. 'Everyone! Let's not start flapping. We've been set up. The whole op is a bust. Adapt!'

He saw Craddock and Robirchenko, pressed flat with their backs to the wall on either side of the tunnel entrance. Close to, Griffith was crouching down near the bunker doorway, holding his little Glock 17.

Gunfire from two separate sources boomed and whanged from within the tunnel. AKs, it sounded like to MacGowan.

Craddock and Robirchenko swung into the tunnel entrance, opened up simultaneously with their MP5Ks, then leapt back for cover. Craddock had emptied his clip. In a series of quick, deft movements he replaced it with a fresh clip from his belt.

Griffith tapped MacGowan on the elbow and pointed straight ahead, into the depths of the reactor chamber. 'Over there,' he said. 'Think I saw someone moving.'

MacGowan followed the line of Griffith's finger but could see nothing but the water-logged floor and darkness filled with luminous blue speckles like phosphenes.

'You're sure?'

'Aye. I don't think they're just in the tunnel. I think they're in here with us as well.'

'Oh, great.' MacGowan turned. 'D.B.?'

But Uphadhyay did not need to be asked. He was already stalking across the reactor chamber, keeping low.

Three more shots resounded from the tunnel, and all of a sudden Craddock was screaming, 'Fuck! Fucking *cunt*! I'm hit!'

A spurt of submachine-gun fire. Robirchenko, crossing the tunnel entrance.

Robirchenko: 'I come!'

A frantic splashing.

Craddock, still screaming, writhing on the floor: 'Ah, fuck! Jesus fucking arse!'

Robirchenko: 'We have a man down, Bill.'

MacGowan: 'I bloody know! Where's he hit?'

Robirchenko: 'Stomach. Looks bad. He broke cover . . .'

Craddock, grinding out the words urgently through the pain: 'There's no one there, Bill! Aah! Christ alive, shit, fuck, shit, that hurts! Bill! I had to have a look. They're firing at us but they're *not fucking there*!'

'Vasily, hold your position,' MacGowan said. 'Bob, this way. Let's get under cover.' He jerked his thumb behind him, and he and Griffith retreated into the shelter of the doorway.

Robirchenko: 'They are coming up the tunnel, Bill. I think I can see . . . No, they are gone. What is happening? They are like ghosts. One moment they are there, the next – not there.'

MacGowan: 'Get a grip, Vasily. We have to think of a way to get the fuck out of here.'

Uphadhyay: 'Mr Bill?'

MacGowan: 'What is it, D.B.?'

Uphadhyay: 'Mr Bill, I am sorry. They have found me. I did not see them. I could not see them.'

MacGowan looked across to where the Tibetan was. He could just make him out, fifty metres away. He was standing upright, hands raised, kukri aloft. And around him there were vague shapes. Nebulous outlines of men moving, flickering phantom-like into and out of perception. MacGowan counted three of them. They were closing slowly in on Uphadhyay. When they reached him and halted, they disappeared.

Lightwarp generators, MacGowan thought. The fuckers are carrying lightwarp generators.

And, all at once, everything was clear to him.

Gene Genius had set this up. No doubt thanks to Anarch-influenced members within the company, Gene Genius had got wind of the fact that the Guardians were

180

going to raid Seal Point, and had moved the laboratory elsewhere, leaving a small force of mercenaries in place of the bioweapons scientists in order to ambush the Guardian squad – a small force of mercenaries equipped with the one piece of kit that could compromise the effectiveness of paraterrestrial-grade available-light enhancement technology: the lightwarp generator.

Uphadhyay's voice interrupted his thoughts: 'Mr Bill?'

'D.B., just surrender to them,' MacGowan said, his tone heavy with resignation. 'Don't try anything. We may get lucky.'

'These are men like us, Mr Bill. They do not take prisoners.'

'That's an order, D.B., all right? Give yourself up. Do not resist.'

'I regret, Mr Bill, that I must disobey. I want to say that it has been a pleasure knowing you and working with you.'

'D.B.! No!' MacGowan yelled, but at that same moment he saw Uphadhyay dip his head forwards momentarily, as though in prayer. Then, suddenly, the Tibetan sprang into life. Fast as a snake striking he brought his kukri down and around.

The knife, finding its mark, made the invisible visible again. A blue blur appeared next to Uphadhyay, a smeary azure sketch of a man tumbling backwards, one hand clutched to his throat.

Without pausing, Uphadhyay whirled around and aimed for the spot where another of the three 'ghosts' had been just before it vanished. His intended target shimmered back into view, moving to evade the attack. The kukri dealt a glancing blow somewhere around the man-shaped blur's midriff. The 'ghost' staggered sideways, uttering an oath.

From nowhere, a shot rang out. Uphadhyay was hurled backwards, landing on the floor in a graceless gangle of limbs. He tried, shudderingly, to rise. Another shot was fired, a muzzle-flash igniting in mid-air. MacGowan saw

Uphadhyay's head lose its solidity and the Tibetan's body slump limply flat.

Then Robirchenko started firing again into the tunnel. His Heckler and Koch was on tri-burst setting, and he accompanied each triplet of bullets with a grunted curse in Russian: *'Khuesosy! Yeblany! Pediki! Gavnuki!'* He was shooting blind, laying an arc of fire across the tunnel's breadth, hoping rather than aiming.

Two salvoes of return fire doubled Robirchenko over and brought him down. He toppled face-first to the floor, was racked by a single powerful convulsion and a handful of twitching aftershocks, and lay still. A set of concentric rills radiated out in the water around his body, ebbing and fading.

Near the dead Russian, Craddock continued to groan, inarticulately now, his torso twisting from side to side with agony, his legs working uselessly, heels slipping and splashing.

MacGowan heard and saw all this. He saw, too, that the phantom that had killed Uphadhyay and the one the Tibetan had wounded were making their way across the chamber towards Griffith and him. The wounded one lurched as he walked, creating more of a blue disturbance in the air than his uninjured associate.

'Bob?' MacGowan said to Griffith. 'Maybe you could put together something from your knapsack? Like a little mini-bomb?'

'Nowhere near enough time.'

'Yeah. Thought so. Just felt I should suggest it. Bob, I'm really fucking sorry.'

'Not your fault, Bill,' Griffith replied gamely. 'We were outgunned, and they've got some way of confusing our night-vision, haven't they?'

'They have.'

'We can't see them when they stand still, and barely see them when they're moving. Sneaky buggers.'

MacGowan's throat was dry. He coughed to clear it. 'Want to go out shooting?'

'Aye, well, why not? For all the chuffin' good it'll do.'

'Hey, it's the principle of the thing.'

Griffith uttered a grim laugh and ratcheted the slide of his Glock, chambering a round.

As he prepared himself for death, MacGowan felt at once hollow and warm and weirdly serene. The certainty of knowing that everything would shortly be over was, in a strange way, a comfort. It meant that nothing mattered any more, that all the failures and fuck-ups he had made in his life were inconsequential, that he could shrug off the memory of them and feel lighter for it, freer. It was not important that this mission had gone to shit. Nor was it important that he had been a bad husband to his wife and a bad son to his mother, or that he had killed numerous times both in the SAS and as a Guardian, had ended countless lives just as someone was about to end his. All of that, suddenly, was done with. Behind him. Over. He was embarking on a new phase of his existence, a final few minutes of guiltless simplicity, a last brief redeeming taste of innocence.

He had only one regret, he realised – that he had not tried to make amends with Sarah after the divorce. Maybe they could have patched things up, after he had joined the Guardians and stopped drinking heavily and got his life back on an even keel. Maybe he should have at least have gone to visit her, to talk things over, see how the land lay. He had refrained from doing so purely for her sake, feeling that he had caused her enough pain already and that it was unfair on her to risk causing her more. Perhaps if he had tried, though, things might have worked out between them. You never know.

But that was it. That was his one and only regret, as he faced imminent death.

He exchanged looks with Griffith, faceplate to faceplate, both of them signalling with a nod that they were ready to make their valiant last stand.

Then MacGowan felt something small and hard and round pressing into the back of his neck and heard a muffled voice say, 'Drop the pistol.'

MacGowan slowly swivelled his head. There was

another of those glimmering blue phantoms standing beside him. The ghost-man had stolen up on him from behind – had been lurking in the empty bunker all along, unseen – and the object pressing into the nape of his neck was the tip of a rifle-barrel. MacGowan could just distinguish the rifle, its outline vibrating into view with every slight movement made by the man holding it.

'Drop the fucking pistol,' the half-glimpsed man repeated, with a slightly pedantic edge to his voice.

A chance to live? MacGowan wondered. Or should he just go ahead with the Butch-and-Sundance routine and try to take the bloke out? A moment ago he had been entirely reconciled with the idea of dying. But, then, a moment ago there had seemed to be no choice about the matter. Maybe Uphadhyay had guessed wrong and these men *did* take prisoners. If so, then he might not have to die. When you were taken captive, after all, there was always the possibility of escape.

The tide of fatalistic calm within him receded. Mac-Gowan realised, with a certain amount of surprise, that he had more to live for than to die for.

Bending at his knees, he lowered the Browning to the floor, and when he stood up again he was no longer the pure, raw, fearless creature into which acceptance of death had temporarily transformed him; he was once more just an ordinary, troubled human being.

'You, too,' said the ghost-man to Griffith.

Griffith hesitated, then reluctantly complied and laid down his Glock.

The ghost-man who had killed Uphadhyay reached MacGowan and Griffith, along with his wounded accomplice. At the same time, another pair of ghost-men emerged from the mouth of the tunnel. One checked Robirchenko's body, nudging it with his toe. The other went over to Craddock and swiftly and summarily put the Australian out of his misery, silencing his groans with a single clean shot to the forehead.

'This is the one we want,' said Uphadhyay's killer, and

184

a disembodied arm shimmered bluely in the air, gesturing at MacGowan. 'The big fellow.'

'What about the other?' asked the one holding the rifle to MacGowan's neck.

'Nonessential.'

Instantly Griffith lunged for his Glock, but he had barely got his hands on the pistol when Uphadhyay's killer shot him in the right shoulder. The bullet entered Griffith's deltoid at point-blank range and exited at his scapula, all but severing his arm. Griffith uttered a horrifyingly inhuman screech and crashed to the ground, rolling over on to his back, his arm dangling from his body, no longer seeming a part of him, now just some flopping appendage attached by a few shreds of skin and tendon.

Uphadhyay's killer shot him again, this time in the heart. As the percussive echoes of the second gunshot faded, Griffith twitched and spasmed. MacGowan was forced to listen to his dying gurgles via the comms-link. Eventually the Yorkshireman fell silent and was still.

MacGowan turned to the ghost-man who was now personally responsible for the deaths of two of his team.

'You bastard,' he snarled icily. 'You cold-blooded fucking bastard.'

'Shut it,' snapped the man holding him at gunpoint, jabbing MacGowan's neck with the rifle barrel.

Uphadhyay's and Griffith's killer stepped forward and raised a hand to MacGowan's faceplate. He depressed the release buttons, and MacGowan saw a sizzle of blue light. Then he was blinking into perfect blackness. He felt cold, damp air on his face and breathed in the odours of brine and stagnant water.

He heard the man who had removed his faceplate say, 'All right, do it,' and a second later he heard a hiss like an aerosol-can spray.

He caught a whiff of something that smelled like cinnamon.

And then he was engulfed by a different kind of blackness – one that was empty, and all-enveloping, and silent, and still.

PART 3

19

Some time later, MacGowan came to with a start, with a sudden sharp intake of breath.

His surroundings were immediately familiar: his room at the Ship Hotel, Carvingdean. The curtains were drawn, but the daylight framing them was bright enough for him to make out everything clearly. The functional table and chairs. The basin, with mirror. The galleon print on the wall above the dresser. The Adidas gym bag he used as a holdall, unzipped on the floor where he had left it the previous night, clothes spilling from its opening like the pinched-out insides of a baked potato. The bed on which he was lying.

For several befuddled moments he struggled to remember how he had come to be here. Then, as though a dam in his mind had burst, memory-images came flooding in.

The power station.

The infil.

The contact.

The ruthless elimination of his team.

Capture.

Capture!

He leapt from the bed, scanning around the room. Where were they, the men who had taken him prisoner? Surely one of them was here, keeping watch over him.

There was no one in the room with him. He hurried over to the door and tried the handle. The door was not, as he had anticipated, locked.

Peering out into the corridor, he saw a maid lugging her basket of cleaning things into the room across the landing. The maid glanced round at him, and then, with a grimace of embarrassment, turned away again.

MacGowan looked down at himself. He was wearing nothing but his boxer shorts. Hastily he drew back into the room and closed the door.

He sat down on the bed and gazed dully around, all of a sudden aware of pain at his temples – a dim, distant throb similar to that which, back in his heavy-drinking days, used to denote the onset of a hangover.

He was not a captive. The Anarch mercenaries had brought him back to the hotel and left him here.

What the hell was going on?

At about the same time as MacGowan, Rattray also awoke.

What first drew him back to consciousness was sounds. Creaks and rattles. The churn of metal wheels on tracks. The clatter of those same wheels passing over points. And now a steam-whistle letting out a staccato tattoo of shrill peeps, and a far-off, muffled chuffing.

He felt a smooth leather-upholstered seat beneath him.

He became aware of an insistent, irregular rocking motion that swung him gently from side to side, with an occasional abrupt juddering jolt lifting him upwards.

Gradually, in a series of widening blinks, he opened his eyes.

Had it merely been that he was sitting in a compartment in a train carriage straight out of the Age of Steam, Rattray might not have been too concerned. He might have wondered *how* he had got where he was, but his immediate surroundings, in themselves, would not have presented him with a problem. After all, steam enthusiasts all over the world kept vintage locomotives and rolling stock operational and in pristine condition, offering paying punters short, nostalgic round-trips along disused branch lines. If it was merely that he had awoken to find himself on board one of *those* trains, Rattray might have had trouble fathoming Emperor Dragon's motives for putting him there, but at least he would have been in an environment he could comprehend.

Nothing about the compartment itself, therefore, with its straight-backed seats, its brass fixtures and its wood panelling, would have caused Rattray to begin to question his own sanity.

The view from the compartment window, however, was a different matter.

It was a view at once oddly familiar and completely extraordinary. A view of a world that could not – did not – exist.

20

Slowly, methodically, in order to give himself time to think things through, MacGowan went through his regular morning ablutions – washing his hands and face at the basin, brushing his teeth, shaving. The familiarity of the ritual, the orderliness of it, was comforting.

The Anarch mercenaries at Seal Point had gone to the effort of singling him out and taking him alive, while killing every other member of his team. They had hit him with a knockout spray, doubtless paraterrestrial-grade, but instead of carting him off to a secure location somewhere, they had brought him back to the hotel. (In his own car, and all. He had found the keys lying on the dresser, and a quick glance out of the window had revealed the Saab sitting in one of the parking spaces outside the hotel.) Then, once they had got him here, they had dumped him on the bed in his skivvies and just left him. Why? It made no sense. Anarch agents killed Guardians, just as Guardians killed Anarch agents. That was their job. And yet here he was, definitely alive, and with a headache to prove it.

Having wiped away the last few blobs of shaving foam from his face with a handtowel, MacGowan peered at himself in the mirror. His skin was weary and pale; his eyes were bloodshot, their lids puffy and grey. Unless you had known what had happened to him recently, you might have thought that he was simply someone suffering the consequences of a hard night out on the town.

The situation was all too confusing, and he was finding it hard to think clearly. His brain seemed to be operating at reduced capacity, doubtless owing to the oncoming headache. Absentmindedly he scratched at an itch on the underside of his left forearm. There was a small, reddened swelling there, just above a vein. He must have been bitten by a mosquito while he was out cold on the bed.

Aspirin.

That was a good idea. He would get dressed, go down to the reception desk and ask someone there for some aspirin to knock his headache on the head, so to speak. Then he would drive to Bretherton, grabbing breakfast at a service station on the way. He needed to have a debriefing with Lucretia. The action-to-suppress had been the world's biggest balls-up, and he had the deaths of four men – one of whom, Uphadhyay, he considered a friend – on his conscience. The sooner he reached Bretherton and got down to assessing with someone else what had gone wrong and how much, if at all, he was to blame, the better.

At the reception desk there was aspirin, which was good. There was also a hotel manager who felt it her duty to inform MacGowan that the conduct he had displayed the previous night was not to be tolerated in a respectable establishment such as this one.

'Conduct?' MacGowan said, as he blearily examined the bill the manager had handed him.

'Yes, you wouldn't remember, would you?' replied the manager with a sniff and a sigh. She was young, too pinch-cheeked to be considered pretty, but she looked coolly efficient in her charcoal-grey suit and rimless spectacles, with her hair fastened back in a tight plait. 'The night clerk reported that shortly after four a.m. you were brought in by two of your friends, in a state of undress and clearly the worse for wear. Your friends took you up to your room and then went out again, presumably to carry on with their revels, wherever they were having them. Now, I don't know how they do things up in' – she consulted the registration form MacGowan had filled out when checking in, supplying his usual false name and address – 'Basingstoke, Mr Cameron, but here in Carvingdean we're decent people and we lead decent lives. I'm not saying that you and your friends aren't welcome to stay at the Ship Hotel again. You are. I'm simply saying that we expect a certain level of decorum to be observed by our guests.'

Her didactic, patronising tone MacGowan found, for some reason, extremely grating. What made it worse was that she could not have been much older than twenty-five. Who was this person, this *girl*, to lecture him about behaviour and decorum? And who, for God's sake, in this day and age used a word like *revels* in ordinary everyday speech, unless they were buying a packet of sweets? Mind you, she was no oil painting, and that suit and those glasses and that hairdo made her look as frigid as a schoolmarm. She had probably never had a day's fun in her life.

He was tempted to give her a piece of his mind, tell the frigid, repressed bitch where to get off, but he checked himself. The intensity of his irritation surprised him, but he managed to rein it in. There was no point in losing his rag with this woman. She was just doing her job. He was tired and he was thoroughly perplexed. He was letting little, inconsequential things get to him.

'I'm sorry,' he said, sincerely. 'These "friends",' he added. 'They weren't the same ones who were staying here, were they?'

'Well, I imagine so. Why shouldn't they be?'

'But the night clerk . . .' His voice trailed off. He nodded to himself, understanding. The night clerk had barely glanced up as he and his team had left the hotel just after midnight, so it was hardly surprising that he should have failed to notice that the two men who brought MacGowan back four hours later had not been two of the men he had originally departed with.

'Yes?' said the manager.

'Nothing.' MacGowan opened his wallet, fished out a

thick wad of cash and counted off several tens and twenties. 'I'll be paying for all five rooms.'

The manager took the money and gave him change. 'Your friends are aware they have to be out by midday, of course.' It was partly a question, partly a warning.

MacGowan wondered how he could explain to her that his 'friends' were not in their rooms and would not be checking out any time ever. He could not. He could not think up any decent cover story that would account convincingly for their disappearance. He merely said, 'Yeah,' signed the bill, picked up his gym bag and went outside.

It was a brisk, bright morning. The tang of briny air stung his nostrils, and the sunshine, reflecting in sequin sparkles off the surface of the sea, hurt his eyes. Squinting, he took the two aspirin the manager had given him, popped them into his mouth and dry-swallowed them.

He unlocked the car, tossed his gym bag onto the back seat and clambered in behind the wheel. As he inserted the ignition key, he wondered whether the Anarch mercenary who had driven the car last night had realised, as he had held MacGowan's puzzle-egg keyring in his hand, just how important the keyring was, what it signified, what it was capable of. Probably not.

He twisted the key. The engine turned over, choked, guttered. He tried again. The engine turned over, choked, guttered. Both times the ABS indicator light on the dashboard flashed, so he knew the battery must be fine. He tried the key a third time, but still the car would not start. He thumped the steering-wheel. Fucking thing! What was *wrong* with it? Fucking Swedish fucking piece of shit! All he wanted was for the damned buggering fucking thing to *start*! Was that really too much to ask?

He pounded the steering-wheel again, and again and again, hammering it until his fist hurt. The headache was clenching at his skull now, pain throbbing around his eye sockets and at the back of his jaw. He caught sight of himself in the rearview mirror – wide-eyed, haggard, ashen-complexioned. There was a vein twitching prominently in his forehead. He was breathing fast.

'Cool it,' he murmured to his reflection. 'Just cool it, Bill. It's all right. A little technical problem, that's all. Nothing to get worked up about.'

He took a look under the bonnet. As far as he could tell there was nothing amiss with the Saab's engine, but he was no mechanic, and his headache was not helping, making it difficult for him to concentrate. How long before the aspirin began to take effect? He jiggled the spark plugs and tugged at a couple of cables, not expecting that this would do any good but simply so as to have tried *something*. Then he got back into the driver's seat, reached down and twisted the key again. Turn over, choke, gutter. No use. The Saab was not going anywhere today.

He had two options. He could call the breakdown company and sit tight and wait until they reached him, or he could take the train. Carvingdean had a small railway station. He could head up to London and then down to Guildford, and Lucretia could collect him from there. The prospect of spending another hour or so in Carvingdean did not fill him with joy, and there was no guarantee that the breakdown repairman would be able to get the Saab started, so the whole business of getting to Bretherton by car might wind up taking the best part of the day. Moreover, if his headache got any worse – and he thought it was going to; it felt deep-seated, there for the long haul – then he probably ought not to be driving anyway. His priority was to get to Bretherton. His impulse was to get away from Carvingdean as soon as possible. Need and desire, urge and urgency, coincided. He decided to take the train.

21

The train on which Rattray was a passenger was travelling along a viaduct through a city. But the viaduct was so immense that it could not conceivably exist, and the city, though in many ways it resembled Victorian London, was not any Victorian London that he remembered.

With his forehead pressed to the window's rain-flecked glass, Rattray stared out, amazed and perturbed.

By his estimate, the viaduct rose a good half-mile above the ground. He could see it curving ahead, arch stacked upon arch in narrowing tiers, a great vaulting symphony in brick. As for the city, it was spread out beneath a louring, overcast, drizzly sky, a labyrinthine expanse of tented roofs running in parallel rows. Here and there a huge soot-caked factory arose, its tall chimneys gouting plumes of black smoke, and here and there could be seen a tottering, buttressed cathedral crowned with a steeple or a dome. He glimpsed a glass edifice on the horizon that reminded him of Alexandra Palace and Crystal Palace but was considerably larger than both combined, and he saw a silvery, cylindrical shape in the sky that he identified as an airship. It was tacking towards a distant aerodrome where dozens of its kind were tethered at mooring masts like fish on hooks. Down, deep down between the terraced buildings he could just make out backyards that clustered against other backyards, with narrow alleyways between them. The streets and the alleyways teemed with people so tiny he could not distinguish individuals, just a mass of motion like blood cells pulsing through veins. He was reminded of the tenement slums which Dickens had dubbed 'rookeries'.

If this *was* Victorian London, however, then it was a vastly exaggerated version of the Victorian London that he (and Dickens) had known. It was Victorian London amplified to the nth degree.

He was so preoccupied with staring out at the city – or, more accurately, from this dizzying height, *down* on the city – that someone who had just entered the compartment and was standing behind him had to clear his throat several times to attract his attention.

It was a ticket inspector in a navy-blue uniform, with a silver watch-chain strung between the pockets of his waistcoat and a cap with the letters 'VR' emblazoned above its peak in embroidered gold thread. Rattray's assumption, reasonable enough under the circumstances, was that the initials stood for Victoria Regina.

'Good day, sir,' said the ticket inspector. He was rotund and plum-cheeked, with a bristling walrus-moustache. 'Might I trouble you for your permit to travel?'

With some difficulty Rattray found his voice. 'I don't believe I . . . I'm not sure I . . .' He could not think how to answer. It seemed simpler just to go along with the situation for now; figure out the whys and wherefores as he went. He surely would not be on this train if he did *not* have a ticket, so he stood up and began patting his pockets down, discovering as he did so that he was dressed in unfamiliar clothing – a black serge lounge suit with a starched, wing-collared shirt and a plain navy tie. He noticed at the same time that, folded up on the luggage rack above his seat, there was a double-buttoned ulster overcoat, presumably his.

In the inside pocket of the suit jacket his fingers encountered a small rectangle of card. A ticket. He held it out to the ticket inspector, who took it from him, examined it and handed it back.

'Enjoy the trip, sir,' he said, and turned to go.

'Excuse me,' said Rattray.

'Yes?'

'I'm – I'm from out of town.'

'You don't sound it to me, sir, if you don't mind my saying. You sound like a Londoner born and bred.'

'Yes. Well. I've been away for a while. Abroad. So, if you could possibly help me – where, exactly, is this train heading?'

'Why, Middle London, of course, sir. Not far now. Should be' – the ticket inspector glanced out of the window – 'another ten minutes, I'd reckon.'

'Yes, quite. London,' said Rattray. 'And which terminus?'

'Are you telling me you bought a ticket and boarded this train without knowing what your destination was?' The ticket inspector pushed back his cap and scratched his forehead, fixing Rattray with a bemused look. 'That's a bit of a rum to-do, don't you think?'

'Yes, yes, terribly absentminded of me.'

'Well, it's Empire Station. That's where we're going. Now do you remember?'

'Empire Station. That's right. Yes.'

'Good. I'm glad we got that sorted out, sir. So. If you'll not be needing anything further, I've other passengers to attend to.'

'Of course. I apologise.'

The ticket inspector exited the compartment, and Rattray sat back down in his seat, half convinced that he must be dreaming. There was no other explanation for what was happening to him, other than that he had been transported a hundred years or so back in time to a London that had never existed, which was a scenario so absurd as not to be even worth contemplating.

He resumed staring out of the window at the impossible city below.

Yes, he was dreaming. That had to be it.

Dreaming, or going mad.

22

At Victoria, MacGowan disembarked and headed through from the platform on to the station concourse. There, the brightness of the lighting, the hard, reflecting surfaces, the hubbub, the crowds of people milling and meandering in cross-colliding trajectories – all of this made him wince. Too much motion, too much visual information to assimilate at once.

Locating a payphone, he slotted in a twenty-pence coin and dialled Lucretia's number.

'Bretherton Grange.'

'Lucretia, it's Bill.'

'Bill! How are you?'

The headache was raging now, like a tiger loose inside his skull. The aspirin had not worked. The packet had probably been sitting behind the hotel reception desk for years and was long out of date. He dug a thumb and forefinger into the inner corners of his eye sockets and pinched the top of his nose hard, but this brought little relief.

'Been better,' he said. 'Listen, I'm at Victoria, and I'm going across to Waterloo to catch a train to Guildford. Can you pick me up from there?'

'From Guildford station? Of course. Bill? Something's happened, hasn't it? Something bad.'

'I can't explain anything right now. Not here. I'll give you a bell from Waterloo, let you know which train I'm going to be on.'

'Bill, please tell me you're all right.'

'Lucretia, to be honest, I don't know *what* I am at the moment. Fucking knackered, that's for sure.' The little display that showed how many seconds of conversation remained was counting down fast to zero. 'Look, my money's running out. I'll speak to you again in quarter of an hour or so, once I'm at Waterloo. OK?'

'All right. Bill—'

Zero seconds left. Her voice was cut off.

MacGowan hung up the receiver and rested his forehead against the payphone unit. The metal felt refreshingly cool against his skin.

How had Lucretia known that the action-to-suppress had gone pear-shaped? She had guessed from his tone of voice. Yeah, that had to be it. And from the fact that he was taking the train, not driving.

Or perhaps she had known all along that the mission was destined to fail.

No. MacGowan shook his head, even though it hurt to do so, but needing to reinforce the mental denial with a physical action. No. Not possible. Rattray and Lucretia would never have sent him off on a dead-end, no-return-ticket mission. The Army might do that to its rank-and-file, but not the Guardians. No. Ridiculous thought. The action-to-suppress had been a cock-up, pure and simple. The Librans had supplied bad information, or else the Anarchs had somehow rumbled that the Guardians were coming. Shit like that happened, even to the best-regulated fighting force.

Picking up his gym bag, MacGowan turned away from the payphone and headed off across the concourse to a concession branch of Boots. There, he bought a packet of Nurofen and a large bottle of Evian. The girl at the pharmacy counter eyed him curiously, and a little warily, as he paid. Hardly surprising. If he looked half as bad as he felt, then he must look pretty fucking awful indeed.

He swallowed three of the Nurofen, one more than the recommended dosage, washing the pills down with half of the bottle of mineral water. Then, stashing away the

Evian and the painkillers in his gym bag, he headed for the entrance to the Underground.

He managed the first leg of the Tube journey from Victoria to Waterloo without much trouble, although sharing a carriage with a gaggle of French teenagers did little to alleviate his headache. The youths seemed to have no control over the volume of their conversation. Toting identical, garishly coloured rucksacks emblazoned with the logo of the tour operator responsible for bringing them over here, they shouted and laughed and made jokes and jeered at one another simultaneously. Within the close confines of the rumbling carriage their raucous babble resounded deafeningly. The noise set Mac-Gowan's eardrums ringing and pierced his brain like a skewer, but he was only travelling three stops on this train, so he grinned and bore the discomfort.

It was as he was transferring from the Circle Line to the Northern Line at Embankment that things began to go really awry.

Navigating the network of tunnels and escalators between platforms, he came across a beggar – a stooped, straggle-haired figure in a combat jacket who was holding out a hand and mumbling imprecations to passers-by.

Normally, whenever he passed a beggar, MacGowan would at least shake his head and say, 'Sorry, mate.' If he was in a charitable mood and the bloke looked really hard-up, he might fork over some spare change. On this occasion, though, helping out a fellow man was the very last thing on his mind. He just wanted to get to Waterloo and on a train to Guildford as quickly as he could.

He strode straight past the beggar, and as he did so, at the periphery of his vision, he glimpsed the man reaching into his pocket and pulling out a shiny, silvery-metallic object.

He knew immediately, instinctively, that it was a knife.

Without hesitating, he dropped his gym bag and lunged for the beggar. Before the beggar had a chance to raise the weapon, he smacked his head against the wall, punched him in the gut, then kicked his legs out from under him and sent him crashing to the floor. Straddling him, pinning his arms with his knees, he battered the beggar repeatedly in the face until blood was flowing freely from the man's mouth and nose, and then kept battering him until he had ceased to struggle or scream.

When the beggar was no longer conscious, MacGowan sat back on his haunches, breathing hard. His heart was pounding, his ears singing. He felt invigorated. The sensation of the man's teeth cracking loose beneath his fist had been exhilarating. Whether the man had been an Anarch stooge or simply a mugger seemed, at that moment, almost inconsequential. Beating him up, neutralising a threat, had felt good. Had felt right.

A small crowd of onlookers had gathered. MacGowan peered up and around at appalled faces.

'Bastard was going to rob me,' he explained between panting breaths.

'But that's George,' one of the onlookers said, a suit-wearing executive-type. 'I see him here nearly every day.'

'So what?' MacGowan snapped. 'That doesn't mean he isn't going to try and fucking nick your wallet at knifepoint. Look!'

He pointed to the beggar's hand, which was still clasped around the silvery-metallic object.

That was when he realised that the silvery-metallic object was not a weapon of any sort.

'That's his harmonica,' the executive-type said, accusingly. 'George busks sometimes.'

MacGowan blinked and peered at the musical instrument. No. Not possible. It had been a knife. Definitely a knife. No way had it been anything else. No fucking way.

He clambered to his feet, and all the onlookers edged back several paces, giving him plenty of room. He stared at them and they stared at him. They thought he might be about to attack one of them; he thought they might be about to gang up and attack him. The stand-off lasted several seconds, and then MacGowan – sensing that, contrary to the Clash song, if he went there would be trouble but if he stayed it would be double – snatched up his gym bag and made off along the tunnel.

Nobody moved to stop him. Nobody even considered *attempting* to stop him. He was far too big and crazy-looking. Instead, one of the onlookers, a nurse, went and knelt beside George the beggar to attend to his injuries, while the executive-type, announcing that he was going to notify the transport police, turned and jogged off in the direction of the ticketing hall.

MacGowan quickened his pace, and shortly arrived at the staircase that led to the Northern Line platforms. The rumble of an approaching train sent him hurrying down the stairs. He emerged onto the platform just as the train was pulling in. Doors hissed open. He leapt aboard and made his way to a seat. The doors rolled shut and the train lumbered off.

One stop to Waterloo. As rushing darkness filled the carriage windows, MacGowan peered down at his hands. His knuckles were spattered and smeared with the beggar's blood. Discreetly he wiped off the bloodstains on the seat-cover fabric.

Maybe, he thought – and he was having to battle against the headache in order to pursue the line of reasoning – maybe it had been some kind of Anarch knife that only *looked* like a harmonica. Yes, maybe that was it. A disguised paraterrestrial weapon.

But more likely he had made a terrible blunder and had bludgeoned an innocent man half to death.

How? How could he have done such a thing?

Actually, he could think of several reasons why he had perceived an assault when there was none and had responded with such force. He was not normally prone to nerves and jumpiness, but after the ambush last night and its perplexing aftermath this morning, it was hardly surprising that he should be on edge. And the man had been wearing a combat jacket, which had probably triggered an ingrained chain of association in his mili-tary-trained mind: uniform = enemy = danger. Then there was a Guardian's natural paranoia. Anarch attacks could come out of nowhere, at any time. A Guardian had to be constantly on his guard. And, of course, there was the headache. The headache which the Nurofen, like the aspirin, did not appear to be making a dent in. Indeed, the pain, if anything, was worsening.

The train approached the next stop, and slowed, and MacGowan reached up for the strap that hung overhead and hauled himself unsteadily to his feet. The effort of the movement sent a tremor of unprecedented agony through his head. He reeled off balance and, as the train braked, tumbled back into his seat. He thought, at that moment, that his skull was about to implode.

The doors rolled apart and through pain-dimmed eyes MacGowan glimpsed the name of the station. Charing Cross. Not Waterloo. Charing Cross.

Shit.

In his hurry to catch the arriving train, he had not paused to check whether the platform was for the north-bound service or the southbound.

Shit shit shit.

Even more reason to get off here. He had to change trains, get onto a southbound one. But still he could not stand. He thought, if he did, he might pass out from the pain. It felt as though the sutures in his skull were knitting together even more tightly, squeezing his brain within its cranial casing.

The doors closed again and the train lumbered off. Darkness filled the windows again, and against the background of passing buttresses and ribboning pipes and cables picked out by the carriage's interior illumination MacGowan saw his own reflection hovering like a greasy, ghastly ghost.

What had the Anarch mercenaries done to him? What? Poisoned him? Denied him a quick death by bullet in favour of a slow death by some sort of toxin? Was that it?

The train stopped at Leicester Square. People got on and off. MacGowan could not bring himself to move. The same at Tottenham Court Road. All he knew was agony and strangers' faces, strangers' faces and agony. At some point one of a pair of nuns leaned forwards and asked him if he was all right. He could not answer. A couple of other passengers pointed at him in a none-too-discreet manner and whispered.

Up and onwards along the Northern Line. Where would this train terminate? Edgware or High Barnet? Hardly mattered. This was the route (he recalled, deep in his cocoon of pain) that he and Sarah always used to take after they had been for an evening out in the West End. Sitting side by side, his arm around her shoulders, her head pressed against his neck, and the feel of her ringleted hair, the smell of it – coconut-oil shampoo and her own sweet secretions . . .

Sarah.

She still lived in Camden, didn't she?

God, he could do with seeing her now!

And why not? Why not? If the Anarch bastards *had* poisoned him, if he *was* dying, and since providence had propelled him in this direction, then why not make the best of it? Why not go and see his ex-wife one last time?

At Camden Town station, with a superhuman effort MacGowan struggled to his feet and, gritting his teeth against the grinding pain, staggered off the train.

23

Empire Station was the terminus to end all termini. The terminal terminus, if you will. What seemed like a hundred separate railway lines fed into its entrance, some carried by viaducts of varying heights, others running along the ground, all incurving into the station like ribbons of seaweed being sucked into the maw of some gigantic marine behemoth. Rattray's train was just one of dozens he could see, either pulling in or departing. As the station's canopy of arched glass roofs loomed overhead, for all his continuing bewilderment he could not help but feel a little awed.

With a huff and a settling sigh the train came to a halt, and Rattray picked up and donned the ulster and stepped out of the carriage. Still convinced that he must be dreaming, he could think of nothing better to do than go along with the flow of events. Until he got to the bottom of what was happening, oneiric acquiescence seemed his best strategy.

The station was arranged on three levels – a ground level and two upper levels, the lower of which Rattray was on. The platforms of the upper levels were constructed from cast-iron plates welded together and perched atop a framework of pillars and cross-braces that rose from the platforms on the ground, which were brick and marble. The tracks on the upper levels were suspended between platforms on iron sleepers – horizontal girders, in effect – and the entire three-tier edifice boasted a soundly riveted sturdiness of construction. There were trains coming and going on all sides, above and below, and the piston hisses and whistle shrieks echoed through the vastness of the station like the clamour of an immense battle being waged.

Rattray joined the throng of passengers who had also alighted from his train and moved along the platform with them. Like him, they were dressed in Victorian garb – suits, chesterfield overcoats, high shirt-collars and top hats for the men, and, for the ladies, bonnets, pointy-toed ankle boots and either crepe blouses and skirts or bustle gowns of taffeta and velvet.

Following the crowd, Rattray passed through the billows of steam issuing from beneath the stationary locomotive and came to the end of the platform, where the passengers were queuing up at a pair of waist-high trellis gates made of brass. As each person inserted his or her ticket into a slot in a device located next to the gates, there was a whirr of mechanism and the gates folded flat into their uprights with an abrupt rattle. When it was Rattray's turn at the gates, he did as everyone else had done, inserting his ticket in the slot, and was permitted access to a descending flight of iron steps.

He reached ground level and, via one of a row of brick archways, entered a cavernous, marble-paved concourse. There were hundreds of people here, milling around. Among them were several uniformed railway officials, and, as he crossed the concourse, Rattray noticed a pair of police constables patrolling in step, hands clasped behind their backs, revolvers holstered at their hips. He passed shirtsleeved, waistcoated vendors at barrow stalls who were peddling newspapers, periodicals, penny dreadfuls and a variety of snacks in greaseproof-paper bags, hawking their wares, not by the traditional method of shouting, but by means of gramophones that played prerecorded street-cries through trumpet-shaped speakers. These competing, crackling come-ons were intermittently drowned by passenger information announcements that echoed out over a Tannoy system, delivered in crisp, received-pronunciation tones.

Outside the station's main entrance, in the shade of a vast iron awning that sported filigree-work so elegant and amazingly intricate it looked like cast-moulded Nottingham lace, Rattray found a cab-rank where a dozen hansoms were parked in a row. Each cab had a bowler-hatted driver perched in the raised seat at the rear, and each had what Rattray at first took to be an armour-clad horse tethered between its shafts. On closer inspection, however, he discerned that the horses were actually mechanical beasts, and that what he had taken for armour was a hide composed of interlocking metal plates, heavily segmented at the joints, where the greatest range of movement was required. Most of the horses' hides were brass, but a few were stainless steel, a couple were iron and one was copper. Their tales and manes were made up of fine strands of wire spun from the corresponding metal, and gave a shimmery rattle whenever the horses tossed their heads or stamped their feet. The horses' eyes, beneath spiky-lashed metal lids, were empty orbs of glass.

Rattray could see no other form of transport immediately available, and decided that if he was going to explore this London and try to find some way of leaving it, he would be able to cover ground more quickly by hansom than on foot.

He joined the queue at the rank and was soon at the front of it and being accosted by a cab driver.

'Lovely weather, innit, guv'nor,' the driver said, pushing back his felt Derby hat and rolling his eyes at the rain. 'Should turn out nice around noon, though. Least, that's what the Met. Office've said. So, where'll it be?'

'I'm not entirely certain,' Rattray replied. 'Perhaps you could just drive.'

'That's no good, is it, guv'nor?' said the driver with a lopsided but kindly grin. 'I mean, I can't rightly take you somewhere if I don't have some idea what the destination's going to be. Stands to reason, dunnit?'

'Then start driving, and I'll tell you where I want you to stop when we get there.'

'What, just drive anywhere?'

'Anywhere.'

The driver shrugged. 'All right. Fair enough. After all, you're the guv'nor, aintcha.'

Rattray clambered aboard the hansom, and the driver raised his whip and, uttering a loud 'Yah!', lashed the back of his horse. There was an electric crackle as the whip made contact with the horse's brass hide, and the startled mechanical nag let out a tinny neigh and began to trot, metal hooves clanging on metalled road.

The street which led away from the station was given over to commerce, with shops along either side. Pedestrians sauntered along the pavements, perusing the merchandise on sale in the shop windows, most of them from beneath the shelter of umbrellas. Looking out from the hansom, Rattray examined the shops' bow windows with their bottled-glass panes; the hanging shop-signs executed in ornate, curlicued fonts; the names emblazoned across storefronts in enamel lettering or mosaic tiles; the handwritten price-tags marked in pounds, shillings and pence, or occasionally in guineas. All these details were much as he remembered them from the nineteenth-century London he had known. As on the station concourse, however, there were also numerous anachronisms and anomalies, readily perceived. The streetlamps, for instance, were fitted with sodium bulbs instead of gas jets, and the trams that burred along the tracks embedded in the centre of the road were sleek, multi-carriaged and driverless.

Turning his attention to the items in the shop windows, Rattray saw that they, too, were a curious mixture of the period-authentic and the retrofuturistic. A gentlemen's outfitters offered both traditional woollen and cotton apparel alongside clothing manufactured from 'the Very Latest Extruded-Chemical Fibres'. A bookshop boasted not only leather-bound print collections of the partworks of Mr Dickens, Mr Trollope, Mrs Gaskell, *et al.* but also 'Magnetophone Editions for Domestic Auditory Consumption'. A chemist's promised 'Bactericidal Compounds most Efficacious in the Treatment of Infectious Disorders' – antibiotics by any other name – in addition to the usual crude nostrums and potions. A barber's, complete with rotating candystriped pole, advertised both traditional cutthroat and 'Electro-Vibrational' shaving techniques, while a ladies' *coiffeur* announced the imminent arrival of a 'New Electrical Method for the Permanent Removal of Undesired Feminine Luxuriance – a Process which has met with Considerable Success and Much Approbation in the French-Speaking Colonies'. There was even a shop selling what appeared to be transistor radios, along with bulky wooden cabinets with calibrated ivory dials and convex oval glass screens that could only be television sets – several of them manufactured, it transpired, by a firm called Wᵐ Morris & Co. Utilitarian Products.

It was clear to Rattray by now that this London was a London of Progress unchecked, a London of contratemporality gone mad. How it existed and where it existed, he had no idea. It seemed both too realistic to be a dream and too dreamlike to be real. Perhaps, he thought, he was trapped in some feverish fugue of his mind's own devising. At any rate, whatever the explanation for this highly abnormal situation, the simplest course of action still seemed to be to play along, be a passive participant in events, until some kind of rationale became apparent. Then he could figure out a means of escaping, or awakening, or snapping out, or whatever process was required to bring him back to his normal state of existence.

The hansom turned a corner into a broad thoroughfare flanked by massive, many-windowed buildings of a decidedly administrative and governmental aspect. At the far end of the street, which reminded Rattray of Whitehall, there was a plaza. At the centre of the plaza rose a tall Doric column that supported a giant globe. The globe was relief-mapped with the oceans and continents, and on top of it sat a statue of Britannia, imperious with

211

trident, helmet and shield. Pigeons roosted on her head, skirts and shoulders, and had coated her and most of the Arctic at her feet with their guano (in the case of that icebound continent, the whiteness was amusingly appropriate). The pigeons also thronged the plaza, surrounding pedestrians in fluttering flocks like wind-blown clumps of ashes.

Rattray rapped on the roof of the cab and the driver slid open the speaking-hatch.

'Tell me, please,' said Rattray, gesturing ahead. 'What's the name of that?'

'The name of what, guv'nor? That monument?' The driver snorted with ill-disguised incredulity. 'You're having me on, surely.'

'It was a straightforward question, politely phrased. Perhaps you'd do me the courtesy of answering it.' Rattray had decided, following his experience with the ticket inspector, that the simplest way to obtain information here was not to make elaborate excuses for his ignorance but merely to demand.

The tactic worked. 'It's called Britannia's Column,' the driver said, adding under his breath, 'as even the most dim-witted darkie from Her Majesty's Basutoland would be able to tell you.'

'I see,' said Rattray. 'And Britannia rules the waves, does she?'

'Britannia rules the *world*, guv'nor!' exclaimed the driver. 'The whole bloomin' world! Blimey, to hear you talk, anyone would think you were from Mars or something.'

'No, not from another planet. Just from very far away.'

'Well, wherever you come from, it's got to be somewhere that's under British control, dunnit.'

'Is that so?'

'Of course it's so! Every square inch of the map is Empire red these days. Even where we've let them carry on using French as their official language, they know who's boss, who owns them. It's a Golden Age, that's what it is, guv'nor. I read that in the *Imperial Clarion* yesterday, so it must be true. A Golden Age for all mankind. Thanks to us British the entire planet's at peace, except in those countries where they're still rebelling against us, but *they'll* be at peace soon, you mark my words. And we're inventing new things left, right and centre. Miracles of modern science. And good Queen Victoria – the Lord bless her, may she reign for ever – watches over it all like a goddess. Yes, a goddess, guv'nor! I know it sounds like I'm coming on a bit strong, but I'm not the only one who thinks that way. Why, just the other day I had the Governor-General of the States of Columbia in the front of my cab, right where you're sitting now, guv'nor. He's over here for the Annual Governors' Conference, and he told me, confidential-like, that there's a move afoot in Parliament to declare the Queen constitutionally a divine being, just like they used to do with their emperors in the Nipponese Protectorates before we put a—'

By now the hansom had reached the plaza, and Rattray interrupted the driver mid-sentence by announcing his wish to alight here. The driver duly reined in his horse, crying, 'Whoa!', and Rattray opened the low twin doors that half enclosed the interior of the cab and stepped down.

He realised then that he had no money with which to pay the driver. While searching his pockets on the train he had found the ticket, but nothing else. In desperation he tried the pockets of the ulster, and, lo and behold, one of them contained a crocodile-skin wallet, and inside the wallet there were several pound notes, neatly folded to fit, as well as what appeared to be a couple of credit cards, fashioned from sturdy Bakelite.

Rattray tendered one of the pound notes to the driver, who pursed his lips and said, 'Ooh, I'm not sure I've got change for that.'

'Never mind. Keep it.'

'That's very generous of you, guv'nor, but really . . .'

Rattray tapped the credit cards in the wallet. 'I've always got these if I need them.'

'Yeah, but not everywhere accepts Bakelite, you know.' The driver chuckled. He flapped the pound note. 'If you're absolutely sure . . . ?'

'Positive.'

The driver thanked Rattray, bade him good day, and urged his horse into motion again with another crackling lash of his whip.

Rattray crossed the plaza to the foot of Britannia's Column and stood gazing up at the monument and blinking against the gentle but persistent rain. Pigeons gathered at his feet, waddling around and pecking suggestively at the bare ground. Other people in the plaza were feeding them bags of breadcrumbs, which an old woman was selling from a tray slung about her neck.

Observing that Rattray was attended by pigeons but breadcrumb-less, the old woman came over to him. He saw her approach from the corner of his eye.

'Feed the birds, sir?' she said. She was a withered, twinkly-eyed creature with a shawl wrapped around her narrow shoulders and, on her head, a bonnet whose trimmings of feathers, lace, ribbons and artificial flowers had seen far better days. 'It's a ha'penny a bag.'

'I regret to say I have no coins on me,' Rattray replied. 'Only notes.'

'That's a proper tragedy, that is, sir. Why, I wish I had such problems in *my* life.' The breadcrumb seller' s tone was as much sarcastic as teasing.

'I'm sorry that we can't do business, then.'

'Well, sir, as a matter of fact, I think I ought to let you have a bag anyway, for free. Seeing as you've a nice face. A gentlemanly face. And nice eyes, too, though they're eyes that have seen plenty of sadness, if I don't miss my mark.'

'Perhaps,' said Rattray. 'Perhaps.'

'A bag *gratis*, then, for the nice but sorrowful gentleman.'

Rattray, shrugging, reached for her tray and selected a bag.

'No, sir,' she said. 'Not that one. Try the one in the corner.'

Rattray, with a flicker of a frown, replaced the bag he had chosen and took the one she had suggested instead.

'I wish you luck, sir,' the breadcrumb seller said, and turned to go.

As she walked away, she began trilling a song to herself in a reedy, warbling, old woman's soprano:

'I have a love and he loves me
We make our love near the cedar tree
The cedar tree with branches dark
That grows in Victoria and Albert Park . . .'

Neither the lyrics nor the tune were familiar to Rattray, but it sounded like a typical popular sheetsong, one that doubtless went down well in the music halls. A piece of innocent, sentimental nonsense, but he listened to it anyway, with a vague, deep-rooted pang of nostalgia, until the breadcrumb seller had strolled out of earshot. Then he delved into the bag and began distributing breadcrumbs among the impatient, purring pigeons.

About halfway down into the bag, his fingers came across something that was not breadcrumbs. He withdrew it.

A slip of paper, folded several times.

He unfolded it.

And for several moments could only stare at it, astounded.

24

Even though it was not the weekend, Camden High Street was bustling. The day had turned out milder than usual for autumn, and as it was past noon the lunchtime crowd was swelling the ranks of the shoppers who had come to sample the delights of Camden Market. Pedestrians were spilling over from the broad pavements into the roadway and threading around the traffic that was grumbling slowly, nose-to-tail, in both directions. The market's stalls and the cafés and restaurants along the High Street were doing a brisk trade.

Through all the hurly-burly MacGowan strode, head down like a rhino, expecting people to get out of his way, barging past those that did not. Smells and sounds assailed him: body odours, exhaust fumes, human chatter, vehicle engines. Every sensation was amplified by the headache, turned into an overwhelmingly powerful version of itself. Kerbside comments were shouts. A whiff of perfume was as caustic as bleach. The toot of an impatient car horn was like a blare from one of Joshua's trumpets.

Struggling to stay focused, MacGowan kept going. He wanted to lash out at everyone and everything around him. He wanted to bellow 'SHUT UP!!!' at the top of his lungs. But he just kept on walking and thinking to himself, Sarah, Sarah, Sarah, as if mentally beaming out her name like a sonar signal in order to help him home in on her.

Just past the canal he crossed a side-street without looking left or right and was almost hit by a Fiat Uno. The car had not been travelling at great speed, but its driver still had to brake sharply to avoid the hulking man who had stepped out in front of him. Immediately he laid on with his horn and yelled abuse at the careless pedestrian. The hulking man spun around and, with a furious snarl, pounded the Fiat's bonnet once, then resumed crossing.

The blow resounded hollowly through the car. The Fiat's driver wrenched his handbrake on and scrambled out to inspect the damage. The dent in the bonnet was the size of half a football. He turned and glared at the back of the man who had inflicted it. By now the man had reached the other side of the road, and the Fiat driver considered running after him and accosting him, but – wisely, under the circumstances – decided against doing so. The man was huge and looked half-mad, and the Fiat driver was not so annoyed that his sense of self-preservation had deserted him.

Instead, fuming with impotent rage, he got back into his car and drove on, ruminating darkly on the ineffectiveness of the Thatcher government's Care in the Community programme, and then wondering how he was going to explain the dent when he made his insurance claim. A falling piece of masonry, maybe, or a midnight act of vandalism.

At the next junction he came to, MacGowan turned off the High Street. He knew the route to Sarah's flat without having to think about it. The flat, after all, used to be *their* flat.

Within minutes he had reached the quiet, terraced cul-de-sac which had once been where he lived, his home address. The street had changed little. The trees were taller, some of the houses had been done up a bit, but everything was still essentially as he remembered it. He and Sarah had left a drab MoD housing estate in Hereford to move here in 1988, intending to stay here until their first child came along, at which point they would

217

look for somewhere larger, somewhere in the suburbs perhaps.

That, at any rate, had been the plan. But then Codename: Bearskin had come along and fucked everything up the arse with a bargepole sideways.

He came to a halt outside his old address. Number 48. There, in the slot next to the doorbell button for Flat C, was a slip of paper with 'Kingsley, S.' written on it. Sarah had gone back to using her maiden name, of course. And why not? They had been divorced for longer than they had been married. Longer, even, than they had known each other.

MacGowan jabbed the bell button. Distantly within the house a buzz sounded.

No reply.

He jabbed the bell button again.

Still no reply. She was out.

He dropped his gym bag on the doorstep and leaned against the house's spiked iron railings to rest and collect his thoughts. It seemed, at last, that his headache was abating. This might, of course, just be a lull in the proceedings, the calm before an even greater storm of pain. Equally, it might mean that the worst was over. Was he still dying? It seemed an absurd question. He was aware of numerous, vague little aches and pains that had sprung up all over his body. In his limbs, in his muscles. His clothing felt uncomfortable on him in several places. Maybe he had some kind of flu. Maybe he had caught a chill in the damp power station. It was a marginally more plausible explanation for his symptoms than being exposed to some kind of lethal toxin. For surely, even with a slow-acting poison, he would be dead by now.

He did not know what to think. Nothing made sense any more. Why, for fuck's sake, was he standing on his ex-wife's doorstep? Visiting her had seemed a reasonable enough idea at the time, but now, with the headache gradually relaxing its grasp, undamming his thoughts, allowing a trickle of rationality to flow, it just seemed like a dumb thing to have done. Simply because he happened to have been on the wrong train and heading up Camden way. Christ, what kind of shock would it give Sarah, to find him here, standing on her doorstep, the husband she had not seen for eight years?

'Bill? Is that you?'

MacGowan turned around, and there she was. Sarah. A bag of shopping in one hand. And a man beside her, holding her other hand.

25

My name is John Rattray, he said to himself, and for nearly a hundred years I have served as a Guardian, shaping and regulating the course of Progress.

He repeated the sentence over and over in his head while he stared at the slip of paper in his hand, which argued a different truth.

You are John Rattray, it said, and for seven years you have served with Her Majesty's Metropolitan Police. You have recently been promoted to Detective Inspector, and this is the first time you have actually held one of these notorious artefacts in your hand, although for the past couple of years you have been hearing a great deal about them. You have heard how one first appeared in the winter of 1876 pinned to the mutilated corpse of a police constable which was dumped mysteriously one thickly fogged night in St James's Park, virtually on the front doorstep of Great Scotland Yard – a kind of calling card, a statement of intent. And you have heard how, in the ensuing months, as more of the slips of paper turned up all over the capital at the scenes of various crimes, whispered rumours began circulating through the East End underworld about a man, a physician whose name was not to be found on the records of any hospital or surgery in the land, a criminal mastermind whom no one had actually met or even seen but whom all feared as they feared the Devil himself. And you have heard how the slips of paper then started appearing in various public locations *before* a crime had taken place, the barely legible messages they contained no longer commenting enigmatically on a felony that had just occurred but giving cryptic, taunting clues to a misdeed which was due to happen somewhere in the city in the near future and which inevitably, and in spite of the best efforts of the police, did.

Abstruse announcements of impending robberies. Frustrating forewarnings of murders and outrages not yet committed. Puzzling predictions of kidnappings and acts of extortion to come.

Prescriptions from Roderick Greatorex, the Bad Doctor.

It was 1878 when Rattray was first called upon to decipher one of those arcane and atrociously scribbled messages. Superintendent Williamson, head of the Detective Branch, had assigned him to the case, saying, 'That medical so-and-so is up to his "grey tricks" again, John. You have a mind for this sort of thing. Let's see if you can succeed where others have failed.'

With some trepidation, and some eagerness, Rattray took the prescription to his office and set to working out what it might mean. The brains of several of Scotland Yard's finest had been applied to cracking the Bad Doctor's riddlesome warnings, with little success. Though not exactly a young man any more, but with the hunger of youthful ambition still not quite sated, Rattray was determined that he would be the first to penetrate the meaning of one of the prescriptions in time and foil the villain's plans.

On that occasion he was not successful, and the Bad Doctor's henchmen got away with the abduction of the five-year-old daughter of a prominent Member of Parliament. The little girl was returned to her parents shaken by her ordeal but alive and unharmed. This, however, was only after a substantial sum in ransom – several thousands of pounds – had been handed over.

Rattray's failure to prevent this crime, far from disheartening him, served only to stiffen his resolve. And over the ensuing twelve years, as the Bad Doctor continued to mete out what he called his 'treatments' all across London, Rattray was able to thwart his nefarious schemes at least half the time. He worked on other cases during that period, of course, including the Whitechapel Murders, but it was the Bad Doctor whom he came up against time after time and whose nemesis, with every small victory and every exasperating setback, he became more and yet more resolved to be.

Although the Bad Doctor's crimes frequently hit the headlines, Rattray's campaign against him was carried out quietly, with the minimum of publicity, one man's secret vendetta against another. How often did he so nearly catch up with the villain, only to lose him at the last moment to a twist of fate or a well-planned and deviously contrived escape route? How often did that shadowy, nebulous *éminence grise* slip through his fingers and live to plot and plan anew? More often than he cared to admit. But he nailed him finally, that was the main thing. In 1890, in a burning warehouse on Cheapside, he brought an end to fourteen years of the Bad Doctor's malicious practice. In the words of his colleague Fred Abberline, he 'struck the bastard off the register permanently'.

These memories returned to Rattray in an instant as he gazed at the slip of paper he had found in the bag of breadcrumbs. He had not thought about the Bad Doctor much over the past hundred years. The case had been closed, after all, and Greatorex was dead. But now it was as if the year was 1878 again and his twelve-year-long pursuit was beginning once more.

The prescription was headed, as each had always been, with the words 'From the Surgery of Roderick Greatorex, MD', printed in Times bold. Beneath this were a few lines of scrambled, jagged writing reminiscent of a seismograph readout of a medium-to-strong earthquake.

Not long after the prescriptions first began appearing, a system for interpreting the Bad Doctor's cacography had been arrived at through the combined efforts of a handwriting expert and a retired pharmacist, the latter able to draw on years of experience of unscrambling the scrawl of general practitioners. The system meant that detectives would not have to devote precious time to working out what the words themselves were and could concentrate on the prescriptions' content instead. Rattray, however, had never had any need of it. He had quickly become intimate with the scarps and fells of Greatorex's appalling penmanship, until he was able to read the prescriptions as easily as if he himself had been their author.

This one said:

To prevent three oleaginous Hellenic navigators being fatally brought to light: take diamonds to the value of 2,000 guineas and deposit in the mail coach of the noonday train to Calais.

Three oleaginous Hellenic navigators?

The next thing he knew, Rattray was chasing down avenues of thought, travelling along pathways of possibility, his mind throwing up suggestions to be sifted and assessed. He could not help himself. It was a kind of instinct, a reflex that had been cultivated over ten years and had lain dormant since but had clearly not atrophied. He actively had to stop himself trying to solve the prescription; had to call a halt to the turning of his mental cogs, throw a cutoff switch in his brain. He should not be wasting time trying to solve clues to a crime. That was not his priority. He should be concentrating on finding a way to escape this unreal dream-London.

Three oleaginous . . . ?

He tore his gaze away from the prescription. Enough! A way out of here. Think. Perhaps the aerodrome he had glimpsed from the train. Yes, maybe an airship would take him beyond the borders of this place, back to where he belonged.

The idea made no practical sense, but, then, in that regard, it suited his situation perfectly. Perhaps that was the way to tackle the eerie dream-logic of this place: by thinking in similarly dream-logical terms. At least, if nothing else, heading for the aerodrome represented a plan.

Glancing briefly at the prescription again, Rattray, for the first time since waking up on the train, remembered Kim. The causal link between her and the prescription was the prescription's contents, reminiscent in a way of Cecil's visions, which Kim was so adept at interpreting.

Rattray had left Kim in Emperor Dragon's clutches. Emperor Dragon had vowed that she would not be harmed, but there was no guarantee that he was, despite his claims, a man of his word. For Kim's sake, as well as his own, Rattray's primary objective had to be to escape.

He looked around for a hansom that could take him to the aerodrome, and as he did so he caught sight of someone striding purposefully towards him, twirling a silver-knobbed ebony cane.

The person's outfit – striped waistcoat, top hat, lilac silk cravat, lacy shirtcuffs, green carnation buttonhole – was pure *fin-de-siècle* dandy. The face was one that Rattray knew very well indeed.

And when he spoke this individual's name, his voice was a hoarse, incredulous shadow of his usual speaking voice.

'Valentina?'

26

'Piers?'

'Lucretia old girl. I'd say it was nice to hear from you, but your tone of voice leads me to suspect that you're not ringing up with good news.'

'You'd be right.'

Piers settled the coffin-handle receiver of his ornate ormolu rotary-dial telephone in the crook of his neck and began neatening up the cuticles of his right hand with the edge of his left thumbnail. 'Go on.'

'Bill called over an hour ago from Victoria Station. He was on his way to Bretherton and said he'd call me from Waterloo when he got there to confirm train times to Guildford. He hasn't.'

'Might he not have been delayed between Victoria and Waterloo?'

'For an *hour*, Piers? I doubt it.'

'Maybe he forgot to ring, then.'

'Not Bill. When he says he's going to do something, you can count on him to do it. But that's not all. It was pretty clear from what he said, or rather what he didn't say, that the action-to-suppress went badly. And I have this feeling. I don't know why, but I think Bill's in trouble. And if you dare make some offhand, chauvinistic remark about "women's intuition", Piers, I will drive up to Chelsea right now and personally give you a biff on the nose.'

Piers smiled to himself. 'My dear Lucretia, how could you say such a thing? The thought hadn't even occurred to me. Moreover, while I've always admired the greater sensitivity of the female of the species when it comes to matters of instinct, the fact is that the evidence you've presented me with would seem to be solid, logical grounds for concern. So what should we do?'

'I'm not sure. I would have called John, of course, but he's off gallivanting around Japan.'

The subtly harsh emphasis Lucretia laid on the word *gallivanting* was not lost on Piers. 'And I'm the next best thing to John,' he said.

'No offence, Piers, but he has abilities you don't.'

'Yes, we do tend to rely on our Captain Scarlet rather, don't we?'

Now it was Lucretia's turn to detect a subtext. 'And we'll continue to do so for a very long time,' she stated in such a way that there could be no doubt about the matter.

'Yes, of course,' said Piers. 'So, would you like me to go out and search for Bill?'

'He could be almost anywhere in London by now. Needle in a haystack. No, I think the best plan is if you come down to Bretherton. If Bill does manage to make it here, I'd feel better if there were more than one of us on hand to greet him. Just in case.'

'Just in case of what?'

'I don't know, Piers. Like I said, it's a feeling, that's all. And if that's not good enough for you . . .'

'No, Lucretia, a feeling will more than suffice.' Especially since something like this had been predicted in Colloquy. Danger from within. 'I'll be with you as soon as I can.'

'Thanks. Look, Piers, I'm sorry if I was a little . . . short with you just now. I'm worried, that's all.'

'Perfectly understandable, old girl. Have no fear. Piers Pearson, Freelance Facilitator, is here.'

Having replaced the receiver, Piers leapt to his feet with a clap of his hands. 'Right!' he said to Lady Grinning Soul, who was lying on the mohair rug that was spread out in front of the imitation gas-log fireplace in his living room. 'I think this calls for some undercranked-camera high-speed preparation, don't you?'

For the next five minutes Piers was a blur of motion, quickstepping from one room of the house to another as he packed an overnight bag, locked windows, donned a sheepskin flying jacket, tried on different combinations of sunglasses and neck scarves, and fetched out a couple of tins of dog food and a box of dog biscuits from a kitchen cupboard.

Up until this last activity Lady Grinning Soul had been observing him with mild interest, one eyebrow idly raised, but as soon as she heard the familiar chunky clunking of the dog-food tins and the rattle of the biscuit box she lifted her head alertly and got to her feet. Seeing her master getting ready to leave, she had thought that she was going to be left in the house for a while, perhaps in the company of one of her master's ladyfriends who, though they adored her and petted her and spoiled her rotten, were no substitute for the man himself. Now, however, food sounds were being made and it was nowhere near mealtime, which could mean only one thing. Her master was taking her on a trip with him!

Lady's tail began to swish to and fro as Piers, slowing to normal pace again, approached her carrying certain familiar buckled leather accessories.

'Come on then, Lady,' he said. 'There's no time to arrange a babysitter for you, so you'd best get your travelling togs on.'

A couple of minutes later, with a *blatt* of unmuffled exhaust, Piers's canary-yellow Caterham 7 convertible raced out from its garage into the cobblestoned mews in which Piers lived, with Piers at the wheel and Lady Grinning Soul in the passenger seat beside him. Both were wearing matching flying helmets and goggles, and Lady sat with her muzzle raised above the level of the Caterham's windscreen, her nose in the air, her tongue lolling deliriously and her fur flowing, as her master steered the roadster through the streets of south-west London towards the Guardians' Surrey headquarters.

27

'Bill MacGowan, what in God's name are you doing here?'

Sarah's tone was partly bemused and partly aghast. MacGowan, in defensive mood, heard only the latter.

'I have a reason,' he said.

Had, Bill, he told himself. *Had* a reason. Only you can't really remember what it is and you're not sure if it was much of a reason in the first place.

'But, Bill . . .' Sarah's face writhed with conflicting emotions. 'We haven't spoken, haven't seen each other in Christ knows how long! And now you just *turn up* like this, out of the blue?'

She had cut her hair short. The long lion's mane of blonde curls was gone. Now she had what amounted to a short back and sides. MacGowan was of the opinion that short hair looked good on very few women, making them appear too masculine for his liking. Short hair had not done any favours for Kim Basinger or Sharon Stone, to name but two, and it did not do much for Sarah. When had she had it cut off? Shortly after the divorce? As a kind of symbolic gesture? She had known how much he liked her hair being long.

'Bill.' Her voice had softened. She took a step forward, letting go of the hand of the man with her. 'Are you all right? I mean, not to put too fine a point on it, but you look like death.'

MacGowan ignored the remark and turned his attention to Sarah's companion. He was not a particularly tall bloke and his carrot-coloured hair was shaved Number Two short all over for that I'm-not-really-going-bald look. He had a kind of wistful, limpid face – sensitive behind his wire-framed spectacles – and he was dressed in a black polo-neck, jeans with the cuffs turned up, and Dr Martens. North London arts-and-media type, MacGowan decided. Probably one of those middle-class Arsenal fucking supporters as well.

'Who's this?' he said to Sarah, jabbing a finger in media-man's direction.

Sarah bristled at the way in which he had spoken the question. Proprietorially. As if, after all this time, he still had some claim on her.

'This, Bill, is Tim. Tim Andrews, this is Bill. My *ex*-husband.'

That 'ex' had spikes on it.

Andrews reached out manfully to shake MacGowan's hand. 'Bill,' he said. 'Sarah's told me a lot about you.' His tone was neutral, but his eyes glittered behind his spectacles. Smug. Telling MacGowan who was Sarah's stud now.

'Piss off, wankstain,' MacGowan said.

That wiped the smugness from Andrews's face. His hand dropped.

'Bill—' Sarah began.

MacGowan interrupted her. 'You two married, then?'

'It's none of your business whether we are or not, Bill,' Sarah said frostily. 'And you have no right to come just barging in here and start asking questions like—'

'I haven't barged in anywhere.'

'You know what I mean.'

'Well, you should choose your words more carefully.'

'Bill, why are you being so aggressive? You're the one who's in the wrong here. In fact, you really shouldn't be here at all.'

'Aren't you glad to see me?'

'Not like this I'm not, no. You've been drinking, haven't you?'

'No.'

'Don't lie, Bill. You know, I'd heard though the grapevine that you'd given up. Cleaned up your act. Obviously the rumours were wrong.'

'I have *not* been drinking!' he yelled, taking a step towards her.

Sarah did not flinch. She stood firm. 'Please, Bill. Go. It doesn't matter why you came. Just go. Leave. I don't want to see you.'

Andrews stepped forward, moving close to Sarah to offer moral support. 'Yes, Bill,' he said. 'I think you should do as she says. Sarah's got a new life now. You're not a part of it.'

'Shut it, twat.' MacGowan raised a fist.

'Bill!'

Sarah was furious now, but MacGowan kept his attention fixed on Andrews. He remembered thumping the bonnet of the Fiat that had nearly run him down. That had been cool, putting a dent in that Italian sardine-can and then just strolling on. And he remembered, too, how good it had felt to beat up that beggar at Embankment. Mistake or not, he had enjoyed smashing the guy's face in. Kicking the crap out of this carrot-topped tosser in front of him would be just as much fun, if not more.

No. No, what was he thinking? What was wrong with him? Andrews had done nothing to deserve a beating. He was guilty of being Sarah's boyfriend and a bit of a prat, but these were not offences that merited violence.

'Listen, Bill,' Andrews said. There was a slight quaver in his voice, but he was doing everything he could to sound rational and calm. 'There's no need for fighting. I'm sure we can sort this out like grown-up, sensible people.'

'Tim, don't,' Sarah warned. 'Leave this to me.'

'I've always believed, Sarah,' Andrews said loftily, 'that whatever the circumstances, violence can always be overcome by reason.'

MacGowan had been on the point of lowering his fist, but this last comment, for some reason, pressed all the wrong buttons. What a load of pious old toss! That kind of statement was just asking to be disproved.

And, lunging at Andrews, MacGowan did exactly that.

It was brief and it was brutal, and it culminated in MacGowan holding Andrews's head above the sharp tip of one of the railings, shoving down, trying to impale him through the ear. Andrews was resisting with all his might, struggling and screaming, and Sarah was pounding at MacGowan's arms and shoulders and back, begging him, telling him, *commanding* him to let Andrews go. Anger and joy surged through MacGowan in a volcanic rush. The blood and fear on Andrews's face were intoxicating, an aphrodisiac. He roared with ecstatic glee.

He scarcely noticed when Sarah stopped hitting him. However, he had no choice but to notice when, a few seconds later, something hard and heavy struck him on the side of the head with stunning, concussive force.

He reeled sideways, relinquishing his grip on Andrews. Clutching his head, he rounded on Sarah, who was standing on the pavement, legs apart, panting. Her eyes were startled-wide, as if she had surprised herself by her own actions. In both hands she was holding an economy-size tin of chickpeas, badly dented. The shopping bag, which had provided her with this weapon, was at her feet, open.

MacGowan took his hand away from his head and examined it. There was blood on his fingers. Not just Andrews's. His own.

He could hardly believe it. Sarah had made him bleed. She had whacked him with a can of chickpeas and made him *bleed*. How dare she!

With a savage grunt he brought his gaze to bear on his ex-wife again, while, from somewhere to his right, he heard Andrews slump against the railings with a groan.

Bitch, he thought. Fucking bitch. Trying to brain me with two pounds of fart-fodder. I'll teach *her* a lesson . . .

Sarah's expression shifted. She saw what was in MacGowan's eyes and her look of startlement turned to plain fear.

That was good. MacGowan liked what the fear did to her face. He thought it would be a thrill to wrap his hands around her throat and throttle her – see what *that* did to her face.

He raised his hands. Tensed, ready to attack.

'Bill . . .' Sarah said, in a soft and very scared voice.

MacGowan hesitated.

Her eyes were glistening. 'Bill, I'm sorry,' was all she said.

And something that was dwindling inside MacGowan, slowly dying, gave a last valiant flutter.

He blinked.

He had been about to attack her. He, who had never laid a finger on her or any woman. He, who thought men who beat their wives or girlfriends were the scum of the earth. He had been so consumed by rage that he had been about to attack *Sarah*? It was almost inconceivable.

Shame flooded through him. Christ. What could he say that would make amends? Nothing. Nothing he could say, nothing he could do, could make up for that kind of behaviour. He was the lowest of the low. He was beneath contempt.

He lowered his hands. He turned. He loped off down the street. Sarah called out his name once, but he kept going all the way to the end of the street without looking back. Turned the corner. Kept going.

28

'Quickly now,' said the dandy who looked and spoke exactly like Valentina Aleksandrovna Popkova. 'We must hurry.'

Rattray, dumbfounded, did not move.

'Please, John,' Valentina insisted. 'I understand that this is a shock, but we have to get moving. We have to get you out of here. I will try to explain everything as we go.'

It was her. Despite the man's outfit, it was definitely her. That accent, curling like a cat around the back-of-the-throat consonants. That stalwart, somewhat pudgy jawline, identical to the jawline of the man reputed to have been her father, Tsar Alexander III himself. Those tawny-verging-on-yellow eyes which, for two years of Rattray's life, had gazed on him, first with approval, then compassion, and finally love. Standing before him, dressed in male drag, in this strange, impossible London, a strange and impossible sight herself – Valentina, exactly as he remembered her.

'You *are* Valentina, aren't you?' said Rattray, as the drag dandy took him by the arm and led him across to the edge of the plaza.

'In one sense, yes,' she replied. 'In another sense, no. It's somewhat complicated.' She raised her cane. 'Cab!'

A passing hansom clattered to a halt alongside them.

'In,' she said to Rattray, with an ushering gesture.

As Rattray climbed obediently aboard, Valentina

instructed to the driver to take them to Victoria and Albert Park.

'The Marionette Gallery?' the driver enquired.

'That will do.'

Valentina hauled herself in, sat down beside Rattray and closed the doors in front of their legs. The hansom rolled off.

Pointing to the Bad Doctor's prescription, which Rattray was still holding in his hand, Valentina said, 'Let me put you out of your misery. "Three oleaginous Hellenic navigators". The Ancient Greek for navigator is "gubernater", from which the English word "governor" is derived.'

'Then this has something to do with the Governors' Conference,' Rattray said, with a nod at the prescription.

'It does. And as for "oleaginous" – well, some would argue that the adjective might be fairly applied to almost any individual in a position of political power, but in this case the oiliness referred to is not to do with behaviour but with natural resources. Three of the governor-generals who are over here for the conference preside over regions where crude oil is produced: the Arab Protectorates, the States of Columbia and the North Russian Territories. Those three have been abducted and are, at this very moment, in peril of their lives. "Fatally brought to light". There is no way you could know this yet, but illumination at the Greenhouse Palace is provided by giant reflecting mirrors, which swivel on motorised gymbals to reflect the sun.'

'I saw a big glass building on the way in.'

'That, indeed, is the Greenhouse Palace. And the governor-generals are, even as we speak, lying bound and gagged up on the gantries that run between the mirrors. When the sun comes out—'

'As it's supposed to this afternoon.'

Valentina nodded. 'They will be slowly roasted alive. Unless, of course, the ransom is paid. As the message says, diamonds to the value of 2,000 guineas are to be placed in the mail coach of one of the cross-Channel trains. The kidnappers plan to take the diamonds and leap off the train as it passes over the Trans-Channel Bridge. Parachutes will see them safely down to the sea's surface, where they'll be picked up by a waiting submersible.'

'And I was supposed to work all this out and foil the kidnappers' plot.'

'Yes. It is a sort of game, you see.'

'A game? People's lives are at stake.'

'No, they are not. None of this is real, John. Do you not see that? None of this exists. This place, the people in it – it is all an artefact, an artificial construct.'

Rattray paused to let this sink in. 'Constructed by whom?'

'Partly by your enemies and partly by yourself.'

'*I* helped make this? But that can't be. I've always been against imperialism, and this place, as far as I can see, is a British imperialist's utopia.'

'The setting was created by another, but the inhabitants and the events that occur here are all your own work.'

'Even the Bad Doctor's prescription and the crime pertaining to it?'

'Even that.'

'This is fantastic,' Rattray said, using the word in its most literal sense. He shook his head, as though by doing so he could shuffle loosened brain-parts back into alignment, but it did not seem to make any difference. 'So where do *you* fit in here, Valentina? Are you an artificial construct as well?'

'Not exactly. I am that part of you that helps defend you against attacks. That part whose task it is to heal you and keep you safe.'

'You're—' Rattray hesitated. It seemed absurd, yet he could not think that she meant anything else. 'You're my immune system?'

'A manifestation of it, yes. I originate from the region of your subconscious that autonomically oversees the constant, regular maintenance of your body and carries out repairs without being asked to. I am its avatar, in a sense.'

235

'And you've come to me in the guise of Valentina Popkova because . . . ?'

'Because mine are a face and voice you instinctively trust,' came the reply.

There was no denying that. Rattray could not think of any other person whom he would have obeyed as automatically, as unhesitatingly, as he had her.

'So why are you taking me to Victoria and Albert Park?' he asked.

'Because it is my job to look after you, and in this instance looking after you means getting you out of here. There is a "back door", so to speak, in the park. A point of access from the outside world that also serves as an exit.'

An exit. A way out of this insane, implausible place. The thought that he might never be able to escape, that he might be trapped here for ever, was not one that Rattray had permitted himself to entertain, even though it had been there, hovering at the back of his mind, almost from the moment he had woken up and found himself on the train. A feeling like claustrophobia, he had been steadfastly suppressing it until now, at first burying it in the belief that he was wandering through some bizarre, hyperreal dream-realm and then sublimating it with his resolution to discover a means of getting back to Kim. Logic quelling panic. Now that he knew that escape *was* possible, however, he was able to admit that he had been scared and at the same time dismiss the fear. Relieved of this unacknowledged burden, he felt in command of himself once more, no longer a victim of events. He had recovered the phlegmatic self-possession that, more than his quick brain and his near-indestructible body, was, in his view, his greatest asset.

The hansom was nearing a pair of imposing wrought-iron gates. On one was a representation of Queen Victoria, on the other Prince Albert, monarch and royal consort both picked out in brightly coloured enamelled relief and both ten times larger than life. The gates were shut fast, but the hansom passed through an open archway to the side, entering a park that resembled Hyde Park, only lusher and more expansive, its lawns and groves and gravelled pathways reaching as far as the eye could see.

Rattray turned to his companion again. 'I last imagined I saw you when I was in the Nevada desert,' he said. 'I thought I was dreaming. Was that *you* then, or was it another Valentina?'

Valentina smiled in the way he had always remembered her smiling. Furtively. As if smiling went against her better judgement. 'It was and it wasn't,' she said. 'Remember your Jung, John. Animus and anima.'

Rattray thought hard for a moment. He had never been much of a one for Jung. 'So you're not just my subconscious, you're the feminine component of my personality – is that what you're saying?'

She nodded. 'The real Valentina and I share many traits. That is why you and she were so compatible.'

'No,' said Rattray, shaking his head ferociously. 'No, no, this is altogether too mystical for my tastes.'

The dandy Valentina laughed. 'Yes. You have always denied that side of life. You, who works for a race of mysterious, unseen beings, yet will not believe that there are also mysteries – greater ones – that lie within the human soul.'

'Who doesn't even believe that there is such a thing as a soul.'

'Well, you are entitled to your opinion,' Valentina said. Her expression and voice turned sly. 'I didn't *have* to appear to you as Valentina, you know, John,' she said. 'Perhaps you would have preferred it if I had come as that young Oriental girl, Kim.'

'So now you're implying . . . ?'

'Nothing,' said Valentina, feigning stony-faced seriousness. 'Nothing at all.' Her expression went sly again. 'But she likes you very much, I think.'

'There's nothing going on between us. We're colleagues.'

'You could do with a woman in your life.'

237

'Arguably so, but what woman could do with being in my life? What I am, what I do – it wouldn't be fair to inflict that on another person.'

'But it was fair on me?'

'Are you speaking as my anima now or as Valentina?'

'Either. Both.'

'That was different, back then. I was younger. My role as a Guardian was less . . . established. Besides, how can I consider the idea of long-term involvement with someone, knowing that she will age and die and I won't?'

'Who said anything about long term?' said Valentina. 'I am merely suggesting that you should admit to yourself that you like this Kim girl. You like her for her mind, and her body quietly interests you, too.'

'Valentina, I'm old enough to be her' – he performed a swift mental calculation – 'great-great-great-grandfather.'

'That is true. But it is not an insurmountable problem.' Valentina tapped his shin with her cane. 'Think about what I have said, at any rate, John.'

'As long as I have *you* lodged in my subconscious, I fear I don't have any choice.'

'Quite,' said Valentina, with a slow, sublime blink of her tawny-yellow eyes.

The rain was letting up and the sun was beginning to shine glassily through the cloud cover as the hansom drew to a halt outside a one-storey building which the driver announced as their destination, the Marionette Gallery. The gallery had high arched windows and was adorned on top with Gothic spires, onion domes, minarets, pagoda roofs and various other architectural motifs from around the world. The mishmash of styles was clearly intended to commemorate the ubiquity of the British Empire, but the overall effect was cluttered and somewhat vulgar.

Valentina and Rattray stepped down from the hansom. Valentina tossed a shilling to the driver, who caught the coin smartly. Then she gently steered Rattray away from the gallery, towards which he had begun walking, and onto a path that bypassed the building.

'We're not going to see the marionettes, then?' he said.

'What for? To look at a few scenes from imperial history acted out by mechanical puppets? "Gordon's Glorious Repulse of the Arabs at Khartoum"? "Burton and Speke's Conquest of the Antarctic"? "The Bombing of Bombay"? A waste of time. *There* is where we are going.' She pointed to a broad stretch of water, not quite a lake, not quite a river, a hundred yards ahead. Its surface gleamed placidly in the emerging sunshine. 'The Serpentine.'

They walked towards the Serpentine arm-in-arm, on the way encountering a middle-aged married couple promenading, also arm-in-arm; an elderly, red-faced gentleman taking a brisk midday constitutional; a triumvirate of nannies pushing prams; and two parents accompanied by their children – a young daughter in pantalets and frock, twirling a hoop along with a stick, and a slightly younger son in a Little Lord Fauntleroy suit, who was absorbed by some kind of handheld electric puzzle housed in tin. They must have made for an unusual-looking pair, the dandy and the sober-suited middle-aged gentleman, but no one they passed offered them anything more than a polite 'good day' and a tip of the hat or a wave with a rolled-up umbrella. Certainly no one looked askance at Valentina, but, then, Rattray recalled, even in the real world (wherever *that* was) Valentina had always been able to pull off a male disguise convincingly. Her features were boyish, and she could convincingly adopt a masculine gait as swaggering as the next man's. He recalled, too, that she had been the match of any man when it came to holding her drink and holding her own in a fight. But he had seen her feminine side as well. In private, intimate moments, Valentina had revealed herself capable of ineffable tenderness.

He missed her still, he realised, even after a hundred years. The entity beside him, whom he was content to accept was not Valentina, only made him the more acutely aware of the impact the genuine Valentina had had on his life. Not only had she been responsible for his becoming a Guardian, she had opened up a side of himself

239

that had thitherto been closed to him. As a policeman he had had just one mistress, the Law, and to her he had been faultlessly faithful. Then Valentina had come along and brought an end to the monk-like existence he had been leading . . . and then, two years later, she had gone again, and the extraordinary flowering she had effected within him had withered with her departure, and he had thrown himself relentlessly, singlemindedly, and with a certain guilty relief, into the duties of Guardianship.

But maybe she was right, this anima-creature walking beside him. Maybe, after a century, it was time he opened himself up to that side of life again. Let the withered flower bloom once more. Maybe.

The path they were on led them towards a granite bridge that traversed the Serpentine in a series of low spans. As they neared the bridge, Valentina said, 'Whatever happens now, John, your task is escaping. Do not be concerned for me. I am no less illusory than everything else here. No matter how it appears, I cannot be harmed. Do you understand that?'

'Inasmuch as I don't have a clue what you're talking about, no,' Rattray replied. 'But I trust you.'

'That is all that I can hope for.' Valentina patted his forearm. 'When we reach the bridge, you must jump. There will be a defence mechanism, a sentry, whose purpose is to prevent you entering the water by whatever means it can. Let me deal with it. You must concentrate on getting yourself into the Serpentine. Once you are fully immersed, you will no longer be here.'

'All right. So do we say our goodbyes now?'

'No need, John,' Valentina said, with another of those furtive smiles. 'We're never really parted.'

She unlinked their arms and, grasping her ebony cane halfway along its length with her left hand and by its silver knob with her right, drew the cane apart to reveal a straight steel sword. Having discarded the sheath portion of the cane, she whisked the sword through the air in a series of swift practice patterns. The sword's blade flickered mercurially in the burgeoning sunlight.

'Well,' she said to Rattray, '*I'm* ready. How about you?'

Rattray glanced ahead at the bridge, whose flagstoned roadway was free of pedestrians, deserted. He nodded, and together he and Valentina strode forward.

No sooner had they set foot on the bridge than the Serpentine's smooth surface started to bulge and roil as something immense began to rise from below, looming up as though from great depths – something with a thick, long body that glimmered greenly in the lead-grey waters.

Rearing abruptly from the Serpentine on a great surge of seething foam, the creature raised its head skyward. Its head, perched on a scaly neck as broad as an oak trunk, was as big as a caravan and had beachball-sized ruby eyes and a gold-rimmed maw filled with fangs, which the creature exposed in all their manifold, sickle-shaped glory as it let out an ear-shattering roar.

Rattray recognised the creature immediately as a vast Japanese dragon, Emperor Dragon's online symbol magnified to monstrous proportions. Its roar was as loud as a clap of thunder detonating directly overhead.

The dragon towered over him and Valentina, water pouring off its body in freshets, the Serpentine churning around it. Its jewelled gaze was pitiless and wild. One three-taloned paw emerged from the water and grasped the parapet of the bridge. Then, without warning, the dragon lunged at the two humans, its head descending at a terrific velocity, fangs bared.

Valentina shoved Rattray one way and leapt the other, and the dragon's jaws slammed shut on empty air between its intended targets, missing both of them by inches.

Valentina rolled nimbly to her feet as the dragon drew back its head for a second attack. Her top hat had fallen off, revealing her pinned-up hair. Rattray picked himself up, too, and prepared to shift into his accelerated mode, all neurons firing at ultraspeed, muscle-twitch responses sharpened to an uncanny degree. His plan was to sweep both himself and Valentina to safety, but Valentina,

241

realising what he was about to do, shouted, 'John! No! You must jump!'

Rattray hesitated, and the dragon swooped for him, butting him with its snout, sending him crashing to the flagstones. The dragon's head glowered over him, eyes aglow with a vermilion inner light. It opened its mouth, and Rattray glimpsed flames fomenting deep within its throat, rising up towards its tongue like fiery, lambent vomit. He began scrambling frantically backwards on all fours, and then Valentina came charging in from the side, sword levelled.

Rattray would not have thought that the sword's slender blade – like a sewing needle to the dragon – could have pierced the dragon's jade-scaled hide. Valentina, however, sank the weapon into the beast's neck up to its hilt, and when she withdrew it, dark crimson blood spurted from the wound.

The dragon wrenched away, bellowing in pain and shaking its head, and Valentina grabbed Rattray by the arm and hauled him to his feet.

'What did I say?' she yelled. 'Do not be concerned for me. You must get off the bridge and into the water. Now go!'

The next instant she was knocked off her feet, swept flat by a swipe from the dragon's paw. The dragon then stamped on her, enclosing her in a cage of its talons. One of its claws penetrated her left shoulder, skewering her in place. Screaming with agony and indignation, Valentina brought her sword up and slashed at the underside of the paw, but though she repeatedly drew blood, the dragon ignored her, focusing its attention on Rattray, who was backing away across the bridge to its further parapet.

Valentina kept slashing at the paw and at the same time urged Rattray to hurry, to leave her, not to worry about her. He hated the idea of abandoning her, but he had to trust that she had been telling the truth. She could not be hurt. She was not real.

Reluctantly he turned and sprinted for the parapet.

He reached it just as the dragon opened its mouth wide

and unleashed a jet of flame at him. The flame roared towards him as he scrambled up onto the parapet. He felt heat reaching for him, as though a furnace door had been opened. Orange billows of fire surrounded him, their crackle drowning out Valentina's desperate exhortations, as he launched himself into the air.

There was a moment when he thought he might have been too slow. He heard the sound of singeing. Smelled burning.

Then the surface of the Serpentine leapt up to greet him, and he plunged into the water.

Which was neither cold nor warm.

Which was not wet.

A zone of silence.

Toneless.

Neutral.

Dead.

29

Neither running nor walking, but at a loose, loping pace somewhere in between, MacGowan hiked through London in a southerly-tending arc. He travelled, not by street-knowledge but by instinct, following his inner compass. The boroughs he crossed and the city landmarks he passed meant nothing to him. The street signs with their names and their postcode suffixes – NW1, W9, W2, W14, SW6 – might as well have been written in Serbo-Croat for all he cared. Pedestrians were merely obstacles to be circumnavigated. He had set out with no particular direction in mind, his only goal to put distance between himself and Sarah, but now his one concern, the thought that overrode all others, his imperative impulse, was *Get to Bretherton Grange.*

He crossed the Thames at Putney, skirted the rim of Wimbledon Common and headed into the suburban hinterlands of Morden and Surbiton, still maintaining his steady, semi-jogging speed. After his experiences earlier that day, he had no desire to take public transport again. This method of travel – on foot – seemed altogether simpler, purer, cleaner. Besides, he did not appear to be tiring, or at least, if his limbs and lungs *were* starting to feel the strain, he was not conscious of it. He felt like a machine, or a force of nature, inexhaustible, relentless, with a well of limitless energy within him from which to draw. Time passing was something he was no longer aware of, except in the form of the lowering of the afternoon sun, which seemed to occur in fits and starts – whenever he happened to glance up at the sky, the sun had changed position. And one thought chimed through his brain like a dinner bell, summoning him on: Bretherton Grange.

The two days and nights he had spent adrift in the Iraqi desert must have been like this. He had no clear recollection of the long, meandering journey he had made back then. His memory had stored it as a kaleidoscope of impressionistic images – sunburn, blisters, sips of water from the rapidly depleting supply in his canteen, brief rest stops, pain, hunger, thirst, endless horizons of flat bedrock plains, the agonising subzero cold of night and walking, walking, walking. Then, however, as now, it had all been about purpose, a goal. Then: the Saudi border. Now: Bretherton Grange.

A translucent early moon appeared in the sky, like a fingernail-paring on a blue-grey carpet. The sun was low and MacGowan was nearing the M25. Still he did not feel tired, although he remained aware of the numerous small aches and pains all over his body that he had first felt back in Camden. One leg of his jeans felt too tight. One of his Berghaus walking boots seemed a better fit than the other. His jersey had become snug around the chest. But all these discomforts were minor. He had suffered worse in the past. On he went towards Bretherton Grange.

The suburbs gave way to a series of villages and small towns. At one point, a carload of youths hurtled past him. He must have looked a bit of a state – what with a slight limp thanks to the ill-fitting boot and one side of his face caked with dried blood from the wound Sarah had inflicted – because the passengers in the car started flicking V-signs and jeering at him out of the windows, while the driver honked the horn. He would have killed them all. Had he had a 66 rocket launcher with him, he would have blown their car clean off the road. Had they been on foot, he would have slaughtered them with his bare hands. It would have delayed him only briefly on his long, remorseless trek to Bretherton Grange.

Onward into dusk he went, across London's orbital motorway via an A-road bridge, onward into the wilds of Surrey. Still he did not feel tired. His body remained strong. He felt like he could keep this pace up for ever, walk halfway around the world if he wanted, without pausing, without once breaking his stride, his arms swinging limberly, leg muscles pumping. He had pretty much forgotten why he had originally set out for Bretherton. Perpetual forward motion, footfall after footfall, had drummed the reason out of his brain. But in its place there was a new reason, a new conviction in him, a new purpose. A seed of an idea, sown earlier that day, had germinated in his mind while he was travelling through London, and now the idea was breaking into full bloom. There was, he saw now, only one explanation for the abysmal failure of the Seal Point action-to-suppress. He would surely have realised it earlier, had it not been for the headache and the hassles he had experienced in London – the beggar/mugger, the confusion over Tube trains – and then the confrontation with Sarah and that Tim person in Camden. There was only one way to explain why the Anarch mercenaries could have been expecting him and his team. Only one way to explain how they could have picked his men off so easily. Like the Codename: Bearskin mission, the action-to-suppress had been a set-up. And it was obvious who was responsible. And that was why he was making his way to Bretherton Grange.

Twilight and country roads. Hedgerows rustling with animal activity. The last gloaming gleaming of the sun on the western horizon. His destination was near now, the miles to Bretherton counting down on signposts he did not need to consult. His feet were beginning to grow sore, but he kept striding. Stars were coming out overhead, hanging crystalline alongside the fingernail moon. How far had he come? A good thirty klicks at least. Hard tabbing. Fast. Some kind of a record, maybe. What he had been trained for all those years ago at Stirling Lines and in the jungles of Belize. No bergen to carry, mind you. No weapon, either.

But still, impressive. And now he was entering Bretherton Village – a sleepy hamlet, one pub, one post-office-cum-corner-shop, a duck pond surrounded by weeping willows, all very sodding picturesque. Half a mile to go. Half a mile to Bretherton Grange.

Into the dark depths of a lampless rural lane. Night wind and stubbly, recently harvested cornfields. A fence, then a high brick wall. The perimeter of the estate. And soon, the gates. And through the bars of the gates, just visible at the far end of the driveway, windows ablaze, the distant building. He had arrived. Bretherton Grange.

All at once MacGowan felt exhausted, as though his body had been holding out till this moment, refusing to succumb to weakness until it had got him to where he wanted to be. He was enveloped by tiredness, almost a physical weight dragging on him. Suddenly all of his limbs were aching and all his clothing was constricting him, as though somehow everything he was wearing had shrunk a couple of sizes. He was hungry, too, although not desperately so.

He weighed up the alternatives and came to a conclusion. Now was not the time to go marching into the Grange, he decided. He needed to rest up. Wait till first light. Then he would go in.

Opposite the gates, on the other side of the lane, there was a small beech copse. The trees still retained much of their summer coverage. The copse would make for a good lying-up position. MacGowan stretched himself out in the middle of it, still within view of the gates. He made himself comfortable on the ground and heaped a blanket of fallen leaves over him for warmth. Surrounded by the rustling of the tree branches and other countryside sounds – small creatures scrabbling through the undergrowth, the occasional far-off screech of a barn owl or eerie bark of a vixen – he settled down to sleep.

He was looking forward to seeing Lucretia again.

He was looking forward to killing her.

PART 4

30

The flight attendant, the very epitome of the petite, chic Frenchwoman, presented the young oriental couple in First Class with their dinner menus.

The young oriental woman set the menu down in her lap without so much as glancing at it, but the young man next to her, whom it was reasonable to assume was her boyfriend, said *merci* to the flight attendant and eagerly fell to perusing the list of hors d'oeuvres and entrées.

From their behaviour during the flight so far, it was clear to the flight attendant that the young couple had had an argument – a lovers' tiff – prior to leaving Tokyo, and that discord was still simmering between them. One noticed these things in First Class, where one had fewer passengers to look after and the passengers, consequently, were individuals and not, as in Economy, cattle. Since embarkation two hours earlier, the young woman had had little to say to her boyfriend, greeting each of his conversational overtures with a few terse remarks followed by stony silence. Evidently he had done something to displease her, and she was making him pay for it. The scratch-marks on the young woman's chin and hands might or might not have been evidence of domestic violence, but whatever their origin they were clearly doing nothing to improve her disposition.

Never mind, thought the flight attendant as she moved on to the next row of seats. A holiday in Paris – for that was surely the purpose of the young couple's journey –

would help them sort things out. A few days in the world capital of romance, and they would soon put past disagreements behind them and kiss and make up.

Kissing and making up with Emperor Dragon was, of course, something Kim had no intention of doing. Killing and maiming him, maybe. Hurting him in some way, certainly. But kissing and making up? That was surely the furthest thing from her mind.

'French airlines are reputed to have the best in-flight cuisine,' Emperor Dragon announced. 'Not the hardest field in the world to excel in, I admit, but really, the food is supposed to be very good.' He pointed at the menu. 'I'm torn. I don't know which to choose, the *poulet au poivre* or the *boeuf bourguignon*. What are you going to have?'

'Screw you,' Kim replied in English.

Emperor Dragon squinted at the menu. 'No, I don't see that here,' he said, still using Japanese. 'Is that some Cantonese dish?'

Kim rewarded the witticism with a sarcastic sneer.

'Honestly, Kimiko.' Emperor Dragon shook his head in a parody of weary exasperation. 'Why the attitude? What have you got to complain about? Your *gaijin* friend is alive and well, and you, as long as you behave yourself, will not be harmed in any way. You're getting a free first-class trip to Paris.' He said this like a gameshow host informing a contestant of the prize he has won. 'So why not relax and enjoy the ride?'

Kim remained silent. There were several questions she wanted to ask Emperor Dragon, but she was reluctant to give him further opportunity to mock and patronise her.

She knew by now who he was. At customs he had produced two passports, one for her, one for himself. Hers was a forgery, but it was his that she had been more interested in. As he had passed it to the customs official, she had craned her neck and, by peering over his shoulder, had, unbeknownst to him, glimpsed the name inside.

And everything had fallen into place. How he knew her

family name. The veiled references he had made to their previous acquaintance.

Even now, more than two hours later, she was amazed at herself for not having recognised him sooner. Not that knowing the real identity of the man sitting next to her and his erstwhile connection with her would have done anything to improve the situation, but it did at least give her an additional reason to hate him.

A person's face could change considerably in the course of a few years, not least when those years covered the span from adolescence to early maturity. And, of course, the tinted contacts had thrown her off. In Emperor Dragon's case, however, the changes in his features were not simply physical. They were behavioural as well. The personality that animated his face had altered significantly. When she had first known him, the teenage boy who would become Emperor Dragon had been unintelligent and self-obsessed. The self-obsession remained, but the young man beside her was, loath though she was to admit it, anything but unintelligent.

Back when she had known Emperor Dragon at high school, he had been plain old Jun Shirow, the school baseball star. Neither inclined nor encouraged to be academic, Jun had boasted the highest batting average in the school's history, as well as the highest turnover in girlfriends. Never a star pupil, he had compensated for what he lacked in the brains department with good looks, a good physique and a good chat-up technique. He was one of those people who never seem to have to strive for anything, to whom everything comes effortlessly. He made success on the baseball diamond look easy. He made being charming look easy, too.

And Kim had been charmed by him. Oh, had she been charmed!

To begin with, she had been just one of many at school who knew little of Jun other than his face and his reputation. She had considered him handsome, but, then, there were few of her contemporaries at school who *didn't* fancy Jun, including several members of his own

253

sex. So, in this respect, Kim was just one of many, and by the same token Jun was just one of a number of boys whom she admired from afar but was too nervous, too unsure of herself, ever to approach. Besides, it was a large school, and academically she and Jun were poles apart, she a fast-stream student, he slow-stream. Hence there was little opportunity for them to meet.

The first instance of direct contact between them occurred one day when she and Jun happened to be approaching each other in an otherwise deserted corridor of the school. It was late afternoon. Most other pupils had gone home, but Kim was working in the school library, while Jun was serving out a detention for poor grades. The moment Kim saw who it was that was coming towards her, she shrank against the wall and buried her face in the armful of books she was carrying, trying to make herself as small and innocuous as possible. Jun duly walked by without appearing even to register her presence. However, as he passed, Kim saw a sheet of blank paper slip out of the ring-bound exercise folder that he was dangling loosely from his right hand, as if to symbolise how casual his grasp of learning was.

Breathlessly, scarce able to believe her own audacity, Kim bent down, retrieved the sheet of paper from the floor and, in a hoarse, halting voice, called out Jun's name. Jun stopped and turned, and Kim held up the sheet of paper and explained that he had dropped it. He peered at her for a moment, blinking slowly – unsure what to make of her, it seemed. Then, with a courteous statement of gratitude, he told her that she should keep the sheet of paper if she wanted to. She was welcome to it. He had no need of it.

It was such an inconsequential thing for him to have done, not even a gesture of generosity, really – more one of indifference. Yet he accompanied it with such a warm, gracious smile, such a twinkle in his eye, that in that moment, against all her instincts, against her better judgement, Kim fell for him. Hard.

For weeks thereafter she nurtured her crush on Jun in

secret. Sometimes it was like a foetus inside her, something that was wonderful to be carrying, something to gloat over and protect. Other times it was a parasite that caused her pain and put her off her food and leached her strength. Either way, it was always there, constant, inexpressible, and ever-developing.

The ridiculous fantasies she had! That Jun would come up to her in the refectory one lunchtime and ask to share her table. That Jun would beg her help with a problem in maths or computer sciences, her strong subjects, and this would be a pretext for them getting to know each other better. That Jun would invite her out on a date and take her to a burger restaurant, and all her classmates would happen to pass by while she and Jun were sharing a milkshake with two straws, and her classmates would see them together through the window and go green with envy. That Jun would publicly dedicate the school baseball team's next victory – in which he, it went without saying, would have played an instrumental role – to Kimiko Harada, his best girl. That Jun would be the one who, with a tenderness and sensitivity that he kept hidden from the rest of the world, relieved her of her virginity.

She remembered how, once her infatuation took hold, she started attending baseball games, having hitherto been indifferent to the sport. How she began positioning herself within Jun's line of sight in the refectory at lunchtime, just in case he might chance to look up and catch her eye. How she composed endless notes and letters to him, intending to pass them to him but never plucking up the courage to do so. How she even hung on to the blank sheet of paper that had fallen from his folder, keeping it stowed in a drawer at home and taking it out every so often to hold and gaze at reverentially, as though it were some holy relic – something Jun had touched, something he had selflessly bestowed on her. It made her blush, even now, to recall the things she had done as a result of her girlish fixation on Jun, the lengths she had gone to in the hope of getting him to notice her.

The vain hope. Thick-bespectacled, bushy-eyebrowed,

pigtailed, awkward, nerdy, shy, Kim was way, way beneath Jun's notice. She was not even a blip on his radar. Jun went out with flighty, flirty, sexy girls, the kind of girls who dared to wear make-up to school, the kind who smoked cigarettes in the lavatories between lessons and often skipped school. Kim was plain-featured and a hard worker, good at her studies, someone who abided by the rules. She was the absolute antithesis of the type of girl Jun preferred.

The crush would probably have run its course, dwindled away of its own accord, had Kim not told her friend Michiko about it. She would never have mentioned it to anyone at all if Michiko had not first confessed her own interest in Jun. Then it seemed to Kim that she had found a fellow sufferer, a sympathetic ear, someone who knew and understood what she was going through, someone with whom she could share her passion, and so she admitted everything to Michiko, everything she felt about Jun, all the silly things her feelings had prompted her to do. She immediately made Michiko swear an oath that she would not breathe a word of what she had just been told to anyone, and Michiko agreed, promising that her lips would be forever sealed.

But Michiko lied. Michiko wanted to get into Jun's good books, and Kim had inadvertently given her what she thought was the perfect way in. Jun, after all, had a right to know that he was the object of a nerd's fantasies, and would look favourably on the messenger who brought him this news.

And Michiko was correct, at least about the first part. Jun was appalled to learn that somebody as lowly and terminally uncool as Kim harboured such feelings for him. It was an affront to his dignity. A slur on his reputation. He did what had to be done. In Ueno-Kōen Park one afternoon in the middle of the late-March Hanami, while Kim was strolling around admiring the cherry blossom that adorned the trees in candy-floss clouds and steering clear of the blind-drunk adult Tokyoites who were reeling, singing and snoozing all over the place, Jun came sauntering up to her, accompanied by assorted friends and hangers-on, including Michiko. Before this audience of their peers, he savagely insulted Kim, calling her vicious names, venting his spite and spleen on her, putting her firmly in her place, making it clear to everyone present that he would not even dream of being her boyfriend, that the very idea of it was abhorrent to him, repugnant. He, Jun Shirow, go out with a girl who clearly had Ainu ancestry and whose parents, committed eco-activists, were such non-conformist weirdos? Never in a million years!

When he was done he turned and strode away, leaving Kim weeping helplessly, tears spilling from her eyes, sobs racking her. She felt as worthless a creature as had ever walked the planet. Her mortification was such that she wished she would collapse and die at that very second, on that very spot. But fate was not so kind. And all the way home the mocking laughter of Jun's friends, and particularly the laughter of Michiko, echoed bitterly in her ears.

At home she found solace in her grandmother's arms, crying some more into the warm fabric of her grandmother's blouse that smelled of fresh-cooked noodles and lilac soap, listening to her grandmother's soothes and croons. Her grandmother managed to comfort her with wise words, and later that evening, in her bedroom, Kim ceremonially burned the sheet of blank paper that had started the whole thing, reducing it to ashes which she then flushed down the lavatory, sending them swirling into the sewers with a curse.

The wound Jun inflicted was a deep one and healed slowly. In the days and weeks following Hanami, Kim went around the school hunched over, head down, starting at every snigger, twitching at every whisper, cowering from every glance, believing that every pupil in the school knew what had been done to her and was laughing at her, both to her face and behind her back. The one tiny scrap of consolation she had to cling to, the one small proof that there was *some* justice in this world, was that Michiko did not profit from her treachery. Jun allowed her to hang around with him for a while, probably out of a sense of gratitude, but it soon became apparent that her presence was no longer welcome in his coterie, and eventually she was cast back out into the wilderness from which she had come. Her humiliation was nowhere near as great as Kim's, but was nevertheless vengefully satisfying to watch.

That was who the young man beside Kim now used to be: a shallow, callous boy named Jun who had somehow transformed himself into this cunning, clever, eloquent foe called Emperor Dragon. Why, Kim wondered, of all the people in the world should Emperor Dragon have turned out to be *him*? Was it sheer coincidence, or had the Anarchs chosen Jun Shirow specially to be her online opponent as a kind of cruel joke, to rub salt in an old wound?

Kim had not yet revealed to Emperor Dragon that she knew his real identity. Much though she resented him, however, she also burned with curiosity to learn how he had made the transition from high-school baseball jock to sophisticated Anarch operative. Perhaps, she thought, if she did interrogate him on the subject, she might in the process glean something about his Anarch employers or why he was taking her and Rattray to France, some fact she could exploit later. She also was desperate to find out what Emperor Dragon was doing to Rattray – the purpose of the bizarre and frightening-looking machine to which he had hooked up her fellow Guardian.

Shortly the flight attendant returned with a drinks trolley to offer Kim and Emperor Dragon pre-dinner aperitifs. Kim refused, but Emperor Dragon ordered a Scotch and ginger ale, no ice. As he was taking his first sip of the drink, Kim decided that now was as good a time as any to obtain the answers she wanted.

'Why?' she asked, simply.

'Why what, Kim? Why am I doing this to you and your friend?' Emperor Dragon smiled. 'For money. Partly for professional reasons, but basically just for money.'

'That wasn't what I wanted to know, actually,' Kim

said. 'I didn't think for a moment you'd have any more noble motive than that. What I wanted to know is, why did you spurn me like that all those years ago in Ueno-Kōen Park? Why didn't you just ignore me, leave me alone? I was of no consequence to you.'

'In Ueno-Kōen . . . ? Oh, yes, of course. You've worked out who I am. Well done, Kim. Although I must say, I'm surprised it took you so long.'

She decided not to admit that his passport had given him away. If he thought she had made the deduction all by herself, then that was a small point in her favour. 'Me, too. I guess I don't usually think much about dogshit. One lump of it looks pretty much like another, after all.'

'Oh, Kim, you wound me.' Emperor Dragon clutched his chest as though he had been stabbed. 'And to think how you used to adore me.'

'I was an idiot back then. I didn't know any better. So, come on. Why did you pick on me like that? Treat me like I was a disease you didn't want to catch? You didn't *have* to.'

'I felt like doing it, that's why. It was fun – just as flaming you on the 'Net has been fun. I admit it, I get a kick out of being vindictive. Being responsible for other people's misery gives me pleasure. And why should I be ashamed of that? I'm only human.'

'Less than, if you ask me.'

'Again, I'm wounded. What a sharp tongue timid little Kimiko Harada has developed.'

'So how did it happen? You were as dumb as a rock when I knew you. Your grades were terrible and the only thing you knew how to do well was play baseball. And yet here you are.'

'I still fascinate you, don't I?'

Kim bristled. The arrogance of him!

'You interest me anthropologically,' she said, with exquisite self-restraint. 'I'm curious to discover how an ape like you could have acquired relatively advanced tool-using skills.'

Other than amusing him, her taunts seemed to be

having annoyingly little effect on Emperor Dragon. He seemed as impervious to insult as she was susceptible.

'Fate,' he said, having paused for a few moments to reflect. 'Fate made me what I am, Kim. After graduating from high school, my only aspiration was to play baseball professionally. Central or Pacific League, I didn't mind. I had tryouts with several teams. The Hiroshima Carp were keen to sign me up. And then I went and injured myself.' He fingered his left kneecap gingerly. 'Ruptured the cruciate ligaments here.'

'Sliding home for base?'

'Regrettably, no. A bit drunk one evening, I tripped and fell down a flight of stairs.'

Kim could not suppress a smile. It was the first genuinely humorous thing she had heard all day.

'Don't worry, the irony isn't lost on me either,' Emperor Dragon said. 'I underwent countless operations, spent the best part of a year hobbling around on crutches, but basically my baseball career was over.'

'I bet you still have trouble with it,' Kim said, thinking of the slight limp he had exhibited at the contemplative garden.

'My knee? From time to time. Cold, damp weather tends to make it ache. Anyway, you're interrupting me.'

'Oh, I do apologise.'

'For a while,' said Emperor Dragon, resuming his autobiographical account with the air of someone narrating the Greatest Story Ever Told, 'I searched around for something else to do with my life. In the end, for lack of anything better to do, I enrolled on a private computer-tuition course, which my parents paid for. It was hard work, but it turned out that I had something of a knack for graphics programming. You must understand, Kim, I was never truly stupid. It was just that, as long as I had baseball, there was never any call for me to stretch myself in any other capacity. Success on the baseball field brought me all that I craved – attention, adulation. Why should I make the effort in any other discipline when I could get everything I wanted doing something that came easily to me? But once that was gone, I had to learn about hard work, about the value of application. I did, and pretty soon I was taken on by one of the big digital entertainment corporations as an entry-level designer. Compositing and texturising backgrounds for computer games. I became a company man, putting in the hours in order to work my way up the ladder. And it paid off. It wasn't long before my employers were giving me greater responsibility, letting me animate sprites and offer input into games concepts. I quite enjoyed the work. None of what I was doing came even close to the thrill of hitting a good, clean home run straight into the bleachers, but as a second-best it sufficed. And then, about three years ago, I met someone. Electronically. Over the 'Net. And things changed again.'

'A girl? Don't tell me you fell in love!'

'Oh, no, Kim. Oh, God, no. Nothing like that. You've been reading too many of those teen-romance manga. No, this person – I'll call him a "he" for the sake of convenience, but I still don't know for sure whether it's a man or a woman – this person e-mailed me anonymously, out of the blue, while I was working late at the office one night. He said he had need of me. He wanted to recruit me as his right-hand man in a secret war. Naturally enough, I thought it was one of my work colleagues in another part of the building playing a prank, so I squirted back a suitably abusive reply. But the person e-mailed me again, saying that I had an important part to play in a grand global game and that my destiny was beckoning me.'

'Which, of course, appealed to your immense ego.'

'Certainly,' said Emperor Dragon, unabashed, as though Kim had just complimented him. 'So I responded a little more cautiously this time, and thus began an exchange of e-mails lasting several months, during which time I learned little *about* the person with whom I was corresponding but a great deal *from*. I won't bore you with the details. Let's just say that he became my mentor in a number of subjects, including the English language –

which before then I'd had only a rudimentary grasp of – and the art of computer hacking. And I must say, I impressed even myself with how quickly I was able to absorb what he taught me.'

Kim thought of how the Windows '95 virus had been inputted subliminally into the mind of that Microsoft employee via his monitor, a kind of software for the brain. It was the classic, tried-and-tested Anarch technique of making knowledge look as if it had been discovered rather than artificially installed. She resisted the temptation to tell Emperor Dragon that he owed his acquired talents to Anarch mind-manipulation. Apart from anything else, he was too conceited to believe her.

'Eventually, when my online mentor considered me ready, he told me about the little secret army to which you belong, the *Hogosha*,' Emperor Dragon continued. 'He described what you get up to, how you are opposed to Progress and human ingenuity, and he asked if I would help in the fight against you. The pay was right, and the job appeared to offer significantly more of a challenge than devising platformers and roleplayers and shoot-'em-ups for consoles and home PCs, and so I said yes. And here I am. Fulfilling my role rather well, wouldn't you agree?'

Kim ignored the last comment. 'And why are you taking us to France? Is it to meet this person, this mentor of yours?'

'No. The man I am taking your friend Mr Rattray to is someone else. An interested third party, you might say.'

'But what does he want with John?'

'That would be telling.'

'All right. Answer me this, then. What *is* that machine you have John hooked up to?'

After the confrontation in the contemplative garden, Kim and the unconscious Rattray had been taken back to the video arcade in Kyoto, and from there transported by van to Tokyo. It was a long drive, and Kim had ridden up front with the driver, Emperor Dragon's broken-nosed cohort, who chain-smoked all the way and, on those rare occasions when she did manage to get him to speak, used terse sentences of few words. The only morsels of information she was able to prise out of him during the entire journey, in fact, were that his name was Ryu and that he was the leader of the gang of *bosozoku* and the owner of the video arcade to which Emperor Dragon's false trail had led her and Rattray. Ryu and Emperor Dragon had some sort of deal going, but she was not completely clear on the terms of their partnership. The use of Ryu's gang-members in return for – what? Money, most likely.

Rattray, meanwhile, had been strapped down to the mattress of a steel hospital gurney and consigned to the back of the van, along with Emperor Dragon and Kenji, the switchblade-wielding *bosozoku*. By the time they arrived at Narita, Kenji had put on a set of white paramedic's overalls over his street clothes, with a matching surgical mask, while Rattray had been stripped of his clothing and dressed in a green hospital patient's gown. IV drips had been inserted into his arms, connecting him to bags of clear fluid that were suspended from armatures attached to the gurney, and his head had been entirely encased inside a kind of matt-black metal helmet. This helmet was linked by a plethora of wires and fibre-optic cables to a heavy, boxlike unit that ran on smooth-rolling castors, which in turn was linked to – and obviously controlled by – a slimline laptop computer. The last Kim had seen of her fellow Guardian, Kenji had been wheeling him down the boarding gangway onto the plane. Both of them were somewhere to the rear, in Economy.

'Mr Rattray can count himself privileged,' Emperor Dragon said. 'He has the honour of being the first person ever to experience what I strongly believe will become the predominant leisure activity of the new millennium. I call it the Hypnagogic Inducer, but I dare say when the time comes to market it we'll have to go with something snappier. "Extreme Dreaming", something like that. I imagine you'll want to hear how it works.'

'I imagine I don't have any choice.'

'It works,' said Emperor Dragon, nodding serenely in agreement, 'through a combination of virtual reality technology and deep-trance hypnosis. You know about temporal lobe epilepsy?'

Kim did, but the question had been a rhetorical one and Emperor Dragon himself duly answered it.

'It's the state of lucid dreaming experienced by people who, for instance, have out-of-body experiences and alien-abduction encounters. Using a battery of LEDs flashing in sequence, the Hypnagogic Inducer brings about this condition in the user, rendering his mind highly suggestible to external stimuli. A computer-generated environment is then projected on to his retinas via low-intensity lasers, with accompanying holophonic sound effects relayed into his ears via stereo headphones.'

'So it's a kind of virtual reality.'

'The Hypnagogic Inducer is to virtual reality what the Lexus is to the Model-T Ford. It isn't even the son of virtual reality, it's the grandson. It's a flawless symbiosis of computer-generated imagery and the human subconscious, the one feeding off the other. At present, as I'm sure you know, the 3D environments offered by virtual reality are crude, limited in scope. The problem is that programmers are forever trying to perfect the look and sound of what's being shown, rather than concentrating their efforts on the end-user, as I've done. Processing power being what it is, perfect VR generated solely by computer is still many years away. But if the mind of the user can be brought into the mix, can be altered so as to enhance the effect of what he is experiencing, then it becomes possible to achieve the pan-sensual digital worlds prophesied by science pundits and SF authors.'

He paused – like an orator, or a salesman giving a sales pitch – before proceeding.

'The graphics themselves are good but nothing exceptional,' he went on. 'If you saw them on a screen, you'd be impressed by the quality of movement, texture-mapping and so on, but would you think them indistinguishable from reality? Hardly. Once you're inside that helmet and in deep trance, however, your mind goes to work, taking the raw data being fed to you through your eyes and ears and smoothing it out, filling in the details, adding nuances, and even extrapolating sensory responses for those regions of the brain not being directly stimulated, the regions concerned with taste, touch, smell and the body's awareness of its own *schema*. Essentially, it's computer-assisted dreaming.'

To punctuate this last sentence, he spread out his hands like a conjuror at the conclusion of a trick.

'Not only that,' he said, 'but the user himself supplies a plotline to go with the environment. You know how it's said that everyone is supposed to have a novel in them?'

Kim nodded.

'It may not be true, but what *is* true is that there's a fundamental human tendency to think in storylines. Even our dreams have plot threads, however bizarre or tenuous. It's a latent ability we all have, and the Hypnagogic Inducer enables the user to access that ability at will. Of its own accord the user's mind comes up with a fully worked-out narrative structure to follow and generates characters whom the user can interact with, hold conversations with, touch, insult, ignore, just as if they were living people. The programmer isn't involved with that aspect of Extreme Dreaming at all. The plots and the characters stem entirely from the user, and so are unique and individual to the user, and different every time. The machine provides the premise, the backdrop, the basic scenario. The user unconsciously does the rest.'

'And does it work?'

'Of course.'

'How do you know that? I thought you said John was the first person ever to try your machine.'

'My mentor assured me that it works, and he's never lied to me.'

'So you didn't come up with this thing all by yourself,' Kim said, permitting herself a small note of triumph.

'I don't deny that I had some help from my mentor. As

well as supplying me with most of the special hardware I needed, he gave me some pretty clever software. He also, by the way, donated the toxin-capsule pistol that I used to put Mr Rattray to sleep and provided me with the verbal bait that, along with your plight, enticed our gallant English friend to come all the way to Japan.'

'John saw through that, though. He knew it was a trap.'

'Yet he came anyway,' said Emperor Dragon, with a shrug.

There was no arguing with that, Kim realised, and so she changed tack. 'It seems, if you don't mind my saying so, a lot of trouble and effort to go to,' she said, 'just to keep one man's mind occupied while you transport him from A to B.'

'It was. A *lot* of trouble and effort. I've been planning and working on this little scheme for more than a year and a half.'

'So why? Why go to all that bother?'

'Because I have to. Your boyfriend is not someone you can simply knock out and keep anaesthetised. His immune system is designed to resist. I'm pouring enough sedative into him intravenously to keep a dozen men out cold, but his autonomic defences are assimilating and neutralising the drug almost as fast as it goes in. Were he even partially to recover consciousness, he would be able to issue a mental command and marshal extra physiological resources to counteract the sedative completely. As long as his mind remains occupied, however, he stays under.'

'And you're sure there's no way he can wake up?' said Kim. 'No way out of the dream environment he's in? Because, if I know John Rattray, he won't be content just to stroll along admiring the scenery. He'll be looking for a means of escape. That's the kind of man he is. You shouldn't underestimate just how resourceful he can be.'

'Is that a note of devotion I hear?' said Emperor Dragon. 'I was joking when I called him your boyfriend just now, but I'm beginning to wonder now if there isn't some truth in it. Are you making it a habit to fall for men who are way out of your league, Kimiko?'

Kim clicked her tongue in contempt.

Emperor Dragon shrugged again. 'I merely asked. At any rate, in answer to your question, yes, there is a way out. It lies at the point of interface between the user and the computer, which marks the threshold between the hypnagogic and waking states – a specific location in the user's mental environment. An unfortunate but unavoidable flaw in the design. Without it, the user could not withdraw from Extreme Dreaming if he needed to. In later models, I'll have to incorporate some sort of shortcut to enable the user to get to the location instantly, a preprogrammed codeword probably.'

'So what's to stop John finding this exit?'

'Unless the user is actually the one who establishes its whereabouts beforehand, he'll only be able to locate it by chance. Therefore it'll be a miracle if Mr Rattray does find the exit from his particular Extreme Dream, and even if he manages to do so, I've installed a safeguard to prevent him actually crossing the threshold. Mr Rattray will remain under the influence of the Hypnagogic Inducer for as long as I want him to.'

'How much money are you making from this?'

'Why do you ask?'

'Because the Guardians will pay you twice as much, three times as much, if you let me and John go.'

Emperor Dragon laughed loftily. 'Oh, appearances to the contrary, Kim, I'm not easily bought. It was my mentor's precondition for helping me create the Hypnagogic Inducer that I employ it first in the war against the *Hogosha*. Thereafter it's up to me what I do with the technology.'

'And you intend to mass-market it.'

'Naturally. As I said, I firmly believe that the Hypnagogic Inducer is going to become the predominant leisure activity of the new millennium. The money I'm making today is earmarked for developing the prototype commercially. We'll begin producing and testing Extreme

Dreaming units at Ryu's arcade – he, of course, getting his cut of the profits. From there, we'll take the units to Tokyo and tout them around the arcades in Akihabara. It won't be long before word spreads and everyone is clamouring to hire one or own one. The global economy may be entering a downturn, but the demand for new forms of entertainment is constant. In fact, I suspect that, if the recession really starts to bite, the kind of escapism Extreme Dreaming provides will be exactly what people will crave. In other words, if all goes according to plan – and it will – it won't be long before Emperor Dragon Incorporated has become a *zaibatsu* to rival the great Sega and Sony. So why should I worry about a few extra yen now, Kim, when in the medium-term future I'm going to be a very rich man indeed?'

'Possibly,' said Kim. 'But what you haven't taken into account is the fact that we *Hogosha* will stop you.' It seemed reasonable to suppose that the Librans would instruct the Guardians to suppress Emperor Dragon at some point. It was clear, after all, that much of the technology he was employing was of paraterrestrial origin.

'No, Kim,' Emperor Dragon replied. 'No. The Frenchman we are going to visit is, I'm quite certain, going to put paid to the activities of the *Hogosha* once and for all. He has the wherewithal and he has the will. Thanks to him, your organisation's days are well and truly numbered.' Emperor Dragon unbuckled his seat belt and rose to his feet. 'Now, if you'll excuse me, I think I ought to check on the "patient" before dinner arrives. And while I'm gone, you bear in mind what I told you earlier while we were embarking. Don't get any funny ideas about trying to alert the cabin crew.'

He pointed along the aisle to where Ryu was sitting, three rows rearward, sipping a glass of beer. Ryu tipped the glass towards Kim in a kind of knowing salute, then opened his jacket to reveal, inserted into his waistband, the toxin-capsule pistol. Ryu had been able to smuggle the pistol aboard the plane because paraterrestrial materials did not set off airport metal detectors.

'So stay put, keep your mouth shut and be a good girl, Kim, and all will be well.'

And with this advice, Emperor Dragon set off in the direction of the Economy Class section of the plane, leaving Kim with nothing to do but fold her arms, sink back in her seat and scowl out of the window at the utter, unremitting darkness of high-altitude night.

31

The rear section of Economy Class was occupied mainly by a large group of holidaymakers bound for France for an intensive two-week coach tour of the nation's cultural sites. They were in a chatty, festive mood, and everyone was taking snapshots of everyone else – heads together, arms around shoulders, cheesy grins, thumbs up. Emperor Dragon made his way through the hubbub, squinting at every flashbulb flare and all the while trying to maintain an air of indifference. It was hard, though. Did these people have *no* self-awareness? Had they not heard of cultural stereotyping?

At the far end of the plane a curtain had been installed to screen off a section of floorspace where four pairs of seats had been taken out. Behind the curtain, the comatose form of John Rattray lay on the gurney beneath a woollen blanket, his head covered by the black helmet and a pair of intravenous tubes feeding into each arm. The tubes quivered with the vibration of the plane.

Kenji, in his bogus paramedic guise, had just finished replacing an empty sedative-solution bag with a fresh, full one when Emperor Dragon pulled aside the curtain and entered the screened-off area.

Kenji greeted his employer's employer with a formal nod, which Emperor Dragon returned.

'How is he?' Emperor Dragon enquired.

Kenji pulled his surgical mask down below his chin. 'Sleeping like a baby. Pulse steady and slow.' Kenji had been coached in rudimentary medical skills – pulse-taking, IV technique – specifically for this occasion. 'He was talking to himself a while ago. In his own language, of course, so it was all gibberish to me. But he's quiet now.'

Emperor Dragon glanced over at the Englishman. Apart from his bare arms protruding from the sleeves of the hospital gown, nothing of Rattray was exposed. He was just a motionless man-shape lying on the mattress of the gurney. The spherical helmet made it appear as though, cartoonishly, his head had been crushed by a fallen bowling ball.

'Good, good,' Emperor Dragon said, surveying his handiwork.

'I'd feel a bit safer around him if I'd been allowed to take my blade on board,' Kenji remarked with a sullen pout.

'Not possible. You know that. Anyway, the *gaijin* is completely incapacitated. As long as we keep pumping sedative into him, he won't be a threat to us.'

'If you say so.' Kenji sounded dubious.

'Oh, I'm certain of it,' said Emperor Dragon. He pulled aside the curtain and stepped back out.

As he was turning to head up the aisle back to First Class, one of the holidaymakers, a middle-aged woman, waved to attract his attention.

'Excuse me, young fellow.'

Emperor Dragon scowled. If she was about to ask him to take her picture . . .

'Please forgive my curiosity,' the woman went on. 'That man on the life-support machine behind the curtain – are you his doctor?'

'Indeed I am, madam,' said Emperor Dragon.

The volume of chatter subsided slightly as several other people tuned in to listen. There had been much debate among the holidaymakers about the mystery man behind the curtain.

'The poor fellow must be very ill,' the woman said. 'What is it he's suffering from?'

'An extremely rare brain disease,' Emperor Dragon replied. The lies flowed with a fluent, rehearsed facility. 'We're flying him to Paris for an emergency operation. There's only one man in the world who can save his life, a surgeon at the Hôtel Dieu hospital.'

'Ah, how fascinating,' said the passenger, nodding. 'Well, I wish both you and him luck. I hope it all goes well.'

'Oh, I'm sure it will, madam,' said Emperor Dragon, and resumed his journey up the aisle.

Of course it was going to go well, he thought. He had planned this whole scheme meticulously. All the variables had been taken into account. All the bases were covered. Nothing was going to go wrong.

As soon as Emperor Dragon had departed, Kenji sat down on a seat positioned next to the gurney and reached into a pocket of his overalls. He took out a small brown bottle, uncapped it and shook out a couple of small white pills into his hand. He popped the pills into his mouth and swallowed them, then returned the bottle to his pocket, which also contained a pack of Marlboro, a Zippo lighter and a single condom still in its foil wrapper. Leaning his head back against the curved interior of the plane's fuselage, he closed his eyes and let the thrum of the turbine engines reverberate into his skull while he waited for the benzedrine to kick in.

It was going to be a long flight and a long night.

At that moment, unseen by Kenji, Rattray's right hand twitched.

Slowly, one by one, his fingers and thumb stretched and articulated themselves.

Then the hand resumed its inert position on the gurney mattress.

32

The changes that had been taking place in MacGowan's body during the day continued as he slept. He spent a fevered night, writhing beneath his blanket of beech leaves as his physiology gradually altered, as muscle tissue thickened, as veins dilated to increase blood flow, as his adrenal and thyroid glands stepped up the rate of production of their secretions.

He shivered. He sweated. He was racked from head to toe with shudders.

And he dreamed.

Torrid, fragmentary dreams.

He dreamed of Gleason and the other three, not as the monsters they had turned into but as the men they had been beforehand. Making preparations for their final mission at the Forward Operations Base. Larking about, taking the piss, as soldiers do to hide their nerves. Four men laughing unsuspectingly in the Saudi sun.

And he dreamed of Intelligence Corps spooks inter-rogating him. Calm, controlled, well-educated voices. Faces blank of emotion.

But then . . .

One of the spooks was Rattray. Another was Lucretia. Another was Piers Pearson. And they were no longer interrogating him. They were standing back and mocking him. Jeering at him. Faces frozen with contempt.

And then he dreamed of Sarah. Sarah with her hair long, the way it used to be, the way it should be. Sarah spitting a stream of accusations at him from the witness box in a courtroom, and then turning to her new boyfriend Tim Andrews next to her and smothering him in kisses. Both of them suddenly naked and on all-fours, rutting like a pair of animals. And Sarah looking round, past Andrews's heaving buttocks, to her ex-husband, and sneering at him as her hair grew shorter and shorter, almost as though it was withdrawing into her scalp.

And he dreamed of real animals. Caterpillars. Snakes. Creatures that metamorphosed. Creatures that shed old skins. Creatures that *became*.

He was dimly aware that he, too, was *becoming*. With every twinge and twang of physical pain, an old self was falling away and a new self was emerging.

He was simplifying. Being streamlined. Casting off conscience, loyalty, compassion.

Throughout the night MacGowan's mind accompanied his body on a slow, twisting journey of transformation until eventually, not long before dawn, the process was complete.

Whereupon a calm fell upon him, and he slept on for another hour, deeply, sweetly, dreamlessly, no longer a man but something that was both less . . . and more.

33

Dennis Holman was by habit and by preference an early riser. He loved to be up and about while the world was still and Bretherton Grange was quiet. Leaving Lucretia asleep, he would dress, slip out of the bedroom, ease the door shut behind him and pad along the main upstairs corridor of the huge old house, heading down to the kitchen, where he would prepare and consume his breakfast while listening to the *Today* programme on Radio 4 with the volume turned down low.

This ritual period of solitary hush was his to call his own, a time to contemplate, to reflect on the demands and duties of the day ahead. Perhaps there were groceries that needed to be bought. Perhaps there were jobs around the grounds needing to be done. There was always housework, which Holman carried out according to a strict weekly rota – bathrooms on Mondays, vacuuming on Tuesdays, and so on – and there were always meals to be cooked. Of necessity, for culinary expertise was not foremost among Lucretia's talents, Holman had become a proficient chef over the years. He had also become something of a dab-hand at DIY, and rarely was he not in the middle of some piece of home-improvement, such as the conversion job he was currently undertaking on the annexe, or else overseeing structural repairs to the house. Like all old buildings Bretherton Grange demanded constant upkeep. Holman likened the maintenance of the Grange to the painting of the Forth Bridge – a task that was never completed.

So every morning, over his bowl of muesli with yoghurt and his pot of decaffeinated coffee, Holman would ruminate on these domestic chores, apportioning time to the day's tasks, prioritising, categorising, composing a mental schedule.

This morning, however, he did not have that opportunity, because he was not alone for breakfast. When he entered the kitchen, one of the two guests who had spent the preceding night at the Grange was there to greet him. Huffing excitedly and lashing her tail, Lady Grinning Soul butted her nose into Holman's crotch and demanded attention, which he gladly lavished on her.

'Good morning, girl,' he said, fondling and stroking the Afghan hound's head and ears. 'Sleep well?' He patted her flanks with both hands. 'I bet you're hungry, aren't you? Well, we'll soon fix that.'

Straightening up, he went to the cupboard where he had stored the dog food that Piers, the other overnight guest, had brought with him. Lady followed and watched, eagle-eyed, as he forked Pedigree Chum into the dog-bowl that was kept at the Grange for the benefit of this particular occasional canine visitor.

Setting the food down on the floor in front of Lady, Holman looked on as it disappeared in a few frenetic seconds of gulping and slurping. Lady then sat and waited patiently while Holman made and, at a somewhat more leisurely pace, ate his own breakfast. The mug he drank his coffee from was an aged, much-used, much-loved, chipped, cracked thing whose handle had broken off and been glued back into place more than once. A gift to him from Daisy and Alice, the mug had the words 'World's Greatest Mum' printed on the side, the lettering eroded to the point where it was only just legible.

When, finally, Holman rose from the table, Lady let out a woof in order to remind him, in case he had forgotten, that now was the time to take her out for a walk.

'Yes, yes, girl, I know,' Holman replied, stooping to place his mug, cereal bowl and spoon in the dishwasher.

Normally Piers left Lady in Chelsea when Guardian business required him to be away from home for a few days, but sometimes he brought her down to be kennelled at the Grange. Holman was in the habit of taking a leisurely stroll around the grounds first thing after breakfast, so it had become a tradition that Lady, whenever she stayed, accompanied him on these walks. Even though on this occasion her master was still present – for reasons neither he nor Lucretia had vouchsafed to Holman and Holman had, with his usual tact and discretion, not enquired about – there seemed no point in breaking with the tradition.

Holman went to the boot-room that adjoined the kitchen and fetched his wellingtons and his quilted Barbour waistcoat. Dressed for outdoors, he summoned Lady with a soft whistle, and together man and dog stepped out through the back door into the brisk, bright splendour of an autumn dawn.

The air was filled with damp, loamy scents. The bird-song in the treetops was a contentedly subdued aubade. Dew turned the Grange's lawns a deeper shade of green and glistened on the triangular planes of Bridget St Swithin's pyramids. Mist was lifting from the surface of the ornamental lake, dissipating in spectral swirls.

Companionably through the hazily lit, long-shadowed tranquillity Holman and Lady Grinning Soul strode, their feet swishing through moist grass and undergrowth. It wasn't long before Holman found himself softly humming the 'Dawn' theme from *Peer Gynt*. It was that kind of a morning.

Usually on his daybreak strolls – and this one was no exception – Holman was moved to give thanks for the life he led and count his many blessings. He had an intelligent, brave, beguiling, successful woman as his common-law wife. He had two daughters who were likewise feisty, smart and intrepid, and who were shaping up to be a pair of fine young women. He and his family enjoyed a high standard of living. He himself was healthy, hale and whole. People as fortunate as he was seldom took the time to appreciate how lucky they were. Holman made a point of doing so as often as he could.

Many men would doubtless have found it hard, if not impossible, to be in his shoes. To have no income of their own. To be financially dependent on their 'other half'. To be a househusband, an implicitly emasculating role. Not Holman. For one thing, he had been a wage-slave once and, frankly, had hated it. Before he met Lucretia and for a few years after he moved in to live with her at the Grange, he had endured the nine-to-five commuter grind as a junior clerk in a City of London firm of accountants. He had been a tiny cog in the vast machinery of Business, and had found it a body-wearying, soul-emptying existence. Then Daisy had come along, and it had been clear that either Holman or Lucretia was going to have to give up work in order to look after their first daughter, and seeing as Lucretia's artistic career was burgeoning and Holman so detested accountancy – a profession he had only joined because his father had been an accountant, too, and *his* father before him – the most logical solution had been that he should be the one to assume the mantle of primary caregiver. In fact, for Holman there had been very little logic involved in the decision. He had jumped at the chance to quit his job. He had left the world of capital gains tax and double-entry bookkeeping behind him without a backward glance, without an ounce of regret, and he would rather lop off his right hand than return to it.

So he had no complaints about Lucretia being the family breadwinner. Besides, these days she made more from her sculpture than he could ever have hoped to earn in his profession.

There was no indignity in domesticity, either. Keeping a house clean and shipshape, cooking a good meal and bringing up children were no less important in the grand scheme of things than bringing home the bacon. These tasks represented Holman's half of the unspoken bargain between him and Lucretia, his contribution to the practical side of their partnership, and he performed them willingly and well.

No, all in all it was not a bad life he led. Not a bad one at all. If there was one aspect of it that he would have changed had he been able to, it was Lucretia's involvement with the Guardians.

Holman knew as much about the Guardians as Lucretia had revealed to him, which was as much as she felt she could in all fairness permit him to know – enough to allay his curiosity, but no more. He had some idea what lay in the cellars beneath the Grange, and he knew, too, that the huge cache of *matériel* and confiscated contratemporal items that was kept down there was patrolled and protected by some large, prowling, catlike entity that he had never seen and had no desire to see. He was not privy to what went on during the Guardians' irregularly and abruptly convened meetings; never knew what was said during those gatherings in the dining room. Nor was he ever told where the Guardians travelled to afterwards on their missions. He knew, though, that they were exposed to a certain level of danger while on those missions, and hence was glad that Lucretia went along with them on average only about one time in every three. He knew that he and his daughters, as close relations of a Guardian, were at some risk themselves; even if they were of no use as a source of intelligence, Anarch operatives might none the less kidnap them and use them for blackmail purposes or as bait for a trap. However, Lucretia had long ago managed to convince him that the threat to the girls and him was minimal. As long as they maintained a reasonable degree of caution while they went about their daily activities, they would be all right. Which advice had been imparted to Daisy and Alice – who were wholly ignorant of matters Guardian-related – in the form of a general admonishment to the effect that, as daughters of an internationally renowned artist and public figure, they had to be aware that there were people whose interest in them might not be entirely wholesome.

The cloistered confines of boarding school and, to a lesser extent, university afforded Alice and Daisy, respectively, a certain intrinsic level of security. Even so, there were times when Holman wished, with a father's fervency, that there was some way he could offer his daughters complete and absolute protection. Of course, short of locking them up in an attic for the rest of their lives, that was not possible. He just had to accept the fact that his daughters would never be perfectly safe as long as Lucretia remained a Guardian, and hope and have faith that no harm would come to them.

This was the one area of his life in which Holman had had to compromise, or at least had had to settle for less than perfection. It was the price of sharing his life with a woman like Lucretia Fisk, and he was prepared to pay it.

He and Lady Grinning Soul walked for half an hour, following a meandering, circuitous route through the grounds of the Grange, taking in the wooded areas, the knolls, the glades. Lady, having got her toilet needs out of the way, took to darting after squirrels and birds whenever she spied either kind of animal on the ground. She pursued them with more enthusiasm than skill, so that her would-be prey invariably detected her approach in plenty of time and scampered or flitted to safety well before she reached them. Short-lived and fruitless though these chases were, Lady enjoyed them, and after each was over she came trotting back to Holman's side with her mouth hanging open in a tongue-lolling grin that seemed to say that she realised she was too urbane and sophisticated for such quaint rustic pursuits, but that didn't mean she couldn't indulge anyway. Besides, her ancestors had been bred as hunters, had they not? It was in her blood.

Eventually their perambulations brought Holman and Lady to the high wall which separated the estate from the lane that described its southern boundary. They followed the line of the wall, Holman's intention being that when they reached the driveway they would turn onto it and head back towards the house. By the time they arrived back at the Grange, Lucretia and Piers would almost certainly be up and wanting their breakfast. As a precaution, Holman had put a half-bottle of Moët in the refrigerator the previous evening. Lady's eccentric master liked a drop of champagne to accompany every meal, including breakfast.

They were approaching the front gates when Lady stopped abruptly in her tracks and started to growl.

'What is it, girl?' Holman asked, halting too. 'Spotted another squirrel, have you?'

He heard the clank of the gates' locking mechanism releasing itself and, peering ahead, saw the gates start to swing open. Meanwhile Lady, head lowered and teeth bared, continued to growl, the hostile noise rumbling and resonating from deep within her throat while she glared intently at the opening gates.

Holman shushed her. 'Oh, come on, Lady, it's nothing to get agitated about. Somebody's rung the bell and Lucretia's let them in from the house. It's probably a delivery van.'

Although we aren't expecting any deliveries, he thought, and I haven't heard a van engine.

A vague, ill-formed feeling of unease began to prickle inside his belly.

The gates clanged against their stops, fully open. A moment later, a man appeared, striding purposefully through the gateway.

Holman, recognising the man, relaxed.

'It's just Bill,' he said to Lady. 'See? No reason to growl. You like Bill. He's your friend.'

He raised a hand and called out to MacGowan.

Lady's growl deepened to a snarl.

34

Inside the Grange, the chime that announced the arrival of a Guardian at the gates sounded, waking Lucretia.

Her first thought was that she needed to pee badly. He second thought, as she swung her naked body out of bed and groped for the satin dressing gown that was draped over the back of the chair near her bed, was that Rattray had returned. He had not said how long he was going to spend in Japan. It could be that he had sorted out that Emperor Dragon business already. She hoped so. With Rattray back, things would seem a little more normal. The status quo would be at least partially restored.

Crossing the bedroom floor to the en suite bathroom, Lucretia considered the alternative explanation for the chime having rung, namely that MacGowan had finally made it to the Grange, perhaps having hired a rental car. She had no idea what could have delayed him by almost a day. The most positive spin she could put on the situation was that, exhausted after the action-to-suppress, he had gone home to rest for twenty-four hours, neglecting to call to tell her that this was what he had done.

That could be what had happened, Lucretia thought as she gathered the dressing gown up around her waist, sat on the lavatory and began to urinate. But there were two reasons why it was unlikely. One, it was not like MacGowan to fail to notify her of a change of plan; and, two, she had tried his home phone number several times the previous afternoon and evening, each time getting his answering machine. He could have left the machine on in order to be able to sleep undisturbed . . . but, again, that was not like MacGowan.

That was what it came down to. That was what was bothering her. None of this behaviour was conventional Bill MacGowan behaviour. And much though she hoped that there was an entirely innocent explanation for the current state of events, her instincts kept suggesting otherwise.

Her fears had prompted her to take the precaution of summoning Piers down to the Grange, but they were too imprecise, too nebulous, too uncertainly founded, to permit her to take any further action than that. For this same reason she had not shared her concerns with Holman. While there remained a chance that MacGowan was all right, there seemed no point in worrying Holman over something that might turn out to be a false alarm.

Accustomed as she was to excluding and shielding her common-law husband from all but the essential aspects of Guardianship, Lucretia had had no difficulty arriving at her decision to keep him in the dark about MacGowan.

She could not have known, as she dabbed between her legs with a folded wad of lavatory paper, that it was a decision she was shortly going to come to regret.

35

A few minutes earlier, MacGowan had awoken in the copse across the lane from the Grange. Shaking off his makeshift blanket of leaves, he clambered to his feet. He was cold, he was hungry, but the energy inside him, the seemingly inexhaustible supply of anger-fuelled strength that had propelled him all the way to Bretherton, was still there. Warmth and food could wait. Business first.

He brushed away the leaves that were clinging to his jersey and jeans, and set off towards the fence.

One thought presided in his brain.

Lucretia. Kill Lucretia.

She had betrayed him. She and Piers and Rattray, together, all three of them. They had, for reasons he neither could explain nor needed to know, sent him on a suicide mission, not expecting him to return. They had set him up, offered him up to the Anarchs like a sacrificial lamb. They were no better than the army top brass, who thought nothing of sending men from the rank-and-file to their deaths. They had no respect for the poor shits at the sharp end like him. A few of them dead, what difference did it make?

What difference? He would show them what difference. He would kill them all. Lucretia first. Then Piers, that sad, deluded Jason King wannabe. Then Mr high-and-mighty John Rattray. For him he would have to use something from the Node beneath the Grange. There was some pretty decisive weaponry in those cellars. He ought to be able to find something down there that would sort out the notoriously hard-to-eliminate Rattray.

He reached the fence and vaulted over it one-handed. Crossing the lane, he approached the front gates of the Grange.

He had thought about this on the way down to Bretherton yesterday. He knew that entering by the gates with his puzzle-egg keyring was going to alert Lucretia that a Guardian was coming. However, the boundary wall was too high to climb and all other approaches to the Grange were guarded by passive intruder-aversion devices: loudspeakers which emitted subsonic resonances so that anyone who came near them began to feel unaccountably dizzy and unwell; infrared stroboscopes which flickered at just the right frequency to cause mild confusion and disorientation; microwave generators which sent out low-average-power electromagnetic energy pulses that triggered auditory hallucinations, the hallucinations most often manifesting in the form of inner voices that urged the listener to leave the vicinity as fast as possible. All these were secreted amidst the woodland and hedgerows around the estate, and all were designed to encourage trespassers and interlopers to turn back of their own accord, without being consciously aware of why they had felt impelled to do so, knowing only that the further away from the estate they went, the less uneasy and uncomfortable they felt.

An invisible barrier, which MacGowan believed he could have penetrated. With sufficient determination and concentration he could have withstood the effects of the passive deterrents and forged on past them. But, then, that would have entailed setting off the intruder alarms that were positioned deeper within the perimeter of the estate, and Lucretia would have been put on the alert. She would have realised that his intentions were hostile and taken appropriate defensive measures.

This way, the direct way, the full-frontal approach, offered him the best chance of achieving his goal. He would walk through the gates and up to the house, acting as if nothing was wrong, as if he was blissfully unaware that Lucretia had betrayed him. Whistling a tune. Lah-di-dah. Tum-te-tum. Lucretia might be on her guard purely on the strength of the fact that he had survived the Seal Point mission, but she could have no way of knowing for certain that he had rumbled her game. As long as he kept a poker face, gave nothing away, she would not suspect anything until they were face to face. And then it would be too late for her.

That, at any rate, was the plan, and as the gates of the Grange parted obligingly for him, like the Red Sea parting for Moses, MacGowan took this as a good omen. Everything was going to go smoothly. All potential obstacles were simply going to sweep themselves out of his way.

He heard a man's voice calling his name.

Buggeration.

He turned to find Dennis Holman standing some twenty yards away from him, hand raised in greeting. With him was a dog, an Afghan hound. Piers Pearson's dog, Lady Grinning Soul. (MacGowan used to think the name was endearingly daft, but now it just seemed inane.) If she was here, Piers was probably here, too. Well, that would not be a problem. If anything, it made his job easier. Two birds with one stone and all that.

Lady looked none too pleased to see him. Holman, on the other hand, was smiling.

Smiling.

He *knew*. He was part of it. Part of the Guardian conspiracy against MacGowan.

Which meant he would have to die, too.

36

'Bill,' said Holman. 'This is a pleasant surprise. Lucretia didn't . . .'

Holman's voice tailed off as he got a better look at MacGowan.

MacGowan's already bulky physique was appreciably larger. His neck was thicker and the veins stood proud. The same was true of his hands. Parts of him, indeed, looked almost *inflated*. Similarly, the familiar contours of his face were distorted and distended. His jaw had developed a prognathous jut and his eyes were sunken into their sockets and rimmed with purple. His posture was different, too. He held himself with a heavy, menacing stoop.

He regarded Holman with an expression of intense hatred that was all the more disturbing and alarming because Holman had never seen him exhibit anything like it ever before. It was as though some possessing demon had manifested inside MacGowan, transforming his features into a gargoyle grimace of loathing.

MacGowan's hands balled into fists, and he came running at Holman.

Holman was too stunned even to think of moving. He watched, rooted to the spot, as the big ex-soldier bore down on him.

Head lowered, MacGowan collided with him, brow-butting him on the bridge of the nose. Pain exploded across Holman's face and he crashed backwards to the ground. Next thing he knew, a pair of immensely power-ful hands were clamped around his neck and thumbs were digging into his throat, crushing his Adam's apple into his windpipe. It hurt, but worse than the pain, more terrify-ing, was the sudden realisation that he was no longer able to breathe. He was sucking air into his mouth, in through his nose, but it was not going anywhere. His lungs were demanding oxygen but, hard as he tried, none was reaching them.

He grabbed at MacGowan's shoulders, clawing at the sleeves of his jersey. His attempts at resistance were feebly ineffectual. MacGowan's arms felt like concrete. Nothing Holman could do was going to dislodge his throttling grasp.

Holman's vision filled with miniature Catherine wheels and sparkling bubbles of light. His lungs seemed to be expanding within his chest, straining at his ribcage as though they were going to burst through. His head felt as if it was bloating with blood. He was dimly aware of Lady barking nearby. MacGowan's altered, hate-filled face loomed over him, a mad moon.

I'm going to die, Holman thought with a sudden, strange, aloof calmness, as though from somewhere distant within himself. This is it. Bill's strangling me and I'm going to die.

The world grew foggy and grey. There was a rushing and roaring in his ears.

Then, as though from miles away, he heard a grunt and a yell, and suddenly the pressure was gone from his throat. The inhalation reflex kicked in. He heaved in air. His head sang with relief.

Deliverance!

How?

37

Lady Grinning Soul identified the man's scent well before he came into view. He was a member of the pack her master ran with, the one she thought of as the tall man (all humans were tall to her, but this one was taller than most).

She liked the tall man almost as much as she liked the packmate of her master with whom she was walking, the one with the bushy hair on his face and not as much hair as usual on the upper half of his head. *He* was her second-favourite man in the world, after her master. The tall man came a close third.

But today the tall man smelled different from normal. Always there was a particular undercurrent to his scent, a sharp, vinegary tang that Lady associated with killing. Her master did not have it, nor did the hairy-faced man, but her master's white-haired packmate did, and so did the tall man. It was similar to the smell of blood but subtly distinct. A predator's odour. The smell of someone who, often and without compunction, *spilled* blood.

And today it was not just a faint tinge among all the tall man's other scents, a single ingredient in the complex recipe of odours he gave off. Today it was the dominant smell, a reek that overpowered the rest.

The growl came to Lady's throat unbidden. And when the tall man came through the gateway and she got a full, downwind sniff of him, she knew then that he was not her friend any more. He was a killer, plain and simple.

Deadly. Dangerous. He looked different, too. Larger and more intimidating.

The hairy-faced man said something to the tall man in that motley, mongrel barking that humans use. His tone was friendly. Did he not realise that the tall man was about to attack him? Apparently not.

And then it was too late.

Lady watched, appalled, as the tall man lunged in for the kill, wrapping his paws around the hairy-faced man's neck. She could not think of a situation more *wrong* than this. Apart from anything else, the tall man should not be trying to kill a packmate, even if he was higher up in the pack hierarchy than the hairy-faced man. The hairy-faced man had not provoked him or shown him any aggression.

She started leaping from side to side, voicing her protest. But her complaints seemed to be falling on deaf ears, and so finally she realised there was nothing for it but to get involved. She launched herself at the tall man from behind, snarling and sinking her teeth through his layers of false fur, into the meat between his shoulder and neck. The taste of blood was shockingly, guiltily delicious. Likewise the scream the tall man uttered. It was wrong to enjoy such things, Lady knew, but she could not help herself. Besides, she was trying to save the hairy-faced man.

And it worked. The tall man let go of the hairy-faced man, tumbling off sideways, taking Lady with him. Lady could not sustain her jaw-grip on him and was sent rolling over onto her back. Righting herself, she saw the tall man, on his knees, clutching the wound she had inflicted. He started bellowing at her. Fearlessly, ferociously, she hurled herself at him again.

38

'Bitch!' MacGowan yelled at the dog, oblivious to the fact that, technically, this was not an insult. Bitten him! The fucking animal had bitten him!

Bloodied fangs bared, Lady Grinning Soul came at him again.

MacGowan raised his arm defensively. The Afghan managed to get his wrist between her teeth, but the cuffs of his shirt and jersey prevented her from taking a firm bite. He twisted his forearm around, and her teeth meshed together on fabric rather than flesh. He staggered to his feet and yanked his arm away from the dog. Lady dug her heels in and pulled against him. His sleeve stretched. The tug of war lasted several seconds. Then there was a ripping sound, and Lady went skidding backwards with a torn scrap of wool in her mouth. She spat the scrap out.

MacGowan, incensed, went for Lady, aiming a kick at her with his booted foot. Lady managed to twist out of the way in time so that the kick, intended for her ribs, connected with her hind leg instead. It was a glancing blow but it hurt all the same, and Lady yelped and scrambled hurriedly out of MacGowan's range before he could deliver a second kick.

MacGowan had forgotten all about Holman, who was lying on his side, propped up on one elbow, wheezing hard, with blood streaming from his nose. He charged at Lady again. Lady, realising that she had become the tall man's prey now, not the hairy-faced man, took to her heels. MacGowan, howling his rage, gave chase.

39

The devil (as the saying went) was in the details, but so, in Gérard de Sade's opinion, was the truth.

Truth was not to be found in government statistics or in scientific surveys, in official statements or in mass marketed popular culture. Truth shied away from the limelight, inhabiting the grey shadows at the edge of things. Truth lurked in the twilit realm of unprovable facts and untestable hypotheses, at the outer limits of all that was commonly seen and known. What mankind collectively believed was not necessarily everything that was true or real about the world. Reality was a shared hallucination, an illusion people had agreed to accept as real for convenience's sake. And the same was true of truth.

De Sade had spent years exploring the hinterlands of knowledge, poking around in the cracks in history, peering sidelong at news reports and eyewitness accounts of events, ignoring the main picture and concentrating on the corners, the background, the edges. For a man who was scared to step outside his home, he had roved far, both mentally and electronically. He had pored over the myriad works of reference that filled the library in his château. He had searched the downloaded texts of major libraries in other countries via modem. He had trawled the Internet, where information was not constrained by the fetters of acceptability and convention, where wilder theories could be freely aired and one could publish without fear of censorship or concern for commercial considerations. Unsurprisingly, this meant that there was a lot of madness out there in the electronic ether, a lot of contradictory evidence and a lot that was just plain wrong, but amid the insanity and the ambiguity and the inaccuracy, that was where the truth might be unearthed. In the places where people felt at liberty to think and dare and speculate. In the metaphorical margins of the main text, where open-ended questions and comments were scribbled. In the footnotes and fine print that few ever read. In the details.

The events surrounding Jean-Claude's death had taught – forced – de Sade to look at the world in a new way, with new eyes. Gradually, painstakingly, he had amassed a body of evidence against *les Gardiens*, a database of the crimes against humanity committed by their organisation. Possibly he was the only person on the planet who could have done this, the only person who had the requisite combination of incentive, persistence, resources and financial independence to devote himself fulltime to the task. For nearly a decade he had done nothing but hunt for the truth about that band of international terrorists. Their motives still eluded him, their geographical whereabouts still evaded him, but some of the deeds they had done – not least in that Balkan village where Jean-Claude had died – were pretty clear to him. The evidence he had gathered was comprehensive and conclusive. He thought so, and he was convinced that the International Court of Human Rights would think so, too.

That morning he was up by five. Emperor Dragon was not due till midday, but there were last-minute preparations to be made for the arrival and containment of the Englishman, and, anyway, de Sade had been finding it difficult to sleep. The night had been a sequence of fitful naps interspersed with long periods of anticipatory wakefulness, and long before dawn de Sade had decided that there was nothing to be gained by staying in bed. He rose, put on his running vest, shorts and trainers, and went for one of his long rambling jogs through the interior of the château, switching on the lights in each room as he entered it, switching them off as he exited.

Next he fed the cats, who congregated around him in the kitchen in a great mass of mewling mouths and rubbing cheeks and shin-insinuating tails. Nowadays there were a good 150 of the animals in the château, so the fifteen tins of Ronron that de Sade opened each morning satisfied only a third of them, the greediest and most aggressive ones. Luckily there was still a sufficient supply of rats and mice in and around the château to cater for the remainder, although the feline population was expanding at such a rate that the day was surely going to come when demand for rodent sustenance would outstrip supply and some kind of Malthusian correction would have to be brought into effect. Whether there would be a spontaneous mass exodus of cats from the château or whether he would have to call in the vet, de Sade did not know. He hoped that it would be the former, that a proportion of the cats would simply sense that they had to go elsewhere and leave of their own accord. He shuddered at the prospect of decreeing the euthanasia of dozens of perfectly healthy, innocent felines.

After a shower, de Sade dressed in a suit that had not been out of its wardrobe in years and smelled mustily of mothballs. He ran a comb through his coarse, salt-and-pepper hair, applied some cologne to his stubble-bedecked cheeks and chin and inspected himself in the bedroom mirror. He had looked better. He had also looked much worse.

At seven-thirty, he made a phone call to Xavier Barraud in Paris. Xavier had let de Sade down so badly during his first abortive attempt at wrecking a *Gardien* operation that de Sade had vowed never to employ him again. However, Xavier had begged so insistently to be given a second chance, had bombarded de Sade with so many piteous, pleading e-mails, that eventually de Sade had relented and offered him another job. This one would not call on Xavier to exercise his much-vaunted computer-hacking skills, in which department he had been found so sorely lacking. This job, in fact, was a straightforward chauffeuring assignment, the kind of thing a trained monkey could not screw up. None the less de Sade felt impelled to ring Xavier and make sure that he was completely clear on his instructions.

Together, they went over everything Xavier had to do. First and foremost, had Xavier got hold of an ambulance, as he had said he was going to?

Xavier had. In the *banlieue* where he lived – situated in one of Paris *quartiers sensibles*, its difficult areas – it was possible to obtain just about anything, if you had the money and you knew whom to ask. One ambulance, stolen to order? No problem. He would be picking it up shortly, he told de Sade.

'That's good,' de Sade replied. 'And you know when precisely the plane from Tokyo is coming in?'

'I do,' replied Xavier. 'I checked the arrival time with the airline just a few minutes ago. The flight Emperor Dragon is on is running a quarter of an hour ahead of schedule.'

'And you received the directions to the château that I e-mailed to you yesterday?'

'I did, and I've committed them to memory. Gérard, please. I understand why you might want to check up on me, but really, I have everything under control.'

'I wish I shared your confidence,' de Sade said with a sigh, but in truth, such was his mood this morning that he was prepared to give even Xavier the benefit of the doubt. Perhaps he had been judging the kid too harshly. Xavier's previous failure, after all, had not *really* been his fault.

'You know, I'm looking forward to meeting Emperor Dragon,' Xavier added.

'You remember, of course, that he will not make himself known to you as he steps off the plane.'

'I know, I know. He needs to preserve his anonymity.'

'And he will be making his own way here. You will be travelling with two of his associates.'

'As well as the Englishman. Yes, Gérard, I know all this. But I will get a chance to talk to Emperor Dragon when we arrive at the château, won't I? There's so much I want to ask him. He is such a great hacker.'

De Sade was not sure that Emperor Dragon would have the time or, from what de Sade knew of his personality, the inclination to chat with Xavier. Emperor Dragon would probably linger at the château just long enough to see the Englishman safely delivered and make sure that de Sade paid him the rest of his money, and then would head back to the airport. De Sade did not want to dash Xavier's hopes, however, in case this somehow caused him to perform the task entrusted to him less efficiently, so he merely said, 'I can't see why you might not be able to exchange a few words.'

Xavier either failed to detect or chose to ignore the equivocal phrasing of this sentence. He said that he would see de Sade in a few hours, and hung up.

Madame Laforgue appeared punctually at eight. Drawing up before the front door of the château in her puttering, spluttering 2CV, de Sade's housekeeper was surprised to find her employer waiting on the doorstep, with a couple of his cats sitting pertly at his feet. She was even more surprised when the habitually lugubrious de Sade greeted her with a cheerful smile and offered to help her unload the week's groceries from the car. She knew about de Sade's fear of the outdoors, and it was clear that to move even a few paces away from the building was discomforting for him. Nevertheless he made several journeys to and from the 2CV, ferrying the bags of groceries into the château, and all the time he chatted with Madame Laforgue and listened with unprecedented attentiveness to her update on recent events in the nearby town: who had started an affair with whom, who had bribed the mayor how much to nod through a planning application, who had disgraced himself messily with his drunken antics ('*Dégueulasse!*') at the recent town festival.

Finally, when the groceries were stacked away in the pantry, de Sade invited Madame Laforgue to take the day off. This, too, was unprecedented. Or, to be precise, in all the years she had worked for de Sade Madame Laforgue had been asked to take the day off on a number of occasions but never in so cordial a manner. Usually when her employer sent her home it was because he had sunk into one of his recurrent black depressions and could not bear to have any living creature around him save his blessed cats. His voice would be a strained whisper, as though his whole body was enfeebled by the effort of striving to keep inner demons in check. Today, however, he was so polite and friendly as he dismissed her that Madame Laforgue could only assume he wanted to be alone for a different reason from normal. 'If I didn't know better,' she said to her husband later, 'I'd have sworn he was expecting company.'

After Madame Laforgue departed, de Sade collected a roll of paper towel and a cloth-draped porcelain chamber-pot from a cleaning cupboard and headed downstairs into the château's clammy, cobweb-hung cellars. Passing along the aisles between the racks of wine bottles, he noted the absences in the collection – like fresh gouges – that were the result of yesterday's visit by Monsieur Chaigne, the wine dealer.

On most days, an examination of the depleted state of his principal financial asset would be guaranteed to inspire melancholy and mild despair in de Sade as he thought of the money he had spent, the sacrifices he had made, in his pursuit of *les Gardiens*. This morning, though, he felt only a serene sort of equanimity, for he knew that at long last something good was going to come of all those thousands of wines his grandfather and great-grandfather had purchased and laid aside, all those vineyards and vintages they had selected and stored away for succeeding generations of de Sades to savour. It seemed (at this moment, at any rate) that de Sade had put these liquid heirlooms to the best possible use. He could not possibly have drunk them all on his own – not unless he wished to spend his entire life in a permanent state of inebriation – and he was quite confident that he was going to produce no progeny to inherit them.

In a remote corner of the cellars there was a room, a chamber ten metres by ten metres, whose walls, floor and ceiling were of solid rock. The chamber had been hewn out of the raw sandstone on which the château was founded, and had a solid, ten-centimetre-thick oak door, to which de Sade had yesterday added a pair of stout iron bolts to supplement the heavy inbuilt lock. He had also carried out some amateur carpentry at the base of the door, sawing a rectangular aperture just large enough for a food tray and, of course, a chamberpot to be passed through.

De Sade had no idea what the chamber had been used for in the past, but judging by its appearance and location and by the Judas hole in the door, it could well have been a dungeon. Certainly it was going to be that as from today.

He set the roll of paper towel and the chamberpot down in one corner of the room. Then he made sure that the light which he had installed in the ceiling, and which could be operated only from outside the chamber, was working. Then he checked the Panasonic mini-DV camcorder which he had affixed to the door so that its lens and microphone were pointing through the Judas hole. He had run a feed from the camcorder up from the cellars to the dining hall, where it was plugged into his PC via a high-speed serial port. The plan was that his interrogation of the Englishman would be broadcast live across the 'Net to members of his *Société Pour la Vérité*, the loose-knit association of hackers and 'Net buffs whom de Sade had banded together with the common goal of exposing conspiracy and secrecy of all kinds. The previous afternoon he had posted a general alert to all *Société* members that a major development was in the offing, and by evening he had received several e-mails expressing interest and requesting further data. The appetite of the *Société* had been whetted, and when the time came there would be dozens, if not hundreds, of online witnesses to the Englishman's confession. The confession would also be downloaded onto diskette – a digital film-clip that would, de Sade was confident, prove more historically significant than the Dead Sea Scrolls, the Rosetta Stone and the Zapruder footage combined.

The camcorder was charged and fully operational. The image reaching the screen of his PC was sharp and clear, as was the sound quality, which he tested by leaving a portable stereo playing in the chamber.

Taking one final appraising glance around the chamber, he realised that the conditions in which he was going to be keeping the Englishman *were* somewhat primitive. He was not entirely inhumane. He went upstairs and fetched the only two English-language books in the château: a UK translation of *Astérix Chez les Bretons* that Jean-Claude had brought back from a trip to London as a gift, knowing how much de Sade loved *Astérix* albums, and an old, crumpled American paperback edition of a Jeffrey Archer novel that de Sade had bought on holiday twenty years ago in an effort to improve his English (although he had given up reading the book three chapters in, sensing that the atrociousness of the prose was, in fact, doing his English considerable harm). He laid the two books down beside the chamberpot. Archer novel notwithstanding, it was a small, charitable gesture.

He climbed back up the stairs to the ground floor and there picked up the first cat that came to hand, a ragged, soot-black creature which had been fast asleep inside an overturned umbrella stand. The cat was a veteran of innumerable fights, with tiny triangular slivers missing from both ears to prove it, but, though it yowled disgustedly as de Sade draped it over his shoulder, it swiftly succumbed to his strokes and nuzzles and soon had its eyes closed and was emitting a contented, seamless purr.

Strolling along the château corridors, de Sade spoke softly to the animal.

'I am not a cruel man, *minou*,' he said. 'You know that. I feel bad that I am going to be imprisoning this Englishman for who knows how long. I do it only in order to get him to break down and tell me what I want to know. I am hoping that he is a rational man and that he will realise that there is nothing to be gained by holding out on me. However patient he is, I will be more patient. I need from him enough information to confirm the evidence that I have on his organisation. That is all. If he has any sense, he will give it to me quickly and willingly. If not . . .' De Sade shrugged his cat-less shoulder. 'It will be bad for him. But I must do what I must do. I must steel myself, be strong. I cannot allow my conscience to stand in the way of what needs to be achieved. It is for all our sakes. For the benefit of the whole world. You understand that, don't you? You who have fought in many battles. You understand that sometimes the harsh way is the only way.'

The black cat, whether it did or did not agree with the philosophy it was being invited to ponder on, continued to purr.

40

Lucretia emerged from her bedroom dressed in trainers, a sweatshirt and a pair of tracksuit bottoms. She was holding a slim black trapezoid box that she left on her bedside table at night and, by day, always kept close to hand. The box was adorned with a trio of blue studs in triangular formation, each stud engraved with a different hieroglyph.

Her brother Ron had first shown her the box and told her what it was for on the very day he handed over custody of the Grange and cellars to her. He had described the box as the ultimate line of defence against intruders, and had gone on to explain to her the function of each of the studs: which one summoned the Domestic to attack an intruder; which one put the catlike sentinel, once summoned, into temporary stasis; and which one returned the beast to her lair. 'It's like on a reel-to-reel tape deck in a recording studio,' he had said, lightly fingering the studs one after another in turn. 'Play, Pause and Stop. And only one person can use it. Right now that's me. In a few moments, once I've reconfigured its user-recognition capability, it'll be you.'

The box fitted snugly into Lucretia's palm. It was as light as a wafer, but what it represented lent it a certain comforting weight and solidity.

Sliding the box into her pocket, she headed along the

upstairs corridor. She was met near the top of the stairs by Piers coming out of the guest room. He was wearing a pair of flamboyant – and, frankly, purple – silk pyjamas, accessorised with a pair of scarlet Chinese slippers. His pyjama jacket had a monogram, two entwined Ps, stitched in silver braid on the breast pocket. The cut of its lapels exposed enough of Piers's chest to reveal his crystal puzzle-egg medallion, which dangled, glittering, just below his collarbone.

Piers yawned extravagantly. 'Way too early for me, this is. I'm normally a cornflakes-at-noon kind of chap. Who's turned up? Do we know?'

'Not yet,' Lucretia replied tensely. 'But whoever it is ought to have reached the house by now.'

She set off down the staircase to the entrance hall. Piers ambled after her, ruffling a hand back and forth through his hair.

The Grange's double front doors were half-glazed, their small square panes affording a clear view of the last hundred yards of driveway and the turning circle where *Da Vinci's Dreams Downcast* stood, a frozen whirlwind of fused metal. No car had pulled up yet. The Holman-Fisk family fleet – comprising a Range Rover, a Volvo estate and a Rover Metro for the girls' joint use – was garaged around the side of the house, so the turning circle was empty of vehicles except for Piers's Caterham.

Lucretia stopped at the doors and, clasping her upper arms, looked out. Piers joined her a moment later.

'I think we're in deep trouble,' Lucretia said.

'Is this that woman's intuition of yours at work again?' Piers enquired.

'Don't you feel it, too?'

'I feel a gnawing emptiness inside, but that's probably because I haven't had my breakfast yet.'

'Oh, for God's sake, Piers!' Lucretia snapped. 'Be flippant if you must, but only when it's appropriate.'

Piers decided it would be wise, for the time being, to keep any further amusing comments to himself.

Lucretia drummed her fingertips against her triceps muscles.

Both she and Piers caught sight of movement out on the driveway at the same time.

41

Lady had never run so fast in her life. She could hear the tall man behind her – his pounding feet, his rapid, thumping heartbeat, the air hissing in and out of his throat. The sounds were diminishing as the gap between her and him widened, but Lady did not dare slacken her pace. On she went, driven by fear.

Her only hope of escaping the tall man's clutches, she knew, lay in beating him to the house. She could not maintain top speed indefinitely, and unless she found refuge soon she would weaken and falter and slow, and the tall man would catch her up and then she would be killed. Simple as that. Despite his human appearance, the tall man was truly a feral creature now. He would have as much compunction about tearing her apart as a fox would about tearing apart a rabbit.

The only problem was, no matter how far ahead of him Lady was when she reached the house, there was no guarantee she would be able to enter it. She lacked that talent, exclusive to humans, of opening and closing doors. She had observed how humans used their long, spindly paws to manipulate the small, revolving protuberance that doors had, halfway up, but she had not worked out how to do it for herself. She would have to scratch and bark at the front door of the house and hope that someone inside heard her and came in time to let her in.

She ran alongside the driveway, sprinting like a greyhound along the grass verge with her long fur streaming horizontally backwards. The tall man followed, still falling behind, but dogged and relentless in his pursuit.

The house hove into view. Lady veered towards it, making a beeline for the front steps. She darted across the driveway, her claws tick-tacking on the gravel, and continued across the front lawn. It was several seconds before she heard the tall man's footsteps crunching as he, too, traversed the driveway's gravel. She felt a surge of hope. She might just make it. She might just survive.

Hope turned to ecstasy as she saw the front doors open outwards and caught a whiff of the distinct, the unmistakable, the one-and-only, the sublime odour of *her master*! He was there at the entrance to the house, along with his female packmate, the alpha-bitch who was in many ways the pack leader. He was there, urgently barking the name-sound he used for her: *Luh-duh! Luh-duh!*

Lady crossed the turning circle, bounded up the steps and hurtled through the doorway.

Safe!

42

At first, seeing the dog and the man coming towards the house across the front lawn, Lucretia thought it was Lady Grinning Soul who had gone berserk. Observing the blood-flecked, foamy saliva around Lady's mouth, and then turning her attention to Lady's pursuer and observing his torn clothing, the dried blood on his face and the wound to his neck, her assumption was that Lady had gone mad and attacked MacGowan.

A closer look at MacGowan forced a reappraisal. While he was still unmistakably Bill MacGowan, he was not the Bill MacGowan she knew. He was a shambling, swollen, warped version of the original – a distorted, funhouse-mirror reflection. His cheeks were flushed purple, his mouth was open in a silent, lunatic roar of rage and the whites of his eyes were visible clear around the irises. This was not a man aggrieved to have been bitten, seeking revenge on the dog that had wounded him. This was a savage beast intent on slaughter.

Piers barely paid any attention to MacGowan, having eyes only for Lady's obvious terror. He threw open the doors and called to her twice. Lady came sprinting up the front steps and into the house, her momentum carrying her halfway across the hallway before she was finally able to skid to a stop. Piers hurried over to her, arms outstretched, and crouched to enfold her in an embrace. Lady, panting and trembling and wagging her tail so hard that her entire hindquarters shook, covered her master's face and neck in slobbery licks of gladness and gratitude.

Lucretia, meanwhile, could only stand and watch in horror and dismay as the funhouse-mirror parody of Bill MacGowan came closer.

Reaching the foot of the steps, MacGowan looked up and caught sight of Lucretia in the open doorway. Emitting an inhuman cry, he cleared the steps with a single bound and charged straight at her.

It was only then that it dawned on Lucretia that Lady was not the sole object of MacGowan's murderous intent.

She lunged for the handles of both doors and yanked them towards her, managing to slam the doors shut a split-second before MacGowan got there. Glass cracked and woodwork creaked as MacGowan smashed headlong into the doors. He careened backwards with a stunned grunt. Lucretia hurriedly groped for the key in the right-hand door, turning it with a shaking hand. There were bolts at the top and bottom of the left-hand door, but she did not have time to throw them. MacGowan, having collected his wits, drew himself back and launched himself, shoulder-first, at the barrier between him and the object of his murderous intent. The doors juddered in their frame at the impact. Lucretia flinched and recoiled. More glass cracked. But the doors held.

'Lucretia!' MacGowan roared through the panes. He started hammering on the doors with both fists. 'Lucretia, I'm going to get you, you slag! And that timewarped tosser with you, and his fucking dog, too!'

Lucretia backed away, staring at the raving, raging creature outside who had once been a man. A decent, level-headed man. Someone she trusted implicitly. A friend.

MacGowan threw himself at the doors a couple more times, then, seeming to realise that there might be a less strenuous means of opening them, drew back his fist and punched one of the windowpanes. After three blows, the glass began to give way, sagging inwards, small shards of it falling out.

'Oh, God, I didn't take the key out,' Lucretia whispered. 'He's going for the key.'

Without a word, Piers let go of Lady and darted forwards.

MacGowan, seeing Piers coming, redoubled his efforts to smash the windowpane. The jagged glass was lacerating his fingers, but he seemed neither to feel the cuts nor to care. Within the space of a couple of seconds he had knocked out all the glass. Thrusting his torn, bloodied hand through the empty pane, he started groping for the lock.

Slithering to a halt at the doors, Piers crouched down, grasped the lower of the two bolts and shot it home. MacGowan abandoned his attempt to reach the key and made a grab for Piers instead. His hand latched on to Piers's hair, but Piers jerked his head sideways and his hair slipped through MacGowan's blood-slicked fingers before they could obtain a firm grip. MacGowan, snarling through gritted teeth, thrust his arm further inwards and groped for Piers again, but Piers, standing up, twisted himself sideways out of range of Mac-Gowan's hand. With a desperate lunge he reached for the upper bolt and drove it home with the heel of his hand. Then he scurried back across the hall to Lucretia and Lady.

Thwarted, MacGowan let loose a torrent of epithets and began hurling himself at the doors once again, as before using his shoulder as a battering ram.

'I don't think even the bolts will keep him out for ever,' Piers remarked.

'What do you suggest?'

'I would say "panic", but there are those who would consider the remark inappropriately flippant. So instead I recommend we take sanctuary in the cellars.'

The thumps of MacGowan's efforts to gain ingress echoed thunderously through the hall. The door frame was splintering and fissuring in several places now, and starting to give way at the lintel. Flecks of paint and flinders of wood were falling onto the doormat and the surrounding floor, joining the broken glass already lying there.

'Yes,' said Lucretia. 'Yes, of course. Come on, then.'

Together the two Guardians and Lady Grinning Soul made their way over to *Daedalian*, the bas-relief Fisk that adorned the hallway's west wall. Amid the sculpture's archipelagic terrain and the moving parts that flitted mothlike to and fro across its contours, there was a cog-shaped depression located at waist-height. Lucretia raised her right hand, clenched it into a fist and extended it, knuckles-first, so that the puzzle-egg ring on her middle finger was poised directly in front of the depression. She was just about to insert the egg portion of the ring into the hole when the thumping at the doors abruptly ceased.

As one, Lucretia, Piers and Lady Grinning Soul turned.

MacGowan had hunched down and was leering at them through the frame of the windowpane he had dislodged.

'Oh, Lucretia,' he said in a sinister, singsong tone. 'Lu-u-u-*cree*-tia. Where are you going? Don't you want to know where Dennis is? Where dear old hubby has got to?'

'Dennis?' Lucretia echoed.

Her face fell.

Of course. Lady Grinning Soul had been outdoors. She liked to accompany Holman when he went for his early-morning stroll. If Lady had encountered MacGowan, then so had . . .

Lucretia cursed herself for failing to make the connection earlier, not that it would have made any difference. Through clenched teeth she demanded, 'Where is he, Bill? Where's Dennis? What have you done with him?'

'Come here and I'll tell you,' said MacGowan through the empty pane. Whether or not he was consciously emulating the wheedling intonation used by Jack Nicholson in that famous scene in *The Shining* when he menaces his wife and son with an axe, the cinematic echo only served to emphasise the grotesqueness of the whole situation.

310

Lucretia said, 'If you've harmed him in any way, Bill, so help me God, I'll . . .'

'You'll do what, Lucreeetia? Call me bad names?'

'Where *is* he? Tell me!' Lucretia took a couple of steps towards the doors. Piers intervened, seizing her by the arm.

She turned and glared at Piers's hand. 'Let me go.'

'Ignore him, old girl. He's taunting you. Trying to get to you.'

'I'm perfectly aware of that. But he's done something to Dennis. I have to know if Dennis is all right.'

'Come on, Lucreeetia,' said MacGowan. 'Come over here where I can talk to you.'

'Don't go, Lucretia,' Piers urged, tightening his grip. 'He'll kill you if he gets the chance.'

'Piers, let go of me. Now.'

Piers debated whether to slap her or not. That was what a chap had a duty to do under these circumstances, when females started acting irrationally. A quick smack across the cheek usually was enough to bring them back to their senses. But these days, alas, slapping a girl – like patting her bottom – was more likely to get you a knee in the groin than gratitude. So he decided to persist with reasoning.

'Whatever's happened to Dennis has happened,' he said. 'Getting yourself killed isn't going to make any difference to that.'

'This is my husband we're talking about, Piers. The father of my daughters.'

'And if you want to do what's best for him, save yourself. Get down into the cellars. That's what *he'd* want you to do, I'm sure.'

Lucretia looked over at MacGowan, then back at Piers. Piers's words were sinking in. She knew he was talking sense. But the man she loved like no other, with a love that had been tempered by time, a love that had withstood thirty years of cohabitation and family life and several fiery arguments and still remained passionate and strong, a love that was now so deep she scarcely recognised it as love any more, for it had become as visceral, as essential, as hearing or breathing – that man was out there somewhere in the estate. He might be injured, perhaps severely. He might be suffering in terrible agony. Dying. Dead, even. She had to know what had happened to him. The uncertainty, the fear, was almost too much to bear.

But Piers was right. Damn him. Getting away from MacGowan was the priority. The sane, sensible course of action. It might not be what she wanted to do, but it was what she had to do.

Piers felt her relent, her shoulders sagging, the muscles in her arm slackening in his grasp. He let go of her.

'There, that's a girl,' he said.

Stalwartly, without a word, Lucretia turned and inserted her ring into the depression in *Daedalian*. Segments of the puzzle-egg shot outwards, fitting into the depression's cog-teeth slots. The sculpture's moving parts pounced into a fixed configuration and the outline of a door cracked open in its surface, just to Lucretia's right. The door sank inwards and sideways with a hiss, revealing a descending flight of stone steps.

'God forgive me, Dennis, I'm sorry,' Lucretia sighed, and headed through the entranceway.

Piers and Lady followed.

'BASTARDS!!!' The word came out of MacGowan's throat as a barely articulate howl of frustration. Stepping back, he commenced barging at the doors again.

43

Sequestered in one of the toilets at the rear of the plane, hunkered on the ring-seat of the lavatory unit in the classic pose of contemplation (elbow on thigh, chin on fist), Kenji took a long, deep drag on his cigarette and exhaled the smoke in twin plumes from his nostrils.

It was his sixth cigarette-break so far during the flight, and as on the previous five occasions Kenji found himself resenting the no-smoking policy that this particular airline had recently instituted. You would have thought, wouldn't you, that such a vigorously pro-cigarette nation as France would have held out against banning smoking on its long-haul carriers, especially on flights to and from another vigorously pro-cigarette nation like Japan. You would have thought that the French, of all people, would have resisted the tide of health fascism that was sweeping the planet. But no. They, like almost everyone else, had capitulated to the demands of a bunch of do-gooders who pretended to have people's best interests at heart but really just got a kick out of spoiling other people's fun.

And what made it worse, as far as Kenji was concerned, was that the anti-smoking lobby originated in America. America, which had given the world so many great things, so many great sports, fashions, icons, slang terms, movies . . . *This* was the newest worldwide export from the so-called Land of the Free: the demonisation of smokers.

So now, in order to enjoy a quick puff on a plane, Kenji

and others like him were forced to go to absurd lengths. They were forced to skulk in the cramped confines of a toilet, disable the smoke detector and light up furtively, as though they were perverts indulging in some kind of unspeakable secret vice. It was not right.

And Kenji needed his cigarette-breaks. Oh, yes. Needed them badly. The bennies had him wide-eyed and wired. He had popped so many during the course of the flight that he thought he was never going to sleep again. His leg kept jiggling, his hands were trembling and his insides were knotted. Benzedrine gave most people the squits, but Kenji it left constipated. Here he was, sitting on a lavatory, and he probably was not going to take a decent dump for a week.

The cigarettes served to calm him a little. Took the edge of the benny buzz. So fuck the health nuts, fuck airline regulations – he had to smoke, and, God damn it, he was *going* to smoke.

He filled his lungs with another inhalation of burning, acrid, delicious fumes.

If Ryu found out that he had deserted his post, he would be furious. But Kenji had no doubt that Ryu was fast asleep in his comfy First Class seat. Fast asleep and dreaming of all the money he and Emperor Dragon were going to make together from that machine they had plugged the Englishman up to, the – what was it called? The Hypnagogic Inducer.

Kenji also stood to make money from the Hypnagogic Inducer. All the members of Ryu's gang did. Nowhere near as much as Ryu and Emperor Dragon would be making, but Ryu was pretty conscientious about giving a cut of his profits to the gang members. When business was going well, the *bosozoku* received nice bonuses in their pay-packets. Equally, when business was slow, the *bosozoku* also felt the pinch. But, then, as Ryu's couriers and enforcers, Kenji and the other gang members had to be prepared to share in the downs as well as the ups of economic fortune. Besides, whatever they got paid, it was usually money for nothing. Money for doing what they

314

liked to do: hanging out, smoking, riding their motor-bikes, looking cool, intimidating people. Only occasion-ally were they actually called on to fight on Ryu's behalf. When they did fight, though, they were expected to give it their all, which meant, if necessary, sacrificing their lives – as had been demonstrated back in the contemplative garden during that set-to with the Englishman.

Shaking his head, Kenji recalled how easily the English-man had taken out three of his fellow *bosozoku*. He had never seen anyone move as fast as that guy had. And the way he had taken all that punishment from Katsuhiro's brass-knuckled fists and come up *smiling*. Incredible! Emperor Dragon had warned the gang beforehand that the Englishman was no slouch when it came to hand-to-hand combat, but none of them, Kenji included, had had an inkling how quick and tough and lethal he would prove to be. He would have wiped the floor with them all if Kenji had not taken the girl hostage and Emperor Dragon had not produced that weird-looking pistol.

Kenji tapped ash into the sink and took another drag. The cigarette coal was nearly down to the filter. Another minute in here, and then he would resume his position at the Englishman's bedside, put on his surgical mask again and try to look expert and medical.

Ryu was going straight. That was why he had hooked up with Emperor Dragon. After a few recent brushes with the police and a much scarier run-in with the Kyoto branch of the yakuza, Ryu had decided that the time was right to get out of the narcotics trade and stake a claim in something legitimate. Emperor Dragon's virtual-reality-type device was Ryu's ticket to respectability – although, ironically, in order for that to happen it seemed that the Hypnagogic Inducer had to be first used for a decidedly *il*legitimate purpose.

From what Kenji had gleaned about the Hypnagogic Inducer's capabilities, it seemed to him that what it offered, with its vivid trips that could take you almost anywhere in your subconscious mind, was a non-pharma-ceutical equivalent of the effects of a psychoactive drug.

He wondered whether it might not in its own way be as addictive as a real drug, with all the attendant problems of come-downs and withdrawal. Maybe, when it became publicly available, people would take to it for the same reasons they took to drugs – as a release, a way of escaping from the crushing anxieties and mundanity of life. Maybe, in the end, the Hypnagogic Inducer would have to be outlawed, just as opium, cocaine and LSD had been.

(And tobacco, too, Kenji thought as he finished his cigarette with one last crackling, smouldering suck. If the health fascists got their way, tobacco might well be next to join the list of the world's proscribed substances.)

Still, whatever ultimately happened to Emperor Dragon's machine in the future, Ryu seemed confident that in the medium-to-long-term future it was a valid financial enterprise, and that was good enough for Kenji.

He ground the cigarette out in the sink, then dropped the butt between his legs into the lavatory bowl. Standing up, he turned on the tap and swilled the ash down into the sink plughole. He checked his reflection in the mirror. His pupils were two gaping black holes surrounded by blood-shot flares, like eclipsed red suns.

He used a dab of water to slick a few stray strands of hair back into place. Then he waved a hand to disperse the last few lingering tendrils of smoke that were hanging in the air. When the atmosphere in the toilet appeared clear he reached up to the ceiling and removed the condom with which he had covered the smoke detector. Some people stuffed the smoke detector's vents with lavatory paper in order to disable it, but a condom, if you came prepared with one for this purpose, was far more efficient.

Kenji flushed the lavatory, picked up his cigarettes and Zippo, tucked them into a pocket of his overalls along with the condom, and exited the toilet.

All but a couple of the passengers within view were asleep. People were contorted into the most comfortable positions they could achieve within the narrow confines of their seats. Those lucky enough to have an empty seat adjacent to theirs had raised the dividing armrests and were lying on their sides, foetally curled to fit the available space. Rolled-up coats and cardigans were being used as pillows. This, along with the plain, poor-quality airline-issue blankets that people had draped over themselves and the bags and personal belongings that littered the floor, gave the cabin something of the appearance of a refugee camp. The only sounds were the occasional cough or snore and the constant hissing roar of the jumbo's turbine engines. Early sunlight glowed behind the lowered window-blinds.

The screened-off section where the Englishman was being kept was almost directly next to the toilets. Kenji plucked aside one end of the curtain.

He had just enough time to register the empty gurney. The unbuckled straps. The IV tubes hanging uselessly down, their needle-tipped ends leaking droplets of clear fluid on to the floor. The black metal helmet lying upturned on the gurney mattress, its intricate inner mechanics exposed.

He had just enough time to ask himself where the Englishman was.

Just enough time to begin reaching for his switchblade, which he normally kept in the back pocket of his jeans, and then to realise that he was wearing overalls, not jeans, and to recall, with dismay, that he had not been allowed to bring his blade on board.

Then he glimpsed a flicker of motion at the periphery of his vision.

Hands clutched his head.

There was an instant of whitesteel agony.

And after that, the absence of everything.

44

On the reverse of *Daedalian* lay an arrangement of cogs, ratchets, pulleys and levers of Heath Robinsonian complexity. Lucretia had contrived the sculpture so that each of its moving parts was effectively a tumbler in a safe lock. When a Guardian's puzzle-egg was inserted into the cog-shaped hollow in the sculpture, this completed a circuit that triggered the unlocking sequence. The 'tumblers' ceased cycling through their myriad permutations and settled into the correct formation to release bolts within the hidden door and cause the door to open inwards pneumatically. In order to secure the door from the inside, all that was required was to close it and depress a lever which disengaged several crucial components. Then access to the cellars was impossible for anyone, even a Guardian, except by force.

When all three of them – Lucretia, Lady Grinning Soul and Piers, in that order – were safely through the doorway, Piers turned and heaved the door shut behind them, muffling the sound of MacGowan trying to batter down the front doors of the Grange. Outside, as soon as the door was snugly closed, the bas-relief's moving parts resumed their flitting and darting. Piers threw the lock-disabling lever, and several of them became stationary again.

Lucretia sagged against the wall.

'What's happened to him, Piers?' she asked, in a faint, appalled voice.

318

'Unclear, old girl. I think the only thing one can say with any certainty at the moment is that he means to kill us and he's not going to stop until he's achieved that goal.'

'So what should we do?' She thought of the box in her pocket. 'Should we unleash the Domestic on him?'

'The Domestic would make pretty short work of him,' Piers agreed. 'But she won't attack anyone carrying a puzzle-egg, and we know Bill has his on him because he used it to open the front gates.'

'What if we somehow managed to get his puzzle-egg off him?'

'And, assuming that was possible, then set the Domestic on him? That would most likely solve the problem. Only . . .'

'Only?'

Piers shrugged. 'Call me a sentimental old fool, but that's Bill out there. Our cohort and ally Bill MacGowan. And if what's been done to him is reversible, if he can be cured, then we've an obligation to find a way of doing that.'

Lucretia assented with a nod. She knew that, as earlier, Piers was talking sense, but at the same time, secretly, in the ruthless, vengeful deeps of her soul, she quite liked the idea of letting loose the Domestic on MacGowan. If it turned out that he *had* harmed Holman, then friend or not he deserved no better fate than death.

Just then, audible from the hallway through *Daedalian*, came a thump louder than all the others preceding. It was immediately followed by a huge, heaving, splintering, shattering *CRACK*. Something heavy toppled loudly to the hallway floor, and both Lucretia and Piers heard a guttural yell of triumph.

'He's in,' Piers said.

Lucretia pushed herself away from the wall. 'All right. Let's get downstairs.'

As they reached the top of the stone steps they heard MacGowan crossing the hallway and arriving at the sculpture. There was a jangling of metal as he produced his keyring and attempted to unlock the door with the keyring's brass puzzle-egg. The sculpture mechanism whirred impotently. Infuriated, MacGowan swore and began pounding at the sculpture. Lucretia and Piers exchanged grim glances and set off down into the cellars. Lady, perhaps wiser than both of them, was already at the bottom of the steps.

Entering the cellars beneath Bretherton Grange was like entering some bizarre treasure trove, an Aladdin's cave filled not with jewels and gold but with weaponry and inventions that gleamed and shone with a dark value of their own. Here were artefacts which had had no part in history, which belonged to futures that had never arrived. Here, stored on shelves and in alcoves, were devices the Librans had deemed mankind unready to possess, most of them covered in a patina of dust like exhibits at a never-visited museum. Here were armaments and equipment bequeathed over the centuries by the Librans to the Guardians for the Guardians' exclusive use, hoarded alongside manmade items brought back from missions by past and present Guardians. (As a rule, Guardians destroyed all traces of the contra-temporal technology they were sent to suppress, but exceptions were made for things that might prove useful to them.)

The cellars were divided up into chains of vaulted chambers, one chamber leading to the next, arranged over several levels. Lucretia knew the cellars' geography better than anyone else, but there were remote corners that even she had yet to discover, lower levels that even she had yet to plumb.

She, Piers and Lady hurried away from the cellars' entrance, putting behind them the dully reverberating clang of MacGowan's assaults on *Daedalian*. Lights came on automatically in each chamber they entered, switching off the moment they moved on to the next chamber. Eventually, when neither Lucretia nor Piers could hear MacGowan any more (though Lady, with her sharper ears, still could), they halted.

'OK,' said Lucretia. 'We're safe for now. So what's our plan?'

'I was rather hoping you might be able to tell *me*,' Piers replied.

'If only John were here.' Lucretia's tone was more petulant than wistful. 'Christ, he really couldn't have picked his time worse.'

'Still, nothing we can do about that now, eh?' said Piers. 'Spilt milk and all that.'

Lady was licking the spot on her hind leg where MacGowan had kicked her. Suddenly she stopped, catching a scent. She started barking. In reply, from a long way off, deep within the bowels of the cellars, came a low, menacing, wavering yowl.

'The Domestic,' said Lucretia. 'Ssh!' she called out to the Node's sentinel. 'You're not needed!' Under her breath she added, 'Yet.'

The Domestic huffed and fell silent. Piers quietened Lady, too, with a few soothing strokes, though the Afghan remained agitated. The Domestic's scent was both perplexing and arousing to her – arousing in that it was feline, perplexing because it was like no feline scent she had ever smelled before.

'Well, then,' said Piers. 'Perhaps it would help us with our plan if we go through a brief recap of events leading up to this episode.'

Lucretia nodded. 'This is how things stand, as far as I can tell. The day before yesterday Bill led an action-to-suppress on a bioweapons laboratory set up by a company called Gene Genius that used to be known as PetriTech. Something went wrong, we don't know what, and now a monster-mutated version of Bill has come back and is trying to kill his fellow Guardians.'

'And their pets.' Piers patted Lady's head. 'Well, given the historical connection between Gene Genius and PetriTech, I believe there's only one conclusion to be drawn.'

'Bill's been infected by the Codename: Bearskin berserker agent.'

'Correct. Although apparently not as extreme a form of the agent as the one that was used on his comrades in the Gulf War.'

'But we suppressed Codename: Bearskin, didn't we?' said Lucretia. 'Back in 1990?'

'All but the one batch of the agent, remember? The one the British army got their hands on before we hit the PetriTech laboratories.'

'The batch that was field-tested on Bill's patrol.'

'Yes, but was all of it used then?' said Piers. '*That* is the question.'

'You think the army held some back?'

'Held some back, and then returned it to PetriTech – or Gene Genius as the company had become – for further development.'

'Enabling them to create a refined version. Of course. A Mark 2 berserker agent. Slower-acting than the original, with some kind of growth inhibitor introduced into the bacillus to suppress its reproductive rate and so lessen its effect on the human body.'

'But the Mark 2 version may still be ultimately terminal, like its predecessor,' said Piers gravely. 'Which makes it all the more imperative that we attempt to cure Bill. Now, you have an all-purpose paraterrestrial vaccine down here, don't you? One that can eradicate harmful bacteria within the human body.'

'I do. In fact, I supplied Bill with some for the mission.'

'Then our objective is clear. We have to vaccinate him.'

Lucretia uttered a sardonic laugh. 'Easier said than done.'

'Most things are,' Piers said. 'Except silence, which is easier done than said. Nevertheless, I take your point. The vaccine pressure-guns, as I recall, are designed for administering the vaccine either to oneself or to a comatose or compliant second party. In order to deliver the vaccine properly they require direct contact with the subject's skin for at least two seconds.'

'Two seconds which Bill isn't going to give us. And then, of course, there's the small matter of the vaccine not

322

taking effect immediately. It takes a couple of minutes to work, and Bill will still pose a danger to us for those couple of minutes.'

'The vaccine gun wasn't made for use on an unwilling subject,' Piers said resignedly. 'But, then, the Librans could hardly have foreseen such a need.'

'Perhaps we could hit him with a tranquilliser first.'

'There's no guarantee that a tranquilliser, even a paraterrestrial-grade one, will be effective on him in his present berserker form. And that's assuming one of us would be able to get close enough to him in the first place to get a clear shot.'

'John would probably be able to manage it.'

'Yes, well, indestructible Captain Scarlet is currently unavailable, so we'll just have to try to muddle through without him.' Piers said this with just a hint of exasperation.

Lucretia gave a tight, contrite smile. 'Yes, you're right. Sorry, Piers.'

'Apology accepted. So now, let's think about this. The only way we have a chance of administering the vaccine to Bill is if we can find some way of capturing and containing him.'

'Perhaps,' said Lucretia, frowning, 'if we were to lure him into a room and lock him in?'

'But then someone would have to remain in the room with him in order to administer the vaccine, and there's still that other problem – Bill isn't just going to stand still and obligingly let himself be injected.'

'Yes. Good point.' The furrows in Lucretia's forehead deepened. 'Unless . . .'

Piers grinned. 'Oh, I like the sound of that "unless".'

'There is *one* way Bill could be safely corralled. I think I could do it. I'd need about ten minutes to get things ready, though. And he'd still have to be lured to a specific place. But it's possible, Piers. God, I think it might just be possible.'

'Excellent. Tell me more.'

Lucretia told him more, and when she had finished,

Piers arched one eyebrow and said, 'And is there anything else you'd like me to do while I'm about it? Turn some water into wine, perhaps? Walk on water?'

'You're not prepared to do it?'

'Oh, I didn't say that.'

'I wouldn't blame you if you weren't.'

'Oh, no, I'm quite happy to give it my best shot,' said Piers. 'I'm just not sure I'll succeed. But, then' – he shrugged – 'that's what Freelance Facilitating's all about.'

'Really?' said Lucretia, with a faint glimmer of a smile. 'I've often wondered.'

45

An announcement was repeated over the plane's PA system in three languages, first French, then halting English, then very halting Japanese. Passengers were wished a good morning and informed that the plane would be landing at Charles de Gaulle in one hour and that breakfast would be served shortly.

Rattray listened as he dressed himself in the street clothes the dead *bosozoku* had been wearing beneath his white overalls. The young Japanese was large for his race, and Rattray was of medium build, so the clothes were not a bad fit. He could not do up the waistband button of the jeans, but the belt, buckled on its last notch, kept the jeans up. The sneakers pinched his feet slightly but the discomfort was tolerable.

As he dressed, he did his best to disregard the ghostly warmth lingering within the fabric of the clothes, the borrowed heat of the body they had moments earlier clad. It was a disagreeable sensation, but things could have been far worse. He counted himself fortunate that the *bosozoku* had not voided his bladder and bowels at the instant of death, as often occurs.

He pulled the white overalls on, and as he did so a rattling sound coming from one of the pockets drew his attention. Delving in, he took out a pack of Marlboro Lights, a Zippo lighter, an unwrapped condom and a small brown bottle of benzedrine. He examined all four items in turn, then returned them to the pocket. Tying the ribbons of the surgical mask around his neck, he turned to the *bosozoku*'s body, which he had laid out on the gurney, naked and face-up. He picked up the hospital gown that he himself had been wearing and set about clothing the body in it. With quick, quiet movements he pulled the sleeves up around the young man's arms. Then he rolled the body over onto its side. Shattered cervical vertebrae grated against one another as the *bosozoku*'s head lolled loosely, a dead weight on the end of his neck. He knotted the gown's ties at the back, then lowered the corpse back down into the lying position. He drew the hospital blanket up over the body, leaving the arms uncovered as his had been, then secured the restraining straps and set the black helmet firmly on the *bosozoku*'s head. Finally he inserted the four IVs into the *bosozoku*'s forearms, securing them in place with their attached pieces of sticking plaster.

He gave his handiwork a quick once-over. Nobody who took a good look was going to mistake the young man's ochre skin for his own, but at a distance, and to the casual observer, the switch was probably undetectable.

He went to the curtain and teased one edge of it aside to peek out into the cabin. Passengers were stirring, straightening up, stretching. Flight attendants were making their way along the aisles, raising the window blinds, letting in more light. From the galley halfway up the plane came the smells of coffee and tea brewing.

Tea. What Rattray would have given then for a lovely, steaming cup of Earl Grey.

Letting the curtain fall gently back into place, he turned, went to the rear of the screened-off section and let himself out that way. He checked over his shoulder. The passengers were facing away from him. The cabin crew were preoccupied. Unobserved, he slipped into the nearest toilet – by coincidence the same toilet in which Kenji had enjoyed his final cigarette.

No sooner had he closed and locked the toilet door than a wave of dizziness swept over him, nearly overwhelming him. He braced himself against the sink, willing himself not to pass out, to remain conscious. His system was still fighting the effects of the sedative and he could feel that his inner resources were at low ebb. But he could not allow himself to weaken. Not now.

He spun the tap and splashed cold water on his face. The water was wonderfully refreshing. He peered up at his droplet-speckled face in the mirror. The dizziness was abating; clarity was returning to his brain.

'Well,' he said to his reflection, 'now to see if this brilliant scheme of yours is going to work.'

It was not really a scheme, more a hastily conceived idea whose parents were lack of time and lack of alternatives. Rattray was going on the assumption that Emperor Dragon must be somewhere aboard this plane, along with perhaps a couple more of his rent-a-thugs. Obviously he could not deal with them while still on the plane, not without putting the lives of innocent passengers at risk and drawing unwanted attention to himself. A violent in-flight incident would mean French police waiting on the Tarmac at Charles de Gaulle, and for many reasons Rattray did not want a run-in with the authorities. The best course of action available to him, *if* he could pull it off successfully, was the one he was about to attempt.

He remembered what Kim had said at the restaurant in Tokyo. Sometimes a thing was so obvious, so simple, that you just could not see it until someone else pointed it out to you. The following morning at the *ryokan* in Kyoto, shortly before waking Kim, Rattray had had a go at putting her suggestion into practice. A limited experiment, but the results had been encouraging.

Now to find out just how far he could take it.

He concentrated on his hair first. Before the strange and terrible surgery that had altered and immortalised him, his hair used to be pure raven black. It had turned snow-white after the surgery was over – an unavoidable side-effect, he had been told. Now, he imagined it black again. Staring at his reflection, he willed this to be so.

And just as when he willed his legs to move fast and

they did, or when he willed his muscles to perform a feat of superior strength and they did, his hair complied.

At first, for several seconds, he noticed no apparent change in colour, and was disheartened. Perhaps he had been expecting too much. Then, at the roots at his crown, he detected a darkening. The darkness spread slowly out across his scalp, each strand of hair gaining colour from its follicle towards its tip like ink being drawn up the tube of a fountain pen. It was not long before all that remained of his former whiteness was a tidal ring at his fringe, his temples and the nape of his neck, and this, too, soon succumbed to black.

He examined his reflection from all sides by the lilac-tinged light of the toilet's overhead strip-bulb. The John Rattray peering back at him from the mirror was a John Rattray he had not seen in a century. His eyebrows had also gone black, as had the fine hairs on the backs of his hands.

Satisfied, he proceeded to the next phase.

Holding an image of the dead *bosozoku*'s skin colour in his mind, he commanded his own epidermis to take on a similar pigmentation. All at once he was tingling all over, as though there was a subcutaneous layer of liquid electricity rippling up and down his body.

An increase in melanin levels, he thought as he watched his face and neck pass from pale white through deepening shades of light brown until it finally attained the correct ochre hue.

Again, he paused to inspect himself. His hands matched his face. He fixed his mouth into a grin. The contrast between his teeth and skin had never been so marked.

Emboldened by his continuing success, he embarked on the third and final phase of self-modification.

The first phase had been painless. The second had felt peculiar but not uncomfortable. The third – altering the colour and shape of his eyes – wound up being by far the least pleasant of the three.

He knew, from having tried it out at the *ryokan*, that changing his irises from grey to brown would be straightforward and would not hurt. However, when he willed his eyelids and the skin around his eyes to adopt an oriental cast, the sensations that accompanied the process – the stretching, the pulling, the membranous tightening, as skin, blood plasma and lymph all redistributed themselves – were exquisitely repulsive. His eye sockets throbbed with a heat like an infection and his vision blurred and doubled as the changing pressure on his eyeballs distorted his corneas out of true.

Eventually the stretching sensations subsided, the heat ebbed away, and clarity of vision returned. He peered, blinking, at the results.

It was quite possibly the strangest sight he had seen in two lifetimes' worth of strange sights: a hybrid, half-Japanese man in the mirror who was himself and yet not himself, eyeing him back warily through heavy, upturned, epicanthic lids. It might have been some ghastly joke, had it not been so deadly serious.

Examining his metamorphosed face, both marvelling and mildly disturbed, he realised that the eyelids were not quite there. They bulged too thickly, making him look like an occidental actor in bad oriental make-up. With reluctance he set to altering them again, submitting to the feverish discomfort of the process. It was a question of fine-tuning, and after several attempts he finally managed to get the appearance of the eyelids right.

He ran his hands through his hair, arranging it into a rough approximation of the *bosozoku*'s swept-back style, and pulled the surgical mask up over his mouth and nose.

With his face half-hidden, he looked more convincingly oriental. His prominent forehead was still a giveaway, but he did not think he could quite stomach rearranging the bones of his skull, especially given how unpleasant the relatively superficial alteration to his eyes had been. Besides, with his hair restyled he did actually bear some resemblance to the *bosozoku* – perhaps enough of a resemblance to fool even an acquaintance of the young man such as Emperor Dragon, at least from a distance, although probably not close up. That was fine. The main thing was that the disguise was not instantly penetrable. If luck was on his side, he would be able to pass himself off as the dead *bosozoku* and keep the bluff going until the plane was on the ground, at which point he would be in a considerably better position to make a bid for freedom.

Another wave of tiredness sucked at him. The effort involved in modifying his features had further drained his already dangerously depleted reserves. He felt a yawning, enervated emptiness inside him, and sensed that he was on borrowed time. If he did not rest or eat soon, his body would take an executive decision and forcibly shut itself down in order to give itself a chance to recuperate.

Breakfast was about to be served, he reminded himself. But before that, he needed to do a bit of reconnoitring.

He demanded a boost of adrenaline, and was given it. Tinglingly invigorated, he cast a final quick glance at his unfamiliar reflection, then let himself out of the toilet.

The seats in the cabin were divided by two aisles. He headed up the left-hand aisle, bending against the shallow incline of the plane and casually surveying the faces of passengers on either side of him as he went. He reached the galley halfway along the Economy section, having confirmed that neither Emperor Dragon nor any *bosozoku* were in the rear portion of the plane.

He proceeded through into the other section of Economy, and soon ascertained that Emperor Dragon and his lackeys were not there either.

That left only First Class.

A second, smaller galley and a bulkhead doorway separated the privileged occupants of First Class from the riffraff to the rear. The galley was empty, since the cabin crew in charge of First Class had already begun serving breakfast. No one, therefore, challenged Rattray as he sidled up to the bulkhead doorway and peered through.

The attention of the First Class passengers was trained either on their meals or on the LCD television screens fixed into the headrests of the seats in front of them, which meant that Rattray was able to observe them unnoticed. Almost straight away he spotted the broken-nosed *bosozoku* who had handed him the envelope in Kyoto. He was in the middle row of seats, avidly tucking in to a croissant.

Rattray's gaze roved on. Three rows further up, across the aisle from the broken-nosed *bosozoku*, he saw a head of hair he recognised. He was viewing the hair from behind and could see that it was scraped back and bunched into a ponytail that was secured by an elasticated loop. As he continued to watch, the owner of the ponytail leaned across to speak to the person in the adjacent seat. This enabled Rattray to catch a glimpse of his profile between the headrests, and he saw that the owner of the ponytail was, as he had suspected, Emperor Dragon.

He then noticed the back of the head of Emperor Dragon's neighbour. That person's hair looked familiar, too.

A girl's cropped bob.

Of course. Rattray nodded grimly to himself. He should not have been surprised. He should have expected no more, and no less, from Emperor Dragon.

Kim's presence complicated matters, but not, Rattray thought, to the point where he would have to radically rethink his plans. He quickly scanned the rest of the First Class cabin, establishing that Emperor Dragon and the broken-nosed *bosozoku* were his only remaining opponents. That was good. Those odds were manageable.

Someone tapped him on the shoulder. He snapped his head round, one hand clenching reflexively into a fist.

It was a member of the cabin crew, a slim-hipped, moustachioed young man. '*Excusez-moi, m'sieur,*' he said.

Rattray spoke softly so as not to attract attention from the First Class passengers. 'English, please?' he said. 'You speak?'

The flight attendant held up a thumb and forefinger. '*Un peu.* You are a First Class passenger, sir?' The tone of his enquiry, and the look in his eyes, indicated that he knew Rattray was not.

Rattray shook his head. 'I am sorry. I am looking for the . . .' He mimed washing his hands.

'The toilets are to the rear of the plane.' The flight attendant pointed sternly in that direction. 'Where your patient is.'

'Thank you.' Rattray gave a little bow and headed back into Economy, where passengers were now also receiving their breakfast. He waited at the halfway galley until the flight attendants had finished wheeling their tall trolleys along the aisles, dishing out meals on trays. Then he ambled down to the screened-off section. With a dumb-show of eating he indicated to a female flight attendant that he, too, would like breakfast, and was duly handed a tray. He begged a second one.

'You are hungry, *m'sieur*?' the flight attendant asked.

Rattray nodded. The flight attendant, in generous mood, and surprised to find someone keen enough on airline meals to eat two of them, produced another tray for him. Rattray took both trays behind the curtain. There, sitting beside the dead *bosozoku*, he wolfed down both breakfasts gratefully and with gusto.

The ingestion of two meals was enough to offset his energy deficit for now. Making himself comfortable in the seat, he waited quietly for the final approach for landing to commence.

46

The cellars had a secondary point of access, to which Lucretia led Piers and Lady by means of a circuitous route that took them through two specific chambers along the way.

The first chamber they visited housed a collection of guns and pistols, mostly of the black-and-blue paraterrestrial design, but some of earthly manufacture, including a belt-loading repeating shotgun, an outlandish-looking prototype that had been expropriated from the New Bond Street workshops of London gunsmiths Messrs Griffin and Tow back in the early 1800s. This was kept inside a glass cabinet, as were an antique, arabesque arquebus with half a dozen trumpet-shaped barrels and a selection of muskets and flintlocks that incorporated contratemporal innovations such as rifling and hand-cranked revolving cylinders. All of these would have been collector's items of incalculable value, had any collectors even known they existed.

From this chamber Lucretia obtained a small handheld pistol, standard Guardian issue for most missions. It fired a beam of coherent light and was lethal at any range.

'Just in case,' she said to Piers, and Piers nodded.

From the second chamber, where medicines and triage materials were kept, Lucretia collected a trio of clear plastic ampoules containing an opaque, milky-blue fluid – the vaccine. She loaded one of the ampoules into the breech of a small, tubular, compressed-air gun, also obtained from the chamber. Snapping the ampoule into place like a shotgun cartridge, she tucked the gun into her pocket along with the two extra ampoules. She did not know how likely it was that they would have a second or third shot at vaccinating MacGowan if they failed the first time, but it seemed prudent to take along a couple of spares.

To get to the secondary point of access it was necessary to leave the network of chambers and pass along an arched, brick-lined tunnel. The tunnel was dimly illuminated by wall-mounted lightbulbs and smelled strongly of damp earth and less strongly, but distinctly none the less, of feline musk. The latter odour further upset the already unnerved Lady, who stuck close by her master's slippered heels, drawing comfort from his proximity, for the entire length of the tunnel.

At the far end there was a flight of stone steps whose breadth and shallowness seemed to imply that they were not designed solely for human use. The two Guardians and the Afghan hound ascended, Lucretia taking the lead. After climbing twenty feet they found themselves just below ground-level, their way impeded by a flat, square slab of stone lying horizontally overhead. The slab was in fact a sliding trapdoor operated by a switch, a raised nub of stone set into the wall beside the top step. As Lucretia reached up to the press the switch, Piers stayed her hand.

'Bill could be lying in wait, old girl,' he said, nodding upwards. 'He might have reasoned that we'd be coming out by the back door.'

Lucretia clucked her tongue. 'I didn't think of that.'

'Let me go first,' said Piers. 'Only the keeper of the Node can call up the Domestic, so if Bill gets you then that's both of us in trouble. In this particular situation I'm expendable. Although not,' he added, 'irreplaceable.'

'Yes, you're right. On both counts.'

Lucretia and Piers exchanged places. As Piers cupped the trapdoor switch with one hand, Lucretia produced the coherent light pistol, grasped it by the grip and curled her index finger around the trigger.

'Ready?' said Piers.

Lucretia nodded.

'On three, then.' Countdowns, Piers knew, were essential for heightening dramatic tension, and he paused portentously between each digit. 'One . . . Two . . . Three.'

He pressed the stone nub. It sank inwards, and with a ponderous, grinding heave the slab began to slide open, reeled into a recess by hidden pulleys. Cobwebs tore. Dirt fell in crumbling sifts. Daylight flooded down the steps, and with its brilliance came a clean-smelling waft of outdoor air.

As soon as the aperture was wide enough, Piers poked his head up through and looked around, gopher-style. He was in the middle of a square of lawn enclosed on all four sides by a neatly clipped, nine-foot-high yew hedge, with a gap at one corner. No one was in sight.

When the slab door was fully retracted, Piers hopped up out of the opening. Lady followed; then came Lucretia, brushing dust and dirt off her shoulders.

They were at the epicentre of the oval hedge maze which, like the constellation pyramids, had been planned and constructed by Bridget St Swithin. When closed, the trapdoor looked like a simple square of stone embedded in the grass, similar to the covering of a grave, with one of Bridget's poems carved into its surface. The words of the poem were still just discernible through an encrustation of grey and yellow lichen. In three doggerel verses maze-solvers were congratulated on having successfully 'penetrated to the heart of an ages-old mystery' but warned that there remained further mysteries 'known only to the initiated, / Those who ensure that what is good survives / Whilst what is bad is eliminated'.

Leaving the slab door open, since it was the only way they could re-enter the cellars if they needed to, Lucretia, Piers and Lady negotiated the maze in reverse, from the centre outward. Lucretia was almost as familiar with the layout of the maze as she was with the layout of the cellars. She guided Piers and Lady through its tortuous, yew-hemmed pathways unerringly but cautiously, pausing at every junction not so that she could get her bearings but to make sure that the coast was clear. From a bird's-eye view directly overhead it would have been perceivable that the route the three of them took to negotiate the maze traced the outline of an old-fashioned key.

They halted at the maze entrance and peered out. They were looking at the rear of the house, with its terrace and high windows. At one end of the building was the turret and dome of the observatory added on by Bridget's father, Archibald St Swithin, while at the other lay Lucretia's conservatory studio, all wrought-iron ribs and curving glass. Dense ivy sprawled across most of the intervening brickwork, fringing the windows and entwining around the railings of the balcony of the master bedroom, which overlooked the studio. The ivy had been the Grange's close companion for the best part of two centuries, and some of its stems were as thick as a child's wrist.

To reach the studio, which was their destination, Lucretia, Piers and Lady would have to cross a hundred yards or so of bare lawn, with only the occasional stone pyramid to hide behind.

'Where *is* he?' said Lucretia, searching the windows of the Grange, in case MacGowan was looking out from one of them.

'With any luck he's still on the other side of the house, banging away at your sculpture,' replied Piers. 'Well, old girl? Ready for a spot of exercise?'

Lucretia gave a reluctant grimace and said yes, and together she and Piers set off across the lawn at a fast lick, with Lady loping behind.

They reached the edge of the terrace without incident, and there paused, squatting out of sight behind the terrace wall, while they caught their breath. Then they crept alongside the terrace to the studio, moving stealthily, keeping low. Lucretia was alert to every whisper of sound, every flicker of movement, her senses strung wire-tight. She was conscious, too, of controlling her

336

breathing, inhaling the bare minimum of air. Every foot-fall the three of them made on the grass – Piers's slippered shuffle, Lady's padding paws, her own trainer-clad tread – seemed excruciatingly loud to her. At any moment she expected the berserker MacGowan to come tearing round the side of the house or leap, howling, from the cover of a shrubbery.

The studio sported a pair of sliding doors tall enough and broad enough to accommodate a lorry. The doors opened onto a concrete loading area, from which a winding sliproad led away, circumnavigating the house and joining the driveway at a point not far beyond the turning circle. All of this was in order to make it easier for Lucretia's sculptures to be transported from the studio to their final resting places. Crossing the loading area with Piers and Lady in tow, Lucretia took a set of keys from her pocket and, selecting the correct one, unlocked the doors and rolled one of them partially open.

They entered the studio, and Lucretia went straight to her workbench, set the vaccine gun down on it and picked up a pair of work-gloves and started pulling them on.

'Ten minutes, then?' said Piers.

'Yes. Be careful, won't you, Piers?'

'Careful's my middle name,' Piers replied. 'Wait a moment.' He frowned and placed a fingertip against his cheek. 'No, it isn't. It's Oscar.'

Lucretia shook her head disbelievingly. 'How can you crack jokes at a time like this?'

'How can I *not*?' Piers replied simply, with a shrug. He squatted down in front of Lady. 'Now, pay attention,' he said fondly to the Afghan, looking her in the eye. 'I've got some heroic stuff to do, so you stay here and be a good girl and look after Lucretia. Got that? Stay.'

Lady whined and raised one of her forepaws, resting it pathetically on Piers's thigh.

'Don't you worry, I'll be fine,' Piers reassured her, scratching her under the chin.

Lady lowered her paw and gave her master's hand a sad, sombre lick as he stood up again.

'I just wish I was better dressed for the occasion,' Piers said, glancing down mock-despondently at his nightwear.

'You look groovy to me, Piers,' said Lucretia, donning a welding mask.

'Really? Groovy? You mean that? Thanks, old girl.'

Lady let out another piteous whine, but stayed put, as Piers turned and strode past the Obstaclimb, heading for the door that connected the studio to the house.

Just as he reached the door he heard the explosive hiss of an oxyacetylene blowtorch being fired up.

Ten minutes.

He let himself into the house.

He was in the Grange's drawing room, which was spacious, high-ceilinged and grandly furnished. The tall windows that paraded along one wall were still shuttered from the night before. Clusters of chairs and tables dotted the room's length, and a trio of bulging-plush sofas surrounded a marble fireplace that was large enough to spit-roast a pig in. Turkish kilims were spread over the polished floorboards, and in one corner stood a Steinway grand piano. Not just any old Steinway, either, but a piece of genuine pop-culture memorabilia, for, as Piers was all too happily aware, it was on this very piano that the Royals' guitarist and main songwriter, Daffyd Morgan, first picked out the sequence of chiming major chords that came to form the intro to 'Strawberry Sunshine'.

Having paused to cast a reverential glance at the piano, Piers stole through the room, threading around the furniture until he reached the door at the opposite end. The hallway lay on the other side of the door, but he could hear no sounds of thumping and banging. Had MacGowan abandoned his attack on *Daedalian*? He grasped the doorknob and turned it slowly, slowly, wincing at every tiny creak of the catch spring. He cracked the door an inch and put his eye to the gap. He was afforded only a limited view of the hallway, enough to see one edge of the bas-relief and the front doors. One of the front doors was lying flat on the floor, encircled by débris, while the other hung askew from a single hinge.

The doors' frame was ragged and shattered, like the edges of a wound.

Piers eased the drawing-room door a couple of inches further open, revealing more of *Daedalian*. There were shallow dents in the surface of the sculpture, mostly around the secret entranceway. Several of the moving parts were limping brokenly along their prearranged paths, and some had been snapped off completely – an act of sheer spiteful vandalism, for MacGowan must have known that damaging the moving parts was only going to make the unlocking mechanism less, not more, likely to yield.

Of MacGowan himself, Piers could see no sign. He widened the door still further and stepped sideways through.

He scanned to the right and left. The hallway appeared empty. He glanced up the staircase. No one there. He took a few wary paces forwards, then halted. The silence filling the house was huge and absolute. He reached for the silver chain around his neck with both hands and lifted his crystal puzzle-egg medallion over his head. He wrapped the chain twice around his right fist so that the puzzle-egg dangled just below his thumb.

Since MacGowan did not seem to be in the immediate vicinity, Piers knew he would somehow have to attract his attention. Shouting was unseemly. Perhaps a very loud 'ahem' would do the trick.

In the event, Piers need not have wasted time fretting over the finer points of offering yourself up as human bait. A hoarse warcry from outside had him whirling around to face the front doors, and next thing he knew, he was staring at MacGowan, who had sprung from a hiding place just to one side of the entrance and was now bearing down on him, a mad-eyed man-mountain, bent on murder, inflamed with hate.

47

With a scrape of tyre rubber and a series of jolting bounces, the plane touched down at Charles de Gaulle. The force of deceleration threw passengers back in their seats, causing many a grimace and a gripped armrest. Groundspeed decreased, and soon the plane was taxiing off the runway towards the terminal. Conversations which had petered out during the turmoil of landing were resumed, and a number of people, regardless of the still-lit signs and a spoken reminder over the PA system, unfastened their seat belts and stood up to retrieve their belongings from the overhead compartments. The tour-group holidaymakers in Economy produced their cameras once again in order to take photographs of the French airport buildings from the windows and, as if for good measure, yet more pictures of one another. There was excitement that the journey was over, and, for nervous flyers, relief.

Behind the curtain Rattray waited, unsure what was going to happen next, knowing only that his best strategy for the moment was to have no strategy; to see what the circumstances demanded and improvise accordingly.

Finally the plane came to a halt and a gangway extended from the terminal building like a robot arm to dock with the main cabin door. Most people were out of their seats by now and queuing in the aisles to disembark. Rattray assumed that he and the substitute Rattray on the gurney would be the last to leave. Emperor Dragon and the broken-nosed *bosozoku* would wait until everyone else was off the plane before coming back here to collect the gurney.

Sure enough, once the exit had been opened and all the other passengers had filed out, Rattray heard a set of footsteps approaching down the aisle and a voice calling out, '*Kenji, o-genki desuka?*'

'OK,' Rattray replied, the surgical mask muffling and to some extent disguising his voice. The phrase '*O-genki desuka?*', meaning 'How are you?', along with the greetings appropriate to various times of day, represented the sum total of Rattray's knowledge of conversational Japanese – although 'OK', of course, was common to many cultures.

The curtain was pulled back by the broken-nosed *bosozoku*. On his own. No Kim, no Emperor Dragon. The *bosozoku* glanced at Rattray and made a comment which he suffixed with a mirthless laugh. Rattray nodded and chuckled. This, it seemed, was the correct response, for the *bosozoku* then addressed himself to the body on the gurney. He said something to the helmeted, blanket-wrapped figure in such a scornful and derogatory tone that Rattray thought it appropriate to chuckle again. The *bosozoku*, with a smile as quick as a nervous tic, turned to the laptop that surmounted the virtual reality unit. Inspecting the laptop's display, he tapped a few keys.

Rattray saw a frown form, and took this as his cue to drew the curtain silently and surreptitiously shut.

The broken-nosed *bosozoku*, not looking up from the laptop, barked out what sounded like a question. When Rattray did not reply, he repeated the question more loudly, still tapping keys. When Rattray again did not reply, he glanced up.

He stared at Rattray. His eyes narrowed. He cocked his head to one side. He examined Rattray's eyes and fore-head closely.

Rattray calmly returned his stare, waiting for the moment of realisation to come.

It came.

The broken-nosed *bosozoku*'s eyes widened. His jaw dropped.

Rattray was on him faster than a mongoose on a cobra. His first punch cracked the young man's sternum. His second dislocated his collarbone. His third stove in several ribs. His fourth and final punch fissured the *bosozoku*'s skull, driving bone fragments deep into the soft tissue of his brain. All four punches were delivered within the space of a second.

The *bosozoku* sagged backwards against the inside of the fuselage, his eyes death-dulled. Rattray grabbed him by his baseball jacket before he could fall to the floor. Supporting the young man's entire body-weight with one arm, he thrust aside the rear end of the curtain with his free hand and bore the *bosozoku* across to the toilets. He pushed open the nearest toilet door and shoved the body inside. The *bosozoku* slumped gangling onto the lavatory, his head flopping backwards, his mouth gaping open in a ghastly, empty yawn.

Slowing to normal speed, Rattray reached into the pocket of his overalls and took out the small brown bottle. He unscrewed the cap and poured a few of the benzedrine pills into the *bosozoku*'s mouth, then tipped the remainder onto the floor. He clasped the *bosozoku*'s hand around the empty bottle, pressing the fingers into place until the bottle was secure.

He cast an eye over the scene, making sure everything looked how he wanted it to look, then closed the door and turned. The rear cabin was empty. There were a couple of flight attendants near the entrance to the Economy Class galley, but they were too far away, and too involved in gathering together their personal belongings and chatting, to have seen or heard any of the brief scuffle at the far end of the plane just now.

Re-entering the screened-off section, Rattray examined the virtual reality unit and the gurney. Clearly he could not leave the VR unit on the plane. It was paraterrestrial-grade technology. He could not abandon it. It had to be destroyed. But he could not do that here, and he could not wheel the VR unit off the plane and leave the body and the gurney behind, not without running the risk of arousing the cabin crew's suspicions. He would have to take the gurney *and* the VR unit with him.

He pulled one of the intravenous tubes out of the dead *bosozoku*'s arm, then tugged the tube free of the sedative bag it was attached to. Gripping the tube midway along with both hands, he pulled it in opposite directions till it stretched thin and snapped. Then he used the two lengths of tube to tie the legs of the gurney to the VR unit's castors.

The end-product looked makeshift and inelegant, but worked. Grasping the gurney by its foot end, Rattray was able to pull both the gurney and the VR unit up the aisle in tandem. It required some tricky manoeuvring, since the VR unit did not always want to go in the same direction as the gurney, but soon Rattray was passing the galley and making his way through the second section of Economy towards the exit. The flight attendants, still busy with their finishing-up duties, eager to be off the plane and home, did little more than glance up as he trundled by. A couple of them offered smiles. Rattray merely nodded in reply. The white overalls and mask made him look medical. Irreproachably official. Orderly, in both senses of the word. The cabin crew left him to get on with what he was doing, and either none of them noticed, or none of them considered it significant, that the young Japanese passenger from First Class who had gone aft a minute or so earlier was not with him.

In fact, Ryu was not found for another half-hour, when one of the airline's janitorial staff happened upon his body in the toilet. Airport security was summoned, and took five minutes to arrive. The police turned up ten minutes later. It was only after the body reached the morgue, however, that it was discerned that the young man had not died of a self-administered drugs overdose, as it appeared, but rather of violent causes. This was nearly two hours after the discovery of the corpse, and although the French police then took prompt action, the delay between thinking they were dealing with an accidental suicide and realising they were dealing with a murder hampered the investigation irredeemably. The plane's crew were interrogated, along with as many of the passengers listed on the flight manifest as could be tracked down, but this was done in the weary knowledge that the culprit, if he had any sense, had already hopped onto a connecting flight and was far, far away.

Inevitably, then, although the investigation was carried out to the very best of their abilities by the Sûreté and Interpol, the case would remain unsolved and the culprit would never be found.

48

Piers leapt backwards so sharply that his left foot slid clean out of his slipper, leaving the elegant silk shoe sitting in the middle of the hallway floor to be trampled, a moment later, beneath MacGowan's hiking boots. Skidding, half stumbling, Piers fetched up against the newel-post of the staircase, which like the two other newel-posts (one at the turn of the stairs, one at the summit) was crowned with a carved wooden puzzle-egg. Still back-pedalling, Piers found himself – somewhat to his surprise – ascending, his feet hammering out a rapid tattoo on the risers, shod sole alternating with unshod, while his left hand provided assistance, hauling him up the banister rail. MacGowan came thundering after him, bellowing his name in a spittle-flecked bray.

At the turn in the staircase, Piers's heel caught the corner of the second flight and he tripped. He was still gripping the banister rail as he fell, so he did not actually hit the staircase but instead, converting vertical momentum into horizontal, continued up the second flight on all fours, propelling himself with thrusts of his arms and legs, MacGowan still in hot pursuit. His other slipper came free just before he reached the top of the stairs, so that he was barefoot as he tumbled backwards into the Grange's upper corridor. He was also mere seconds away from being caught by his comrade-turned-enemy, who, in adopting the easier and more conventional method of climbing a staircase, had gained ground on him.

Then: a moment of sweet serendipity. A gift from the cosmic choreographer.

Two steps down from the top of the stairs, MacGowan trod on Piers's discarded right slipper and slipped. His left leg shot out from under him and he fell sprawling, headlong, hitting the corridor floorboards like a chain-sawed tree-trunk, belly then chest then chin, the last striking with a tremendous, jarring, echoing thud.

The impact left MacGowan momentarily stunned, and gave Piers an opportunity to twist over and push himself to his feet. By the time MacGowan had shaken his head and recovered sufficiently to haul himself upright and resume his attack, Piers was no longer off guard, no longer off balance and no longer in retreat.

Piers held up his right fist, with which he was still clutching his medallion, and thrust it boldly forwards until the crystal puzzle-egg was dangling in front of MacGowan's nose. He stroked the egg with his index finger, and straight away it started to move. In a series of quickening pulsations, as though numerous tiny, invisible hands were manipulating it, the egg began extruding and withdrawing its transparent polyhedral components. No mechanism was apparent. The parts of the egg simply slid themselves in and out and up and down and around one another of their own accord, forming wonderful, spiny, multiplicitous patterns that caught the light dazzlingly, each pattern holding still for a brief instant before the egg smoothly reconfigured itself into a new shape. It was compelling to watch. Once you started watching, you just wanted to keep on looking. You became attentive to each geometrical nuance, mesmerised by the crystalline intricacy of the egg's movements. You fell irresistibly under the puzzle-egg's spell.

Or at least, that was what *usually* happened when Piers deployed his talisman of Guardianship in hypnotic mode. On this occasion, however, the mind of his subject was such a seething confusion of rage and bloodlust and madness that even the split-second of fixed attention which was all the puzzle-egg needed to seduce its beholder was beyond him. He merely eyed the glittering artefact with as much disdain as he would have if Piers had been holding up a Rubik's Cube, say, or a spinning top. Then he batted Piers's arm aside and lunged for him.

Piers sidestepped out of the way and delivered a karate chop to the back of MacGowan's neck. The karate chop ought to have sent MacGowan somersaulting over onto his back, in such a manner that he perhaps collided with a fragile piece of ornamental furniture, smashing it to smithereens. At the very least the chop ought to have laid him out prone on the floor, unconscious. In the event, Piers might as well have tickled MacGowan with a feather duster for all the effect the blow had on him. MacGowan, not seeming to understand that the hand-to-hand combat techniques of a certain era of pop-culture entertainment ought to work in the real world too, merely turned and sneered.

'That the best you can do?' he said. 'Wave your puzzle-egg in my face, then tap me on the shoulder?'

'You can't blame a chap for trying,' Piers replied.

'Oh, this is going to be too fucking easy,' MacGowan said and, drawing himself up to his full height, made to attack Piers again.

'Wait.' Piers held up a hand like a policeman stopping traffic.

MacGowan – amused, and secure in the knowledge that Piers was within easy reach and physically outclassed – paused.

'Can't we talk about this?' said Piers. 'After all, chaps on the same team shouldn't be fighting one another. It's a really bad scene.'

'Perhaps you should have thought about that before you sent me off to be killed at that fucking power station.'

'Is that what you believe?'

'That's what I *know*.'

Piers let out a snort which, not wishing to antagonise MacGowan any more than he already was, he pitched at a level well below contemptuous. 'Trust me, old chap. No one sent you to be killed. Whatever occurred at Seal Point

347

was either an accident or the result of a bad tip from the Librans.'

'You would fucking say that,' MacGowan snarled.

'Well, yes, I would. But only because it's the truth. Look.' Piers raised his puzzle-egg again, which was still gracefully shifting and reconfiguring. Before MacGowan could mistake this gesture for another attempt to hypnotise him, Piers touched the egg with his left index finger. Immediately, the egg retracted its parts, becoming ovoid and inert once more. 'You know how this works,' he said. 'If anyone utters a lie, the egg gives a twitch.'

'Yeah. So what?'

'We did not deliberately send you to be killed at Seal Point.' Piers indicated the egg. 'There. Did you see it react? I think not.'

MacGowan looked from Piers's face to the puzzle-egg and from the puzzle-egg back to Piers's face. He did this three times, then sighed, said, 'Bollocks to this,' and came at Piers, arms outstretched to enfold him in a bearhug.

Piers attempted to dodge out of his way but, unfortunately, ran up against the corridor wall. The next instant, MacGowan's arms were around his torso and he was being pinched like an insect in a pair of pliers. His own arms were pinned to his sides and the breath was being squeezed out of him, his ribs and innards being crushed. He writhed and strained but could not gain any leverage to break free and, anyway, even without the enhancement provided by the berserker agent, MacGowan's strength was considerably superior to his.

One of the many advantages of silk nightwear, however, other than its sheer sexiness, is its sheer slipperiness. And so it was that, by means of a considerable amount of wriggling and contortion, Piers was able to slide his right arm inch by inch up out of its sleeve. MacGowan realised what was Piers was up to, but even by tightening his grip on the Freelance Facilitator yet further he was unable to prevent him extricating his arm entirely from his sleeve. Being slender, and his pyjamas being relatively baggy, Piers was then able to bend the arm in half against his ribs and insinuate it, hand first, out through the neck opening of his pyjama jacket. All at once his arm and shoulder were free.

MacGowan stared at the skinny arm with bullish contempt. He did not believe anything so lacking in musculature could do him any harm, and Piers did not believe this either. The karate chop earlier had been purely for show. Piers had not studied any form of martial art. He knew only that that was how international playboy adventurers were supposed to fight, with karate chops and gentlemanly kicks and possibly the use of a furled umbrella if it came to hand. He also knew that, thanks to the berserker agent, MacGowan was pretty much impervious to pain. He could not hurt him.

But he might be able to incapacitate him.

He raised his hand above his head and aimed a sharp, stiff-fingered jab at the knot of ganglia located at the apex of MacGowan's left trapezius muscle.

The blow had the desired effect. MacGowan's entire left arm went dead. He let go of Piers and staggered backwards, clutching the numbed, dangling limb with his other arm.

'You fucking poncey wanker,' he hissed. 'Trust you not to fight fair.'

They regarded each other across the width of the corridor like two pugilists between rounds, both breathing hard, both slightly hunched over, each injured in his own way. Piers estimated that he had so far bought Lucretia no more than five minutes. Somehow he did not think it was going to be easy to keep MacGowan occupied for another five without getting himself killed. He had tried hypnotising him and reasoning with him, and neither tactic had been effective. What did that leave? Challenging him to a game of Twister?

Tentatively MacGowan straightened up. Feeling and movement were gradually returning to his left arm. He flexed the fingers of his left hand, then clenched them into a fist. There was a grim finality in his voice as he said, 'Right. That's enough farting around. Now to end this.'

And so saying, he started towards Piers.

Oh, well, Piers thought, and resorted to his initial tactic – running.

49

No sooner had Rattray lugged the gurney and the VR unit into the terminal building than he was met by a young Frenchman with a skinny body and a ragged, patently self-inflicted haircut that looked like a bomb had gone off beneath his scalp. The Frenchman's bony frame was draped in a set of paramedic's overalls too large for him and he was wearing a scuffed pair of combat boots. His expression had been anxious, but at the sight of Rattray his face eased.

'I thought I had missed you,' he said, stepping forwards with a hand outstretched.

Rattray shook the young man's hand warily, glancing around. Emperor Dragon and Kim were nowhere in sight.

'The traffic,' the Frenchman explained. 'Terrible. It was only when I was halfway here that I remembered I was driving an ambulance. I put on the siren, and *pffft* – it was plain sailing after that.' His grin revealed the yellow-stained teeth of an inveterate smoker and coffee-drinker. 'I'm Xavier Barraud.'

'Kenji,' said Rattray, remembering the name the broken-nosed *bosozoku* had called out. 'You've come to collect the "patient".'

'And you also.' Xavier peered over Rattray's shoulder. 'I was led to understand there would be two of you.'

'Just me.'

'Ah. Just you. And him.' Xavier indicated the body on

351

the gurney. 'A Guardian, in the flesh. Not so impressive now, hey?' He tapped the VR unit. 'And what is this?'

'It keeps our "patient" manageable.'

'I see. It looks quite . . . sophisticated. Unusual.'

'You know us Japanese. Ahead of everyone else.'

'I see. Yes,' said Xavier. 'And it is this kind of device that these so-called Guardians would prefer it we did not have.'

Rattray affected impatience. 'Do you intend to stand around here talking about such things all day? Don't we have somewhere to go?'

'Yes. I am sorry. Shall we head to the ambulance, then?'

'That would be a good idea.'

'It is not far from here. I was able to persuade the airport authorities to let me park close to the terminal building. The Red Cross – it is like a magic charm, you know? A passport that lets you go anywhere, do anything.'

'Yes, I know.'

'This way. There is an elevator.' Xavier took hold of the side of the gurney, and together he and Rattray wheeled it through the terminal building, past duty-free concessions and seated travellers waiting to be called to embark. Soon they were drawing up to a steel-doored lift that connected the upper, commercial parts of the building with the more functional areas below. Stationed in front of the lift was a security guard with whom Xavier had obviously acquainted himself earlier, for the security guard nodded to him as he arrived and the two of them chatted and joked in rapid-fire French for a while. Eventually the guard turned and used a pass-key to unlock and open the lift doors. Rattray guided the gurney into the lift, and then he, Xavier and the dead *bosozoku* were descending to the ground.

Outside, not far off, an ambulance was waiting. As they headed towards it across the Tarmac, Xavier remarked that he was looking forward to meeting Emperor Dragon later. Rattray had assumed that they would all be travelling together to their ultimate destination, wherever that was, but it seemed that Emperor Dragon was making the last leg of the journey separately from his hirelings.

Xavier then began praising Emperor Dragon's hacking skills, reserving particular approval for the treatment Emperor Dragon had meted out on Kawai Kim. 'That bitch,' Xavier said, pretending to spit. 'It's about time someone cut her down to size. She thinks she is so marvellous.'

'So you are a hacker, too?' Rattray enquired.

'Yes. Although there are some who would claim I was not. That damned aristo, for one.' Xavier rolled his eyes and puffed out his cheeks. 'Just because I let him down one time. One time!'

Rattray framed his next words carefully. 'What do you know about this man? This aristo? Emperor Dragon has not told us much about him.'

'I know that he is as mean with his praise as he is with his money. Otherwise . . .' Xavier gave one of those classic Gallic shrugs, expressive not merely of casual dismissal but seemingly of an entire national attitude. 'Anyway, you will soon be able to see for yourself what he is like. It is, I guess, a journey of about ninety minutes from here to his home, assuming the Périphérique is not too badly jammed. Of course, if necessary we will be able to do the journey more quickly. I think you will like driving with the siren on.'

Rattray felt he could not reasonably ask any more questions about the aristo without arousing Xavier's suspicions and perhaps giving away that he was an impostor, so he said no more.

When they reached the ambulance, Xavier opened its rear doors while Rattray bent and quickly untied the IV tubes with which he had tethered the VR unit to the gurney. There was enough slack in the wires connecting the helmet to the VR unit to allow him and Xavier to manhandle the VR unit and the gurney, which was the kind with collapsible legs, separately into the back of the vehicle. They then clambered in after.

Rattray glanced around. The vehicle's interior was

oddly bare. In one corner there were a couple of white plastic cases marked with a red cross and the words '*En Cas D'Urgence*', but one of them had fallen open and it was empty.

'Where is all the medical equipment?' he asked.

'The ambulance is stolen,' Xavier replied. 'Anything not fastened down has been stripped out and sold.'

'I see,' said Rattray.

'OK,' said Xavier, 'shall we get going?'

'A good idea. I'll stay back here and keep an eye on the "patient".'

'As you wish.'

Xavier scrambled forwards and plumped himself down in the driver's seat. The ambulance's diesel engine grumbled chunkily into life. Xavier shifted into first gear and pulled away from the terminal building, following a route demarcated by painted yellow lines.

Rattray squatted down on the narrow bench-seat opposite the gurney and rested his face in his hands. He could feel that the effort of remaining 'Japanese' was taking its toll on his body. Since the disguise had served its purpose and was no longer vital to his plans, he decided to rescind the alterations to his face, skin and hair. There was a sensation of unclenching, of something coiled unspooling, a feeling similar to the relief of being told good news when you had been expecting bad. Within seconds he knew, without having to look, that he had reverted to his default form; he was fully himself once more.

Xavier had begun talking about hacking again, saying how impressed he had been by the software that had enabled him and his colleagues to break into Kawai Kim's system a few months ago. Was he correct in thinking that Emperor Dragon himself was the one who had sent him the diskette with the software on it?

When there was no reply from the man in the rear of the ambulance, Xavier glanced round to see if he was listening.

He found himself staring into the face of a white-

354

haired, fair-skinned, grey-eyed stranger who happened to be wearing exactly the same overalls that the young Japanese, Kenji, had been wearing.

In his astonishment, Xavier twisted the steering-wheel and the ambulance lurched sideways, skidding. With a yelp of 'Merde alors!' Xavier corrected the vehicle's course. The next thing he knew, he was being hauled bodily out of the driver's seat and flung across the gearstick into the passenger seat. His head slammed into the passenger-side window with enough force to crack the glass and render him instantly unconscious.

Driverless, the ambulance veered off course again, rapidly losing speed. Leaning across the seat that Xavier had involuntarily vacated, Rattray grabbed the steering-wheel. Having steadied the ambulance's progress, he slid agilely into the seat and applied the brake pedal. The ambulance eased to a halt not far from a baggage transporter that was parked, unattended and empty, outside a cargo bay.

Rattray switched off the engine and glanced over at Xavier. The young Frenchman was out cold. Not ideal, since he had been intending to interrogate him further about the aristo. Still, the mysterious aristo could keep for another time. Right now, there were more urgent matters to attend to.

Climbing out of the driver's seat, he returned to the rear of the ambulance, and there set about demolishing the VR unit. First he removed the black helmet from the dead *bosozoku*'s head and, holding the helmet in his left hand, punched inside it repeatedly with his right. Shattered microcircuitry spilled out, along with wires and fragments of plastic and metal components, everything clattering around his feet. Having eviscerated the helmet, he held it up between his hands and applied sufficient pressure to crack it in two.

The laptop he snapped apart at the hinges. He then smashed both sections against the steel rail of the gurney until they were ruined beyond recovery. As for the VR unit itself, a few hearty stomps cracked open its casing and a few further well-placed kicks reduced its innards to so much high-tech scrap.

Not content to leave it at that, however, Rattray began scouring the ambulance for flammable materials. Had this been a fully equipped ambulance he would have found rolls of bandages, bottles of surgical spirit and cylinders of compressed oxygen, all marvellously combustible stuff. As it was, he had to make do with the blanket covering the dead *bosozoku*, which was made from synthetic fibres, and the gurney mattress, which was a pallet of foam rubber. Stripping the blanket off the body, he bundled it up beside the remains of the VR unit. Then he dragged the *bosozoku* off the gurney, removed the mattress and tented it over the VR unit.

He emptied out the *bosozoku*'s pack of Marlboro at the base of this makeshift pyre and arranged the cigarettes into a rough cone, which he set light to in several places with the young man's Zippo. As the cigarettes began to smoulder, sending up a skein of tobacco smoke, he knelt down and blew on them gently, nursing the separate glows until they merged into one, at which point he placed a corner of the blanket over the cigarettes and watched as the fabric slowly turned brown and started to smoulder, too. Soon the blanket was burning. The mattress quickly followed suit. Flames began crackling upwards, reaching ever higher, until their tips were licking the roof and causing the paint there to blister and bubble.

The interior of the ambulance filled with acrid black smoke. The fumes were noxious and toxic, but, of course, even without the surgical mask Rattray would not have been adversely affected. He remained inside the ambulance until he was certain that the fire had taken hold and was going to keep spreading. Finally, eyes streaming with protective tears, he opened the rear doors and jumped out on to the Tarmac. Pulling the surgical mask from his face, he gratefully inhaled fresh air.

He hesitated, wondering whether or not to run round to the front of the ambulance and drag the unconscious

Xavier Barraud out and pull him to safety. After a moment of inner debate, he decided against doing so. The young Frenchman was part of the plot to kidnap him and therefore, unwittingly or otherwise, in the employ of the Anarchs. Not only that but he knew about the Guardians, *and* he had been witness to a seemingly inexplicable phenomenon, a man who was oriental one moment, occidental the next. For all these reasons he could not be allowed to live. However, as Rattray moved clear of the burning vehicle, it struck him as curious that he had felt an impulse to rescue Xavier at all. Normally he would have had no qualms about letting any opponent of the Guardians die. After nearly a hundred years of Guardianship and countless invalidations, he had believed he had become inured to the more dubious aspects of his job. But now it seemed he was no longer so comfortable with the idea of inflicting death, certainly not in the case of people who had barely an inkling of what they were involved in. Maybe in this war between the controlled development and the unbridled proliferation of mankind's technology, between the Libran and Anarch ideologies, the dividing line between combatant and non-combatant was not as clear-cut as he had hitherto believed. Maybe there were grades of innocence.

Having put a good twenty feet between him and the ambulance, Rattray halted beside the baggage transporter and looked round to check on the progress of the fire. Fuelled by the intake of air through the open rear doors, the flames had gathered strength and were burning with an implacable ferocity. The interior of the vehicle was an inferno. Metal was warping and cracking in the heat; the windows were fracturing percussively; plastic and paint were sizzling. The fire was surging up to the ceiling with such force, indeed, that the flames were splaying outwards and lambent orange tongues were flickering all along the top of the rear exit. Wisps of fire were escaping from the vehicle's confines into the open air. Smoke was also escaping, billowing out in a thick, rancorous plume.

A shout caught Rattray's attention. He saw baggage-handlers emerging from the cargo bay to point and stare at the ambulance. It was time for him to beat a hasty retreat. As some of the baggage-handlers started running towards the blazing vehicle and others went to raise the alarm, he crouched down and hurried to the end of the baggage transporter's train of empty flatbed trolleys. Then, launching himself like a sprinter from the starting blocks, he dashed across thirty yards of open Tarmac at superhuman speed. Within a couple of seconds he was crouching behind another parked airport vehicle, one of the sanitation trucks that siphoned off the contents of aeroplanes' waste tanks. From there it was another dash of about twenty yards to the shelter of the terminal building itself.

He flattened himself against the side of the building. Thanks to the distraction caused by the burning ambulance, no one had spotted him. He could see that the crowd of airport employees which had gathered to gawk at the conflagration from a safe distance was rapidly growing. People were running from all directions to join the wildly yelling and gesticulating throng. By now flames were pouring out from beneath the ambulance's chassis. Abruptly two of the tyres exploded, one after the other in quick succession, rocking the vehicle on its axles. The crowd, as one, stepped back several paces, and began yelling and gesticulating even more wildly.

The conflicting sine-wave wails of distant sirens became audible. The fire crews were, Rattray estimated, about half a minute away. No matter. Emperor Dragon's virtual reality device was already nothing more than charred slag, its advanced technology irrecoverable and irreproducible.

Now to locate its inventor and likewise dispose of him. Rattray may have had his doubts about Xavier, but there was no question in his mind that Emperor Dragon had to die.

Hugging the edge of the building, he sidled along until he came to a personnel entrance. The door was locked, and to open it required a pass-key . . . or a single, well-aimed kick from an inordinately powerful leg.

Inside, there was a concrete stairwell leading to the upper level of the terminal building. Rattray swiftly ascended, unbuttoning his overalls as he went.

50

The door to Alice's bedroom, locked with its key and blockaded with a heavy chest of drawers, held Mac-Gowan out for the best part of two minutes. He managed to break in using the same method as he had downstairs: repeatedly throwing himself against the door until its frame gave way.

Shunting the chest of drawers aside, he stormed into the room. There was no sign of Piers. Apart from the displaced chest of drawers, Alice's bedroom was exactly as she had left it the day she had departed for boarding school three weeks earlier at the beginning of the autumn term. The bed was tidily made, its duvet primped and plumped and its pillows piled high with cuddly toys, mementoes of her childhood that the eighteen-year-old Alice was not yet prepared to part with. Posters of rock stars, tacked edge to edge, gave the walls a second papering. (MacGowan recognised the Manic Street Preachers, Jarvis Cocker from Pulp, and that gaunt, mad-looking singer with the Verve; the rest he was too old to be able to identify.) There was a bookcase filled with paperbacks – a mix of Penguin school texts and pastel-cover Aga sagas – and an expensive-looking portable stereo sat on the floor, flanked by messily stacked piles of CDs. A faint, artificially floral scent was detectable in the air – a teenage girl's choice of underarm deodorant.

MacGowan strode over to the bed and checked

beneath. No Piers lying there. He yanked open the doors of the closet and leaved through the clothes hanging on the rail. No Piers cowering behind the dresses and outfits. The bedroom, in common with almost all the bedrooms in the Grange, had an en suite bathroom. MacGowan looked in there. No Piers crouched inside the shower cubicle.

Where *was* the fucker?

Returning to the bedroom, MacGowan scanned around again. He had a good mind to rip the place apart, overturn everything, just for the hell of it.

Then his eye fell on the windows.

The catches were securely closed on all of the windows except one, and on that one the lower sash was not fully shut.

Cunning wanker.

He went to the window, threw up the sash and stuck his head out.

About five feet away from the window, Piers was clinging to the ivy that covered most of the exterior of this side of the house. During the time it had taken MacGowan to force his way into Alice's room, Piers had returned his right arm into its pyjama sleeve and restored his puzzle-egg to its rightful place around his neck. He had also climbed out of the window and managed to get thus far along the wall but no further. When MacGowan opened the window and looked out, Piers was having an especially difficult time maintaining his purchase. His feet could establish no firm toeholds in the ivy and kept losing their grip.

In spite of this, however, his expression was jaunty. 'Ah, Bill, there you are. Lovely day for just hanging around, don't you think?'

MacGowan pointed at him and smiled a darkly menacing smile. 'Don't move.' He ducked back inside the bedroom.

'Oh, don't worry, old chap,' Piers called out brightly.

'I'm not going anywhere.' To himself he added, 'More's the pity.'

He glanced a few feet along to his right, where the balcony of the master bedroom lay. Not far beyond was the beginning of the ribbed glass-and-iron roof of the conservatory studio, which sloped at a shallow angle to meet the top of the conservatory's outer wall at a point approximately twenty feet from the side of the house. He could see bright flashes and sparks down there in the studio, and the figure of Lucretia as she furiously welded, the blaze of her oxyacetylene torch limning her silhouette with pulsing highlights.

He turned his attention to the terrace, some fifteen feet below the soles of his feet. He could probably jump down if he had to, but, barefoot, there was a good chance he might break an ankle or a heel, and then he would be a lame, not to mention sitting, duck. Picking his way painstakingly down was his only other option.

Go down, or try to carry on sideways? He had to decide quickly.

Something crashed into the ivied brickwork, mere millimetres from Piers's left hand. He glimpsed a roughly cylindrical black object, rounded at both ends, swinging away from the point of impact on the end of a length of black flex. He recognised the object as a portable stereo. Holding the other end of the flex – the stereo's wired-in power cable – was MacGowan.

'Found my range now,' MacGowan said. He was leaning half out of the bedroom window, his belly braced against the sill. 'Won't miss *this* time.'

Without any further ado Piers began clambering to his right, away from the window, towards the balcony. His progress was excruciatingly slow. Finding one of the ivy's fibrous tendrils that was both horizontal and thick enough to provide a decent handhold or toehold was a matter of trial and error, of groping around amid the dense, dark green foliage until a suitable stem came to hand (or, as the case may be, foot). All of which meant that MacGowan could afford to take time over his follow-up assault with the portable stereo, paying out the correct amount of cable and oscillating the stereo back and forth like a pendulum several times to build up momentum before once again swinging it at Piers with all his might.

Piers saw the stereo coming, saw it was on a direct collision course with his skull, and took evasive action. He dug the fingertips of his right hand as hard as he could between the ivy stem they were holding on to and the brickwork beneath, then let go with his other hand and both feet, dropping away just as the stereo came hurtling in towards its target. He felt the whoosh of the stereo as it passed over his head. An instant later there was a shattering, resonant crunch. Fragments of plastic casing rained down on him as the stereo lapsed back on its arc of swing, now looking decidedly the worse for wear, its liquid crystal information display cracked, the lid of its CD drive gaping open, one speaker hanging on by a wire, two of the cassette-deck keys snapped off.

Piers dangled by one arm, legs flailing. He knew that his fingers were not going to be able to maintain their grasp for long. His full body-weight, though not great, was still too much for one hand to support more than a few seconds, particularly since he was hanging on – literally – by his fingertips. He scrabbled around in the ivy with his free hand, searching through the slick leaves. Just when his right hand was about to slip, his left found a hold – not another ivy stem but a crevice between two runs of brick where the mortar had crumbled away. He jammed his left fingertips into the crevice and tried not to think about the damage he was doing to his nails. His manicurist was going to have stern words for him at his next appointment, that much was certain. Assuming he was going to live to *make* his next appointment.

He looked around, quickly weighing up his options. The corner of the balcony was now just a few feet away. Within reach? Possibly. At a stretch.

MacGowan began oscillating the stereo to and fro again.

Piers dug his toes into the ivy and disengaged his right hand from its hold.

The stereo whirled towards him on the upswing.

He lunged.

For a moment he was flying. Then his right hand clamped around one of the balcony's ivy-wreathed railings; then his left hand.

The stereo struck the wall where, a split-second earlier, he had been clinging. This third impact proved catastrophic to the integrity of the machine. It split apart, and the speakers and the cassette carriage and the CD drive and bright green wafers of circuit board tumbled out like gifts from the belly of a *piñata*, dropping to the terrace's flagstones, where they shattered into pieces. MacGowan was left holding just a jagged-edged portion of empty casing on the end of the flex. With a snort of disgust he let go of the flex, and the portion of casing fell to join the rest of the stereo on the terrace.

He turned to look at Piers, who was still hanging from the corner of the balcony. Firing a wicked grin at his fellow Guardian, he disappeared into Alice's bedroom again.

Heaving his legs up under the balcony, Piers raised his right foot and hooked his bare toes clumsily between two of the railings. With a far-from-suave grunt he hauled himself up until he was able to seize the balcony's handrail with both hands. Shunting with his leg, he manoeuvred his torso on to the handrail. Then it was merely a question of getting himself over, which he achieved by means of a sort of slithering, rolling motion that left him sitting on the balcony, panting and exhausted.

It would have been nice to sit there for a while and rest, but, of course, that was not an option. Indeed, Piers scarcely had a chance to catch his breath before Mac-Gowan appeared at the french windows that gave access on to the balcony from the master bedroom. This time, because MacGowan was on the inside of a portal trying to get out rather than the other way around, barging the french windows down was unnecessary. The key and bolts were on the same side as he was. A twist, two pulls and he was opening the french windows and stepping out onto the balcony.

In the time it took MacGowan to unlock the french windows, however, Piers was able to leap to his feet and run to the far end of the balcony. He scrambled up onto the handrail. Balancing on this perch in a half-crouch, he surveyed the gap between the balcony and the edge of the conservatory studio's roof. The point where the conservatory roof met the side of the house was about a foot higher off the ground than the balcony handrail. The distance from here to there was, he judged, a little over two yards. Just a very large step. But a very large step across a fifteen-foot drop. Could he make it?

The question was a redundant one, really. As MacGowan came charging along the balcony towards him, Piers knew he had no choice *but* to make it. Standing upright, he launched himself off the balcony.

He cleared the gap and landed with one foot, then the other, on the nearest of the conservatory's wrought-iron roof beams. He teetered for a second, arms pinwheeling, then swung himself forwards. He caught the next beam along with both hands, managing to prevent himself landing on the pane of glass in between.

Over his shoulder he saw MacGowan climbing onto the handrail, obviously planning to copy his acrobatic stunt. He set off across the top of the conservatory, moving from beam to beam on all-fours, careful to avoid treading on the glazing. He did not know how strong the panes were, and did not want to find out.

MacGowan thrust himself off the balcony, landing on the conservatory roof with a thump that sent reverberations through the entire edifice. Almost immediately he lost his footing on the beam, slithering sideways down its sloping edge. Off balance, his only recourse was to throw himself forwards as Piers had done, but unlike Piers he failed to catch himself on the next beam and instead fell knees-first onto the pane in front of him. The pane creaked in protest but held his weight. Easing himself into a push-up position, he began picking his way crab-wise after Piers across the top of the conservatory, hand over hand along the beams.

Piers, who was by now halfway along the roof, paused to look down through the glass at Lucretia below. She was no longer welding. It looked like she was drilling something now. If she had heard him and MacGowan leaping onto the roof, she was evidently not allowing herself to be distracted from her labours. He could see Lady Grinning Soul down there, too. She was on her feet, head craned upwards, watching him and turning around and around in fretful little circles.

He monkey-walked across several more beams. Mac-Gowan was still following. The former soldier was concentrating hard on maintaining his footing, but not so hard that he failed to spot the activity down below in the studio. He frowned, unable to make out clearly through the glass what Lucretia was up to. Working? At a time like this? It made no sense. With a shake of his head, he returned his attention to Piers. One thing at a time. Whatever Lucretia was doing down there, it had no immediate bearing on the task at hand.

Piers glanced behind him. Three more beams to go, and then the conservatory ended. He was out of room. What now?

He racked his brains. There was *one* course of action he could take, but it was a pretty drastic measure and he would probably break his damn-fool neck in the process. Still, in the absence of any better alternative, he could only give it a try.

He had not quite managed to give Lucretia her full ten minutes. He had done the best he could. He hoped it was enough.

MacGowan was now no more than a few feet away. Piers chose his moment, waiting till MacGowan was midway between two beams, his body directly over a pane. Then, with a single scuttling bound, he hurled himself onto MacGowan's back, flattening MacGowan against the glass. There was an ominous creak, followed by a whipcrack sound of splitting. Then the pane gave way beneath the two men's combined weight, and then they were plummeting.

51

If, a few years ago, Kim had been walking through a Parisian airport with Jun Shirow's arm around her shoulders, she might have thought she had died and gone to heaven. Today, it felt like she had died and gone to hell.

The arm was not draped around her affectionately but laid on her like a yoke, the hand gripping her deltoid muscle tightly. Emperor Dragon's other hand was in his jacket pocket, clasped around the butt of the toxin pistol, which Ryu had palmed to him shortly after the plane landed.

He need not have bothered with either of these methods of ensuring her compliance, however. Kim was so wrung out from the flight, so groggy with lack of sleep, her inner clock so skewed by jetlag, that it was all she could do to keep walking in a straight line. Moreover, she was mired in the depths of a misery so abject that she could not even begin to muster the enthusiasm, the optimism, necessary to make an escape attempt. What would be the point? What would she gain? What difference would it make? As far as she could see, the situation was hopeless. Emperor Dragon had won. The Guardians were in serious trouble. And the whole sorry mess was her fault.

The futuristic wonders of Charles de Gaulle were lost on her. As she and Emperor Dragon travelled along a moving walkway through a glass tunnel, one of several that crisscrossed a sunlit atrium at various tangents, all she saw was the mesh of the conveyor belt beneath her feet. The fact that she was on European soil for the first time in her life meant nothing to her. Under other circumstances she would have found the experience novel and thrilling: so many Westerners in one place, and the noises, the languages, the odours, so unfamiliar . . . But today she was oblivious to all that. The foreignness of everything around her only served to reinforce her isolation, her desolation.

Emperor Dragon steered her towards a car-rental desk, where they were obliged to stand in line for several minutes while the customer in front of them, a German businessman, argued calmly but forcefully with the rental agency clerk, a woman whose bleary eyes and weary demeanour indicated that she was at the end of both her shift and her tether. The argument was conducted in the German's native tongue, but while the clerk was answering a phone call, the businessman took the opportunity to explain to Emperor Dragon and Kim over his shoulder, in English, that there had been some sort of mix-up and that the rental agency computer showed no record of the telephone booking his secretary had made for him the previous day. He went on to apologise for holding them up, but there was, you understand, a matter of principle at stake. It was not that he minded that an error had been made, but he was keen to track down the cause so that, whether it transpired that his secretary had been at fault or the rental agency, the error would not be repeated in future.

Courteous though the German businessman was, Emperor Dragon treated his apology with characteristic disdain. Kim, for her part, just looked on, numb, acquiescent, way past caring. Even when she heard the sound of sirens skirling faintly outside, this failed to arouse her interest or her hopes. She had no reason to connect the sirens with Rattray, after all. Neither did Emperor Dragon, for whom – despite the fact that he was presently experiencing a tiny hitch in his plans, in the form of this slight delay – it was still inconceivable that another hitch, a much larger one, might be taking place elsewhere.

Finally, to everyone's relief, the German businessman conceded that nothing was going to be resolved right away, and he let the clerk go ahead and lease him another car, even though it was not the make and model that was supposed to have been reserved for him. He would, he informed the woman, be writing a formal complaint to her company, to which the clerk responded with an as-you-wish gesture that expertly trod the line between polite and facetious – while it was to all intents and purposes the former, no one could construe it as anything but the latter.

With the German dealt with, the rental-agency clerk turned to Emperor Dragon and Kim and enquired how she might be able to help *them*. Her command of English was as good as her command of German. Emperor Dragon requested the best car in the company's fleet. Unfortunately it turned out that all the luxury and prestige models had been hired out already, and the best the clerk could offer him was a Citroën XM hatchback. Emperor Dragon accepted this news with as much good grace as he could manage, i.e., none.

While the clerk filled out the relevant forms and processed Emperor Dragon's credit-card payment, she directed several glances at Kim, puzzled by the scratches on the young woman's face and by her muteness and downcast demeanour. Emperor Dragon, noticing her interest in Kim, allayed her curiosity by explaining that his girlfriend was not a good traveller and suffered badly from airsickness.

His girlfriend. The words filled Kim with a cold, curdled disgust. How dare he? she thought. The bastard!

Her indignation roused her, stirred her back to life. She would show him! She would fight free of his clutches and beg the clerk to help her. She would make a scene. Scream for the police. He surely would not dare shoot her with the toxin pistol right in front of a witness.

Emperor Dragon seemed to sense what she was think-

370

ing. Perhaps she had unwittingly tensed and he had felt it. Softly, in Japanese, he said, 'By the way, Kim, did I mention that Ryu and I are to rendezvous at a pre-arranged place and time? No, I don't think I did. It must have slipped my mind. Of course, should I fail to show up, Ryu is under orders to inflict damage on your friend. Lethal damage.'

Kim's immediate thought was that he was bluffing. She did not believe that it was that simple a matter to kill Rattray, even when he was unconscious. Nor did she believe that Emperor Dragon was prepared to forfeit the money he stood to earn by delivering Rattray alive to the Frenchman, whoever he was. At the same time, she realised she could not do anything if there was the remotest chance that her actions might endanger her fellow Guardian's life.

Her surge of rebelliousness subsided as swiftly as it had arisen. She lapsed back into despondence.

The clerk presented Emperor Dragon with documentation, a complimentary map of France's main *autoroutes* and a set of keys, and gave him directions to the rental agency's car park. '*Bonnes vacances, m'sieur, mam'selle,*' she said, and turned to her next customer.

Emperor Dragon pulled Kim around and marched her off. 'Well done,' he whispered in her ear. 'You're behaving yourself like a good girl. Keep it up and this will soon be over.'

Over, Kim thought. An end to this nightmare. God, how she longed for that.

As she and Emperor Dragon made their way towards the exit that would lead them to the car park, neither noticed that they were being followed.

To Rattray, the car-rental desk had seemed the logical place to start looking for them. Luck, in the form of the delay caused by the over-punctilious German businessman, meant that they were still there when he arrived. Lurking at a nearby newsstand, he feigned interest in the headlines of today's edition of *Le Figaro* and surreptitiously observed them. When they moved off, he set off after them, keeping well back, using the crowd as camouflage, merging with the swirl of tourists and travellers and airline staff and airport employees.

Dressed as he was in baseball jacket, T-shirt, jeans and sneakers, Rattray looked like a man in the throes of a mid-life crisis, unable to age gracefully, still clinging to the fashions of his youth.

Anyone taking a good look at his face, however, would find no evidence to back this up. In Rattray's expression there was no trace of either self-consciousness or insecurity. There was only fixity of purpose. In the set of his jaw, in his steely grey eyes, only a deadly determination.

52

Moments before Piers and MacGowan made their spectacular entrance through the conservatory roof, Lucretia rotated the handwheel that raised the bit-mounting assembly of her precision drill. With a puff of breath she blew away twisted fragments of swarf from the hole she had just bored in one of the two lengths of steel pipe she had joined together a minute earlier. The hole, half an inch wide, penetrated the pipe at a point about an inch and a half from one end. The other end of the pipe was attached by a blobby, burnished weld to the second, shorter length of pipe so as to form a T. The bond between the two pipes was not as secure as Lucretia might have wished, but then what did you expect from a rush job? She began spinning the lever that released the jaws of the vice.

She was aware that her two fellow Guardians were overhead, but had not dared pause from her labours to ask herself what Piers hoped to achieve by luring MacGowan up onto the conservatory roof or, for that matter, how he intended to get down from there. She had carried on resolutely with her work, trusting that Piers knew what he was doing.

The T-shaped fusion of pipes came free of the vice just as Piers leapt onto MacGowan's back. Lucretia's head snapped round as she heard the glass break. She watched with startled amazement as Piers and MacGowan plunged through the roof and hit the studio floor amid a sparkling, tinkling rain of shards.

MacGowan was underneath and so absorbed the brunt of the impact. Piers bounced off his fellow Guardian's back and rolled away, fetching up against the base of Lucretia's lathe.

Lady was by his side in a trice, sniffing at him worriedly. As Piers dragged himself to his feet using the lathe for support, she offered him a beseeching wag of her tail. Piers gave her a quick pat on the head, but the full joyful master-and-dog reunion would have to wait. He crossed over to Lucretia's workbench, limping. Lady followed.

Snatching up the vaccine gun from the workbench, Piers turned round to face MacGowan. Had MacGowan still been lying prostrate on the floor, stunned and insensible, in no fit state to resist, then Piers could have administered the vaccine there and then. MacGowan, however, had recovered from the fall and was pushing himself into a kneeling position.

Piers turned to Lucretia. 'Looks like we're sticking with Plan A.'

Lucretia finally found her voice. 'For God's sake, Piers, are you all right?'

'Bruised but intact,' came the reply. 'Everything ready?'

Lucretia nodded and brandished the steel pipe T. She refrained from mentioning that she had doubts about the integrity of the weld. Piers had enough on his plate as it was. Instead, she bent and picked up a length of solid iron rod which she had set down earlier on the floor next to the drill and, carrying this and the steel T, hurried over to the pulley control panel.

The pushbuttons on the panel were arrayed in two tiers of sequentially numbered pairs, green along the top tier, red along the bottom. Setting down the T and the rod, Lucretia poised her left index finger over one of the green pushbuttons, while with her right hand she took the coherent-light pistol out of her pocket. Just in case.

Piers instructed Lady to go and join Lucretia. Reluctantly, because she loved her master, but obediently, because she loved her master, Lady complied. Slipping the vaccine gun into his breast pocket, Piers then hastened over to a bright red, tent-shaped section of the Obsta-climb. Each of the two sides of this section of the apparatus consisted of a row of angled ladders with a network of ropes serving as rungs. The ropes incorpor-ated excesses of slack and were organised so that the rungs would not pull taut and allow you to ascend or descend unless they were trodden on in a specific order. Standing there, Piers was directly in front of MacGowan. Lucretia and Lady were well out of MacGowan's line of sight.

MacGowan had regained his feet by this time and was shaking fragments of broken glass out of his hair. His clothes were torn in several places and his face and hands were crosshatched with tiny cuts. His expression was, if anything, even more savagely furious than before. Look-ing up, he fixed Piers with a brutish glare. 'That was a nasty trick,' he snarled. 'For that I'm going to tear your fucking nuts off.'

'Well, come along, then,' Piers replied equably. 'I haven't got all day.'

MacGowan went for him with his arms upraised like an attacking grizzly. Piers darted behind the tent-shaped Obstaclimb section and swiftly circumnavigated another section, this one a large cubic cage of orange-painted bars that contained within it sixty-four smaller cubes, each of which gave access to only one of its neighbours, thus forming a three-dimensional maze with a single tortuous solution.

Stationed next to the orange cube was a blue dome-shaped section, like a hollow planetary hemisphere with curved bars for its lines of latitude and longitude. Like the cube the hemisphere contained a maze, this one a lattice of poles crisscrossing and intersecting at a variety of angles. Unlike the cube's maze, which had just the one solution, the hemisphere's had several possible routes through.

There were two short tunnels like igloo doorways on either side of the base of the hemisphere, an entrance and an exit. When all the sections of the Obstaclimb were assembled at its final destination, the hemisphere's entrance would connect directly with the exit from the orange cube. At present, however, with the Obstaclimb's components spaced out across the studio, there was sufficient room for Piers to throw himself prostrate and scramble headfirst into the entrance.

MacGowan was a couple of seconds behind him. Hurling himself flat on the floor, he thrust an arm into the entrance and made a grab for Piers's foot. His fingers made brief contact with Piers's bare heel but failed to gain a hold. Without pausing, he propelled himself into the entrance after Piers, shunting himself along with his elbows, exactly as he had been trained to do on countless assault courses. It did not occur to him that Piers *wanted* to be followed into the hemisphere. All he could think, in his obsession with catching and killing his fellow Guardian, was that Piers had made a final, fatal error of judgement. He had trapped himself. This would all be over and done with in a few short moments from now, and then MacGowan could turn his attention to that bitch Lucretia.

Piers pulled himself clear of the entrance and stood up inside the hemisphere. There was no time to analyse the metal thicket in front of him, no time to plot a course through in advance. Plunging headlong into the intricate network of poles, he groped and grappled and gripped, over, under, between, around, lithely lacing himself into gaps, contorting his body, sometimes bending double, sometimes hanging upside down. He could tell, from the huffs of effort coming from behind him and from the occasional glimpse out of the corner of his eye, that MacGowan was still pursuing him. All according to plan. It was not until he emerged from the other side of the maze, however, that he realised that MacGowan was no longer so close on his heels.

MacGowan, in fact, was making heavy weather of the

maze. The Obstaclimb, after all, was designed for children, not thickset ex-soldiers who stood at over six and a half feet in their socks. Even sinewy, slender Piers had found parts of it difficult to negotiate, but where he had been able to worm his way through, MacGowan had to squeeze, and where he had been able to slither, Mac-Gowan could only wrench himself inch by inch. Several times MacGowan came close to getting stuck, and it was only thanks to sheer, clenched-teeth determination that he was able to force himself onwards. Consequently he was still in the thick of the maze as Piers entered the exit tunnel.

As soon as Piers started crawling into the tunnel, Lucretia punched the green pushbutton. An electric motor whirred, there was a rattle of chains, and the exit end of the hemisphere began to rise from the floor. Hauled by a single pulley, the hemisphere tilted upwards at a rapidly steepening incline. Inside, MacGowan found his battle through the maze made even more difficult by his shifting centre of gravity. Meanwhile, at the exit, Piers hauled himself out and swung himself up and over until he was sitting astride the tunnel, straddling it.

As the hemisphere continued to rise, its weight, coupled with that of its two passengers, was brought to bear on the bars of the entrance tunnel. Gradually the bars started to buckle, the tunnel crumpling into a flattened tangle of metal. This meant that there was only one way in or out of the hemisphere, the exit tunnel, which was now some eight feet off the floor.

Everything that happened next happened quickly.

Lucretia hit the green pushbutton's red counterpart and the pulley mechanism halted. Snatching up the iron rod and the steel T, she ran over to the hemisphere and passed the two items, one after the other, up to Piers. Piers slotted the T in through the bars of the tunnel so that it hung in place suspended by its horizontal portion, its vertical portion bisecting the exit. Then, reaching down underneath the tunnel, he slid the rod into the hole drilled in the base of the T so that the T became an I (or an H on its side). The rod secured the T in place, preventing it from falling out or being pushed out.

Lucretia, meanwhile, grabbed a three-foot-high step-ladder and positioned it below the exit. Then, having fetched her welding mask, a portable propane blowtorch and a straight, silvery length of manganese-coated filler wire from her workbench, she climbed the stepladder. Balancing on its top step, she clamped the welding mask onto her head, flipped down the faceplate, fired up the blowtorch and began applying the filler wire and the blowtorch's flaring blue cone of flame to the points where the rod penetrated the T.

It was not the easiest job in the world. A static weld-point would have presented no problem, but this one kept jiggling and moving about. The entire hemisphere was shaking and swaying, thanks to Piers, who was now busy clambering across its curved surface towards its apex, and MacGowan, who was still struggling inside the maze like a fly trying to extricate itself from a spider's web. Melted filler spattered all over the rod and the end of the T, only about a third of it ending up where it was supposed to, around the edges of the drilled hole. Dribbles of the silvery stuff fell onto Lucretia's workgloves and the floor, but she persevered. She had one chance to get this right, to forge a lock that would hold MacGowan in.

Piers crawled over the hemisphere until he was above MacGowan. He called down through the bars: 'Hey, old chap! Up here!' MacGowan immediately diverted course, wriggling upwards through the maze towards this quarry who had proved so aggravatingly, frustratingly elusive.

He found his way blocked. A nexus of poles stopped him within a yard of the hemisphere's exterior. Stretching out his arm to its fullest extent, he reached through the bars for Piers.

Piers seized MacGowan's hand and bent it back against the bars. With his other hand he pulled the vaccine gun from his pocket. He placed the nozzle of the gun against the glass-scratched skin of MacGowan's wrist and curled his index finger around the trigger.

He did not see MacGowan's other arm come up. MacGowan grabbed a fistful of his pyjama jacket and yanked down hard. The suddenness and violence of the action dislodged the vaccine gun from Piers's grasp. It tumbled through the poles of the maze, bouncing from one to another with a series of tuneless clangs like a brief, mad peal of tubular bells, until finally it dropped through the bottom of the hemisphere and onto the floor.

It hit the floor with a tiny, tinny crash that was unmistakably the sound of its ampoule cartridge shattering.

'Lucretia!' Piers yelled, and MacGowan started yelling, too, spitting out a stream of threats and epithets, and at the same time tugging down on Piers, while Piers strove to maintain his grip on MacGowan's other hand, the one that he was holding on to rather than the one that was holding on to him. Lady joined in, too, adding raucous, panicky *ruffs* to the general medley.

'*Lucretia!*' Piers yelled again, more urgently. 'The gun! Get the gun and reload it!'

Lucretia flipped up her mask. She saw at a glance how the situation had developed while she had been intent on her welding. She flicked off the blowtorch and leapt off the stepladder. She set the blowtorch and filler wire on the floor, tugged off her mask and, getting down on her hands and knees, crawled underneath the hemisphere.

MacGowan started twisting his hand around, trying to loosen it from Piers's grasp. Piers pressed it against the bars with all his strength.

Lucretia reached the vaccine gun, which was lying in a puddle of milky-blue fluid. Tugging off her workgloves with her teeth, she picked the gun up and shook out the remaining fragments of ampoule glass from the breech. She delved into her pocket, thanking God that she had had the foresight to bring spare ampoules along. She slotted a fresh ampoule into the breech. It would not go fully in. Was the gun mechanism broken? Why had she not thought to bring along a spare *gun* as well? She slid the ampoule out and peered into the breech. There was a shard from the shattered ampoule lodged inside. She poked her finger in, knowing that there was no time to waste, that Piers could not keep his grip on MacGowan's hand for ever. This was the best chance – maybe the only chance – they were going to get to inject him. But the shard would not budge. Such a tiny thing, a mere sliver of glass, yet it threatened to ruin everything. For want of a nail the kingdom was lost. She poked her finger further into the breech, hooking it around the shard. She felt a sharp sting as the shard's jagged edge sliced into the pad of her fingertip. She started working at the shard, steeling herself to ignore the deepening pain.

Suddenly the shard came free. She picked it out of the breech. Blood trickled over her fingers as she picked up the spare ampoule and slotted it in. Clasping the gun by its barrel, she slithered out from under the hemisphere.

Piers saw her. He held out one hand. 'Up here, old girl.'

Lucretia tossed the gun up to him. She threw it without thinking, without aiming. Had she hesitated for even a moment, she would probably have missed; the gun would have overshot or fallen short. Reflexive instinct guided her arm, and the gun rose to Piers in a perfect parabola. In a single fluid motion he plucked it from the air, brought it down against MacGowan's wrist and pulled the trigger.

There was a sharp hiss. The ampoule emptied.

MacGowan stopped yelling, not understanding exactly what was going on but sensing instinctively that it did not bode well and that defeat – *his* defeat – was imminent. Letting go of Piers's pyjama jacket, he began hammering at the poles of the maze and throwing his weight around with enough force to set the hemisphere rocking to and fro. Piers hung on for dear life while Lucretia shuffled hurriedly out of harm's way. A safe distance from the hemisphere, she got to her feet, turned and watched the frantic scene: MacGowan raging like a maddened gorilla in a cage, Lady barking alongside, and the hapless Piers clinging on to the hemisphere's blue bars, being thrown about like a rodeo cowboy who has been given a huge and unnaturally vicious bucking bronco to ride.

Then, gradually, the paraterrestrial vaccine started to take effect and MacGowan's anger began to diminish. His struggles grew weaker. The rocking of the hemisphere became less violent. Soon all MacGowan could manage were a few ineffectual, open-palm slaps against the poles. His eyelids were drooping. Unconsciousness beckoned. He slumped backwards, sagging down inside the maze. He came to rest cradled awkwardly amid the network of poles with his limbs poking out at odd angles. It was the kind of position that only a baby could have slept in. And MacGowan was, quite undeniably, sleeping like a baby.

53

The rental agency car park was deserted. No innocent bystanders. No witnesses. As good a place as any, Rattray thought, for a showdown.

Kim and Emperor Dragon were fifty yards ahead of him. He was on one side of a double row of parked cars, they were on the other. Lurking low, he moved from one front bumper to the next, raising his head every so often to check on Kim's and Emperor Dragon's position relative to his. They were walking slowly, Emperor Dragon checking numberplates, looking for one that matched the one listed in the rental agency documentation.

Planes were taking off at a rate of roughly two per minute. Each time, the air was filled with a rumble that seemed to set the entire world trembling.

Rattray closed the gap between him and the two young Japanese, until he was moving parallel with them, keeping pace. When Emperor Dragon halted, having at last found the Citroën he had rented, Rattray halted, too.

Two cars' lengths separated him from them. Rattray tensed, steadying himself in anticipation of a burst of speed. Emperor Dragon, taken unawares, would be dead before he knew what hit him.

Emperor Dragon moved to the driver's-side door of the Citroën and unlocked it. He paused.

Frowned.

The toxin pistol was out of his pocket in a flash. He

seized Kim, wrapped an arm around her neck and swung her around so that he and she were facing in Rattray's direction. He pointed the pistol at her jugular.

'I see you, Mr Rattray!' he called out. 'Come out or I shoot her!'

Kim gasped. Rattray was *here*? How?

She gasped again, this time in pain as Emperor Dragon ground the pistol harder into her neck.

'I won't say this twice, Mr Rattray,' Emperor Dragon snarled. 'I'll kill her, I swear. And then maybe you'll kill *me*, but she'll still be dead. It's up to you. Her life is in your hands. Come out where I can see you, or your ugly little fuck-bitch is toast.'

Another plane roared with the effort of tearing itself free of the bounds of gravity.

Slowly, grimly, Rattray rose to his feet.

Kim could scarcely believe her eyes. Rattray, no longer helpless on that gurney but free, safe. *Here*. How had he managed it? His clothes told part of the story. The rest . . . Well, the rest did not matter right now. He was here, that was all that mattered. And despite the pistol jabbing into her neck, Kim felt a faint fluttering of hope in her heart.

'The wing-mirror,' Emperor Dragon said to Rattray. 'In case you were wondering.' He nodded over at the passenger side of the car. 'I saw your feet. Those are Kenji's shoes?'

Rattray ignored the question. 'I can reach you in the time in takes you to blink,' he said, fixing Emperor Dragon with a flinty, brow-shadowed stare.

'Can you?' Emperor Dragon replied. 'Then why haven't you done so? Could it be because you know that, no matter how fast you move, all I have to do is twitch a finger and she's dead?'

'Kill her,' Rattray intoned, 'and I won't kill you. I'll just leave you wishing you were dead.'

'You don't frighten me,' said Emperor Dragon, and whether this was true or not he certainly did not *sound* frightened. He sounded, in fact, as if he was relishing this standoff, as if this was not a matter of life and death but a delicious game of wits.

Another plane thundered heavenwards.

'Well now,' said Emperor Dragon, as the jet-turbine tumult dwindled. 'What are we to do?'

'You,' said Rattray, 'are to let her go.'

'And then what? You let me walk away scot-free? I very much doubt it. I'm a threat to your organisation, and you people have a policy about threats to your organisation, don't you? A pretty ruthless policy. Kill first, ask questions later – if that isn't the Guardian motto, it ought to be.'

'We do what's necessary in the name of what we believe. But in this instance I'm prepared to make an exception. Let Kim go and you *will* walk free.'

Kim started to object. She did not want Rattray to let Emperor Dragon get away purely for her sake. She did not want to be responsible for any further failures.

Barely had she begun to speak, however, before Emperor Dragon silenced her with a shake and a hissed *ssh*. 'Kimiko, the men are talking,' he said. He had not taken his eyes off Rattray. 'And what if I don't believe you, Mr Rattray? Don't trust you?'

'Then we have a problem. It's a deadlock. A stalemate. Neither of us can win.'

'Maybe not. But one of us can *lose*. You. By stepping back and allowing me to get into the car and drive away with Kim.'

Rattray paused before answering. It was the briefest of pauses, but it spoke volumes. He was considering the idea. 'And what happens to Kim?'

'When I'm a good distance away, I stop and let her out of the car.'

Don't agree to it, John, Kim begged him mentally. Forget me. Kill him now while you can.

'I can't trust you, either,' Rattray said finally.

'Oh, but I'm not asking you to trust me,' Emperor Dragon said. 'What I'm doing is setting out the facts. The only way to resolve this impasse in which we find ourselves is if I and Kim move slowly towards the car, get in and drive away. And that is precisely what we are going to do. Right now.' He tightened his grip around Kim's neck. 'Walk, bitch.'

Indignant anger swelled within Kim again. She did not care any more what happened to her. She did not care whether she lived or died. She had had enough. She would not be treated like this, like some . . . some sort of human bargaining chip. A piece of flesh to be haggled over and shoved around.

It came to her in a flash.

Emperor Dragon's slight limp in the contemplative garden.

His knee injury.

I bet you still have trouble with it, she had said.

From time to time, he had replied.

Which knee was it? The right or the left? She could not remember.

A fifty-fifty shot.

She went for the left. Kicked back violently, viciously with her bootheel.

The heel connected. She felt *and* heard the crunch of hard footwear meeting soft cartilage.

Emperor Dragon's cry of agony could not have been more satisfying to hear. It started low and rose like a wolf howl to a ragged, fraying peak before dissolving into a flood of Japanese invective. She felt him sag behind her, no longer holding on to her neck to keep her still but to support himself. She twisted and turned, trying to writhe out of his clutches, but grimly he clung on to her.

She saw Rattray start to move towards them. Emperor Dragon saw this, too, through his blur of pain. He brought up the toxin pistol and fired. Kim slapped his arm and the shot went wild. Rattray ducked and the capsule of lethal poison splatted against the rear wind-screen of a nearby car.

A mighty shove between her shoulderblades sent Kim stumbling towards Rattray, who was still hunkered down. She could not stop herself. She stumbled into her fellow Guardian, lost her balance and fell haplessly against him. Her momentum carried them both to the ground.

Sandwiched between two cars, it took her and Rattray several seconds to disentangle themselves and get back on their feet. During those precious seconds Emperor Dragon managed to hobble to the door of the Citroën, open it and throw himself into the driving seat. Rattray shoved Kim aside and lunged for the door. He got his fingers beneath the handle just as Emperor Dragon punched down the locking button. The handle flipped up uselessly. Rattray let go of it and thumped the window. The glass went frosty white. Emperor Dragon slotted the key into the ignition and started the car. His foot was pressing hard on the accelerator pedal. The engine over-revved deafeningly. Rattray thumped the window again, clearing a small hole in the glass. Little crystalline chunks showered over Emperor Dragon like hard confetti as he shunted the car's automatic transmission into Drive. The Citroën screeched forwards, zooming across the aisle between it and the next row of parked cars and crashing into a Renault opposite. Rattray sprinted after it. Emperor Dragon threw the Citroën into reverse and stamped on the accelerator, simultaneously spinning the steering-wheel. The Citroën executed a 45° turn backwards, colliding with Rattray on the way. Rattray slammed into the rear of the car, and the Citroën completed its reverse turn with him sprawled across its hatchback spoiler, limbs splayed and flailing. Emperor Dragon jammed on the brakes, and Rattray was jettisoned backwards through the air. He rebounded off the radiator grille of another Citroën, leaving a deep indentation and landing on his side on the ground.

Kim saw Emperor Dragon glance in his rearview mirror. Saw his lips curl into a sickle smile. Saw him turn around in his seat to look out through the rear wind-screen, wincing at the pain this caused his knee.

'John!' she shouted.

Rattray raised his head. The Citroën's brake lights went

off; the reversing lights remained on. Tyres squealed on Tarmac as Emperor Dragon hit the accelerator again. The car came straight for Rattray. He moved as fast as he could, but abdominal muscles had been torn; the orchestra of his body was not playing in perfect symphony. He managed to hurl himself out of the path of the oncoming Citroën, but not quite quickly enough. His right foot was caught beneath one of its rear wheels. Kim heard a crunch like someone popping their knuckles, only five times louder and ten times more sickening. She saw Rattray's face contort into a grimace of pain and relax again almost immediately as the damaged region of his body was flooded with natural analgesics. Emperor Dragon braked sharply and threw the car into Drive once more, intending to run over Rattray's foot a second time, forwards. Rattray pulled his leg towards him, out from underneath the Citroën. The car shot forwards, the rear wheel missing his crushed foot by inches. Rattray slapped his hands onto the bonnet of the nearest stationary car, clawed his way up to a standing position and launched himself in pursuit of Emperor Dragon. The attempt was a valiant but doomed one. His right foot would not support him. He stumbled and collapsed to his knees.

Emperor Dragon did not stop and come back to try to mow Rattray down again. Having inflicted sufficient damage to ensure that Rattray could not give chase, he made his getaway. Kim watched him drive off, powerless to stop him. When the Citroën reached the far end of the aisle, Emperor Dragon let out a couple of defiant blasts on the horn, and then the car turned the corner and was gone.

Kim hurried over to Rattray, who was upright again but standing on one leg, leaning on the car. His right foot dangled loosely from its ankle, hideously twisted and misshapen. The laces of his right sneaker had snapped and several of its rubberised seams had split apart. His gaze was directed at the spot where the Citroën had last been in view; his jaw was tightly clenched.

'John?' Kim said softly.

When he did not respond, she repeated his name a little more loudly. He swivelled his head towards her.

'We should get going. Before someone comes along.' She indicated the damaged cars around them, the fragments of window glass and headlight housing that littered the ground. 'Otherwise we're going to have a lot of explaining to do.'

Very, very slowly Rattray nodded. 'Yes. You're right.'

'Can you walk?'

Rattray tested his foot gingerly on the ground. 'Not for another quarter of an hour, I should think.'

'We can't wait that long. Here.' Kim moved close to him and guided his right arm around her shoulders. 'Lean on me.'

Taking his weight, she helped him hop-hobble back towards the terminal building.

54

'Hello.' Lucretia's voice. 'You have reached the home of Lucretia Fisk and Dennis Holman. I'm afraid there's no one available to take your call right now, but if you leave—'

The answering-machine message cut out and Lucretia's real voice, live and unrecorded, cut in. 'Hello?'

'Lucretia.'

'John! Thank God! Where are you? How are you?'

'In Paris,' said Rattray, 'and I'm fine.'

'Paris? What on earth are you doing in Paris?'

'I'll explain later. How is everything with you? Did the Seal Point job go off all right?'

She told him. She omitted no detail. Her phone call from MacGowan. His attack on Bretherton Grange. His capture and cure. The words spilled out of her. She was glad to have this opportunity to put the events of the past twenty-four hours into order, to be able to make some sense of them.

Rattray did not interrupt her. He said nothing until she had finished. 'And Bill's OK? The vaccine was effective?'

'We think so. He came round just over an hour ago. Weak and hungry. No clear memory of what he did. He had a bit of a surprise when he woke up. We, um . . . We tied him down to a bed while he was unconscious, just in case the vaccine didn't work. Secured him with manacles, in fact. Poor chap. He feels terrible about what he did.'

'And Dennis?'

'His throat looks like a side of raw beef, his nose is swollen and he can only speak in whispers, but with the aid of salves from the cellars he should make a full recovery. He's being very brave about it.'

'Wish him well from me.'

'I will.'

'Do you know yet what actually occurred at the nuclear power station?'

'We've a rough idea. Bill's recollection is hazy, but he's pretty sure he and his team were ambushed.'

'Ambushed? Someone knew they were coming?'

'So it seems.'

There was a long silence from Rattray's end of the line.

'John?'

'Yes, sorry, Lucretia. I was thinking.'

'And?'

'I'm not sure. I have a feeling I may have to have a word with Cecil.'

'All this was Cecil's fault? I don't understand. What could he have done?'

'Nothing. Not deliberately. But the mouths . . .'

Lucretia waited for Rattray to continue. When nothing more was forthcoming, she prompted him: 'You were saying? The mouths?'

'It's something I'll have to sort out with Cecil. Something we'll need to be wary of in the future.'

'That doesn't sound good.'

'I could be mistaken, of course.'

Lucretia knew he had only said that for her benefit.

'The main thing,' Rattray continued, 'is that everyone is alive and well.'

'No argument here. OK, your turn now. How did it go with Emperor Dragon?'

Rattray gave a succinct summary of his and Kim's exploits in Japan, on the flight to France and at Charles de Gaulle, concluding on the downbeat note of Emperor Dragon's escape.

'And you have no clue as to the identity of this French aristocrat who had you kidnapped?' Lucretia asked.

'None, other than that he lives within a 150-kilometre radius of Paris.'

'Well, that narrows it down a bit, doesn't it?' said Lucretia dryly. 'You're only talking about the most densely populated area of France.'

'We'll find out who he is,' Rattray averred. 'You can count on it.'

'So when can we expect you back here? If you were to catch the Eurostar, you could be at Bretherton by this evening.'

'I'm not sure I'm up to travelling just yet. Maybe tomorrow. Apart from anything else, Kim and I both need to go shopping for a change of clothes. And I think Kim ought to take in at least some of the sights before she heads back to Japan.'

'OK. We'll see you tomorrow, then.'

Rattray replaced the receiver of the bedside phone and turned to Kim, who was perched on the end of the bed wearing one of the Paris Ritz's luxurious towelling bath-robes. Her legs were folded decorously beneath her and the bathrobe was done up tight beneath her chin, but for all that there was, in Rattray's opinion, something undeniably alluring both about her pose and about the fact that she was sitting here, in his hotel room, non-chalantly wrapped in just the one layer of borrowed clothing.

He remembered his subconscious avatar, in the guise of Valentina, telling him that Kim interested him not just on an intellectual level but on a physical one, too.

Luckily the blush response, in keeping with all his other physiological processes, was controllable.

'Well, anyway,' he said, 'that's Lucretia brought up to speed. What about you? How are you feeling?'

'All the better for a couple of hours' sleep,' Kim replied. 'And now we have an afternoon and an evening on the town ahead of us?'

Rattray nodded.

'Then let me take a shower and get dressed, and we'll head out.'

'I'm afraid I'm going to have to ask to borrow some money. All my belongings, including my wallet, are back in Japan,' said Rattray. 'Of course, I'll reimburse you every penny once I get home.'

'It's not a problem. I don't mind paying for both of us.'

'I don't want to owe you anything.'

Kim laughed. 'John, I'm the one who owes *you*. For everything you've done for me this past couple of days.'

'Let's not confuse financial debt with any other kind of debt, shall we?'

'Fine by me.' Kim got to her feet and went to the door. As her hand grasped the knob, she paused and turned. 'John, when Emperor Dragon had that pistol to my neck . . .' She dropped her gaze, then raised it again. 'You shouldn't have let him get away. You should have gone for him regardless.'

'And risk your life? I don't think so, Kim.'

She studied his face for a moment. Doubtless what she saw in his eyes was probably there simply because she wanted to see it there. None the less, she was glad to see it.

'All right,' she said, after a short spell of silence. 'Give me quarter of an hour, and then – Paris.'

'Paris,' Rattray echoed.

Only after the door was closed between them did either of them dare to smile.

55

On the island he was known, if he was known at all, as the antiques dealer.

Whether he had actually ever traded in antiques or not was unclear. His house, however, was stuffed to bursting with aged artefacts and fine furniture, and on the strength of this, and in the absence of further evidence, it was generally assumed that this must be how he earned his living. Or rather, *used* to earn his living, for the antiques dealer was no longer in regular employment. Like the island's many other wealthy retirees and tax exiles, he passed his days tending his garden and enjoying brisk, sea-view walks.

He did not socialise. Occasionally he might wander down to one of the island's pubs for a quick half-pint. He might exchange a few trifling words with the landlord while his beer was being poured, and he might bid good-day to anyone who happened to catch his eye, but long, involved conversations with strangers were not for him – and to the antiques dealer everyone on the island was a stranger.

He had a soft, evenly modulated voice. He was not, strictly speaking, well spoken, but there was in his diction and phrasing the unmistakable stamp of intelligence – the kind that comes from experience rather than education. Age-wise, he was probably in his late fifties, shading into his early sixties. His hair was a faded-copper colour with sandy highlights. His eyes were a startling, sparkling blue.

He had pale, freckled skin and, though he was of a generally robust build, his hands were slender and oddly delicate. His sexuality was as much a matter of speculation among the islanders as his erstwhile profession. He was single but showed no interest in any of the island's plethora of well-to-do and still nubile widows, and if his tastes ran in the other direction, then his lifestyle gave no indication of such. It could be that he was the kind of man who, rather than succumb to 'unnatural' proclivities, denied they existed at all. He was of that generation, certainly.

In the event, all that the islanders could say about the antiques dealer with any degree of certainty was that he was one of the most self-contained, self-possessed men they could think of. In his hilltop bungalow, with its panoramic windows and its rooms stuffed with bric-a-brac, he pulled off that most difficult of tricks: successfully living alone.

This evening, as the sun slowly dissolved into a cloud-bank on the western horizon, the antiques dealer was sitting in his drawing room. He was expecting a visitor. His armchair was angled towards the windows, so that he had a commanding view of the Channel and the rooftops of the houses down-slope from his. His elbows rested on the chair's arms and his fingers were steepled, their tips touched to his upper lip. On a side-table to his left, Meissen figurines of a milkmaid and her beau perched with delicate porcelain courtesy next to a Japanese inro box inlaid with shimmering pearl marquetry. African tribal masks glowered down from the wall above the fireplace; another wall sported a Turner etching and a Hockney original. There was a chill in the air, but the fire in the grate was unlit. In twilight silence, the antiques dealer waited.

His guest had stated no precise hour of arrival, saying only that the meeting would occur some time this evening. The antiques dealer, keen though he was to learn what news the visitor had for him, had over the course of his life learned the art of patience. To pass the time, he calmly ruminated.

The trap at Seal Point had been well laid. The Guardians had not suspected a thing. And why should they? The instruction to hit the power station had been conveyed to them by the traditional means, after all. Their oracle had told them what to do, and they, suspecting nothing, had complied.

Confirmation of the trap's success had come from the mercenaries whom the antiques dealer had employed to intercept the Guardian assault squad. The mercenaries had reported back yesterday that all had gone smoothly. The non-Guardian members of MacGowan's team had been eliminated, their bodies disposed of and their paraterrestrial equipment destroyed, while MacGowan himself had been taken captive and injected with the refined version of the Codename: Bearskin agent. With his car disabled, it would take him time to make his way back to his fellow Guardians – time during which the bacillus could slowly take effect, clouding his judgement, altering his physiology. By now, MacGowan's hands were almost certainly stained with Guardian blood. The antiques dealer's imminent visitor would confirm whether this was so, but in the meantime he derived great pleasure in envisioning the former SAS officer, restored to his senses once the effects of the bacillus had worn off, staring around him in horror at the carnage he had wrought. It would not be surprising if, wracked with guilt and despair, MacGowan took his own life. That would be the honourable – the soldierly – thing to do under such circumstances.

And John Rattray. What of him? Doubtless at this very moment he was the prisoner of Gérard de Sade, and that gullible French buffoon was busy trying to pump him for information about the Guardians. Rattray would not stay a prisoner for long – about this the antiques dealer was under no illusion. Someone with Rattray's capabilities could not be kept jailed. That, however, was of no consequence. The point was that Rattray, the only

Guardian who would have been able to defeat Mac-Gowan while MacGowan was under the influence of the berserker agent, had been successfully lured away.

At the thought of Rattray rushing off halfway around the world to save his little hacker friend, the antiques dealer permitted himself a small smirk. Honestly, men could make such fools of themselves over women. All it took was a flash of frightened female eyes, and every man wanted to play the hero, the saviour, to come running to the rescue. This was true even of a someone as seemingly immune to the charms of the fairer sex as John Rattray.

Manipulating Rattray, with the assistance of Emperor Dragon (that jumped-up little halfwit from whose un-promising raw material the antiques dealer had, Pygma-lion-like, fashioned a work of art), had been the most satisfying and rewarding part of the antiques dealer's entire scheme. Now that Rattray had begun to doubt the principles for which he had been fighting and killing these past hundred years, it was important to keep him destabilised and disorientated, unsure what to believe and what not to. His inner world was crumbling, and the deaths of close colleagues could only serve to hasten that process. Eventually, as long as the antiques dealer kept up the pressure on him, Rattray's sense of certainty would give way and he would be left vulnerable and helpless.

Destroying Rattray physically was possible. Extremely difficult, but possible. Destroying his mind, however, breaking his soul – that was an altogether more challen-ging and more satisfying goal. And, ah, how sweet it would be to achieve!

So the antiques dealer reflected, while the daylight dwindled and the night closed in across the sea from the east.

It was fully dark when, at last, his visitor appeared. The drawing room was abruptly filled with azure light, in the midst of which a tall, thin-limbed figure manifested, gazing down on the antiques dealer with large, impassive black eyes. There was not a conversation as such, just a silent exchange of information, data flowing from one mind to the other, and when it was over, the visitor and the light vanished, leaving the antiques dealer with the afterimage of a nebulous glow in his retinas . . . and the sour, galling taste of defeat in his mouth.

For the rest of the night, tirelessly, sleeplessly, the antiques dealer brooded. He did not dwell on what had gone awry. Endlessly rehashing failures was for lesser minds. Greater minds glanced over their shoulders for one look back, then moved on, scouting ahead. He began formulating new stratagems, turning over possibilities, thinking of all the seeds of schemes he and the Anarchs had sown over the years and wondering which of them had grown to ripeness, which was ready for use.

By the time dawn came, he had chosen one.

The town in Bedfordshire. Yes. Now was surely the time for that particular card to be played.

Reaching this conclusion after several long hours of thought, the antiques dealer grinned – and in the early-morning glimmer, his teeth shone very whitely indeed.

Epilogue

The message was waiting for Cecil at one of the homeless shelters where he regularly stayed. 'Call me,' it said, and was signed simply, 'John'. Cecil phoned Rattray straight away, trying his home number first. Rattray was in. He asked if Cecil would meet him at noon the following day in Soho Square, next to the statue of Caius Cibber. Cecil agreed, knowing better than to enquire about the reason for the meeting. He was curious as to why Rattray might want to talk to him, but only under extreme circumstances were Guardian-related matters discussed over the telephone.

They met at the appointed time at the appointed place. The weather had deteriorated overnight. Yesterday had been bright and autumn-benign; today was chilly and squally. But at least the cold, the rain and the blustering wind meant that he and Rattray had Soho Square's small area of park virtually to themselves. Side by side on a bench they talked.

The conversation lasted a little over ten minutes, and Rattray did most of the talking, Cecil's dialogue being confined to the occasional 'Yes' and 'I see'. When it was over, they shook hands, and Rattray strolled away while Cecil remained sitting on the bench, trying to absorb the implications of what he had just been told.

There had been many times during his career as a Guardian oracle when Cecil had felt less than human, a machine rather than a man, a mere instrument, a tool. But at least he had always felt useful. Until now. Now he just felt *used*.

How often in the past had he been – *hijacked* was the only word he could think of for it. How often in the past had he been hijacked like this? How often had he unwittingly served as a conduit for false and treacherous information from the paraterrestrial world? Surely never. Otherwise more Guardian missions would have gone disastrously awry than just this most recent one. Still, it was possible that it had happened before, and it was even more possible, now, that it might happen again.

From this moment on he would be vigilant, just as Rattray had requested. He would pay careful attention to Mr L. Brain's signature-symbol, his two mouths.

The mouths would tell him whether a communiqué from Mr L. Brain was to be trusted or not. Whether the instructions that he was being given to relay to the Guardians were from the Librans . . . or from the Anarchs.

For the next few days Cecil was, if not exactly in a state of shock, then certainly in a state of disarray. He wandered his usual London haunts, moving with the pavement-flow of pedestrians or sometimes stopping to watch people pass by. He endured the usual insults as he begged for spare change, the usual averted gazes, the usual hostile glares, and he mumbled his usual thanks whenever somebody bothered to acknowledge his existence and hand him money. He ate at the usual fast-food outlets and read the usual discarded newspapers and binned magazines. He followed old, ingrained habits while, inside, his mind was in turmoil. Rattray had been perfectly polite about it, had laid not one jot of the blame on him, but the fact remained that Cecil Evans was no longer simply a valuable asset to the Guardians – he was a potential liability as well.

Coming to terms with this revelation was not going to be an easy process.

Cecil was still brooding on the matter when, two days

after his meeting with Rattray, he found himself being approached by a tall, broad-shouldered man in a concrete underpass near the South Bank Centre. The man came hulking towards him, and Cecil was stirred from his introspection by a vague prickling of fear. The man looked like trouble, and the last thing Cecil wanted right this moment was trouble. Could he still rely on Mr L. Brain to look after him? What if Mr L. Brain refused to protect him any more?

Cecil was inordinately relieved, therefore, when the man reached into his pocket, took out all the loose change in it (the total, when Cecil counted it later, amounted to over six pounds) and dumped the coins into Cecil's fingerless-gloved hands.

'There you go, mate,' the tall man said, and hulked on.

Cecil pocketed the money and thought no more about the encounter.

There was no way he could have known, because Rattray was his sole point of contact with the world of the Guardians, that his tall benefactor was also a Guardian.

MacGowan had decided on a new policy while taking the train up to Waterloo from Guildford, and Cecil was the first person to benefit from it. MacGowan now remembered enough about what he had done while under the influence of the berserker agent to recall beating up the beggar in the combat jacket at Embankment Tube. The only way he felt he could begin to atone for that act was by giving money to every homeless person he came across. He would not always be as generous as he was to the raggedy, mad-bearded bloke in the South Bank underpass. He might be suffering pangs of guilt but he was not *crazy*. In future a twenty pence here, a twenty pence there – that would help make him feel better, and with any luck improve life a little bit for the recipient, too. And he would make a point of buying the *Big Issue* whenever a new issue came out.

And so, having offloaded the contents of his change

pocket into Cecil's hands, MacGowan walked on, crossing the lead-grey Thames via the pedestrian portion of Hungerford Bridge, and forging on up into the West End. He had elected to make his way home on foot rather than take the Underground because the memory of that agonising Northern Line journey was etched indelibly in his mind. It would be some time, he thought, before he felt brave enough to travel by Tube again. Besides, the walk to Crouch End would do him good. Blow away a few cobwebs.

The past four days had been spent recuperating at Bretherton Grange. Lucretia and Holman had looked after him solicitously. After what he had done they would have had every right to spit in his face and turf him out, but instead they had treated him with nothing but kindness and forbearance. The same went for Piers, who had left the Grange the day after MacGowan's attack, once he was satisfied that the berserker agent had been thoroughly eliminated from MacGowan's bloodstream. Even Lady Grinning Soul was MacGowan's friend again. As soon as she was let into the guest room to see him, she came bounding over to the bed and licked his hand happily. This, for Piers, was the final confirmation that MacGowan was fully cured.

No one, in short, held MacGowan responsible for the injuries he had inflicted or for the damage to property he had caused. All the same, in his own opinion his actions were unforgivable. He had tried his best to slaughter people who were his allies, his friends. And, worse, throughout it all he had been convinced that he was doing the right thing, taking revenge on those who had betrayed him. Never mind that he had been under the influence of the berserker agent. What worried him was that his loyalties had been perverted so easily. Was his faith in his fellow Guardians really so weak that it could be demolished by a few *germs*?

'You were the perfect foil for the Anarchs' plan,' Rattray had told him on the second day of his convalescence, after each had finished recounting to the other in person the details of his less-than-successful mission. 'You were betrayed once before, by the army, and that left a kind of psychological rift in you. The berserker agent simply reopened the rift. Exposed an imperfectly healed mental scar.'

Which was intended as a comfort, and should have been one, but in the event only made MacGowan all the more acutely aware of his own shortcomings. He prided himself on his professionalism, on being utterly one hundred per cent reliable when called upon to do his job. Yet now his effectiveness as a Guardian was open to question. For all their kind words, for all their sympathy, would the Guardians (and Holman) ever completely trust him again? Would he ever trust himself?

He remembered the look on the faces of Lucretia and Piers when he first woke up in the brass bed in one of Lucretia's guest rooms, a few hours after he was hit with the paraterrestrial vaccine. The two of them had been standing on either side of his bed. A safe distance away. Arms folded. Nervous. Tense. He remembered realising that he was not able to move his limbs and being shocked to discover that he was bound to the bedposts, his wrists and ankles secured by figure-eights made of what looked like liquorice – paraterrestrial manacles fashioned from an oily-black rubbery substance of an incredibly high tensile strength. He remembered feeling the cumulative sting of the cuts on his face and hands, the pain in his ribs and the dog bite in his neck, and having no idea why. Why he was hurting. Why he was shackled to the bed. Why there was that unmistakably wary look in Lucretia's and Piers's eyes. Phantom thoughts flitted through his head, like memories from someone else's mind: hating these two people, detesting them enough to want to murder them, pursuing them, battling them.

Why?

And that was the first word he spoke to them. Croaked out in a voice made hoarse by shouting:

'Why?'

They exchanged glances, and Piers nodded to Lucretia,

and she began to explain. The whole sorry saga. And everything she said, appalling though it was, made sense, rang true.

Not long after that MacGowan had fallen asleep again, and when he had next awoken the manacles were gone and Lucretia was standing over him carrying a tray of food. Holman was there, too, looking a hell of a sight. He was wearing a blue paraterrestrial healing pad around his neck, and his nose was distended and whitish-purple across the bridge, and his eyes were blackened.

'Christ, I'm sorry,' MacGowan rasped.

And that had become his refrain over the ensuing three days. No matter how many times he was told that it had not been his fault, that he should not hold himself accountable, that he should not go around torturing himself for no good reason, all the same he had found himself endlessly repeating those three guilt-ridden words: 'Christ, I'm sorry.'

On the third day he had felt well enough to leave, but Lucretia had insisted on him staying one more night, just to be on the safe side. Reluctantly he had consented, but on the morning of the fourth day – today – he had been adamant. He would not impose on her any more. Cellular-regeneration gels had healed the cuts to his face and hands and the teethmarks in his neck. His chest, an impressive action-painting of brown, purple and yellow bruises, no longer ached too severely (Rattray – something of an expert in the field of bodily injuries – had determined that there were no broken bones there). It was time for him to leave, to head back to his flat and continue his convalescence away from the scene of his crimes. Away from the sheets of plywood that Holman had erected as temporary front doors. Away from the missing pane in the conservatory roof that Piers had covered with a tacked-down sheet of polythene. Away from the buckled Obstaclimb hemisphere and the battered *Daedalian*, both of which Lucretia had begun the laborious task of mending.

Holman had given him a lift to Guildford station. As

they pulled up at the passenger set-down point outside the station, MacGowan had attempted to tender one last apology, but Holman had stalled him in mid-sentence, holding up a finger and saying: 'Bill, whoever attacked me at the gates, it wasn't you. It wasn't the person who frequently visits my house and is always welcome there. It wasn't the person my elder daughter thinks is the best thing since sliced bread. It was someone else, someone entirely different, and I know he's not coming back again. And that's the last I ever intend to say on the matter, and I hope you'll do me the courtesy of never raising the subject again.'

'Consider it never raised,' MacGowan had replied, and the two men had shaken hands and he had climbed out of the car and headed into the ticketing hall.

One rail journey and a lengthy cross-town walk later, he reached his flat. He no longer lived in the bedsit hovel where he had ended up after Sarah chucked him out of their place in Camden. His current abode was more spacious, tidier (these days he could afford a cleaning lady) and situated in a far smarter part of Crouch End – on the borders of Highgate, in fact. He had the top floor of a big, three-storey Edwardian semi-detached house to himself, and his neighbours all knew him as that nice Mr MacGowan who kept himself to himself and every now and then went away on business trips at very short notice.

His post was stacked in a neat pile on the sideboard in the hallway. Mrs Kapoor, who lived in the ground-floor flat with her wheelchair-bound husband, was the building's self-appointed mail monitor. As usual, everything addressed to MacGowan was either a bill or a piece of unsolicited junk, but on top of the pile there was a note to him from Mrs Kapoor herself, lodged inside a small, floral-patterned envelope. 'I have something for you,' she had written.

The something turned out to be his Adidas gym bag. 'A young woman dropped it off the day before yesterday,' Mrs Kapoor said. 'A pretty thing,' she added with an inquisitive lift of her eyebrows.

She was visibly disappointed when MacGowan did not take the bait and reveal who the woman was, and instead merely thanked her for looking after the bag, then made his excuses and went upstairs. He knew that the woman in question could only have been Sarah. He must have left the gym bag sitting on her doorstep when he had turned tail and fled from her. Shit, *there* were two more people he ought to apologise to – Sarah and that bloke with her, her boyfriend.

In his flat, he picked up the phone and dialled the first few digits of Sarah's number. He did this several times, but each time his nerve failed him and he set down the receiver before completing all seven digits of the number. Finally, after a stiff shot of Macallan, he had another go and managed to dial the number in full. He heard the ringing tone burr at the other end of the line.

Sarah picked up. 'Hello?'

He was struck dumb, unable to think of anything to say. Under the circumstances, though, his silence was as good as announcing his name.

'Bill,' Sarah said, in a voice dripping with icicles. 'That *is* you, isn't it, Bill?'

MacGowan mumbled that it was.

'OK, Bill, you listen to me now. I was planning on saying this to your face when I brought your bag round, but you weren't there so I suppose the phone will have to do.' She paused, collecting herself. 'You are never, ever to come round and see me again. Are you clear on that? Never. If I so much as see you in my street, I'll call the police. After what you did the other day I'm tempted to take out a restraining order on you as well, but I'm hoping that won't be necessary. I'm hoping that telling you to stay away will be sufficient. And I've managed to persuade Tim not take legal action either, though God knows you deserve to be banged up for attacking him like that. Jesus, all your training. You were taught to kill people for a living, and Tim directs *television adverts*, for heaven's sake. You're just lucky you didn't do him any permanent injury, that's all I can say. Bloody lucky.'

'Sarah, I—'

'No, Bill, let me finish. I've been thinking hard about why you might have turned up the way you did, out of the blue, after we hadn't seen each other, hadn't even talked in God knows how many years. And it seems to me that it's something to do with the way things ended between us. They ended on an unresolved note, didn't they? I threw you out and started divorce proceedings, and you just sort of accepted it, went along with it without a fight. I realise that must have seemed pretty harsh to you, pretty callous. But that was never my intention. I didn't want to hurt you. In any way. I only did what I did back then, back when you were drinking heavily and staying out all night, because I had to. Because I thought it might bring you back to your senses. A short, sharp shock, you know? And I'd tried everything else. It was the only thing I could think of left to do.'

Her voice had softened. The indignation had been replaced by sorrow.

'It hurt me, too,' she continued. 'Christ, I *loved* you, Bill. But when you came back from the Gulf you were a different man. I don't know what happened to you out there, and sometimes I wanted you to tell me and sometimes I didn't, but it was this thing that was between us, this thing that only you could know, this thing that, out of pride or for some other stupid reason, you wouldn't share with me, and I couldn't cope with that, Bill, I simply couldn't deal with it. And you kept having those nightmares, and you couldn't even tell me what *they* were about. I'd wake up with you thrashing around and crying out beside me, and there was nothing I could say, nothing I could do, to comfort you when you woke up except tell you that it wasn't real and that I loved you, and that wasn't enough, was it? What happened to our marriage, Bill, wasn't your fault and it wasn't mine. Your job showed you Hell and you were never the same again, and I'm sorry, Bill, I'm truly sorry that our lives were screwed up for us, but neither of us was to blame. You do understand that, don't you? Neither of us. And whatever you may have been thinking or hoping these past few years, we can never recapture what we had. I wish it wasn't so, but it's the only way. We can never go back. You're just going to have to come to terms with that and do as I've done. Move on. Get on with life. Let the past lie.'

She paused for a deep breath.

'There. I've said all I'm going to say. Goodbye, Bill. And good luck with . . . well, with everything.'

She cut the connection before he could speak again.

The bottle of Macallan was a welcome source of solace that night.

Sarah was right, of course. MacGowan knew that when he woke at dawn the following day in his favourite armchair, the whisky tumbler still in his hand, a mild hangover buzzing in his head. The only way to carry on with life was to let the past lie. Even when the past would not let *you* lie, even when it had its hooks deep in you, even when it insisted on trying to drag you down with nightmares and regrets and misplaced hopes, still you had to keep going forwards. Keep looking for the next prospect. Keep walking towards the next horizon.

Over the past four days he had been toying with the idea of quitting the Guardians. For their sake as much as his, they would probably be better off without him. But now he saw that, as long as they were prepared to maintain their trust in him, then the very least he could do was return the favour.

New horizons. New prospects.

And there was something else he could do, something else that might help him shake off the tethers of the past. Something he perhaps should have done months ago.

He obtained the phone number from Directory Enquiries.

He waited until a decent hour to call, then left a message with the porter at the college lodge.

Daisy rang him back that lunchtime.